P9-DEK-981

FALLOUT

BY HARRY TURTLEDOVE

The Guns of the South

THE WORLDWAR SAGA

Worldwar: In the Balance
Worldwar: Tilting the Balance
Worldwar: Upsetting the Balance
Worldwar: Striking the Balance

COLONIZATION

Colonization: Second Act
Colonization: Down to Earth
Colonization: Aftershocks

Homeward Bound

THE VIDESSOS CYCLE

Volume One:
The Misplaced Legion
An Emperor for the Legion
Volume Two:
The Legion of Videssos
Swords of the Legion

THE TALE OF KRISPOS

Krispos Rising
Krispos of Videssos
Krispos the Emperor

THE TIME OF TROUBLES SERIES

The Stolen Throne
Hammer and Anvil
The Thousand Cities
Videssos Besieged

A World of Difference
Departures
How Few Remain

THE GREAT WAR

The Great War: American Front
The Great War: Walk in Hell
The Great War: Breakthroughs

AMERICAN EMPIRE

American Empire: Blood and Iron
American Empire: The Center Cannot Hold
American Empire: The Victorious Opposition

SETTLING ACCOUNTS

Settling Accounts: Return Engagement
Settling Accounts: Drive to the East
Settling Accounts: The Grapple
Settling Accounts: In at the Death

Every Inch a King
The Man with the Iron Heart

THE WAR THAT CAME EARLY

The War That Came Early: Hitler's War
The War That Came Early: West and East
The War That Came Early: The Big Switch
The War That Came Early: Coup d'Etat
The War That Came Early: Two Fronts
The War That Came Early: Last Orders

THE HOT WAR

Bombs Away
Fallout
Armistice

THE HOT WAR

FALLOUT

Harry Turtledove

DEL REY • NEW YORK

The Hot War: Fallout is a work of fiction. All incidents and dialogue, and all characters with the exception of some well-known historical and public figures, are the products of the author's imagination and are not to be construed to be real. Where real-life historical or public figures appear, the situations, incidents, and dialogues concerning those persons are entirely fictional and are not intended to depict actual events or to change the entirely fictional nature of the work. In all other respects, any resemblance to persons, living or dead, is entirely coincidental.

2017 Del Rey Mass Market Edition

Published in the United States by Del Rey, an imprint of Random House, a division of Penguin Random House LLC, New York.

DEL REY and the HOUSE colophon are registered trademarks of Penguin Random House LLC.

Originally published in hardcover in the United States by Del Rey, an imprint of Random House, a division of Penguin Random House LLC, in 2016.

This book contains an excerpt from the forthcoming book *The Hot War: Armistice* by Harry Turtledove. This excerpt has been set for this edition only and may not reflect the final content of the forthcoming edition.

ISBN 978-0-553-39075-9
Ebook ISBN 978-0-553-39074-2

Cover design and illustration: David G. Stevenson, based on images © Shutterstock

Printed in the United States of America

randomhousebooks.com

9 8 7 6 5 4 3 2 1

Del Rey mass market edition: June 2017

Acknowledgments

With thanks to Viktor T. Toth for help with the Hungarian.

FALLOUT

IT WAS A BRIGHT, warm, sticky day in Washington, D.C. Summer wasn't here yet, but it was less than two weeks away. President Harry Truman turned his swivel chair away from the desk in the Oval Office. For the moment, all the urgent papers demanding his attention could damn well shut up and wait. The green of the White House lawn seemed far more appealing.

Three or four robins hopped across the neatly mown grass. Every so often, one would pause and cock its head to one side, as if listening. Maybe the birds were doing just that. Pretty soon, one of them pecked at something. It straightened with a fat earthworm wrapped around its beak. The worm didn't want to get eaten. It wiggled and clung. The robin swallowed it anyway, then went back to hunting.

"Go get 'em, boy," Truman said softly. "Maybe you'll catch Joe McCarthy next. I can hope, anyhow."

The robins didn't know when they were well off. Here in Washington, they didn't need to worry—too much—about getting blown to hell and gone by an atom bomb. Lord only knew how many robins the Russians had just incinerated in Paris.

Of course, robins in Europe weren't the same birds as the ones here. Truman had seen that as an artillery officer in the First World War and then again when he met with Stalin and Attlee at Potsdam, outside of Berlin. Robins over there were smaller than the American ones, and had redder breasts. He supposed the local ones had got their name by reminding colonists of the birds back home.

But, when you got right down to it, what the French robins looked like didn't matter. The A-bomb didn't care. It blew them up any which way. It blew up a hell of a lot of French people, too.

When the telephone rang, Truman spun the chair back toward his desk. He picked up the handset. "Yes?"

"Mr. President . . ." Rose Conway, his private secretary, needed a moment before she could go on: "Mr. President, I have a call for you from Charles de Gaulle."

"Jumping Jehosaphat!" Truman said, and meant it most sincerely. He couldn't stand de Gaulle, and was sure it was mutual. At the end of the last war, French and American troops had almost started shooting at each other when the French tried to occupy northwestern Italy. De Gaulle had been running France then, and Truman had cut off American aid to him.

These days, de Gaulle was out of French politics—or he had been. *Damn shame,* Truman thought unkindly. If he'd been in politics, he'd likely have been in Paris, and the bomb could have fried him along with all the poor, harmless little robins.

Here he was, though, unfried and on the telephone. And since he was . . . "Go ahead and put him through, Rose. I'd better find out what he's got to say."

"Yes, Mr. President. One moment," she said. Truman heard some clicks and pops. Then Rose Conway told someone, "The President is on the line, sir."

"Thank you." Charles de Gaulle spoke fluent if nasal English. But he sounded as if he were calling from the Cave of the Winds. The connection was terrible. Well, most of France's phone service would have been centered in or routed through Paris. De Gaulle might have been lucky to get through at all. The Frenchman said, "Are you there, President Truman?"

"I am, General, yes," Truman answered. "Where exactly are you, sir?"

"I am in Colombey-les-Deux-Eglises, about two hundred kilometers southeast of martyred Paris." Or maybe de Gaulle said *murdered Paris.* Both were true enough—all too true, in fact.

Two hundred kilometers was just over a hundred twenty miles. Truman remembered that from his days as a battery commander. He'd hardly had to worry about the metric system since. "Glad to hear you're safe," he said, thinking what a liar politics had turned him into.

"I am safe, yes, but my beloved country has had the heart

torn out of her." De Gaulle seemed matter-of-fact, which made what he said all the more melodramatic.

"That is tragic, General, but it's not as if America hasn't taken plenty of hard knocks, too," Truman said.

"Seattle. Denver. *Hollywood.* Such places." Charles de Gaulle's scorn was palpable. "This is *Paris,* Mr. President!"

In lieu of *Screw you, buddy, and the horse you rode in on,* which was the first thing that sprang to mind, Truman said, "Well, the United States is hitting the goddamn Russians harder than they're hitting the Free World."

"All the Russian hovels added together do not approach equaling Paris." De Gaulle's contempt was plenty big enough to enfold the USSR as well as the USA.

Instead of calling him on it, Truman tried a different tack: "Why exactly are *you* calling me, General? You haven't been part of the French government for five years now. Or are you again?"

"In a manner of speaking, I am, yes," de Gaulle replied. "You will understand that the explosion eliminated large portions of the country's administration. Certain individuals have approached me to head a Committee of National Salvation. I could not refuse *la belle France* in her hour of need, and so I have assumed that position for the purpose of restoring order."

"I . . . see," Truman said slowly. It made a certain amount of sense. De Gaulle was a national hero for leading the Free French during the war and for putting France back on her feet once England and the USA chased the Nazis out of the country (with, yes, some help from those Free French).

But both Churchill and FDR had despised him (by all accounts, that was mutual). Harry Truman didn't agree with all of Roosevelt's opinions, but about de Gaulle he thought his predecessor had got it spot-on. He hadn't been a bit sorry when the tall, proud, touchy Frenchman left politics for his little village in the middle of nowhere to write his memoirs.

If de Gaulle was back, though, Truman would have to deal with him. The Red Army wasn't far from the French border. In spite of everything America and Britain (and the French, and the West Germans) could do, it was getting closer by the day. If de Gaulle cut his own deal with Stalin, a free Western Europe would be just a memory, even if American A-bombs flattened most of the Soviet Union.

And so he needed to keep the new boss of this French committee at least partway happy. De Gaulle understood he needed to do that, of course, understood it and exploited it. Trying to hide a sigh, Truman asked, "What do you need from the United States, General? Whatever it is, if we can get it to you, it's yours."

"For this I thank you, Mr. President. I have always known how generous a people Americans are." De Gaulle could be gracious when he felt like it. The one drawback to that was, he didn't feel like it very often. "Medical supplies of all sorts are urgently needed, naturally. And if you have experts on the effects of what you call fallout and how to mitigate those effects, that, too, would be of great value to us."

"I'll see what I can do," Truman promised. Both sides had fused most of their A-bombs to burst high in the air. That spread destruction more widely and also cut down on the amount of radioactive crud that blew downwind after the blast. But the Paris strike was a low-altitude, hit-and-run raid. The A-bomb had gone off at ground level or very close to it. And now the French would have to clean up the mess . . . if they could.

"Has the fallout reached, uh, Colombey-les-Deux-Eglises?" Truman asked, with a certain amount of pride that he'd remembered the name of the place and brought it out pretty well for a Yank.

"The Geiger counters say it has, yes, but not to any serious degree. This place lies in the direction of the prevailing winds," de Gaulle said. "Closer to Paris, you will understand, the situation is more dire. We have many cases of radiation sickness."

"That's nasty stuff. Horrible stuff. We'll send you doctors who have some experience with it, yes." Truman didn't tell de Gaulle that nothing the doctors tried seemed to do much good. You watched and you waited and you kept people as clean and comfortable as you could, and either they got better or they didn't. But then, de Gaulle might well already know that. Paris wasn't the first French city to have had hellfire visited on it, just the biggest. And the war still showed no signs of ending.

Boris Gribkov, Vladimir Zorin, and Leonid Tsederbaum joined the queue in front of the field kitchen near Munich. The bomber pilot, copilot, and navigator carried tin mess kits the Red Army men holding this part of what had been West Germany gave them.

Nose twitching, Zorin said, "I smell shchi."

"That'll fill us up," Gribkov said. With shchi, you started with cabbage, as you did with beets for borscht. Then you threw anything else you happened to have into the pot along with it. You let it simmer till it all got done, and then you ate it.

That was how Red Army—and Red Air Force—field kitchens turned it out, anyway, in enormous sheet-metal tureens. No doubt fancy cooks fixed it with more subtlety. Gribkov cared not a kopek for subtlety. Filling his belly was the only thing he worried about.

A Red Army noncom saw his blues and his officer's shoulder boards and started to step out of line. "Go ahead, Comrade," he said.

"No, no, no," Boris answered. "We won't starve to death before we get up there. Keep your place."

"You're the guys who gave it to the froggies, aren't you?" the sergeant said.

"Well, some of them," Gribkov told him. The Tu-4 that he flew had a crew of eleven.

"Good," the noncom said. "You ought to drop a bomb on these German pussies, too. Blast 'em all to the devil so nobody has to worry about 'em any more. You ask me, every one of 'em's still a Nazi under the skin."

"I wouldn't be surprised," Zorin said. Gribkov wouldn't have, either. By everything he'd heard, German troops still fought the Red Army as fanatically as they had when Hitler called the shots.

He glanced over at Leonid Tsederbaum. The *Zhid* looked back, his handsome, swarthy face showing nothing. If anybody hated Germans and Nazis even worse than a Russian, you had to figure a Jew would. But Tsederbaum didn't say anything that would show he did.

As a matter of fact, Tsederbaum hadn't said one whole hell of a lot since he guided the Tu-4 back from the attack on Paris. He'd already made it plain that he didn't like dropping atom bombs on famous, important cities. Boris Gribkov didn't like it worth a damn, either. Liking it had nothing to do with the price of vodka.

Your superior told you to do something. You saluted. You said *I serve the Soviet Union!* And you went out and did it or you died trying. If you screwed it up, your superior gave it to you in the neck. If he didn't, somebody would give it to *him.* How else could anyone run a military? The Germans, the enemy whose example the Russians knew best, had the same kind of rules.

All the same, Boris kept sneaking glances at Tsederbaum as men with mess kits shuffled toward those bubbling, fragrant cauldrons. The navigator had never been one of your talky guys. When he did open his yap, what came out of it was dryly ironic more often than not. But yeah, he'd been even quieter than usual lately.

When Gribkov reached the shchi, the chubby-cheeked corporal with the ladle—who ever heard of a skinny cook?—beamed at him. "Here you go, sir!" he said, and dug deep into the pot for the good stuff at the bottom. He did the same for Zorin and Tsederbaum. Gribkov didn't think he *was* a hero, but he didn't mind getting treated like one.

That sergeant who wanted to bomb the Germans waved the flyers to a commandeered bus bench. Then he and the rest of the Red Army men politely left them alone. They were heroes to the ground-pounders, enough so that Gribkov wished he felt more like a hero to himself.

He dug into the shchi. "Not half bad," he said. "I do wonder what the meat is, though."

"You mean whether it'd neigh or bark or meow?" Zorin chuckled, for all the world as if he were joking.

"As long as I don't see the critter it came from, I'm not going to worry about it," Boris said. "I just wonder, that's all."

"Curiosity killed the cat—which is why it's in the shchi." By the way Zorin shoveled in the soup, he didn't worry about it, either.

The crack, though, was more one Gribkov would have expected from Tsederbaum. When he stole another look at the Jew, Tsederbaum caught him doing it. Raising his spoon in mock salute, the navigator said, "The condemned man ate a hearty meal."

Nobody'd condemned them. They'd won medals for bombing America and then making it back to the *rodina.* Boris pulled a small metal flask off his belt. "Here," he said. "I've got some vodka. That's good for whatever's bothering you."

Leonid Tsederbaum's smile called him a Russian, or possibly a small, stupid child. As if humoring such a child, the

Zhid took a knock. But he said, "There's not enough vodka in the world to fix what ails me."

"How do you know? How much have you drunk?" Zorin asked. Tsederbaum's chuckle was on the dutiful side. Boris Gribkov, who drank himself before passing the flask to Zorin, thought it was a good question. Sometimes if you got smashed out of your skull, whatever you'd been chewing on didn't seem so bad in the light of the morning-after hangover.

In a day or two, the crew would fly the Tu-4 back to the Soviet Union. Chances were they'd pick up another gong for their tunic fronts. And then somebody would tell them what to do next, and they'd do it—or die trying.

They slept on pews in a gutted church. With enough blankets cocooning you, it wasn't so bad. At least you had room to stretch out. At some point in the middle of the night, Tsederbaum got up and headed outside. "Sorry to bother you," he whispered to Gribkov, who sleepily raised his head.

Heading for the latrine, Boris thought. He wondered if he ought to do the same. Instead, he yawned and submerged in slumber again.

Then somebody shook him awake. It was predawn twilight. Even in the gray gloom, he could see how pale Vladimir Zorin looked. "What is it?" Gribkov asked. Whatever it was, it wouldn't be good.

But it was worse than he'd dreamt. "That stupid fucking kike!" Zorin sounded furious. "He went and blew his goddamn head off!"

"Bozhemoi!" Gribkov untangled himself and scrambled to his feet. "I knew something was eating him, but I never imagined—"

"Who would? Who in his right mind would, I mean?" the copilot said.

Boris pulled on his boots. "Take me to him."

"Come on." Zorin led him out just past the stinking trenches where Soviet fighting men eased themselves. There lay Leonid Abramovich Tsederbaum. He'd put the business end of his Tokarev automatic in his mouth and pulled the trigger. The back of his once-so-clever head was a red, ruined mess. Flies had already started buzzing around it.

Going through his pockets, Gribkov found a note. He recognized Tsederbaum's precise script at once. All it said was *Men a hundred years from now will know what I have done.*

Let them also know I did not do it willingly. Maybe then they will not spit whenever they say my name.

He showed Zorin the note. Then he fumbled in his own pockets till he found a matchbook. He lit a match and touched it to the edge of the paper. He held it till it scorched his fingers, then dropped it and let it burn itself out. Once it did, he kicked at the ashes till nothing discernible was left.

"Good job," the copilot said. "Now they won't be able to go after his family."

"Right," Gribkov said tightly. The world would never know just why Leonid Tsederbaum had killed himself. Boris wished *he* didn't know. Better not to start thinking about things like that. You only got into trouble when you did. He had to keep flying. He wondered how he'd manage.

First Lieutenant Cade Curtis wondered where the devil he was. Oh, he knew in a general sense: he was in Korea, and in the southern part of it. He even knew in some detail—he was south of the town of Chongju, which lay southeast of Seoul. The Americans (if you wanted to get fancy about it, the United Nations forces, but most of them *were* Americans) and the Republic of Korea had been attacking "in the direction of Chongju" for quite a while now. They hadn't got there yet, and didn't seem likely to any time soon.

When Curtis got to Korea in the fall of 1950 as a newly minted shavetail straight out of ROTC, it was the most important fight in the world. He'd been part—a tiny part, but part nonetheless—of General MacArthur's triumphant drive to the Yalu River. That drive was going to take care of North Korea and Kim Il-sung once and for all.

It was going to, but it didn't. Winter and the Red Chinese made sure of that. The UN forces—there were Englishmen and Turks along with the Americans—had reached the Chosin Reservoir, near the Yalu. Then the mercury dove somewhere south of twenty below, and Mao's band of merry men drove south across the Yalu.

MacArthur hadn't figured they would. It was one of the nastiest surprises in the history of surprises, especially if you happened to be on the receiving end, as Cade was. He'd got lucky. He'd slipped through the Red Chinese net, one of a handful who did. The Reds destroyed three or four divisions trying to retreat to safety at the port of Hungnam.

Because they did, Truman dropped A-bombs on several Manchurian cities to fubar their logistics. Because he dropped them on Red China, Stalin dropped them on the USA's European allies. Because Stalin did that . . . the Free World and the Communists had been climbing the ladder of devastation one rung at a time ever since.

Those Manchurian cities, and several in the Soviet Far East, glowed in the dark now. So did ports on the American West Coast from Seattle all the way down to Los Angeles. Both sides had trouble getting men and weapons into Korea these days. Both sides had trouble caring, too—the big fight now was in Europe.

But the war here, the little war that had touched off the bigger one, ground on with whatever was at hand and whatever Truman and Mao and Stalin could spare. The outside world forgot it? You hurt just as much if you got maimed in a fight nobody back home gave a damn about, and you were just as dead if you got killed in that kind of fight.

Cade walked along the trench, here somewhere south of Chongju. Dust scuffed up under his boots. When he noticed, he could smell his own stink, and the stink of his fellow dogfaces. He couldn't remember the last time he'd bathed. If the wind blew down from the north, he could smell the different but no more pleasant stinks of the Red Chinese and North Koreans. And the stench of death was always in the air. It was sometimes stronger, sometimes weaker, but it never went away.

To get it out of his nose, he lit a Camel. He hadn't smoked at all before he got here. Of course, he'd been just nineteen. He sure smoked now. Like so many other soldiers, he hardly knew what to do without a cigarette dangling from the corner of his mouth.

He ground the match out under his bootheel. The smoke did let him forget about the other charming aromas for a little while. And it made him more alert and relaxed him at the same time—for a little while. Pretty soon, he'd fire up another one to get the same effect all over again.

In the meantime, he cautiously stuck his head up out of the trench to make sure the Reds weren't up to anything. He looked around for a couple of seconds, then ducked down again. A few seconds after that, a rifle bullet cracked past, not far enough above where he'd just been. If he'd shown himself for much longer, that sniper might have put a round through the bridge of his nose.

"Anything cookin' out there, Lieutenant?" asked Sergeant Lou Klein. He was old enough to be Cade's father. An Army lifer, he'd fought in North Africa and Italy the last time around. He could have run the company at least as well as Cade did. They both knew it. Since the days of Hammurabi, one of the many things veteran sergeants were for was riding herd on eager young officers.

After this long in Korea, Cade might still have been young, but he was eager no more. He shook his head. "All seemed pretty quiet."

"Good." Klein hedged that by adding, "Unless they're cooking up something sneaky, anyway."

"They don't seem to try cute stuff a whole lot," Cade said. "When they fight, they just get in there and slug."

"That's on account of most of 'em carry pieces like yours." Klein pointed at Cade's PPSh submachine gun, a Russian weapon he liked much better than the M-1 carbine American officers were supposed to carry. The sergeant went on, "Hard to get fancy when you can't hit anything out past a coupla hundred yards."

"Yeah, but when they get in close—" Cade didn't go on, or need to. An awful lot of combat took place at ranges where the PPSh and its older cousin the PPD were world-beaters. They sprayed a lot of bullets at anything that looked dangerous, they hardly ever jammed, and they were easy to strip and clean. What more could you want?

"Hey, they ain't tryin' to kill me right this minute. I won't worry about it till they do," Klein said.

That attitude was wonderful—if you could manage it. Cade had always been a worrier. He fretted over what would happen next, what might happen next, what could possibly happen next. The sergeant didn't. Whatever happened, he tried to deal with it as it came up. He was still here, still breathing, still fighting. His way worked as well for him as Cade's for him, and he probably had lower blood pressure.

But he wouldn't be promoted to officer's rank if he lived to be ninety. Cade didn't have much chance of making general if he stayed in the Army. Few without a West Point class ring scaled that mountain. But major, light colonel, maybe even bird colonel wouldn't be unreachable. Men at those ranks needed to care about possibilities, not just take things as they came.

Off in the distance, an American machine gun spat a burst

at the Communist lines. The Red Chinese didn't have so many machine guns. They had plenty of rifles, though, and plenty of men to shoot them. They shot back. Firing picked up on both sides.

Klein swore under his breath. "Somebody's been eating his spinach, so he thinks he's fucking Popeye," he said. "If it's quiet where you're at, why do you want to go poke it with a stick?"

"Beats me." Cade was far more willing to let lying dogs sleep than he had been when he got here.

Not everybody was. The hothead disease afflicted guys on both sides. They figured Uncle Sam or Chairman Mao had gone to the trouble of issuing them a rifle or a PPSh and the ammo to go with it, so the least they could do was start shooting as soon as they got the chance—or imagined they did.

Somebody on the American side of the rusty barbed wire started screaming and wouldn't stop. The noise was horrible, terrible, dreadful, whatever was worse than those. It was the noise a dog makes after a car smashes it, when it's dead but hasn't finished dying yet. Sometimes a kind human will cut a dog's throat when it's hurt like that, or bash in its head with a brick.

Cade wished somebody would bash in that poor GI's head with a brick. The man's shrieks made him want to stuff his fingers into his ears till his fingertips met between them. The awful cries just wouldn't stop.

"Sorry bastard," Klein said, which only went to show how useless words were at times like that.

"Yeah." Cade's nod felt every bit as inadequate. General Sherman had known what he was talking about, even if he was a damnyankee (Cade grew up in Tennessee). War was hell.

Vasili Yasevich looked around the hamlet of Smidovich with unbridled curiosity and amazement. It was a tiny little place compared to Harbin, where he'd lived his whole life up till now. Before the Americans dropped an atom bomb on it, Harbin had held three quarters of a million people. No more than three or four thousand lived here.

But that wasn't what was amazing about the place. What was amazing was that everybody here looked like him. In Harbin, he'd been part of a tiny, dwindling Russian minority drowning in a rising tide of Chinese. The past few years, he'd used Mandarin far more often than his birthspeech.

Here, though, everybody—well, everybody male—grew a thick beard. Everybody's skin was pink or swarthy, not golden. Some people had black hair. Some people, not just about everyone. Some people had brown hair, some straw-colored like Vasili's, some even red. There were brown eyes and blue ones and green. Everybody had a big, strong-bridged nose.

For the first time in his life, then, Vasili didn't look like a foreigner—a round-eyed devil, as the Chinese so charmingly put it. You couldn't tell by looking that he hadn't been born and raised here.

Which was funny, only the joke was on him. No matter what he looked like, he'd never felt so alone, so different, so foreign, in all his life.

He'd been a baby when his father and mother brought him to Harbin after the Reds won the Russian Civil War against the Whites. They'd lived through the Japanese occupation, when Manchuria turned into Manchukuo. Japan and the USSR stayed neutral through the Second World War, which suited them both. Japan worried about China and America, while Stalin was in the fight of his life against Hitler.

Then Hitler shot himself, the Germans gave up, and Stalin finally turned on the Japanese. After smashing the Nazis flat, the battle-hardened Red Army found them easy meat. Soviet tanks roared through Harbin, bound for Korea and other points south.

And the NKVD followed the troops. The Chekists didn't care that the scores they were settling were a quarter of a century old. They had their lists, and they used them. Uncounted thousands of Harbin's Russians disappeared, either into the gulags or into shallow, unmarked graves.

Vasili's parents hadn't waited for the midnight bang on the door. His old man was a druggist, and knew what to take. They died almost as soon as the poison hit their stomachs.

For reasons known only to them, the Soviet secret police hadn't bothered with Vasili. He'd stayed in Harbin, doing carpentry and bricklaying and compounding medicines on the side . . . till he fell foul of a Chinese big shot when he wouldn't sell him opium. Mao's camps were just as delightful as Stalin's. So Vasili ran away.

He trudged toward the town hall near the center of Smidovich. He had no Soviet papers, but he was in the process of getting them. Normally, the MGB—the NKVD by a new set of initials—would have jugged or shot any Russian it caught without proper documents. But these weren't normal times. Atomic fire had fallen on Khabarovsk, not far east of Smidovich. Even the secret police recognized that people might have escaped from the city on the Amur without waiting to gather their paperwork.

Although Vasili hadn't, he might have. The Chekists seemed willing to believe he had. A couple of the ones he'd dealt with even seemed like halfway decent human beings. He wondered what they were doing working for the MGB. Then again, Smidovich wasn't the kind of place where hotshots were employed.

"Good day, Vasili Andreyevich," one of those functionaries said when Yasevich walked into the building, which looked like nothing so much as an overgrown log cabin.

"Good day, Gleb Ivanovich," Vasili replied. No, he'd never expected to be on familiar terms with an MGB man.

Gleb Ivanovich Sukhanov waved toward a samovar bubbling on a corner table. "Fix yourself a glass of tea. Then we'll talk."

"Spasibo." Vasili did. He was used to drinking tea from a handleless cup and without sugar, Chinese-style. But he remembered how his folks had done things when he was small and they still clung to Russian ways as tightly as they could. He brought the tea over to Sukhanov's table and sat down in the chair on the opposite side. The MGB man's chair was padded; the one people who saw him used was of plain wood. One way or another, the Reds let you know who ran things.

Sukhanov pulled a manila folder off a pile. "So let me see," he said. "You tell me your flat was on Karl Marxa Street near Lenin Square."

"That's right." Vasili hoped it was. What Soviet city wouldn't have a street named for the founder of Communism and a square named for the founder of the USSR?

Frowning a little, Sukhanov said, "It's a wonder you survived. The bomb went off right above the square, I am told."

"I wasn't home when it went off, sir." Vasili tried to sound faintly embarrassed. He did have his backup story ready.

But Gleb Sukhanov's frown deepened. "Don't call me *sir.* I'm just a comrade like everybody else."

"Sorry, Comrade Sukhanov." Vasili cursed himself for his slip. He might speak Russian, but he didn't speak Soviet Russian. The exiles in Harbin kept *gospodin* and *gospozha, sir* and *madam*. In the USSR, those were counterrevolutionary. Everybody was a *tovarishch,* a *comrade.* Even the written language looked funny to Vasili—the Reds had simplified the alphabet, getting rid of several characters.

"Hmp," the MGB man said. "Where exactly were you, then?"

"Comrade"—Vasili did his best to look shamefaced—"I was coming back from visiting a woman on the edge of town. A building shielded me from the worst of the flash and the blast, or I wouldn't be talking with you now."

He could talk with conviction about what happened when an A-bomb went off. He'd been working near Pingfan, outside of Harbin, when the Americans hit the Chinese city. However much he wished he didn't, he knew what happened at a time like that.

"You should have kept your identity card with you," Sukhanov said severely.

"Have a heart, Gleb Ivanovich," Vasili said. "She was somebody's wife, but she wasn't mine. I wanted to keep everything as quiet as I could. How was I supposed to know the Yankee sons of bitches would choose that particular night to murder people?"

" 'Why is this night different from all other nights?' " Sukhanov sounded like a man quoting something, but Vasili had no idea what. He must have looked puzzled. The MGB functionary let out a self-conscious chuckle and said, "Now I know I've worked in the Jewish Autonomous Oblast too long."

Vasili had had Jews for friends in Harbin, though times got harder for them after the Japanese seized the city. Here in Smidovich, some of the shop signs were in Yiddish instead of or along with Russian. It made less sense to him than Chinese would have: he read that language less well than he spoke it, but he could manage.

He could manage a chuckle of his own for the Chekist, too. He wanted Gleb Sukhanov to like him. If Sukhanov did, maybe he'd quit asking so damn many questions and making Vasili tell so many lies. If anyone who really did live in a block of flats near Lenin Square on Karl Marxa showed up in Smidovich, he was screwed.

For now, though, he was golden. Sukhanov signed an official-looking document, stamped it in red ink with a hammer-and-sickle rubber stamp, and slid it across the table. “Here is a temporary identity card,” he said. “Keep your nose clean while you’re in these parts and everything will be fine. If you cause trouble . . .” He let that hang.

“I’m no troublemaker, Comrade,” Vasili said. He even meant it. Why not? He had a place here, and he didn’t any more in China. Now he was a Russian among Russians. What would come of that?

RUSSIAN TANKS RUMBLED PAST Luisa Hozzel's flat in Fulda. She was close to a window, so she looked out. If she hadn't been, she wouldn't have bothered. It wasn't as if she'd never seen tanks before.

During the days when Hitler ruled the *Reich,* there'd been military parades through town. Goose-stepping soldiers in *Stahlhelms* and panzer crewmen in black coveralls and black berets ornamented with the *Totenkopf* were plenty to set a girl's heart aflutter.

She'd married one of those soldiers. Gustav had gone off with millions of others to knock the Soviet Union over the head. Unlike so many of those millions, he'd come home again after the Russians—with American and English help—knocked Germany over the head instead. Fulda became part of the American occupation zone, though the border with what the Russians still held didn't lie far to the east.

She'd seen plenty of American tanks over the next few years. The Amis said they were protecting this part of Germany from the Red Russians. They even seemed to mean it. The Marshall Plan helped western Germany get up off its knees after the war, the same way it helped the rest of shattered Western Europe.

Then this horrible new war started. If Russian tanks were going to make any progress in western Germany, they had to break out through the flat country of what people called the Fulda Gap. The Americans fought hard to hold them back, but couldn't do it.

So now the red flag with the gold hammer and sickle flew here, not the black, red, and gold of the new Federal Republic of (West) Germany and of the old Weimar Republic. The black, red, and white of Hitler and, back in the day, of the Kaiser didn't mean Germany any more.

Like everybody else, she'd heard stories about the Russians' rapes and murders when they swarmed into the *Reich* at the end of the last war. She was one of the lucky ones. She couldn't judge those stories from personal experience. She'd never seen a Russian in her whole life till this past winter.

The Ivans in Fulda didn't drag women off the streets or shoot people for the fun of it. That was about as much good as any of the locals could find to say about them.

But when the knock on Luisa's door came, a few minutes after those tanks clattered by, she didn't panic. She just went to the door and opened it. Two Soviet officers stood out there. She still didn't panic. She didn't know what their blue *Waffenfarb* meant. Had it been a German arm-of-service color, she would have, but the Ivans used a different system. She didn't know blue meant MGB.

"You are *Frau* Luisa Hozzel?" one of them asked in palatal German.

"Yes, that's right." Luisa admitted it. Why not?

"Your husband is Gustav Hozzel?" the Russian persisted.

"Yes." She nodded. "Why?" Fear seized her—was he going to tell her Gustav was dead?

He didn't. He asked, "Where is Gustav Hozzel now, please?"

"I don't know," Luisa said truthfully. "I haven't seen him since the war started." A Russian bomb or bullet might have killed him right outside of Fulda half an hour after he left the flat then. But if none had, he probably had a rifle in his hands right now. He'd left intending to fight the Reds again, in the German auxiliary force that rapidly turned into a German army.

Luisa didn't say that. She still owned a working sense of caution. She thought the Russians were asking questions about her husband, though, not about her.

They talked to each other in their own language for a moment. Luisa didn't know any Russian, though Gustav had. They both drew their pistols at the same instant and pointed them at her. The one who spoke German said, "You are under arrest. Come with us. Immediately!"

"What?" she blurted. She understood him, all right. She just didn't, or didn't want to, believe him. "I haven't done anything!" That was true, too.

True or not, it did her no good. The Russian slapped her in

the face. "Immediately, I said!" he snapped. "Come now, or you will be even sorrier later on."

Numbly, she preceded him and his silent chum down the stairs. The slap didn't hurt her so much as it left her stunned. Whatever Gustav did in the war, he'd never laid a hand on her like that. No one had, not so callously, as if she were nothing but an animal that needed a smack to get it going. She was going, all right, straight into a nightmare.

A captured American jeep sat waiting, half on the street, half on the sidewalk. No German would have parked it in such a disorderly way. The Russians had painted red stars on it in place of the white ones the Amis used. The two officers waved for her to get into the passenger seat. The one who'd been quiet slid behind the wheel. The other fellow, pistol still ready, took the back seat.

As they jounced away, he said, "The charge is counterrevolutionary activity."

"That's insane!" Luisa said. "All I've done is stayed here and tried to keep out of trouble."

"We have reason to believe your husband is fighting against the progressive vanguard of the workers and peasants," he said implacably. "This also shows your own political unreliability."

"But I haven't done anything!" Luisa said again. "What are you going to do to me?"

"You will go into the authority of the Chief Administration of Corrective Labor Camps," the Russian officer replied. In German, it sounded impressive and bureaucratic, even pompous. The Russian acronym was *gulag*. He didn't mention it to Luisa, and it wouldn't have meant anything to her if he had.

Whether she knew now what it meant or not, she'd find out.

The jeep bounced along. All those tank tracks had torn up Fulda's streets, and no one had bothered fixing potholes. The Russians didn't care what happened to German towns.

They didn't bother with jail. They took her straight to the train station. As things turned out, they had what amounted to a jail there, in what had been a storeroom. A bored-looking soldier with a machine pistol guarded the door. But for him, you could walk past it without having any idea it was there.

Half a dozen other dejected women stood in there or sat on the floor, that being the only place to sit. A slops bucket in the corner made do for a toilet. Luisa vowed to hold everything as long as she could. She didn't want to have to use it.

She wasn't altogether astonished to discover she knew one of the other women the Russians had grabbed. Trudl Bachman's husband ran the print shop where Gustav had worked. Like Gustav, Max was an old *Frontschwein* who'd fought the Red Army as long as he could before.

"I bet they went off together to play soldiers again," Trudl said bitterly.

"I bet you're right," Luisa said. Max had vanished from Fulda at about the same time as Gustav.

"And then they left us behind to catch the devil for whatever they're up to." Yes, if Trudl had got her hands on her husband just then, she would have made him sorrier than the Ivans ever could. Or so she imagined, anyhow.

Luisa had a better grip on things. "They aren't just playing at soldiers, remember. For them, it's real, especially if . . . if things go wrong."

Before Trudl could answer, the door opened again. The Russian sentry gestured with his weapon. *Come out.* Warily, the women did. He and a couple of other soldiers herded them to a waiting train. The windows on the cars had bars and shutters on them. The Red Army men stuffed Luisa and her fellow victims into a car that was already full of miserable women. The door slammed behind them with a horribly final sound. A bar thudded down to make sure they couldn't force it.

A few minutes later, the train pulled out of the station. All Luisa knew was that it was heading east.

Gustav Hozzel lit a Lucky from a K-ration pack. The cigarette and the rations were both American. So were the pot-shaped helmet on his head and the olive-drab uniform he wore.

The rest of the Germans spooning food out of tins and smoking looked like Yanks, too. The USA had plenty of weapons and equipment for all its own men and for anybody who fought alongside them. When you saw just how much the Americans had, and how they took it all for granted, you couldn't very well not be daunted.

Some of his own countrymen—most of them retreads, a few kids who'd been too young to fight in 1945—carried Springfields. The U.S. rifle worked so much like the Mauser; the biggest difference was the caliber of the ammo they fired. Some had what the Amis called grease guns. The American machine pistol fired .45 cartridges. If you got in the way of one, it would do for you, all right. Others, Gustav among them, used PPDs or PPShs, as many *Soldaten* had last time. There was nothing wrong with the Ivans' submachine guns. They might be ugly, but they sure worked.

After blowing a smoke ring, Gustav said, "I want to get my hands on one of those Red assault rifles—that's what I want. You can spray like a machine pistol with 'em, but they've got almost as much range as a rifle." He pointed toward somebody's Springfield.

Max Bachman paused halfway down a tin of ham and eggs. He liked that one better than Gustav did. "I wouldn't mind getting one, either, but keeping it in cartridges would be a bitch." The new Russian weapon fired a round halfway between those for ordinary rifles and submachine guns.

"It's nothing but a goddamn copy of the *Sturmgewehr* we rolled out in '44," Rolf said. Gustav had fought beside him for weeks, but still didn't know his last name. He did know Rolf had served in the *Leibstandarte Adolf Hitler,* one of the crack SS panzer divisions. Rolf still had the headlong bravery—and the taste for blood—that had marked the *Waffen*-SS.

Gustav remembered the *Sturmgewehr,* too. He'd craved one, but he hadn't got one. The Germans never had enough of them. More and more Russians were using their version, though.

"Whatever it is, it uses funny cartridges. That's the drawback," Gustav said. He didn't feel like arguing with Rolf right now. He was too goddamn tired. He hadn't been pulled out of the line since he started fighting. He'd gone west with it.

Now he was in the town of Wesel, a few kilometers north of Duisburg and only a few kilometers east of the Dutch border. If the Russians forced the Americans, English, and French—and the Germans like him who fought on their side—out of West Germany, they won a big chunk of the war.

Not far enough away, artillery thundered. Gustav cocked his head to one side, gauging the guns. They were Russian, all right: 105s and 155s. Since the shells weren't screaming in on his buddies and him, he relaxed again. He fished another Lucky out of the five-pack that came with the rations and lit it. Some other sorry bastards would catch hell from those Russian presents, but he wouldn't.

He wouldn't this time.

American guns answered the Ivans. As long as the gunners

murdered one another, that was fine by Gustav. He only hated them when they came after the guys who couldn't shoot back at them.

Sometimes, in fast-moving battles, foot soldiers overran the other side's artillery. Somehow, the assholes who served the guns hardly ever got taken prisoner. They wound up dead instead, stretched out beside the weapons that had dished out so much murder. Artillery was the big killer. Everybody knew it.

The Russians sure did. They used cannons as if they feared somebody would outlaw them tomorrow morning. Man for man, the Germans had always been better than their Red Army foes. But the Russians not only had more men, they had way more guns, sometimes ten or fifteen times as many as the *Wehrmacht* on the same stretch of front. When that hammer dropped, it dropped hard.

And they were fighting the ground war the same way this time. Their panzers were bigger and nastier than they had been during the last round. More of their guns were self-propelled. That just let them have an easier time putting all their firepower right where they wanted it.

But they didn't have everything their own way. American jet fighters screamed by, no more than a couple of hundred meters above the ground. They had rockets under their swept-back wings. They looked like Me-262s, but the Amis used far more of them than the *Luftwaffe* ever had. For that matter, so did the Russians.

Max Bachman dug his right index finger deep into his ear. "Between the guns and the jets, I'll be deaf as a post by this time next week," he said.

"What?" Gustav asked, deadpan.

Bachman started to answer him, then stopped and gave him a dirty look instead. "Funny, Gustav. Funny like a truss."

Gustav blew him a kiss. "I love you, too."

Then a heavy machine gun coughed into angry life. It was a Russian gun; the rhythm and the reports differed from those of the American equivalent. Almost before he knew how it had got there, Gustav's PPSh was in his hands, not at his feet. The others had grabbed their weapons just as quickly.

"Back in business at the same old stand!" Rolf sang out. He sounded positively gay about it. Gustav was plenty good at what he did in the field, but he didn't take that kind of delight in it.

Something went *whoosh-crash!* That was an American bazooka, not a Russian rocket-propelled grenade. The bazooka had inspired the German *Panzerschreck;* the German *Panzerfaust* seemed to be the model for the Red Army's RPG. Both kinds of weapons could wreck a tank with a square hit. Both were also good for flattening anything else that needed knocking down.

This one knocked down a shop a block from where the Germans had been eating and smoking and were taking cover. Somebody inside the shop started screaming and wouldn't shut up. Gustav couldn't tell whether the wounded man was an Ivan or a German civilian who'd been too stupid to refugee out of Wesel before it turned into a battleground. One nationality's mortal anguish sounded pretty much like another's.

Ten meters away from Gustav, Max grimaced behind a beat-up stone wall. "I wish he'd be quiet," Bachman said, and then, after a little while, "I wish somebody'd *make* him be quiet."

"Tell me about it," Gustav said with feeling. "You keep listening to that, you start thinking about making those noises yourself. It's the goddamn goose walking over your grave—with jackboots on."

"You got that right," Max said. "Why don't the Russians finish him off, the sorry son of a bitch? That kind of horrible racket has to drive them around the bend, same as it does with us."

Both Germans bitched about the suffering man in the smashed shop. Neither broke cover to go over to finish him off. The Russians wouldn't be sure that was what they were doing. It would look as if they were trying to advance and take control of the shop's ruins. The Ivans would shoot them before they got there.

And the Red Army men couldn't have had a clear path that way, either. They had to figure Germans or Americans would plug them if they put the wounded fellow to sleep. After all, one bazooka round had already hit that building. Another could follow.

So the screaming man in there went right on screaming for the next two hours. As far as Gustav could tell, he fell silent of his own accord, not because anyone killed him. Even after he did, though, the noises he made echoed and reechoed inside the German's head. *That could be me,* they said. *That could be me.*

* * *

A Red Army man with a sergeant's shoulder boards said something in Russian to Istvan Szolovits. "I have no idea what you're talking about, pal," the Hungarian Jew replied in Magyar.

That was as much gibberish to the Ivan as Russian was to Szolovits. *"Yob tvoyu mat'!"* the noncom snarled.

Istvan did understand that particular unendearment. Not letting on that he did, though, seemed the better part of valor. The Russian looked very ready to use the PPSh clamped in his hairy paws. Since it had a seventy-one-round snail drum attached, if he started shooting he wouldn't stop till he'd puréed whatever had pissed him off.

Taking a calculated risk, Istvan asked, *"Sprechen Sie Deutsch?"* If a Hungarian and a Russian had any language in common, German was the top candidate. Of course, if the sergeant did speak German, he was liable to order Istvan to do something that would get him killed. That was where the risk came in.

But the Russian just looked disgusted. *"Nyet!"* he answered proudly, and spat at Szolovits' feet. Istvan stood there with his best stupid expression plastered across his face. The Russian spun on his heel and stomped off. Every line of his body radiated rage.

"He's a sweetheart, isn't he?" Sergeant Gergely said from behind Istvan. Istvan jumped. He hadn't heard his own superior coming up. Gergely could be cat-quiet when he chose.

"Sure is, Sergeant," Szolovits said.

Gergely's chuckle had a nasty edge to it. It often did. Coming from that ferret face, the wonder was that sometimes it didn't. "You're thinking the asshole was just like me," he said, daring Istvan to deny it.

Deny it Istvan did: "No, Sergeant, honest to God, I wasn't thinking that at all. That Russian, he was only a bruiser."

"And I'm not . . . only a bruiser?" Gergely could be most dangerous when he seemed smoothest—which went a long way toward proving he wasn't only a bruiser.

"You know damn well you're not," Szolovits blurted.

For a split second, Sergeant Gergely preened. He had his share of vanity: maybe more than his share. But he came by it almost honestly. He'd worn a *Stahlhelm* and fought in Admiral Horthy's *Honved* when Hungary joined Hitler's invasion of

Russia. Not only that, he'd survived the horrible Russian siege and conquest of Budapest near the end of the war.

And he was still a soldier, now for the Hungarian People's Army. A Soviet-style helmet covered his dome. Instead of the old *Honved*'s tobacco-brown khaki cut almost in Austro-Hungarian style, his uniform, like Istvan's, looked Russian except for being made from greener cloth. No mere bruiser could have performed that handspring of allegiances so acrobatically. He might be ugly and nasty, but his brains worked fine.

He carried a PPSh like the Russian's, though he fed his with thirty-five-round boxes rather than snail drum—he said he could change and charge them faster. He gestured with the muzzle. "C'mon, kid. Let's see what's going on up there. What we don't know can kill us."

"So can what we do know," Istvan said in hollow tones, but he followed Gergely through the ruins of Raesfeld. The village lay east of Wesel, in the middle of the forest called the Dämmerwald. The forest had also been pretty comprehensively ruined; eye-stinging woodsmoke hung in the air, partly masking the wartime stink of death.

He knew he wouldn't move with such smoothness and silence as the sergeant showed if he stayed in the Hungarian People's Army for the next fifty years. He was tall and loosely put together—shambling, if you wanted to get right down to it. With light brown hair, hazel eyes, and a nose-shaped nose, he didn't look especially Jewish. Only his mouth really gave him away.

Out in the forest, an American rifle cracked. Whether an American or a German fired it, Istvan didn't know. The Red Army and its fraternal socialist allies seined the areas they occupied with a coarse net. Little fish could slip through the mesh and make trouble later on.

Most of the soldiers in Raesfeld were Russians. They either ignored the Hungarians or sneered at them, depending on whether they took them for countrymen or recognized that they belonged to a satellite army. There was that sergeant who'd growled at Istvan. He'd liberated a bottle of wine from somewhere and was guzzling it down. Of course, he'd be more used to vodka. If that was what you drank most of the time, you could pour down a lot of wine before you felt it.

That American rifle barked again. A Russian major not ten

meters from Istvan threw his hands in the air and let out a high-pitched, bubbling screech as he fell over. Blood puddled on the paving under him. A Red Army private ran up to drag him to safety, and the sniper shot him, too. He went down without a sound and lay motionless. Istvan had seen enough horror to be sure he wouldn't get up again.

A machine gun started hosing down the edge of the Dämmerwald. Maybe it would punch the rifleman's ticket for him, maybe not. The bastard had already earned his day's pay any which way.

And, as soon as the machine gun quieted, a defiant rifle round spanged off brickwork too close to Istvan for comfort. A furious Soviet officer ordered men into the forest to hunt the sniper down.

"Those fuckers are like cockroaches," Sergeant Gergely said. "You can never step on all of them, no matter how hard you try." *An A-bomb would do it,* Istvan thought. How could you have people hiding in the woods if you eliminated both woods and people?

The machine gun banged away to help the hunters advance. As soon as it eased back for a bit, the sniper out there squeezed off a couple of rounds to remind the Russians they hadn't killed him. A Red Army soldier near the edge of the woods bellowed in pain and let out a horrible stream of profanity. Istvan understood only bits of it, but admired the incandescent flow of the rest.

"That Yank or Fritz out there will be disappointed," he remarked as aid men brought the wounded soldier back to Raesfeld. "He didn't kill that guy—he just put him out of action for a while."

"Half the time—more than half—that's all a sniper wants," Sergeant Gergely said. "Look. Two guys are taking him back to a hospital tent. A doctor will have to work on him there. He'll lie on his ass in a bed for a while, and more people'll need to feed him and wash him and change his bandages. A wounded man makes more trouble than a dead one. If somebody catches a round in the ear and just drops, you plug in a replacement and go on. This way, a whole bunch of people have to waste days dealing with the fucker."

"Huh." Istvan wasn't a dope, or he didn't think he was, but he'd never looked at war's economics from that angle before. The Russian machine gun started up once more, and Ivans with machine pistols wasted ammo on whatever their imaginations fed them. When they stopped, the sniper took another shot at somebody. That made Istvan say, "They ought to drop an A-bomb on the woods. That would settle the son of a bitch, sure as hell."

To his surprise, Gergely cuffed him on the shoulder, hard enough to stagger him. "You wanna watch what you say, sonny, to make sure it doesn't come true."

"How do you mean?"

"Say the Russians throw the Americans out of West Germany. Only thing I can see stopping Truman from using A-bombs here is, the West Germans are on his side. But if they're all in Russian hands, how much does he care any more?"

"Gak," Istvan said when he'd worked that through. "You make me want to cross myself, and I don't even think it does any good."

Sergeant Gergely cuffed him again, this time with a chuckle. "Cute, kike—cute," he said. From his lips, the insult sounded almost affectionate. Szolovits had heard plenty worse from his alleged countrymen, anyhow.

Marian Staley dreamt about her large, comfortable house in Everett, Washington. She wandered from room to room to room—so many rooms, and all of them hers! The only thing wrong in the dream was that she couldn't find Bill in any of those rooms. She kept wandering. Her husband couldn't have gone very far . . . could he?

Her eyes opened. The house disappeared, swallowed up by wakefulness rather than the atomic fire that had really wrecked it. She lay curled up on the front seat of her Studebaker, where she'd slept every night since the A-bomb fell. Linda, her five-year-old, lay on the back seat. She was still small enough not to need to curl up to fit. She was also getting over a cold. Her snore would have done credit to somebody three times her age.

As for Bill, the waking Marian knew she could hunt from room to room forever without finding him. He'd been the copilot in a B-29 that went down over Russia. Marian didn't *know* his plane was carrying an A-bomb, but she figured it must have been.

So here she and Linda were, living in the refugee camp outside of shattered Everett. Camp Nowhere, the inhabitants called it. Nobody used the official name, Seattle-Everett Refugee Encampment Number Three. Who would, when Camp Nowhere fit like such a glove?

There were other camps like this outside of Everett and Seattle. There were more on the outskirts of Portland, and around the San Francisco Bay, and in Los Angeles, and next door to Denver, and in Maine. Marian had no idea how many people they held, not to the nearest hundred thousand. She wondered whether anyone did.

She supposed there would be refugee camps in Russia, too, and in Red China, and in the European countries one side or the other had bombed. Those places wouldn't be just like Camp Nowhere, though . . . or would they? The people in them might speak different languages and live under a different flag, but wouldn't they be disgusted and bored and irritated, too? They were people, weren't they? How could they be anything else?

It was getting light outside. Now that summer was arriving, sunup came early and sundown came late. Daylight here, almost as far north as you could go and stay in the USA, stretched like taffy in spring and summer. Marian liked that . . . when she had her house with all those rooms, and with curtains and windowshades on the windows. When you were sleeping in a Studebaker, all of a sudden these long days didn't seem so wonderful any more.

The outlines of tents of every size and shape made dark silhouettes against the brightening eastern sky. Most people lived in one of those. Most people here had no car. Plenty of autos—the dark-painted ones—on Marian's block had gone up in flames when the bomb fell. The Studebaker was bright yellow. It survived.

She wondered if it would start now. She had her doubts. She couldn't remember the last time she'd turned the key. What was the point? She wasn't going anywhere. She had nowhere to go. People with anywhere else to go didn't wind up in places like Camp Nowhere.

When her stomach told her it was getting on toward breakfast time, she woke Linda. Her daughter was no more happy about getting up than any other little kid. "You've got to do it," Marian said. "Potty and then food and then kindergarten."

"Yuk!" Linda said. Marian didn't know which of those she was condemning, or whether she meant all of them. Any which way, she sounded very sincere.

Sincerity, though, cut no ice with Marian. She made herself sound like a drill sergeant: "You heard me, kiddo. Get moving!"

Every once in a while, Linda would mutiny and need a smack on the behind to get her in gear. Marian didn't like to do it. No doubt her folks hadn't liked to spank her, either. But they had when she earned it, and now she did, too. She was glad it didn't come to that this morning. Linda looked sullen, but she got out of the car with her mother.

Marian didn't like the latrine tent any better than Linda did. The seats were just holes in plywood set above metal troughs with running water. Even those were an improvement on the slit trenches that had been here at first. Still no stalls. No privacy, not even when you had your period. And in spite of the running water, it smelled horrible.

Breakfast wasn't wonderful, either. The choices were sludgy oatmeal or cornflakes and reconstituted powdered milk. The milk that went with the oatmeal was reconstituted, too. The milk Marian poured into her instant coffee (which reminded her of hot mud) was condensed. To her, it tasted like a tin can; before the bomb fell, she'd used half-and-half or real cream. The sugar, at least, was the McCoy. Linda slathered it on her cornflakes. Marian couldn't cluck. Without it, they had all the flavor of soggy newspaper.

Fayvl Tabakman came into the refectory tent a few minutes after Marian and Linda sat down. The cobbler gravely touched a forefinger to the front of his old-style tweed cap. Marian nodded back. He was a familiar face; she'd gone to his little shop before the bomb hit. And he was a nice man.

He and his friends—also middle-aged Jews from Eastern Europe—never groused about the food or the latrines or the sleeping arrangements here. Tabakman had a number tattooed on his upper arm. After Auschwitz, Camp Nowhere had to seem like the Ritz by comparison.

"You are good, Marian?" he asked. Considering that he'd been in the country only a few years, he spoke excellent English.

"Yes, thanks," she answered. He'd lost his whole family to the Nazis. Of all the people she knew, he best understood what she was going through now that Bill was dead. "How are you?"

He shrugged. "Still here." She nodded; she knew what that meant, all right. But then Tabakman smiled. "How are you, Linda?"

"These are blucky cornflakes," she said.

"Blucky." He tasted the word—if that was what it was. Then he nodded. "Well, I would not be surprised. Now you will excuse me, I hope." He lined up to get his own breakfast. Odds were it would be blucky, too, but not next to what the Master Race had fed him in Poland, when it bothered to feed him at all. From what he'd said, he'd been down to about ninety pounds when the last war ended. He wasn't big, and he remained weedy, but at ninety pounds he would have been a walking skeleton.

The Germans, of course, had done their best to kill off the Jews and queers and Gypsies and other undesirables they shipped to Auschwitz and the other concentration camps they set up. The Americans were trying to keep the people in Camp Nowhere and the other refugee camps as comfortable and healthy as they could. Somebody like Fayvl Tabakman, with standards of comparison, had no trouble telling the difference.

To someone like Marian, who was used to a comfortable, middle-class life, this seemed much too much like a concentration camp.

It had started to drizzle while they were eating breakfast. Linda made theatrical noises of despair. Marian had lived in Washington long enough to take the rain in stride. She didn't suppose real concentration camps had kindergartens. This one reminded her that people here *were* doing their best, not their worst.

Then four National Guardsmen in fatigues came by carrying a stretcher with a body on it. Definitely a body, not someone hurt—a towel covered the face. She'd seen that a lot in her earliest days here, as people died of radiation sickness and injuries from the bomb. She'd got a dose of radiation sickness herself, as had Linda, but luckily they were both mild cases. This might have been someone who'd lingered till now and then at last given up the ghost.

More likely, though, it was somebody who couldn't stand it here and killed himself: the corpse had been a man. Plenty of people got sick to death or bored to death of living like this, and chose to end things on their own terms. Without Linda to worry about, she might have thought of it herself, especially after she learned Bill was dead. If hanging on seemed a living death, it was better than the other kind.

She supposed.

SOME THINGS CAME BACK to you as if you never left them behind. When the Red Army dragged Ihor Shevchenko off his collective farm outside of (now radioactive) Kiev, he didn't need long to get the hang of things again, in spite of the wounded leg that gave him a limp. He'd served the Soviet Union from 1942 to 1945. It was like riding a bicycle. You didn't forget how.

Take footcloths. Most countries' soldiers wore socks under their boots. On the *kolkhoz,* Ihor had. Red Army men didn't. They did things the way the Tsars' troopers had before them—probably the way everybody had, till some smart cookie thought of socks. They wrapped a long strip of cloth around each foot to protect it from blisters.

Learning how to wrap your feet was an art of sorts. It took practice. A corporal had beaten Ihor black-and-blue when he learned too slowly for the noncom's taste.

No corporal would get that kind of chance this time around. A bored sergeant gave Ihor a uniform. Most of the men getting theirs with him were retreads, too. A few were fresh conscripts. They looked shit-scared at what was about to happen to them. And well they might. A lance-corporal with a clipper hacked off everyone's hair. Then it was time to don the clothes Ihor had been issued.

His tunic and trousers were too big. Well, that was better than the other universal size, too small. He'd just tighten his belt. His helmet was too small. He traded with somebody who had a smaller noggin and a bigger metal pot.

He got the footcloths wrapped without even noticing what he was doing. He hadn't messed with the goddamn things since 1945, but his fingers still knew what to do, the same way they did when he lit a cigarette. Thinking consciously about either one would only make him mess it up.

"How—how did you do that, uh, Comrade Veteran?" The kid next to him on the bench had no idea how to go about it. He also had no idea whether Ihor would whale the snot out of him for daring to speak at all.

Some guys who'd been through the mill would have, just as a kind of warming-up exercise. Ihor wasn't that kind, any more than he found enjoyment from kicking a kitten. "Here. I'll show you," he said. And he did, quickly and deftly.

As quickly, he unwound the footcloth he'd done up. "But—" the kid started.

"Shut up," Ihor explained, not without sympathy. "I'm not your mama. You've got to be able to do it yourself."

After a wounded-puppy look, the youngster tried. It wasn't a good job; his foot would blister and bleed in short order. So would the other one, which he did no better. Well, that was how you learned. Pain made the best teacher of all.

Ihor pulled on his boots. They were too small; they'd tear up his tootsies no matter how well he wrapped them. As with his helmet, he swapped with somebody who'd got big ones but had small feet.

A lieutenant with a hook where his right hand should have been carried a rifle in his left. "Listen up, you pussies!" he yelled. "How many of you know how to shoot and how to keep your piece clean?"

Most of the men raised a hand. Only the few pimpled kids hung back. Yes, the Red Army was digging deep, for whatever the USSR could give it. Ihor didn't think that mutilated lieutenant would head for the front with them, but he could serve back here in the Ukraine and give some able-bodied fellow the chance to catch the next bullet.

"I'll take you to the armory next," he said. "Some of you will get a Mosin-Nagant"—he hefted the rifle to show the uninitiated what that meant—"and the rest will use the PPD or the PPSh."

Greatly daring, Ihor raised a hand. The lieutenant aimed the hook's point at him as if it tipped a rapier. He knew what that meant; if the officer didn't like his question, he'd catch it but good. "Comrade Lieutenant," he said, "will any of us get Kalashnikov's new automatic rifle?"

The hook came down at the same time as the lieutenant shook his head. Ihor wouldn't land an AK-47, but he wasn't in trouble, or he didn't think he was. "Not enough to go around," the officer said. "Guards units have first call on them, then other top-of-the-line formations. If this regiment gets them, it will have to earn them."

How did you earn better weapons? If the last war was any guide, by using the ones you had till most of you were dead. People said that in the early days of the fighting against Hitler, some units went into action ordered to pick up fallen comrades' rifles and use those.

Ihor ended up with one of the older PPDs. He didn't care. They both used the same ammo. They were both sturdy. And, at the close ranges he was likely to find in Western Europe, they were both handier and more dangerous than a rifle would have been.

The pup who didn't know how to wrap footcloths got a Mosin-Nagant. He held it as if he'd never touched a firearm before—and he probably hadn't. He followed Ihor around like a real stray dog looking for a master. Ihor found out that his name was Misha Grinovsky and that he came from Podolsk, a no-account town not far south of Moscow. He didn't much care about any of that, but it poured out of the kid like vodka from a cracked bottle.

"Can you show me how to take care of the rifle and shoot it, Comrade, please?" he asked.

"How come you don't know? What were you doing before you got conscripted?" Ihor snapped.

"I was going to start pipefitters' school," Misha said.

"Terrific. Fucking wonderful." Ihor rolled his eyes. Yes, it was like the early days of the last war all over again. They'd give somebody a uniform and shove him into battle in the hope that he lived. There it was, survival of the fittest . . . or the luckiest. If you did live through a couple of fights, you started to have some idea of what you needed to do to keep breathing. If you didn't, well, they'd throw somebody else in after you. Maybe he'd pick things up fast enough to do the *rodina* some good.

Trucks took the new regiment to the railroad station. They had Soviet nameplates, not the American ones that had adorned the trucks Ihor rode in during the last war. But they looked and sounded pretty much the same as those.

By then, the unit had acquired officers and noncoms with a full complement of body parts. The first lieutenant in charge of Ihor's company said, "We're going straight into action, boys. Most of you are veterans and don't need to waste a lot of time with training. The rest of you will pick it up in a hurry."

Had he said *The rest of you will get slaughtered in a hurry,* he would have come closer to the truth. Ihor knew that. So did the rest of the old sweats. Misha Grinovsky's eyes said he suspected as much, too. He opened his mouth to ask, then clamped it shut again. Ihor didn't blame him. Sometimes getting your suspicions confirmed was the last thing you needed.

Up chugged the train. Misha stared at it in dismay. "Those are all boxcars," he squeaked. "Where are the ones with windows and compartments, the ones people go in?"

"They'd cram us into those like you cram herrings into a tin," Ihor answered. "We'll likely have more room in a boxcar."

Misha didn't believe it for a minute. "We're not horses or cows!"

As if they were, the boxcar into which their section got herded had a thick layer of straw over its bottom planks. The straw smelled of animal manure and piss, too, though the buckets the Red Army had provided for its new human passengers even came with lids. By the standards of these accommodations, that counted for luxury. Ihor already knew it. If Misha Grinovsky didn't stop one right away, he'd find out for himself.

Groaning and snorting, the locomotive pulled the train out of the station. Like many of the men it carried, it had seen better years. Yes, they were heading west, toward the fighting. Vodka came out to dull that grim fact. So did cards and dice, to redistribute whatever wealth the soldiers had. Ihor nodded to himself. No, not a goddamn thing had changed.

Herschel Weissman tapped the order form on the clipboard with a blunt, nicotine-stained forefinger. "The refrigerator and the washing machine go to this address," he said. "It's right near Manchester and Vermont."

"I know where it is, boss," Aaron Finch answered quietly.

"Sure you do." The man who'd founded and still ran Blue Front Appliances nodded. "The trouble is, Jim will, too. Don't let him give you any *tsuris,* you hear?" That he let a Yiddish word creep into a conversation other people might overhear showed how important he thought the point was.

Aaron nodded. He was a lean, weathered, medium-sized man five months away from his fiftieth birthday. Ridiculously thick glasses perched on his formidable nose. His eyes were so bad, they'd kept him out of the Army in World War II.

He'd joined the merchant marine instead. The only thing the guys who put together freighter crews cared about was a pulse. They couldn't afford to be fussy, and weren't. On the Murmansk run, in the Mediterranean, and in the South Pacific, he'd seen as much danger as most Army or Navy men. After the war, it got him exactly no benefits. That disgusted him, but what could you do?

"I'll deal with Jim," he promised. "I'm not jumping up and down about going to that part of town myself, you know. I'll do it, but I'm not jumping up and down."

One of the two atom bombs that hit Los Angeles landed downtown. The other tore up the harbors at San Pedro and Long Beach. The delivery address was closer to the first of those. It was out of the zone that had seen a lot of damage, but not very far out. From the Glendale warehouse, the truck would have to go through or around that zone to get there.

Herschel Weissman clicked his tongue between his teeth. It wasn't quite *Et tu, Brute?,* but it might as well have been. "Aaron, we really need any sale we can get, wherever it is," he said. "Those goddamn bombs blew up our business along with everything else."

"Sure, sure." Aaron nodded again. He understood that at least as well as his boss did. He'd seen his hours cut because Blue Front was hurting. When you had a wife and a two-year-old back home, that pinched hard. He would have felt only half a man if Ruth had to go out looking for work because he couldn't make ends meet on his own.

"Tell you what," Weissman said. "I'll give you double time for the run. You don't have to tell Jim about that."

Aaron paused to light a Chesterfield. He went through two or three packs a day, and the little ritual gave him a moment to think. "Give him what you give me, or else don't bother giving me anything," he said after his first drag. "I won't be doing anything he isn't."

Weissman didn't call him a *shlemiel,* but his face did the talking for him. That was bound to be one reason he headed the company and Aaron drove a truck and lugged heavy appliances around. But Aaron didn't care. He had his own stubborn notions about what was fair and what wasn't. Herschel

Weissman must have seen as much. He lit his own cigarette and sighed out smoke. "All right. Double time for both of you. Now get lost."

Even with double time, Jim Summers wasn't thrilled. "Them atoms'll cook you from the inside out," he said. He had a Deep-South drawl and maybe a sixth-grade education. Whatever he knew about atoms, he'd got it from comic books.

Which didn't mean he was wrong. "We'll take the long way around, like we did when we went to Torrance," Aaron told him. "We won't go through downtown." You could do that again; some of the roads were open, and they were working hard on rebuilding the freeways. But even Aaron's lively curiosity didn't make him want to try it.

Jim raised an eyebrow. His weren't as bushy as Andy Devine's, but they were in that ballpark. "If *you* don't want to try it, anybody who does has got to be nuts," he said.

"I'll try not to dance on the lawns and swing from the telephone poles," Aaron said dryly.

"You better not. They'll come after you with a butterfly net if'n you do." To Jim Summers, irony was what his wife used to put the creases in his gabardine work pants.

Aaron drove the big blue truck west to Sepulveda before swinging south. That took him past the veterans' cemetery and UCLA to the east and an enormous refugee camp to the west. Things in the camp were supposed to be getting better, but he could still smell it as he piloted the truck past it. Too many people hadn't bathed or flushed often enough for too long.

He wanted to turn east at Wilshire so he could see more of what the bomb had done. They were almost through tearing down the shattered Coliseum. They hadn't got around to Wrigley Field yet, a mile or so farther south. The PCL Angels were sharing Gilmore Field with the Hollywood Stars. No one seemed to have any idea where the Rams and Trojans and Bruins would play come fall. The look Jim sent him, though, persuaded him not to go east till he had to.

That was at Manchester, most of an hour south of Wilshire. Even then, Jim pulled a bandanna from his trouser pocket and tied it over his nose and mouth. "You look like a bank robber in a bad horse opera," Aaron said. His younger brother, Marvin, had worked in the movies for a while—till people noticed how annoying he could get, Aaron had always thought. Some of the Hollywood slang he'd brought home rubbed off.

"I don't give a shit if I look like a camel in the zoo," Jim said. "I don't want to breathe none o' that radio-action crap."

Aaron thought about correcting him, but decided that was more trouble than it was worth. So was asking how good a screen that none too clean, cheaply woven bandanna made.

The house taking delivery of the washer and refrigerator hadn't got any damage. A colored family was moving in down the block. Jim Summers sighed. "I reckoned the bomb took out most o' the niggers here," he said mournfully. "Guess I was wrong. Oh, well." He didn't like Jews, either. Because Aaron carried an ordinary-sounding last name (it had been Fink till his father anglicized it), he'd never realized his partner was one. No one had ever claimed he was long on brains.

Wrestling the appliances down the ramp from the truck to the street and then into the house was part of what made the job so much fun. Aaron knew he'd feel it in his back and shoulders when he got home tonight. He was sure he wouldn't have ten years earlier. This getting old business was for the birds.

"Thank you very much," said Mrs. Helen McAllister, who'd ordered the icebox and washer. She gave them lemonade made from lemons off a tree in her back yard. After she signed all the paperwork and wrote Aaron a check, she added, "Did you see the coons buying Joe Sanders' place? My God! This is the other side of Manchester! Who ever thought they'd come this far?"

Since Aaron had nothing to say to that, he kept his mouth shut. Getting into political arguments with customers wasn't smart. Jim Summers didn't argue with Mrs. McAllister. He agreed with her. He sympathized with her. Aaron practically had to drag him out of the house and back to the truck.

"Couple more spooks buy around here, poor gal's house ain't gonna be worth the paper it's printed on," Jim said.

"It's not our business any which way," Aaron said.

"It's a damn shame, is what it is." Jim redid his mask, which he'd taken off to bring in the appliances. "'Sides, she was purty."

"She wasn't bad." Aaron could agree about that. He noticed nice-looking women, too. What man didn't? Since finding Ruth, though, he hadn't done any more than notice. If he was happy where he was, why risk messing that up? He made a Y-turn on the narrow street and started the long, roundabout trip back to Glendale.

* * *

Along with the rest of his crew, Konstantin Morozov had slept under their T-54. The tank was stopped on hard ground. Morozov and the other three men did some digging under the chassis to make sure it wouldn't settle and squash them. Then they rolled themselves in their blankets and sacked out. The hardened steel above them and to their right and left would keep them safe against anything this side of an atom bomb. In case somebody dropped one of those on him, Konstantin figured he'd die before he had time to worry about it. So he didn't.

He had enough to worry about without the great destroyer, the ender of worlds. First and foremost came enemy tanks. The American Pershing and Patton and English Centurion were at least as good as his T-54. They were slower, but had thicker armor. Their guns were smaller than his 100mm monster, but carried better fire-control systems. They could kill him and he could kill them. That was what it boiled down to. Who saw whom first, who shot first, who shot straightest—those were the things that counted.

He worried about enemy foot soldiers with bazookas, too. The Hitlerites had had some of those in the last year of the Great Patriotic War. The Americans had more, as they had more of everything. The T-54 carried better protection than the T-34/85 had, but a bazooka round could still torch everything and everybody in the fighting compartment if it burned through.

And he worried about his new crew. The old guys had been fine. He'd been able to count on them. But they were all dead. He'd been blown out of the open cupola with his legs on fire when his last tank got killed. They hadn't made it, poor luckless bastards.

This new tank . . . These new guys . . . Vladislav Kalyakin, the driver, was a kid, but he was all right. He was a Byelorussian, a fellow Slav. The loader, Vazgen Sarkisyan, was an Armenian without much Russian. But a loader didn't need to know much. Like most tank crewmen, Morozov had started there himself. And, as blackasses went, Armenians were pretty much okay. Plenty of other swarthy types from the Caucasus were worse, anyway.

But Juris Eigims, the gunner, he was trouble with a capital T. He was either Latvian or Lithuanian; Konstantin wasn't sure which. Either way, he didn't like Russians. He didn't like it that his little pissant land was part of the USSR, the way it had been part of the Russian Empire before World War I. When he was a kid, it had been its own two-kopek country. Nationalist bandits still prowled the Baltics, the way they did in the Ukraine.

And Juris Eigims really didn't like Konstantin. That was personal, not political. As Konstantin had lost his crew, so these guys had lost their commander. Eigims must have thought he would take charge of this tank. Instead, he got a Russian sergeant dropped on him. By his attitude, he would have preferred an atom bomb.

Morozov would have preferred a puff adder in the gunner's seat. One of those would have been less dangerous. But he had what he had, not what he would have preferred. Somehow, he had to get the best out of Eigims—and keep him from going over the hill first chance he saw.

For now, he wriggled out from under the tank. Half a dozen other armored behemoths had stopped nearby, some with camouflage nets over them, the rest under trees. The Red Army always remembered *maskirovka.* Here in the Ruhr, there weren't that many trees to hide under. Konstantin had never seen so many towns packed so close together. Russia had nothing like this.

Sarkisyan crawled out, too. He'd been sleeping next to Morozov. "I must have woke you up," Konstantin said. "Sorry about that."

"Is of nothings, Comrade Sergeant." The Armenian shrugged broad shoulders. He was built like a brick, a good shape for a shell-jerker. Stubble darkened his cheeks and chin; he really needed to shave twice a day. His hairline came down almost to his tangled eyebrows. He would have made a tolerable werewolf.

Juris Eigims, by contrast, was slim, blond, and blue-eyed. He looked as if he'd come straight from the *Waffen*-SS: one more reason he and Konstantin hit it off so well.

"What's going on?" he asked. He spoke much better Russian than Vazgen Sarkisyan, but it was plainly a foreign language for him. His native tongue left him with an odd, singsong accent that set Morozov's teeth on edge.

"Not much, or it doesn't seem like it," the tank commander answered. And it *was* pretty quiet. It was getting light, but the sun hadn't risen yet. The air smelled of smoke, but of old, sour smoke—nothing new or close. A battery of Soviet 105s boomed, one gun after another, as if going through limbering-up exercises. They too, though, were off in the distance. Up ahead of the tanks only spatters of rifle fire cut the silence—hardly anything.

Corporal Eigims cocked his head to one side, studying the sounds as gravely as if he were a Marshal of the Soviet Union, not a Latvian punk. "Think we'll break into Bocholt today?" he asked.

Konstantin shrugged, as Sarkisyan had earlier. "Depends on what they've moved up to stop us. One way or the other, we'll find out." He scratched himself. "What I think is, I want some breakfast."

Eigims' grin made him almost human, though he still looked too much like a German for Konstantin's comfort. "Breakfast—yeah!"

"Breakfast?" Vladislav Kalyakin emerged from under the T-54 just in time to hear the magic word.

"Breakfast," Konstantin agreed. They ate sausage and stale bread stolen from the last village they'd rolled through, and washed it down with hot tea. Kalyakin had a little aluminum stove he'd taken from a dead Englishman, and enough of the tablets that fueled it to let them brew some without making a fire.

When they were fueled, they checked out the tank. As Morozov went over the engine, he eyed Juris Eigims. The Balt had tried to show him up when he took over the T-54, but ended up with egg on his face instead. He wasn't pulling anything cute today, though.

They had half a load of ammo and half a tank of diesel fuel: enough to go on for a while, anyhow. Both sides were doing everything they could to foul up their foes' supply chains. The bomb that smashed Paris was supposed to make things hard on the Americans that way.

No sooner had Konstantin got into the commander's seat in the turret than Captain Lapshin's voice sounded in his earphones: "Ready to move out?"

"I serve the Soviet Union!" Morozov answered.

Away they went, and straight into trouble. The morning quiet popped like a soap bubble. One of the T-54s in the company took a hit from a 155 that had to be firing over open sights. What the heavy gun was doing so far forward, Konstantin had no idea. But it would have smashed a destroyer, not just a tank. The only hope was, the crew never knew what hit them.

Machine-gun bullets clattered off his own tank's glacis plate and turret. The infantrymen moving up with the T-54s puckered their assholes on account of machine guns. Those rounds would chip his machine's paint, but that was about it. But he needed the foot soldiers, too, to keep the sons of bitches with bazookas at a distance.

Il-10s roared by at rooftop height, gunning and rocketing the enemy. Morozov loved Shturmoviks. They were heavily armored—almost flying tanks themselves. They could take a lot of punishment, and they dealt out even more. They looked old-fashioned in the new jet age, but they could hang around a battlefield better than any jet.

Another T-54 stopped short, spewing smoke from the turret. Hatches flew open. Men bailed out. One of them was burning, the way Konstantin had been when he got blasted out of his tank. He hoped the luckless tanker lived. He hoped this machine didn't get hit the same way.

The Soviet drive stalled. The enemy had too many men, too many guns, and too many tanks in front of Bocholt. This wasn't like the war on the Eastern Front. You couldn't get around the foe and in behind him. He had something nasty waiting for you everywhere. You had to push through him, push him back. But not today.

Daisy Baxter tried to run the Owl and Unicorn the way her dead husband's family had run it for generations. Changes did come to the pub in Fakenham every so often. Flush toilets got added during Queen Victoria's reign, electric lights between the old queen's passing and the start of the First World War. These days, a wireless set—the Yanks from the Sculthorpe air base called it a radio, and so did more and more locals—sat on a shelf behind the bar. Sometimes people listened to it. More often, they ignored it.

But those were cosmetic changes. The smoky air, the potato crisps and meat pies and other salty pub grub, and, most important, the best bitter in wooden barrels in the cellar—those hadn't changed in a long time. Daisy saw no reason they should.

All of Fakenham had flush toilets these days, and electricity, and wireless sets, and automobiles. A couple of prosperous gents even boasted a telly in their homes. People who fancied banging the little East Anglian town's drum said it was modern as next week.

Daisy didn't call them a pack of stupid windbags when they went on like that. She might have thought it—she did think it—but she didn't say it. The way Fakenham looked to her, the externals might change, but the internals never did. Motorcars and televisions be damned. People in a mid-twentieth-century English small town still thought the way they had in a mid-eighteenth-century English small town, and all too likely in a mid-fourteenth-century English small town as well.

She knew they talked about her behind her back. Running the pub by herself didn't quite turn her into a scarlet woman, but it came close. The funny thing was, the USAF and RAF flyers who came to the Owl and Unicorn from Sculthorpe knew bloody well she was no such thing. They would have liked her ever so much better if she were.

They drank her beer and whiskey. They ate her snacks. They played darts in the snug—the locals, better practiced, commonly took their money without the least remorse. And they chatted her up and trotted out all their patented ladykiller routines. And, to a man, they struck out—an American turn of phrase she rather liked.

She knew they talked about her behind her back, too. They called her frigid. They called her a carpet-muncher. She was neither. She liked men fine, thank you very much. When she went to bed not too exhausted, she missed Tom's arms around her almost more than she could bear. He'd been part of a Cromwell crew in northwestern Germany during the last days of the war. A diehard with a *Panzerschreck* made sure he never saw Fakenham again.

But she knew that, if she slept with the customers, they wouldn't come to the Owl and Unicorn for the beer or the pub grub or the darts. They'd come for a go with her. Then she really would be the scarlet woman the Fakenham gossips made her out to be.

She didn't want that. So she always smiled. She was always friendly, but never too friendly. She was always polite. And she was always unavailable for anything more than a smile.

RAF men wore a slaty blue, Yanks in the USAF a darker shade. She wasn't sure which uniform annoyed her more. Some of the RAF officers really were bluebloods, and thought women fell at their feet by divine right. Some of the Americans thought all foreign women were tramps.

And then there was Bruce McNulty, one of the B-29 pilots who visited fire and devastation on cities under Stalin's muscular thumb. He never had come on so strongly as a lot of the flyers did. That left her surprised at herself for slapping him down as hard as she did.

She realized later, when it was too late, she'd done it more because she might be interested than because she wasn't. She wasn't used to being interested in a man. She hadn't been, not that way, since the War Ministry let her know Tom wouldn't be coming home.

She would have chalked it up to water over the damn dam if he hadn't shown up with roses one night after closing time not long before. She made sure she took those upstairs to her flat over the pub. If she'd left them where the customers could see them, everybody would have been sure he knew what she'd done to get them. That she hadn't done that at all had nothing to do with the price of a pint. Her life would have got complicated in ways she didn't need.

Or did she? She'd sometimes daydreamed about a handsome American pilot sweeping her off her feet and carrying her back to the States when his tour of duty here ended. She'd always assumed no Yank she slept with here would want to take her home with him. With Bruce, she wasn't so sure.

Then the locals started coming in, and she had no time for daydreams. Once Sculthorpe became a going concern, the men from Fakenham who visited the Owl and Unicorn mostly began to do it in the afternoon. Except for the darts hustlers, they left the evening to the officers and other ranks who bicycled in from the base. Oh, not always, but more often than not.

Some nights, no one from the base showed up. Those were the nights when the roar of big planes climbing into the darkness—and, much later, landing again—reverberated through Fakenham. Daisy always hoped as many came back as had set out.

Sometimes men suddenly stopped coming in. Sometimes she found out what happened to them; sometimes nobody ever mentioned their names again. You never could tell. When that silence fell, she didn't like to break it by seeming snoopy.

I will, though, if I think anything's happened to Bruce, she told herself. Then they'd know where her feelings lay. She didn't care, which was in itself a measure of how strong those feelings were.

Tonight, though, Bruce walked in early, as cheerful as if he were a commercial traveler rather than a B-29 pilot. How many A-bombs had he dropped? How many cities had he ruined? How many people had he incinerated? Daisy didn't like to think about that, but sometimes she couldn't help it. Bruce and the other pilots didn't like to talk about it, so they probably didn't care to contemplate it, either.

"Pint of your best bitter, dear," he told Daisy, and shoved two silver shillings across the bar.

A pint cost one and three. Daisy started to make change; he waved for her not to bother. That was a ridiculous tip, but not so ridiculous as the ones he'd left when he started coming around. "Thanks," Daisy murmured. "You really don't have to do that, you know."

He laughed. "What better do I have to spend my money on than good beer from a pretty girl?" he said. "Eat, drink—especially drink—and be merry, because tomorrow . . . Well, we're all better off not thinking about tomorrow, aren't we?"

The pilots might not want to talk about their friends and comrades who went down instead of coming back, but they had them on their minds, all right. They knew that what happened to those fellows could happen to them next. They knew it *would* happen to them if they flew enough missions. Sooner or later, the ball on the roulette wheel always landed in the zero slot, and people at the table lost their bets. Casinos never went broke. Pilots didn't keep coming back forever.

After a long draught from the pint, he said, "You know, one of these times, if you can find somebody to ride herd on this place for a while, we ought to go out dancing or something—if there's any place to go dancing around here."

"I expect there is." Actually, Daisy wasn't so sure of that herself. The last time she'd wondered about it, she'd been going out with Tom before . . . well, before.

"Can you get somebody, then?" Bruce asked.

"I expect I can." Daisy wasn't so sure of that, either. But she was very sure she'd try her hardest.

BORIS GRIBKOV and the rest of the Tu-4's crew had lingered in western Germany much longer than he'd ever expected they would. Having your navigator blow out the back of his head would do that to you.

They could have flown back to an airfield in the eastern zone or in Poland or Czechoslovakia. They could have done a little hop like that without a navigator, or with Alexander Lavrov, the bombardier, filling in for poor, dead Tsederbaum. It would have been safe enough.

But no one who outranked Gribkov thought for a moment of letting them get away without interrogation. First came the men from the MGB, the Ministry of State Security. "Did Lieutenant Tsederbaum show any sign of disaffection before committing suicide?" a Chekist with a double chin asked Gribkov.

Of course he did, you dumb prick, Gribkov thought. His face, though, showed nothing of what went on behind his eyes. In the USSR, you learned not to give yourself away . . . or you gave yourself away and paid the price for it.

You also learned not to give anyone else away if you could possibly help it. His voice as wooden as his features, the pilot said, "Never that I noticed, Comrade." They couldn't do anything to Leonid, not now. They could build a dossier against his relatives. Gribkov didn't care to lend them a hand.

"Before his act, was he in any way unsatisfactory in the performance of his duties?" the MGB man persisted. Yes, they were trying to make a case, all right.

"He wouldn't have won a Hero of the Soviet Union medal if he had been," Gribkov said, shaking his head. "We struck Seattle. We struck Bordeaux. We struck Paris. We couldn't have hit our targets without the best navigation."

"Then why did he do it?" the fat fool demanded.

He did it because *we struck Seattle and Bordeaux and Paris,* Boris thought. Tsederbaum made the mistake of seeing enemies as human beings. For a fighting man, that could be fatal. For the thoughtful Jew, it damn well had been.

Try explaining as much to a Chekist, though. To the men who'd been headquartered at the Lubyanka till the Americans turned it into radioactive fallout, enemies were always enemies. Even friends were sometimes enemies.

This fellow badgered Gribkov awhile longer, then gave up and left him alone. But he and his pals also had to interrogate the rest of the crew. They took their time about it. Boris didn't ask if anyone told them more than he had. The less you asked, the less you could get in trouble for later.

He got questioned again two days after the session with the MGB man. The fellow who grilled him this time wore the uniform of a Red Army major. Gribkov rapidly began to doubt that that was what he was, or that it was all of what he was. Everyone knew about the MGB. Hardly anyone heard more than whispers about the GRU, the Main Intelligence Directorate. It was the military's intelligence branch, aimed at the parts of the world that didn't belong to the Soviet Union.

"Did anyone get to Tsederbaum?" the major asked. "Did he talk to or listen to people he shouldn't have?"

"I don't think so, sir," Gribkov answered truthfully. "As far as I know, he spent just about all of his time with us and with other Soviet flyers and soldiers."

The major grunted. He'd introduced himself as Ivan Ivanov, a name so ordinary it couldn't be real. "Did he ever talk with foreigners? When you flew your plane in here, did he go out and find a German popsy to screw?"

"No, Comrade Major." Again, Gribkov told the truth. "Remember, he was a Jew. He liked Germans even less than Russians do, and that's not easy."

Another grunt from "Ivanov." "He was a rootless cosmopolite, you mean," he said, which was what the Party line called Jews when they were out of favor. "Who knows what those people really think? They're masters of mystification. It's part of what makes them so dangerous." Like the MGB man before him, he was working to build a case against the late Leonid Abramovich Tsederbaum.

As with the MGB man before him, Gribkov didn't want to help. "Sir, as far as I know, the only people he was dangerous to were the Soviet Union's enemies. Thanks to him, my bombs hit America once and France twice. How many other crews have done so well?"

"Ivanov" didn't answer, which was in itself an answer of sorts. The likely GRU man did say, "If he was such a stalwart in the service of the working class, why did he shoot himself like a plutocrat after a stock-market crash?"

"Comrade Major, the only person who could have told you that was Tsederbaum, and he isn't here to do it any more," Gribkov said.

"We don't need—we don't want—weaklings in important military positions," "Ivanov" said fretfully. "I have to get to the bottom of this, no matter how long it takes."

"You can't mean we won't fly any more missions till you do!" Boris said. There was a kick in the head for you! As far as the pilot could see, Tsederbaum had stuck the pistol in his mouth and pulled the trigger because he couldn't stand the missions the Tu-4 was flying. Now, because he had, it wouldn't fly them?

Was that irony? No, madness! And Boris knew that if he burst out laughing he'd never be able to explain it to the GRU man, any more than he would have been able to with the Chekist. People who served the Soviet Union in those ways had their sense of humor cut out of them as part of the initiation process, probably without anesthetic.

In any case, Major "Ivanov"—though his rank might be as fictitious as his name—shook his head. He wasn't so porky as the MGB man had been, but he'd never gone hungry for long. "No, no, Comrade, no. We will furnish you with a new navigator so you can keep on carrying the action to the imperialist warmongers. But the investigation will continue until we reach the truth concerning the late Lieutenant Tsederbaum."

"I serve the Soviet Union!" Gribkov said, which here meant something like *I'm stuck with whatever you tell me.*

The new navigator was a round-faced first lieutenant named Yefim Vladimirovich Arzhanov. Boris put him through his paces at the navigator's station, which lay directly behind his own but was separated from it by a bulkhead. As any pilot had to, Gribkov knew a little something about the art of navigation: enough to tell someone who also knew from a clown running a bluff. Arzhanov had a sleepy look to him, but he passed the tests the pilot gave him without needing to wake up all the way.

"You'll do," Gribkov said.

"Thank you, sir," Arzhanov said. "Did you think they were trying to stick a rotten egg in your crew?"

"Of course not," Boris answered, which, to anyone with ears to hear, meant *You bet!* "I just wanted to see how you run."

"Like a stopped clock, Comrade Pilot—I'm sure to be right twice a day," Arzhanov answered with a grin that made him look no more than fourteen.

His voice didn't sound like Tsederbaum's. He looked nothing like the Jew: he looked like the Russian he was. But it was a crack the dead man might have come out with. Gribkov shook his head. "I think the factory that makes navigators stamps them out crazy."

"That's me, sir. Just another spare part, at your service." Yefim Arzhanov came to attention, clacked his heels together, and saluted as if he were flying for Austria-Hungary in what was now the big war before last.

"You'll do, all right," Gribkov said. "Just what you'll do, I'm afraid to ask, but we'll all find out, won't we?"

The first thing Arzhanov did for the Tu-4 was guide the heavy bomber back to an airfield outside of Prague. As the dry run had given Boris confidence he would, he handled the short flight with unflustered competence.

Just getting away from the place where Leonid Tsederbaum decided the weight he carried was too much for his narrow shoulders came as a relief. Now they could get on with the war.

It was the middle of the night, moonless, cloudy, with spatters of warm July drizzle coming down every so often. It was dark as the inside of a concentration camp guard's heart, except when guns and rocket launchers going off lit the clouds' underside with brief, red, hellish glows.

It was, in other words, the perfect time for Gustav Hozzel to pull a sneak. He crawled through the shattered streets of Wesel, away from the blocks on the west side of town that the Germans and Americans still held and toward the Red Army's positions. He didn't tell his friends where he was going. He most especially didn't tell his company CO. Max and Rolf would have tried to talk him out of it. Captain Nowak would have ordered him not to try such a harebrained stunt. What they didn't know wouldn't hurt them.

A snake wouldn't have lifted any higher off the ground than he did. He could feel the buttons on his tunic front scraping the asphalt as he wriggled along. The humid air stank of smoke—most of it the nasty, toxic kind that came from burnt paint and motor oil and fuel—and of death. Except during the coldest stretches of Russian winter, that spoiled-meat reek walked hand-in-hand with war.

More rain dripped from the heavens. That was good, and it was bad. The Ivans would have a harder time spotting him. But he might not hear or see approaching trouble till it arrived. Every few meters, he paused to look and listen before moving on. He wasn't in a hurry. He just wanted to get back.

He had a bayonet in his right hand, a wire-cutter in his left. He hadn't brought his PPSh. Firing it would be nothing but a kind of suicide. He'd scream to the whole world, or all of it that mattered, *Here I am! Kill me!*

The really scary thing was, he'd done worse sneaks than this. That one through the snow in southern Poland during the last winter of the old war . . . He'd come back with a fifteen-kilo ham, enough to let him and his buddies gorge for a couple of days instead of starving. He'd been a hero in his section—till the Russian steamroller started rolling again, anyhow.

He wouldn't make his buddies fat this time. He did aim to make them jealous. Back and to the side of . . . was it this shattered building? Yes, sure enough—the apothecary's shop.

Gustav started to go round the corner, then froze. Somebody was already crouching over what he craved. If another man from his own side had beaten him to it, more power to the sneaky bastard.

But that wasn't somebody from his own side. Even as he watched, the Russian soldier started to drag his countryman's corpse back toward the part of town the Reds held securely. Silent as a hunting hawk, Gustav set down the wire-cutter and eased up into a crouch. Then he sprang on the unsuspecting Ivan's back.

His left palm covered the enemy soldier's mouth. His strong left arm pulled the Russian's head back. And the bayonet still in his right hand cut the man's throat. The Russian gurgled desperately for most of a minute. He thrashed with ebbing strength till he went limp. Gustav held that hand over his mouth for an extra little while, anyway. You didn't get to be an old soldier by taking chances you didn't have to.

So the Ivan was beyond doubt dead when Gustav slid him to the ground. He wasn't what the German was after. The body he'd wanted to recover was. The afternoon before, Gustav had seen that that guy'd bought a plot in spite of his AK-47. Gustav had wanted one for a long time. This was his chance to get hold of one.

Part of the stock was still wet from the blood of the Ivan he'd just disposed of. Swearing silently, he wiped his hand on his trouser leg. But it wouldn't be the first piece he'd carried that was bloodied in the literal sense of the word.

He frisked both dead Russians, and came up with five magazines for the assault rifle. They held thirty rounds apiece. That would keep him going for a little while, anyhow. If he couldn't get more, he'd go back to the PPSh. He wouldn't toss it just yet. He also discovered that one of the Ivans' canteens was full of vodka. That was worth having, too.

"Now," he said, shaping the words but not putting any sound behind them, "let's get the hell out of here."

Sometimes you got careless on the way back after you pulled a stunt like this. When you did, chances were you paid for it. Gustav took even more pains on his way back to his side's chunk of Wesel than he had on his foray into the Red Army's part of town.

The live Russians didn't know he'd been and gone. Neither did the German pickets. That amused and worried him at the same time. What he'd done, some enterprising Ivan could imitate.

He curled up in his blanket and shelter half and went to sleep. He'd snored through plenty worse than this on-and-off drizzle. He slept so hard, Rolf had to shake him awake once it got light. As soon as he uncocooned himself, the ex-LAH man saw his new toy. "Where'd you get *that*?" he demanded.

"Came in one of the cans from my last K-ration," Gustav said, deadpan.

Rolf cussed him out in German, Russian, and what was probably Magyar. Then he calmed down. His gaze sharpened. "First one I've seen close up," he said. "It looks *just* like a *Sturmgewehr*, doesn't it? Except for the crappy wood stock, I mean. Even that banana-shaped magazine's the same."

Gustav had seen only a few of the German assault rifles during the last war. They were made from stamped metal and plastic: no wood at all. "You know how the Russians copy shit," he said. "Monkey see, monkey do." He pulled off the receiver. "Are the guts the same, too?"

Rolf bent over to examine the Soviet rifle's working parts. He whistled softly between his teeth. "No. Not even close," he said, his admiration grudging but real. "Our piece was a lot more complicated. This . . . This is about as simple as it can get and still work, looks like."

"It does, yeah. Makes it easy to take care of, anyway. I like that," Gustav said. The PPSh was the same way. It was far less elegant than a German Schmeisser, but much more robust. Come to think of it, you could say the same thing about the T-34 when you set it in the scales against German panzers.

"You've got blood on you," Rolf remarked.

"It isn't mine. There'd be more if God wasn't pissing on us last night," Gustav said.

"Ganz gut." Rolf had heard enough to satisfy him. The only thing the *Waffen*-SS cared about was spilling the other guy's blood.

Instead of eating K-rations for breakfast, they got last night's stew reheated in a *Goulaschkanone—Landser* slang for a field kitchen. Barley, turnips, carrots, and bits of meat went down easy and put plenty of daub on the wattle of your ribcage.

They did if you got to finish them, anyhow. The Russians started early that morning, raining Katyushas down on the part of Wesel they hadn't seized before Gustav had more than half-emptied his mess kit. He let the little tin basin and spoon fly any which way as he dove for the nearest muddy foxhole. Those rockets screaming in always made him want to piss his pants. The first Germans at whom the Ivans had aimed Katyushas ran like rabbits—the ones the bombardment didn't kill, anyhow. If you wanted to flatten a square kilometer, a couple of launch racks' worth of Katyushas were the next best thing to an A-bomb.

The Ivans didn't have the advantage of surprise any more, though. Gustav huddled in his hole, waiting for the rockets to stop. If they didn't kill him, he'd have to fight them. They didn't. He did. He rapidly developed a deep affection for the Soviet assault rifle he'd killed to acquire. It beat the snot out of the PPSh.

But there were too many Russians, too many tanks. He thought he'd fallen back to the black days of 1945, when there were always too many tanks and too many Russians. He scrambled out of the foxhole to join the retreat. It was that or die.

He saw his mess tin, lying on the pavement. A fragment from a Katyusha had torn it almost in half. *One more war casualty,* he thought. He trotted northwest, toward the new defensive line the Germans and Amis were trying to set up.

"Give them the machine gun, Juris!" Konstantin Morozov shouted.

"I'm doing it, Comrade Sergeant," Juris Eigims replied. The gunner used the weapon coaxial with the T-54's cannon to spray the luckless enemy soldiers—Englishmen, Konstantin thought they were from the shape of their helmets—who had the bad luck to show themselves just as the tank chugged out from behind a burnt-out church.

Some of the Tommies fell over. Some ran back to the stone fence that had protected them till they came out from behind it. Others made pickup on their wounded and dead mates. The machine gun bit some of those guys, too. It didn't care that they were brave and wanted to save their comrades. It only cared that they were there, where it could reach them.

Morozov said, "Why don't you hit that fence with a round or two of HE? Then send in another one and smash whatever's right in back of it."

"Right, Comrade Sergeant." Eigims barked an order to Vazgen Sarkisyan. The loader slammed a 100mm shell into the breech and banged it closed. The Baltic gunner fired. Inside the turret, the roar wasn't too bad. Had he been out in the open air, Konstantin would have thought it took his head off.

Hit by fifteen kilos of speeding metal and high explosives, several meters of the stone fence abruptly ceased to be. So did a good many enemy soldiers behind those meters. The blasted bits of stone made more murderous shrapnel than anything the most fiendish shell-builder would pack into a casing.

"Want me to hit the wall again, Comrade Sergeant? We got good results from that last round." Eigims did understand that killing enemy troops was his own best chance of staying alive. While they were in action, he didn't go out of his way to undercut the tank commander.

Coughing on propellant fumes, Morozov nodded. "*Da.* Say, fifteen or twenty meters to the left of the last one."

"Got you." As Sarkisyan loaded another HE shell into the gun, Eigims traversed the turret. The cannon bellowed again. Another stretch of stone fence turned to deadly fragments. Another swath of Englishmen huddling behind it turned to sausage meat.

"Good shot!" Morozov said. "Now one more, through a gap."

"You want it to burst just behind there?" the gunner asked.

"That's right. That's just right!" Konstantin reached down and thumped Eigims on the shoulder, a liberty he hadn't taken till now. "Now we'll do for the ones the first two rounds only scared."

"Khorosho." Juris Eigims ordered another HE shell from the loader. As soon as Sarkisyan manhandled it into place and closed the breech, the gunner fired. The cartridge case clanged on the floor of the fighting compartment. The shell burst sent bodies cartwheeling through the air, high enough so Morozov could see them above the top of the battered stone fence. Eigims glanced up at him. "Shall I send one more?"

Not without regret, Konstantin shook his head. "I don't want to get greedy. We stay out here in the open too long, they'll give it to us." He spoke over the intercom to Vladislav Kalyakin, who sat all alone at the front of the T-54's hull: "Back us up behind the church again, Vladislav. Some people who don't like us very much will start throwing things at us in a minute."

"You've got it, Comrade Sergeant." Gears ground as the driver put the tank into reverse. The T-54's transmission wasn't what anybody would call smooth. But it beat the hell out of the T-34's. In the older tank, the driver always kept a heavy mallet where he could grab it in a hurry when he needed to persuade the beast to engage the top gear.

The Americans in their fancy Pershings would laugh at that. During the Great Patriotic War, Germans in their fancy Tigers and Panthers would have laughed, too . . . for a while. Then the front stopped moving east and rolled west, west, inexorably west, all the way to Berlin. After a while, the fucking Fritzes started laughing out of the other side of their mouths.

Now the front was rolling west again. Pretty soon, the Americans—and the English, and the French, and the Nazi retreads who fought alongside them—would be laughing out of the other side of their mouths, too.

Juris Eigims tapped Konstantin on the leg of his coveralls. When the tank commander glanced down, Eigims said, "You know what you're doing, hey, Comrade Sergeant?"

From him, Morozov would never get higher praise. Konstantin knew it, but tried not to make too much of it. "Well, maybe a little bit," he answered. "It's not like I'm a virgin inside a tank, you know."

"Captain Lapshin said that, yeah," the gunner replied. "But some people, you put 'em in charge of something and they start thinking they're little tin gods. You aren't like that."

By *some people,* he was bound to mean *some Russians* or perhaps *lots of Russians.* He wasn't even wrong, as Morozov knew too well. Some Russians, perhaps lots of Russians, were like that. No doubt some Latvians and Lithuanians were, too. But in a world where there were swarms of Russians and a handful of Balts, the Latvians and Lithuanians rarely got the chance to show it off.

"Look, all I want to do is get through this mess in one piece," Konstantin said. "We've got to fight. Nobody says we've got to be stupid while we do it." He paused to light a *papiros* and suck in smoke. Then he asked, "How's that sound to you?"

"I've heard things I liked worse." Eigims paused, too, weighing his words. "As long as you're like this, it doesn't matter so much that I didn't get the tank."

The cigarette gave Konstantin the excuse to waste another few seconds before he replied, "You can swing one. You know what to do. If we stay alive, you'll get your chance."

"Maybe. Or maybe not. I'm not what you'd call a socially reliable element." Eigims didn't bother hiding his bitterness.

"In a war, being able to do the job counts for more," Konstantin said.

"Easy for you to tell me that. You're a Russian."

"I've been in the army since halfway through the Great Patriotic War. I'm a sergeant. By the time they make me a lieutenant, I'll be dead of old age." Morozov had no great hankering to wear an officer's shoulder boards. But that was beside the point he was trying to make.

Eigims grunted. Konstantin let it alone, but he was confident he had it right. If you could do the job and they didn't blow you up, you *would* make sergeant and command a tank.

Russian? Karelian? Armenian? Lithuanian? Uzbek? Chukchi from the far reaches of Siberia? He'd seen sergeants from all those peoples, and more besides, in the armored divisions that smashed the Hitlerites. They were still in the Red Army, too.

It wasn't quite the same when you talked about officers. Then Slavs and Armenians and Georgians (Stalin was one, after all) had an edge on the other tribes, mostly because they'd shown themselves to be more trustworthy.

Morozov's musing cut off when Kalyakin asked him, "Comrade Sergeant, what do you want me to do now? Stay here and wait for the enemy or for reinforcements?"

"No, no. Back it up some more. Let's not come out at them the same way. We'll go around to the far side. Juris, swing the turret around so you can fire as soon as you see the chance. Slap a round of AP in there for that. If we need it, we'll need it bad."

"I'll do it," Eigims said. Actually, Sarkisyan would, but it amounted to the same thing. And they did need it. The first thing Konstantin saw when they came around the other side of the church was a Centurion. But it had its main armament aimed at where he had been, not where he was.

"Fire!" he yelled as the English tank's turret started a desperate traverse. Eigims did, and he hit with the first shot. The Centurion exploded in smoke and flame. Konstantin ordered the T-54 back behind the church again. He'd given the Tommies something to stew over, all right.

Somewhere—maybe off a dead Russian officer—Sergeant Gergely had found himself a big, shiny brass whistle. He wore it around his neck on a leather bootlace, and he was as happy with it as a three-year-old would have been with a toy drum. He always had liked to make noise. What sergeant didn't?

He blew it now. It was loud and shrill. "Come on, you lugs! Get moving! It's been a while, but now we're starting to put the capitalist imperialist warmongers on the run!" he said, and blew it again.

Istvan Szolovits didn't giggle. Not giggling took some effort, but he managed. During the last war, Gergely would have shouted Hitler's slogans, and Admiral Horthy's, and those of Ferenc Szalasi, the Magyar Fascist Hitler installed after he stopped Horthy from making a separate peace with Russia.

Now Gergely yelled what Stalin wanted him to yell. He sounded as if he meant every word of what he said, too. Szolovits was sure he'd sounded just as sincere when he bellowed Hitler's slogans, and Horthy's, and Szalasi's.

And he must have sounded even more sincere when he explained to the Chekists or the Hungarian secret police how he'd been lying through his teeth when he made noises for Hitler and Horthy and Szalasi. He'd made them believe him, or give him the benefit of the doubt when there should have been no doubt.

He'd been a noncom for the Fascists. Now he was a noncom for the Communists. If the world turned on its axis yet again and Hungary found itself a satellite of the USA rather than the USSR, Istvan would have bet anything he had that Gergely'd wind up a noncom for the capitalists. Whoever was in charge needed good noncoms, and the sergeant damn well was one.

Which didn't mean Istvan was eager to follow Gergely as the veteran loped forward. An American machine gun was stuttering dangerously up ahead. A man could get hurt if he got close, or even closer, to it.

But the Hungarians weren't the only ones moving to the attack. They had Poles to their left and Russians to their right. The Russians, richer in equipment than their fraternal socialist brethren, had a couple of SU-100 self-propelled guns with them. Those were tank destroyers from the last war. Following the Nazis' lead, Stalin's designers put a 100mm gun in a non-traversing mount on a T-34 chassis with some extra frontal armor. Tanks could do more things, but guns like that were cheaper and easier to make—and when they hit, they hit hard.

Those big mobile guns wouldn't destroy just tanks, either. They were also lovely for knocking even concrete machine-gun nests to smithereens. One of these SU-100s did exactly that. When the nasty machine gun shut up, Istvan let out a whoop like a Red Indian in a Karl May Western.

Andras Orban laughed. "You tell 'em, Jewboy!" the Magyar said.

"Suck my dick, Andras," Istvan answered. *Why didn't the Yankees knock you over before the self-propelled gun got 'em?* he wondered. Most Magyars didn't jump up and down about Jews. Szolovits had no trouble coping with that. But

Andras was one of the minority who, had he been born a German, would have wanted to shove Jews into the gas chambers at Auschwitz.

You couldn't say out loud that you hoped he'd get killed. He and you were allegedly on the same side. But not even the MGB had yet figured out a way to read what you were thinking.

Only a few strands of barbed wire protected the American lines. The men hadn't been here long. They hadn't had time to run up the thick belts that stymied every kind of attack except one spearheaded by heavy tracked vehicles. Some of the wires were already cut. Istvan twanged through others with the cutter he wore on his belt. A bullet cracked by above his head. He was already down on his back, reaching up to work on the wire. He exposed himself as little as he could.

Then he was past the obstacle and rolling down into a trench. A Yank lay there, half his face blown off. Istvan had seen horrors before, but he was still new enough not to be hardened to them. His stomach did a slow lurch, like a fighter pilot's in a power dive.

That didn't stop him from rifling the dead man's pockets and belt pouches for cigarettes, food, and the morphine syrette from his aid kit. Americans were as rich as people said they were, sure as the devil. He'd never seen soldiers with gear as fine as the U.S. Army gave its men. Not even the Germans had come close. Of course, the end-of-the-war Germans he remembered were the ones who'd taken a beating for the past few years. But he didn't think even the victorious Germans of *Blitzkrieg* fame made war as extravagantly as the Americans did.

Sergeant Gergely blew his stupid goddamn whistle again. "Keep moving!" he shouted. "We've got to drive them while we can!"

One of the Red Army SU-100s obliterated another machine-gun nest. An American with a bazooka obliterated the other self-propelled gun. It burned and burned, sending up its own stinking smoke screen. How long had the men in there lived after the rocket slammed into their machine? Long enough to know how screwed they were? Long enough to scream? If they had, the SU-100's armor didn't let their cries escape. More imaginative than he wished he were, Istvan had no trouble hearing those shrieks inside his head, anyway.

He scrambled up and out of the foremost trench, rolled

across the dirt between it and the next, and flopped down into that one. He found himself not ten meters from two live Yanks.

One of them started to bring up his rifle. Istvan shot first, by sheer reflex, from the hip. His round caught the American three centimeters above the bridge of his nose. The man groaned and crumpled like a dropped sack of flour.

That was nothing but dumb luck, but only Istvan knew it. He felt terrible about it. He didn't want to kill Americans. But he was also the only one who knew that.

The dead GI's buddy certainly didn't. He didn't see a scared Hungarian Jewish conscript fighting not to heave. He saw a fierce, straight-shooting Communist warrior whose rifle now bore on him. He threw down his own M-1, raised his hands, and gabbled something in English that had to mean *I give up!*

Istvan frisked him, quickly and clumsily. The American handed him his wallet and wristwatch. Istvan took them, though he cared more about smokes and food and medicine. Then he gestured back toward the rear. Off the new POW went, hands still held high.

He had no guarantee, of course, that some other trigger-happy soldier of the Hungarian People's Army wouldn't plug him for the fun of it or because he had nothing left worth stealing. But that was his problem, not Istvan's. Istvan also did a quick job of plundering the soldier he'd killed. The dead man's identity disk said he was Walter Hoblitzel.

"I'm sorry, Walter," Istvan muttered. He meant it. He would rather things had worked out so he could surrender to an American, not the other way around. You got what you got, though, not what you wanted.

"What are you doing there?" someone asked. Istvan turned. It was Andras Orban.

"What do you think I'm doing, you stupid chancre?" Istvan answered. The best way to treat Andras was like the asshole he was. "I killed him, so I'm getting his tobacco and his ration tins."

"Can I have some cigarettes? I'm almost out," Orban said.

"Kill your own American, hero," Istvan told him, and headed west again. He was lucky—Andras didn't shoot him in the back.

When he caught up with Sergeant Gergely, he did give him some of the tobacco he'd taken from the Yanks. He didn't like Gergely much, but he had an odd respect for him. Gergely nodded back. “Thanks, kid,” he said. “This beats the shit out of retreat, y’know?”

“Does it?” Istvan didn’t.

“Bet your ass it does,” the sergeant said. “Hope you don’t find out, that’s all.” Not knowing how to answer that, Istvan kept his mouth shut.

A MAXIM GUN SPAT DEATH across the line toward Cade Curtis. The Russians and Germans had used the water-cooled murder mills during the First World War, long before Cade was born. The Germans moved on to lighter, air-cooled weapons. The Russians, having found something that worked, kept Maxims through the second war, too. And they passed them on to Mao's band of brigands so the Red Chinese could shoot them at Chiang Kai-shek's men, and now at the Americans.

The water-cooled Maxim gun might be obsolete. Lighter guns were much easier to haul around. When you advanced, they could come forward with you, not after you. But when the front wasn't moving much, any old machine gun was about as good as any new one. If your luck happened to be out, old or new would kill you just as dead.

When the passing stream of bullets wasn't close, Cade stuck his head up over the parapet to make sure the Red Chinese infantry wasn't coming out of its trenches. The gunners spotted him and swung the Maxim back his way, but not till well after he'd ducked again.

"Anything?" Sergeant Klein asked.

"Doesn't look like it," Cade answered. "They're just throwing lead at us."

"Nice thing about a water-cooled piece is, you don't burn through barrels like you do with an air-cooled gun," Klein said. "All that happens is, the cooling water in that metal jacket starts to boil. The limeys in Italy liked water-cooled guns. When the water got hot enough, they'd pour it out and brew tea."

"Yeah?" Cade didn't know whether to believe that or not.

"Honest to God, sir." The veteran raised his right hand, as if in a court of law. "Not like I never drank any of that tea myself. I used to think it was for limeys or fairies, but when it's wintertime in the fucking mountains anything hot goes down good. Italy's got winters a hell of a lot nastier than the steamship lines talk about."

"How's it stack up against the Chosin Reservoir?" Curtis asked dryly. "Near as I could tell, if we went any farther north we'd be fighting polar bears."

"Sir, I wasn't there for that. My hat's off to you for coming through in one piece—a hell of a lot of good guys didn't." Lou Klein actually did sketch a salute. "From things I've heard from you and other people, that would've made the Russians and Germans come to attention in the first winter of their war."

"I wouldn't be surprised." Cade didn't want to talk about it, or even think about it, now that it was over. He'd had a balaclava under his helmet, plus a muffler wrapped around everything south of his eyes. He'd had a tunic, a sweater, and a parka. He'd had two pairs of long johns under his pants—hell when he had to take a dump—and padded, insulated boots. He'd worn mittens. He'd felt like a goddamn popsicle all the time in spite of everything.

The machine gun's stream of bullets traversed past them again. Some of the fiery tracers looked close enough to let you reach up and light a Camel off of them. Cade understood that wasn't a Phi Beta Kappa idea, which didn't make it go away.

Lou Klein spat against the side of the trench. "Hell of a lot of good A-bombing those cities in Manchuria and Siberia did, huh? You can tell the Chinks'll run out of ammo about twenty minutes from now. Boy, did we fuck the hell outa their logistics."

Cade dug a finger into his none too pink and shell-like ear, as if at a loud noise. "Sorry, Sergeant," he said. "My sarcasm detector went off so hard there, it damn near deafened me."

"Heh, heh." Klein gave that two syllables' worth of laughter—about what it deserved. "Yeah, I was just kidding, but I was kidding on the square."

That was pretty much the definition of sarcasm. Saying as much to the veteran noncom struck Cade as one more losing proposition. Klein was old enough to be his father. Just like Cal Curtis back in Tennessee, he assumed he knew better than Cade. That Cade outranked him made him politer than the senior Curtis about saying so, but only to a certain degree. Senior sergeants were the men who taught junior officers their trade in the field. The U.S. Army had inherited that tradition from the English. Cade didn't know or care from whom the Tommies had lifted it.

Little by little, as he showed he had some notion of what he was doing, Lou acted more as if he was his superior after all. That still came by fits and starts, though.

Thinking out loud, Cade said, "We got some more bazooka rounds in last night, didn't we?"

"Sure did." Klein sounded disgusted. "Naturally, they send the fuckers up here when we ain't seen no enemy tanks for a coupla weeks. They can—" He offered a suggestion for where the brass could stick them.

Cade didn't think they'd fit there, even greased. But he said, "I wasn't thinking of tanks so much. If we send out a bazooka or two after it gets good and dark, maybe we can get rid of that stinking Maxim."

Klein didn't answer for close to a minute. He stood there with his whiskery chin cupped in his hand, his eyes far away, weighing the scheme. Almost as slowly, he nodded. "Every once in a while, Lieutenant, you're damn near worth what they pay you, huh?"

"You say the sweetest things." Cade hesitated, then went on, "I'll take one of the tubes myself. I know more about getting through wire than most of the guys."

"You don't gotta do that, sir," Klein said quickly.

"It'll give us a better chance to take out the machine gun," Cade said with a shrug. "That's good for everybody, me included." Klein's lips moved silently. Cade thought he said *stupid kid,* but wasn't sure. He didn't want to become sure badly enough to ask.

He and the other guy with a launcher, a PFC named Frank Sanderson, loaded their rockets before they set out on the crawl across no-man's-land. "Some fun, huh, sir?" Sanderson said.

"Now that you mention it, no." Cade was wishing he'd listened to Sergeant Klein. He'd grabbed the bull by the horns. Now he had to wrestle it down.

The bazooka tube and rocket were awkward slung across his back. If something snagged the trigger . . . In that case, he'd have just enough time to be embarrassed before the Red Chinese killed him.

A couple of hundred yards to the left, an American machine gun started shooting at the enemy's trenches—though not in the direction from which Cade and Sanderson were coming. As Cade had hoped, the Chinks returned fire. The Maxim's tracers and muzzle flashes told him exactly where it lurked.

He snipped one strand of barbed wire after another. He heard every clip and every twang, but the enemy soldiers didn't. The machine-gun duel drowned out softer sounds. His real worry was that the Red Chinese would send out their own patrol and find him. That wouldn't be so real hot.

He worked his way to within a couple of hundred yards of the Maxim, Sanderson literally on his heels. He motioned for the PFC to come up alongside him. "I'll go left now," he whispered. "You go straight. Get in as close as you can. When I fire, you do the same. Then we get the hell out of here."

"I like that part, Lieutenant," Sanderson whispered back.

Cade slithered in to just over a hundred yards from the gun. Then he peered down the bazooka's rudimentary sight and pulled the trigger. *Whoosh! Roar!* As the rocket zoomed away, a wire mesh screen at the front of the launch tube kept its flames from scorching his face.

Sanderson's rocket went off no more than three seconds after his, from almost as close. The Maxim gun, which had been barking away, suddenly shut up. Cade discarded the launcher and scurried off toward the American trenches. He stayed as low to the ground as he could.

More than a little to his surprise, he made it. So did Sanderson. None of what the Red Chinese threw at them struck home. And now they wouldn't need to worry about that Maxim . . . till the bastards on the other side made a nest for a new one.

Ihor Shevchenko methodically shoved 7.62mm pistol rounds into his PPD's snail drum. The big magazine was stamped with a *71* to let you know the most cartridges you could fit in there. Whoever designed that into it was smart—but maybe not smart enough. Some of the dumb bastards the Red Army was sucking into its insatiable maw couldn't even read the number.

Artillery shells flew by overhead with freight-train noises. Those were Soviet 155s, heading for the German town of

Rheine. The Dutch border was only a few kilometers to the west.

Turning to one of the other guys topping up the tank on his submachine gun, Ihor said, "Crazy how you still know what kind of gun it is just by the sound of the ammo in the air."

Dmitri Karsavin nodded. "It is, yeah." Like Ihor, he'd been through the mill the last time around. His limp was worse than the Ukrainian's, in fact. He went on, "It only works for our pieces, though. The Americans' guns don't sound the same as the Hitlerites' did."

"You're right about that." Ihor nodded. "I didn't hear the Americans' guns the last time. A fragment took a chunk out of my leg when we were in western Poland, getting ready to drive on into Germany."

"Sounds a lot like my story," the other retread said. "I got mine in Budapest. A rocket blew up too close to me and bit me in the ass. You see me naked, I've only got half my right buttock."

"No offense, buddy, but I don't want to see you naked. You don't do a fucking thing for me," Ihor said. But no wonder Karsavin limped.

"Well, we're even, believe me. It's not like I'm perfect, but I ain't no fruit." Karsavin hadn't shaved lately. He didn't smell good. His uniform could have used a wash. He looked a lot like Ihor, in other words, even if his stubble was darker than the Ukrainian's.

"I never in a million years figured I'd have to do this again." As Ihor spoke, he went on filling the snail drum. He didn't need to pay much attention to his fingers; they knew what to do on their own. "Once was plenty to last me the rest of my days."

"You do what they make you do, that's all." Dmitri Karsavin spoke with a peasant fatalism Russians and Ukrainians shared. "My father fought against the Kaiser for the Tsar. He fought against the Whites for Lenin. When the Nazis jumped us, he fought them for Stalin. And they killed him outside of Kharkov in 1943."

"Sorry to hear it," Ihor said. To him, the city's name was Kharkiv. He kept quiet about that. Ukrainians learned Russian whether they wanted to or not. It didn't work the other way around.

Lieutenant Smushkevich came over to the fire to see what they were up to. When the company commander saw them doing something useful, he nodded and smiled. "Good job, boys," he said, though he was younger than either of them. "Glad to see you'll be ready. We're going to pound the crap out of Rheine an hour before sunup, and then we're going in and taking it away from the imperialists."

"Comrade Lieutenant, I serve the Soviet Union!" Karsavin said. Ihor's head bobbed up and down to show he did, too. He would have come out with it if the other veteran hadn't beaten him to the punch.

"Ochen khorosho," Smushkevich said. How nervous was he? This might well be his first time under fire. He didn't talk about himself, though. Instead, he went on, "This isn't a brand-new dance for either one of you, is it?"

"No, Comrade Lieutenant." This time, Ihor spoke for them both.

"All right. Try to keep an eye on the new kids, will you? Don't let them be too stupid. They're our seed corn. We don't want to throw them into the grinder if we can help it."

"I serve the Soviet Union!" Ihor got to say it, too. What the lieutenant meant was *Try not to let them get killed because they have no idea what they're doing.* A veteran could do a little of that, but not a whole lot. If you held a rookie's hand for him, you were liable to turn into a casualty yourself. Ihor had seen enough war to have a pragmatic attitude about it. He didn't want to get killed or maimed. If somebody else did, especially somebody he didn't know well or care about, that was the other guy's worry.

"Good luck to both of you," the lieutenant said. "I'll see you in Rheine after we take it." If he was nervous, he made a good stab at not showing it. With a nod, he went off to talk with some more of his men.

Ihor rolled himself in a blanket and tried to sleep. He got more than he expected, less than he hoped for: about par for the course. The old fear was back. *Will I still be in one piece this time tomorrow?* How hard would the Yankees fight?

He was dozing when the Soviet artillery started up in earnest. The thunder from all those guns bounced him awake. He grabbed the PPD. "Luck," he told Dmitri Karsavin, who was also unrolling himself. Then he hunted up Misha Grinovsky. The youngster who wouldn't be a pipefitter just yet was smoking a cigarette in quick, nervous drags. Ihor set a hand on his shoulder. "Stick close to me, kid. It's like anything else. As soon as you've done it once, you'll know how forever."

"I sure hope so." Grinovsky threw down the butt and lit a new smoke.

Before Ihor could offer any consolation—and before he had to start lying—Lieutenant Smushkevich blew a whistle. "Forward!" he shouted. "Forward for the workers and peasants of the Soviet Union and for our glorious leader, the great Comrade Stalin!"

Everybody who heard him cheered his head off. When someone used Stalin's name that way, what else could you do? Somebody would report you for keeping quiet. If the Americans didn't get you after that, the MGB damn well would.

Ihor didn't know how many men trotted forward with him. A couple of divisions' worth, anyway. Tanks went ahead with the foot soldiers, new T-54s and beat-up T-34/85s pulled from storage alongside them. Against a modern American or English tank, the Great Patriotic War's workhorse was a deathtrap. Till it ran into one of those, though, it could smash up a lot of enemy infantry.

Rheine was a town of about 40,000. It lay in a valley between two low ranges of hills. The Americans had guns in the hills to the west. Ihor could see them winking in the distance. That meant shells were on the way. Sure as hell, he heard the hateful rising shriek in the air.

"Down!" he screamed. He had his entrenching tool out and started digging himself a foxhole before the artillery rounds began to burst. He saw that Karsavin hit the dirt with a veteran's speed, too.

Misha Grinovsky . . . didn't. He stayed on his feet a couple of fatal seconds too long. Flying fragments spun him around and tore him apart. What was left lay twitching a few meters from Ihor. He was dead; he just might not have figured it out yet. Once you'd done it once, you were fine. Too many, though, never made it past the first time. So much for one grain of seed corn.

A church steeple more than a hundred meters high dominated Rheine's skyline. The Soviet shelling hadn't toppled it. The American artillery fire was so accurate, Ihor would have bet a Yank spotter lurked up there. He wasn't the only one who thought so. Shturmoviks roared in and rocketed the steeple. The Red Army men cheered when it tumbled down.

Ihor ran forward, yelling to hold fear at bay. Machine-gun and rifle rounds cracked near him, but none bit. He got into the outskirts of town. Something in olive drab moved behind a fence. He fired a quick burst. The something went down. You had to be careful with the PPD. On full auto, it pulled up and to the right even worse than the PPSh.

The Yanks fought street by street, house by house. They didn't know all the tricks, the way the Fritzes had. But they were brave, and they had a lot of firepower backing them. The Red Army had to spend lives to clear them out. Spend lives it did. By afternoon, the hammer and sickle floated over Rheine.

For the first time in his life, Vasili Yasevich found himself among people who all looked like him. No one in the little town of Smidovich stared at him because he didn't have golden skin, black hair, high cheekbones, and narrow eyes. No one here casually said insulting things about him assuming he couldn't follow and wound up gaping when he came back with filthy Mandarin of his own.

He knew he should have felt like a man who'd just fallen asleep on earth and awakened in paradise. If this was paradise, though, he found himself a stranger here.

Smidovich was about as far into the back of beyond as anyone could go while still remaining in the Union of Soviet Socialist Republics. Moscow, even Irkutsk, lay thousands of kilometers to the west. Vasili would have thought that no one in any Soviet center of power would have paid any attention to this village even before atom bombs fell on the two closest cities of any size, Khabarovsk to the east and Blagoveshchensk to the west.

The problem with Smidovich wasn't that it was so far away from everything else. The problem was that the four thousand or so people here had all come from somewhere else—or if they hadn't, their parents had. And they'd brought the rest of the Soviet Union with them. Inside their heads.

Vasili had lived in Harbin while it was part of Japanese puppet Manchukuo. He'd lived on there after Mao's men took over for the Red Army soldiers who drove the Japanese out of Manchukuo and turned it back into Manchuria. He'd been careful during those bad times, and cautious, but he'd never known anything like this.

More and more, he understood why his father and mother swallowed poison rather than letting the Chekists haul them back to the USSR. Everybody here was scared all the time.

That was the biggest part of what isolated him from his own neighbors.

They would say good morning. They would hire him to chop wood or to shape it into a bedframe or cabinet or to lay bricks. Every place needed people who could do those things. He was pretty good at them, even if his old man would rather have turned him into a druggist.

But behind *Good morning* or *How much do you want for laying these bricks?,* they didn't want to talk to him. They hadn't known him for years. They didn't think they could trust him not to rat on them to the MGB if they said anything the least bit out of line. So they didn't.

Something else also showed he wasn't from these parts, something he couldn't possibly have imagined: how fast he worked. He told a plump widow named Nina Fyodorova that he would make a bookcase for her in three days. When he lugged it to her cabin on the day he'd promised, her eyes almost bugged out of her head.

"You really meant it!" she blurted.

"Da." He nodded. "Why not?" He didn't see anything extraordinary about that. The work was as straightforward as you pleased.

But she said, "Two weeks from now, most people would still be telling me lies about how soon it would be ready." To prove she wasn't joking, she paid him half again as much as she'd told him she would. He didn't ask her for the extra—she did it of her own accord.

The same kind of thing happened when Vasili made a little brick shed for Nikolai Feldman, who wanted to use it to smoke fish. Staring at how quickly one course of bricks went onto another, Feldman said, "You're a regular Stakhanovite, aren't you?"

Vasili knew only vaguely what a Stakhanovite was. It had to do with working long and hard; he knew that much. He said, "The sooner I get it done, the sooner I can start something else."

Feldman eyed him. "Were they all like you in Khabarovsk?" he asked—he'd found out where Vasili was supposed to have come from.

If that wasn't a loaded question, though, Vasili had never heard one. "I got along," he answered cautiously. "How come?"

"On account of if they were all like you over there, no wonder the American fuckers bombed the place," the Jew said.

"I'd sooner work than sit around playing with my dick all the time." Vasili's father had smacked him whenever he dropped in some *mat* that he picked up from other Russian exiles in Harbin. The filthy dialect flourished here. His old man had said it sprang from the foul mouths of convicts and political prisoners. Convicts and political prisoners who'd served their stretches in the gulag made up a big part of the population here. Who else would want to, or could be made to, live in this part of the Soviet Union? No wonder *mat* grew like a weed in these parts.

By his cackle, Feldman could have been a laying hen. "You work too hard, sonny, somebody's gonna kick you in the stones hard enough to smash 'em into gravel."

"I don't want trouble," Vasili said: an understatement of epic proportions. "I just want to get by, same as I did there."

"People in hell want cold water to drink, too," the old Jew said. "That doesn't mean they're gonna get it. You keep doing like you're doing, you're the one who's gonna get it—right in the neck."

"What are you talking about?" Vasili didn't get it now. He was behaving the way he would have back in Harbin. If you didn't jump in there and outhustle the Chinese, they'd steal your lunch and eat it before you even knew it was gone. They worked hard all the time. They knew they had to. There were swarms of them, which made every one easily replaceable. Wasn't it like that everywhere?

Evidently it wasn't. Nikolai Feldman cackled some more. "What? I'll tell you what. You make everybody in Smidovich look bad, that's what. How many friends have you got here?"

Vasili hadn't made any, or missed them. These weren't the kind of people he wanted to get friendly with (well, except some of the pretty girls, but that wasn't what Feldman meant). To him, they seemed like a bunch of lazy bums.

And the way they drank! The Russians in Harbin had put it away, but not like this. Vasili hadn't believed some of the stories his old man told. Now he was starting to.

He had to say something. He tried "I'm only trying to get by" again.

"Look, don't get me wrong. I'm not whining. I've got my smoking shed now, and that's great. But people, ordinary people, they don't love Stakhanovites. If you want to bust your balls, that means they got to bust theirs whether they want to or not. You hear what I'm saying?"

"I hear you." Vasili'd gone at top gear his whole life. In China, that was as automatic as breathing. Here? Maybe not.

A couple of days later, a burly bruiser named Grigory Papanin gave him the same message in almost the same words. "You piece of shit, you make me look like a chump," said Papanin, who had been the number one handyman in Smidovich till Vasili got there. Unlike Vasili, he had friends—of about his own size. He also had a hatchet. One friend carried a crowbar, the other a meter's worth of galvanized pipe.

A Chinese would have said *You're breaking my rice bowl.* This also got the message across. Vasili just hoped they wouldn't cripple him. (He also hoped his hand in his pocket would make them worry that he had a pistol. He wished like anything he did.)

"Khorosho," he said. "I won't make like a fucking Stakhanovite any more." He showed his left hand, open in apology. The right stayed where it was. A straight razor wasn't much, but it was all he was carrying.

He waited to see whether they would knock the crap out of him any which way. Three against one made bad odds. But they didn't *know* what was in his pocket. They didn't want to find out, either. Scowling, Papanin snarled, "You better not, cuntface, or you'll be sorry." He stomped off, his buddies in tow. Vasili didn't sag with relief till after they'd gone around a corner.

Daisy Baxter felt giddy and guilty at the same time. She'd gone dancing with Bruce McNulty. Now, though the world was burning all around them, they headed for the seaside. It seemed a mad extravagance, especially since the Russians had hit the airfield at nearby Sculthorpe with ordinary bombs and visited atomic hell on Norwich, less than thirty miles east of Fakenham.

Mad extravagance or not, here she was, pedaling along on a bicycle next to the American bomber pilot. "But you're from California!" she said. "The North Sea will seem like ice to you!"

"I'm from California, yeah, but I'm from San Francisco," he said, and surprised her by laughing. "The way to bet is, the water in the Pacific there'll be colder than it is here."

"You're pulling my leg!" she exclaimed.

"I wouldn't mind," he said, looking at her in a way that

made her cheeks heat and her heart race. But, shaking his head, he went on, "I'm not kidding, though. San Francisco's foggy, and it can get chilly. And the ocean never warms up, not even in summertime."

"I didn't know that," she said. When she thought of California, she thought of Hollywood miles ahead of anything else. But running a distant second were oranges. She knew they needed hot weather to grow.

He must have picked the thought from her brain, because he said, "Sweetie, my state's half again as big as your whole country. It's got room for all kinds of stuff. Cities and mountains and deserts and beaches and farms and . . . well, like that."

A state half again as big as the United Kingdom? And the USA had forty-eight states! California was a big one—Daisy knew that. Even so, was it any wonder the United States was top nation now, with Britain trundling along on its coattails? The wonder had to be that Britain had kept the lead as long as it had.

But that was visibly coming to an end. The two great wars were more than any nation was meant to endure. Britain had won them both, but all the bills were coming due at last. The empire was falling to pieces. India gone, Egypt and the rest of Africa restive . . .

"Mighty pretty countryside," Bruce said. "Flatter than it is where I come from, but everything is so green!"

The land sloped gently down from Fakenham to Wells-next-the-Sea. Cattle and sheep grazed in the meadows. They didn't even look up as the two humans pedaled by; they were used to that. A kestrel hung in the air above a field, looking for grasshoppers or mice or whatever else it could swoop down on and kill. They'd seen only a couple of autos since they set out. Petrol was rationed as tightly as it had been during the last war, and hideously dear even when you could get the coupons.

"It's peaceful," Daisy said.

"Yeah." This time, Bruce's smile didn't reach his eyes. His job was destroying peace—and destroying places like this. After a moment, he went on, "It's gonna heat up again. You didn't hear that from me—I'll call you a liar to your face if you say you did—but it is."

She nodded. The news shocked her less than she wished it would have. With the way the Russians kept coming forward, how else could you stop them than by . . . dropping things on them? "How bad will it be?" Daisy asked after a hundred yards or so.

"Well, it won't be good," he said, and then it was his turn to ride along in silence for a little while. Finally, he went on, "You can hope that, when it's all over, there'll be enough people left to pick up the pieces."

"And enough pieces left that are worth picking up?" Daisy asked.

He nodded. "Uh-huh. And that, too." Perhaps to keep from having to say anything more, he deftly used one hand to take out a packet of Luckies, to put a cigarette in his mouth, to replace the packet, and to light the Lucky with a Zippo. The other hand stayed on the handlebars and kept the bike going straight.

Daisy made a small, needy noise. Bruce passed her the packet and the lighter. Her bicycle wobbled a little while she got the smoke going, but only a little. She blew out a gray stream. "That's very nice," she said. "Smoother than the Navy Cuts I usually get."

"Jesus, I hope so!" he said. "I've had some of those. You can file your teeth on the smoke from 'em."

"Some people like them strong," Daisy said. She didn't herself, or not particularly; she bought Navy Cuts because they were cheap.

"You've got that right," Bruce said. "One guy at Sculthorpe—one of your RAF fellas, not an American—smokes those, uh, darn Gauloises. God, but they're foul! I think there's something about them in the Geneva Convention rules against poison gas."

Daisy nodded. "They're poisonous, all right. The first few months after the war, demobbed soldiers would bring them into the pub. They'd clear out the snug faster than anything this side of a polecat."

"We'd say 'this side of a skunk,' but you don't have skunks over here, do you?" McNulty said.

She shook her head. "No. I saw one, though, at the Norwich zoo. A very neat black-and-white beast, about the size of a cat. It wasn't doing much, not that I recall."

"They mostly go around at night. If you leave them alone, they'll do the same for you. If you don't—watch out! You wouldn't believe how much they stink."

"I suppose not." Remembering the Norwich zoo made Daisy remember that all the animals in it, including the handsome little skunk, were probably dead now. So were all their keepers. That was what happened, or a tiny bit of what happened, when an atom bomb ripped the heart out of a city.

She didn't care to remember things like that. She concentrated on the unblemished countryside here instead. It *was* pretty when you concentrated on it instead of taking it for granted the way she usually did.

Pretty soon, they rolled through the twin villages of Great and Little Walsingham. Added together, they didn't come close to a thousand people. Bruce McNulty exclaimed at some of the half-timbered houses. "Those things must have been here four or five hundred years!" he said.

"Of course." She looked at him. "And so?"

He laughed. "It's not *of course* to me. San Francisco wasn't anything till a hundred and fifty years ago. It wasn't a city till a hundred years ago. There's nothing like this where I come from."

"We must seem as strange to you as you do to us," Daisy said.

"Now that you mention it, honey," he answered, "yes."

Wells-next-the-Sea lay another four miles north. It wasn't quite next-the-sea, or even next to the sea. The harbor had silted up, so the little town lay a mile inland. A narrow-gauge railroad took people to the beach, though.

Daisy and Bruce didn't have it to themselves, but it wasn't crowded. They spread out towels and lay down on the soft yellow sand. A Royal Navy corvette went by not far from shore, fast enough to kick up a big white wake. "He's got a bone in his teeth," Bruce said. "That's what they say, isn't it?"

"That *is* what they say," Daisy agreed. "Are you a naval personage, too?"

"Mm, I have a navel," he said, and she made a face at him. More thoughtfully, he continued, "I wonder if he's hunting a Russian sub or something."

"Just what we need!" Daisy remembered how the U-boats had almost starved England into submission during the last war. There had been sinkings in the Atlantic and North Sea this time, but not nearly so many.

Gulls wheeled overhead, squawking shrilly. The sun was warm—not hot, but at least it wasn't pouring rain. She enjoyed the company. Bruce put his arm around her. She enjoyed that, too. She wished the moment could last forever.

Then he leaned over and kissed her. She kissed him back. It was her first real kiss, her first kiss that meant anything, since the end of 1944. She wondered how she'd ever gone so long without.

6

A CAR DOOR SLAMMED on the street in front of Aaron Finch's little rented house in Glendale. He looked out the window to make sure, then nodded to himself. "They're here, all right," he said. "Such fun." If he didn't sound delighted, it was only because he wasn't.

"Fun!" Leon said. Aaron's son was just past two. He didn't notice tones of voice very well yet.

Ruth Finch did. "You be nice—you hear me? I don't want any trouble," Aaron's wife said.

"Hey, I don't start trouble. That's Marvin," Aaron said, on the whole truthfully.

Truthful or not, he didn't placate Ruth. "You may not start it, but you finish it," she said. "That's all you Finches." She knew the family she'd married into, sure as hell.

The doorbell rang. Muttering under his breath about the family *he'd* married into, Aaron went to open it. Roxane Bauman was Ruth's first cousin. Her husband, Howard, got enough work as an actor to keep food on his table but not enough to be a household name.

Or he had, before the war with the Russians started. His politics, and Roxane's, weren't just pink. They were Red, or as near as made no difference. He'd had to testify before the House Un-American Activities Committee. Since then, and since the bombs started falling, people got much less eager to cast him.

Some of Aaron's relatives owned similar politics. And Marvin had Hollywood connections, though he'd burned through most of them. Aaron was a Democrat, but he let it go at that.

Well, if Ruth had to put up with Marvin, he supposed he could smile at Roxane and Howard. Which he did. "Good to see you," he said, waving them in. "What's new?" Right then, he thought he was a better actor than Howard Bauman at his finest.

"Same old thing," Howard said. He was good-looking in a not particularly Jewish way, and had a thick head of brown hair combed straight back. His nose—small and straight enough to make Aaron wonder if he'd had it fixed—twitched. "Something smells good."

"It's a tongue," Ruth said. "The butcher had some nice ones."

"Mother still makes them, too," Roxane said. Her mother was Ruth's mother's younger sister. Unlike Ruth's mother, Fanny Seraph—you couldn't make up a name like that—was still alive. She spoke more Yiddish and Byelorussian than English, but she managed. And, considering everything that had happened, she was a hell of a lot better off here than she would have been in the Old Country.

By the way Roxane said it, though, only someone fresh off the boat would bother with Old Country food. But Howard said, "Hey, I love tongue." That took the edge off it. How many square meals had he eaten lately? Not so many as he would have wanted, Aaron guessed.

"Can I get you a beer or fix you a drink?" he asked.

"Beer works," Howard said. His wife shot him a startled look. So did Aaron; Bauman usually drank martinis, often in heroic doses. But he explained, "Beer goes with tongue." Aaron had to nod—it did.

"Let me have a scotch on the rocks," Roxane said.

Aaron made one for her and one for Ruth. He poured Burgies for Howard and himself. "Salt, Daddy! Salt!" Leon said. Aaron put salt in beer for some extra flavor. He took it wherever he could get it; the way he smoked, his sense of taste was down for the count like a pug in against Sugar Ray Robinson.

Leon cared nothing for that. He liked the way the salt made the beer bubble. Once he was happy, Aaron took the drinks out front. Leon followed. Howard ruffled his curly hair and tickled him. Leon squealed. He liked Howard, which made Aaron cut the actor more slack than he might have otherwise.

"L'chaim!" Aaron said. They all clinked glasses—two tall, two short—and drank. The beer was cold and smooth. Not expensive beer, but Aaron had never had expensive tastes. His younger brother did. Affording them sometimes got interesting for Marvin.

Everything stayed cheery and familial for about a minute

and a half. Then Roxane pointed to a frame hanging above the rocking chair Aaron was sitting in. "What's that?" she asked. "I don't remember it from the last time we came over."

"I made it myself," Aaron said, not without pride. And he had: he'd done the backing and the wooden pieces, and he'd cut and fitted the glass, too. He was handy with tools. He always had been. Any kind of tools or machinery—he could make them sit up, roll over, and do what he wanted. It wasn't a rare knack or a great big one, but he had it.

"But what did you go and frame?" Instead of waiting for an answer, Roxane came over to see for herself. Aaron downed the rest of his Burgie in a hurry. Things wouldn't stay cheery or familial much longer. Roxane had to lean past his chair to see what the envelope and the letter under it were. She straightened and angrily turned on him. "Oh, Aaron, how *could* you?"

"Because I darn well wanted to, that's how," Aaron answered, setting his chin. No, he didn't start quarrels, but he didn't back away from them, either. "Not every day somebody gets a commendation letter from the President of the United States."

"I wouldn't be so proud of a letter that congratulates you for fighting for the reactionaries and against the working class." Yes, Roxane wore her politics on her sleeve.

"I caught that Russian flyer after he A-bombed L.A.," Aaron said. "If Comrade Working Class dropped it a couple of miles farther west, you wouldn't be here *kvetching* at me. And if I didn't catch him and take him to the cops, odds are he'd've been hanging from a lamppost fifteen minutes later."

"Can we talk about something else, *please*?" Ruth said. She didn't like arguments. Aaron sometimes thought she'd married into the wrong clan. Bravely, she went on, "And can we do it after dinner? It ought to be just about ready." She hurried into the kitchen to check—and, by the way ice cubes clinked, to reload.

"Sounds like a good idea." Howard's politics lay at least as far to the left as his wife's, but he wasn't so strident about them. Roxane was so sure about what she imagined she knew, she might almost have been a Finch.

Ruth had boiled the tongue with potatoes and carrots and celery and onions. Aaron's mother had made it the same way, though his family was from Romania, not White Russia.

Peasants—*Yehudim* and *goyim* alike—must have made it the same way all across Eastern Europe.

He slathered horseradish on the tender, fatty meat now, for the same reason he salted his beer. He hadn't needed to do that when he was living with his mother. Well, that was a long time ago.

Leon ate tongue and carrots and potatoes with a two-year-old's enthusiasm and lack of manners. He used a small, blunt-tined fork. Sometimes the food went into his mouth. Sometimes it ended up all over his face. After he finished, Aaron plucked him out of the high chair and carried him to the kitchen sink under one arm. Something not far from steam cleaning followed. Leon wiggled and spluttered and laughed, all at the same time.

"Coffee?" Ruth asked.

"Sure," Howard said. Roxane also nodded. Aaron wondered how often they could afford it, or a feast like this. By the way Howard stuffed himself, he hadn't eaten so well in a while. And whom did he have to blame for that but himself?

But Aaron couldn't wag his finger at Howard too hard. He'd been light on hours at Blue Front himself lately. Anyone would have thought that atom bombs falling on a city were bad for business or something. Now he'd had a couple of pretty full weeks, so Ruth could splurge a little.

And he couldn't wait for Roxane and Howard to go home so he could tease his wife. He'd said they would pitch a fit when they saw Truman's letter. How often did a man get a legit chance to tell his nearest and dearest *Told you so*? And how often did a prophet turn out to be without honor in his own house?

Marian Staley kissed Linda good-bye. "See you in the afternoon, sweetie," she said.

"'Bye," Linda answered without looking back as she trudged into the tent that held her class.

Do I laugh or do I cry? Marian wondered. Even in a place as awful as Camp Nowhere, her daughter was growing up a pretty normal little girl. She knew she had to go to school, and she also knew she didn't need her mommy while she was there. The teacher would take care of whatever went wrong between now and dismissal time. Having started late, they weren't bothering with summer vacation. That made adults happy, if not children.

Bill would have been proud of his daughter. He might even have been proud of Marian for the job she was doing of raising Linda as a pretty normal little girl. But he wouldn't be proud of anything ever again. Either he'd burned to nothing when his B-29 went down in flames in Siberia or the Russians had dragged what was left of him from the dead plane's wreckage and buried him thousands of miles from where he should have been.

Every so often, usually when she was looking the other way, so to speak, loneliness would reach up and stab her in the back. It wasn't happening so often as it did right after she got word Bill was dead. Whenever it did, though, it hurt as bad as ever.

Fayvl Tabakman said passing time made things easier to bear. If anybody knew what he was talking about along those lines, Fayvl was the one. He'd watched his wife and children go to the gas chambers at Auschwitz. The Nazis had decided he was strong and healthy enough for them to work him to death instead of just killing him.

Somehow, they didn't quite manage to do it before they started losing the war too fast to let them finish. So Tabakman came to America and opened his little cobbler's shop in Everett. The Russian atom bomb didn't quite manage to do him in, either.

And now he was in Camp Nowhere, too. He took all the camp nonsense in stride more readily than Marian could. Unlike her, of course, he'd been in worse places. They gave people enough to eat here. It might not be great food, but there was plenty of it. Doctors in the camp could and would do as much for their patients as doctors outside.

No, Auschwitz hadn't been like that. There, if you didn't starve, the camp doctors might use you for a guinea pig and experiment on you. From the news that came out of the war-crimes trials, they would use you up as casually as if you were a guinea pig, too.

Shuddering at the idea—why, it seemed nearly as inhumane as dropping atom bombs on sleeping cities!—Marian walked over to the enormous tent where the camp's inmates got fed. She thought breakfast was especially bad, but she tried not to complain where Fayvl Tabakman could hear. He worked hard at being a gentleman, so he wouldn't have told her what a jerk she was, but he wouldn't have been able to keep a sardonic glint from his eye, either.

Scrambled powdered eggs this morning, with chunks of sausage as chewy and flavorful as bootsoles. Linda would be getting the same thing in her tent; they'd started bringing breakfast into the school instead of worrying about kids being tardy because they got stuck in long, slow lines. Marian could see why they shipped the sausage to Camp Nowhere by the boxcar. Plainly, it would keep forever. Add in scorched toast and instant coffee and you had a breakfast she wouldn't have given fifteen cents for out in the real world.

Of course, here the bored kitchen hands didn't ask for any money. Except to bet with, you hardly needed cash in the refugee camp. Marian couldn't remember the last time she'd spent any—which was good, because she had so little.

Tabakman came in a few minutes after she did. She waved. He touched the brim of his tweed cap, filled his own tray, and came over to sit across the table (plywood over sawhorses) from her. The sausage was bound to have pork in it, if it held any real meat at all. As she'd seen, he didn't let that bother him. If he'd kept kosher before Auschwitz, he hadn't since.

"How are you?" he asked politely.

Marian shrugged. "I'm here. My husband's dead. My house burned up. Otherwise, I'm not too bad."

"I know what you mean," he said, and she found herself nodding. If anyone did, he would. "Sooner or later, though, we get out. Life starts over. We get on with it again."

Later, Marian suspected. She didn't presume to argue with him, though. He'd used that kind of going from one day on to the next to live through Auschwitz. This wasn't a death camp. It was only a boring, soul-deadening one.

He took a sip of the coffee. Bad as it was, he drank it with the air of a man used to worse. And no doubt he was. Then he said, "So I was thinking—" and broke off more abruptly than he was in the habit of doing.

When he didn't go on without outside prompting, Marian gave him some: "Yes?"

"So I was thinking—" He bogged down again. This time, though, with the air of a man remembering he'd used grenades against his German tormentors before they caught him (which he had), he managed to go on on his own: "So I was thinking, maybe you and Linda could come with me to the moving pictures Friday night?"

Of all the things Marian had looked for, being asked out on what amounted to a date came low on the list. It wouldn't be much of a date, not with a five-year-old along. She wasn't sure she was ready for even that much. But Fayvl Tabakman looked more frightened than he would have if one of those camp doctors aimed an index finger at him like a rifle. If she told him no, would he ever have the nerve to speak to her again? Or would she lose the one friend here she was sure she had?

"We can do that," she said, and then, "Linda likes you, you know."

It wasn't quite *I like you, you know,* but it seemed to come close enough. "Good," Tabakman said. "That's good. Her I also like. So we do that, then." He gulped more coffee. That way, he didn't need to keep talking. *How* nervous had he been, asking her?

She had to do the good-byes herself, the way she had with Linda. Then, when she was on her way back to the Studebaker she called home, the camp's loudspeakers came to rusty-sounding life: "Marian Staley! Please report to the administrative center immediately! Marian Staley! Please report to the administrative center immediately!"

"Christ!" Fear filled Marian. The last time they'd summoned her to the administrative tent, it was to tell her the Russians had killed Bill. What horrible news were they going to hit her with now?

Like anyone in Camp Nowhere with an ounce of sense, she stayed away from the people who ran the place as much as she could. The less they noticed you, the better. But she had no trouble finding it. A big flag flew from a tall flagpole in front of the tent. That flagpole was one of the first things that had gone up here.

Typewriters spat machine-gun bursts of noise. Adding machines clunked—a chugging generator powered them. The twentieth century was alive and well here. Marian gave her name to a clerk who finally looked up from whatever he was doing.

"Oh, yes," he said. "You need to see Mr. Simmons, in accounting."

"I do?" she said. "Why?"

Instead of answering, the clerk took her to Mr. Simmons, who looked more like an auto mechanic than an accountant. He had an envelope on his desk. "This is the government life insurance policy for your late husband, Mrs. Staley," he said. "The check is in the amount of fifteen thousand dollars. Less than his brave service deserves, but the amount prescribed by law."

They'd told her about this when they told her Bill was gone. They'd told her, and she'd forgotten. You could live for two or three years on $15,000. Or you could buy a house free and clear, with money left over. You didn't have to sleep and live in your car for the rest of your days.

Life starts over. We get on with it again. Fayvl Tabakman's words echoed in her head. He was right. Because he was, she didn't think she'd see the movie with him after all.

The train wheezed to a stop. Luisa Hozzel wasn't sure where she was—not which country, not which continent. She'd had no idea a train ride could take so long. She'd never been so hungry, so thirsty, so filthy, so exhausted, in all her life.

She'd had to get off only once after they shoved her aboard in Fulda: at a place with a name she couldn't pronounce but that sounded like a sneeze with a head full of snot. Herded by guards with machine pistols and snarling dogs—or maybe they were wolves; she couldn't have proved otherwise—she got into a truck. She couldn't see much out the back. What she could see looked horrible. Maybe she was crossing land an A-bomb had flattened. She was too miserable too many other ways to care much.

She got into another train on the far side. This time, she rode in a jammed freight car, not a jammed passenger car. It made less difference than she'd imagined it would. She hadn't been able to see out of the passenger car, either, not with bars and shutters over the window.

Somebody—a guard, no doubt—opened the bar that secured the door. Air and light came in. Luisa hadn't had much of either lately. She blinked against the glare, but inhaled gratefully. The smell of a pine forest beat the devil out of her own stink, that of all the other women crammed in here with her, and the reek of the slops buckets, which had long since overflowed.

She could see pine trees, too, uncounted swarms of them, darker and gloomier than the ones she'd known in Germany. The only buildings she could see were made from the trunks of some of those same pines.

More guards with machine pistols stood on the siding. They screamed at the confused new arrivals in Russian. No one in the car spoke the language, or had admitted she did. Even when the guards gestured with their weapons, no one seemed eager to come out. Unlike the halt at the smashed city, this—camp?—in the middle of the vast forest was all too plainly the last stop.

Then someone realized that they'd come from beyond the boundaries of the Soviet Union. A plump man in a better-quality uniform strode up to the freight car and bellowed, *"Raus! Raus sofort!"*

Out! Out right now! Luisa couldn't very well misunderstand him. She also didn't dare misunderstand him. She had little experience of Russian guards, but she could imagine what would happen if she were a Jew with SS men roaring at her like that and she didn't do what they said. She'd never dreamt living under Hitler would give her practice for Stalin, but there you were.

And here she was. Wherever *here* was.

She and the other women in there stumbled out and stood swaying in front of the car. All of them did but one. When a guard went in to get her out, too, he found she was dead. He heaved out the body. It lay on the muddy ground, staring up sightlessly at the gray-blue sky.

The German-speaking officer made a note on a scratch pad. He didn't care whether people got here alive or dead. He just wanted to make sure nothing confused his count from each car.

He stuck the pad into his breast pocket again. "You will come with me," he said. "You will follow my orders. You will follow all orders. You will learn Russian as fast as you can, so you can follow orders in it. We have no time to waste on special talk for reactionaries and counterrevolutionaries."

He and the other guards took them to the closest building, a large one. A sign was mounted above the door. Luisa had no idea what it said. Not only did she not know the language—even the alphabet in which it was written meant little to her.

"You will be made clean before you enter the camp," the officer said loudly. "Your hair will be cut. Remove all your clothing and proceed into the disinfection chamber."

"But—but—" One woman finally managed to get out what Luisa and the rest had to be thinking: "But all you men are still here."

"Ja," the officer agreed. He nodded to one of his flunkies. The lesser guard clouted the woman who'd objected with the butt of his submachine gun. That got the rest of the new camp inmates moving. Luisa tried to pretend all this was happening to someone else, that she wasn't really here in what looked too much like Siberia, that she was back in Fulda going on about her everyday business.

She didn't believe any of that. She knew too well where she was and what was happening to her. But pretending that way let it happen as if to someone else. She wasn't pulling her filthy dress off over her head or taking off her even filthier underwear. No, it was some other person. No guards were peering at *her* naked body the way only Gustav should have. And if they weren't peering at somebody else, then this was all a bad dream. Pretty soon she'd wake up.

The tub was enormous and stank of some strong, nasty disinfectant. Luisa didn't care. Hot water was wonderful after so long without. She scrubbed and scrubbed, trying to get off as much dirt as she could. If she'd had a wire brush, she gladly would have used that.

Worse was to come. The guards drove the women out of the tub. They marched them along, still naked and dripping, to a room where barbers—male barbers with numbers on their shabby clothes, men who had to be prisoners themselves—waited with scissors and clippers. Luisa wasn't one of the very first ones to meet them. She got to watch what happened before she had to go through it herself.

Those barbers sheared their victims convict-close. That, Luisa could almost have lived with. To the Russians, they *were* convicts. But the men didn't stop at the head. They clipped underarms and crotches as tight to the skin as they did with scalps.

If they liked the way a woman looked, they did more than crop her. They felt her up, brazen as you please. When one German slapped a hand away, the barber slapped her in the face, hard enough to stagger her.

Luisa had time to see all that before she had to walk up to one of the men. Her dark-blond hair tumbled from her head and fell to the floor to lie with other locks of assorted colors. The barber gestured for her to raise her arms. She did. He clipped that hair, too. His barber tools weren't all that moved between her legs.

"Stop that, you filthy little man!" she hissed in German—she was five or six centimeters taller than he was.

She didn't expect him to understand her, but he did. "Bitch, you better find somebody to look after you," he answered. "Might as well be me, huh? You'll be sorry if you don't got no connections." He had a thick accent and must have learned the language from somebody uneducated.

She just shook her head. He laughed, gave her a stinging swat on the butt, and pointed down the hall. She told a convict clerk who also spoke German after a fashion her name. He assigned her a number: Г963. Then he sent her on to get new clothes at last.

Only they weren't new. The padded trousers and quilted jacket had seen hard use. So had her shoes. The strips of cloth they gave her instead of socks had old bloodstains on them. Someone had to show her how to wrap them around her feet. Someone else painted over the old numbers that had been on her jacket and pants and applied Г963 with a stencil.

It was official. She wasn't Luisa Hozzel any more, so maybe this truly *hadn't* happened to her. She was this new thing with a number whose initial character she couldn't read.

They took the new thing and her fellow prisoners to the women's barracks, which was separated from the men's by a barbed-wire fence. She wouldn't have kept chickens in the place, much less people. The bunks went up five and six high. She got one. The mattress was thin and stuffed with sawdust. No one bothered giving her a blanket—it was August.

A tough-looking Russian woman who knew some German greeted the newcomers: "Get used to it, cunts! You'll be here a fucking long time! Tomorrow we go out and chop down some trees. Have fun!" She laughed and laughed.

Harry Truman and George Marshall dolefully studied a map of Western Europe in the Secretary of Defense's office. Holes in the map showed where red pins had been a day or two before. The pins themselves almost all sat farther west now.

"Good God in the foothills," Truman said. "It can't get any worse than this."

"Sir, you can't be sure what will happen next," Marshall said. "I was still in uniform, of course, when Hitler invaded Russia. Three weeks into that fight, I was sure Stalin wouldn't last another month. So was every other military man I talked to. Shows how smart we were, doesn't it?"

"Yes, but Stalin looks to be on the winning side this time, too, damn him," Truman said.

"It's taken him as long to get across West Germany as the Nazis needed to go from the border to the suburbs of Moscow, Mr. President," Marshall replied. "He isn't having an easy time of it—not even close."

"Well, neither are we. In spite of everything"—by which Truman meant all the A-bombs the USA had dropped on Russia and her satellites—"the Red Army's just about to the borders of Luxembourg and Holland. If it keeps heading west, that's not a disaster. It's a catastrophe."

"Sir, when Hitler attacked the Soviet Union, Germany was ready and Stalin wasn't. But the Russians still won. They were on the side with more resources and more manpower. They just had to buy the time so they could use them," Marshall said. "I didn't think they could, but they did. We're in the same situation now. We and our allies have more men than the Russians and our industry is more productive than theirs. And our bombs have hurt them worse than theirs have hurt us."

"Every word you say is true, George." Truman had to resist the impulse to call the Secretary of Defense *General Marshall.* Having resisted it, he went on, "Trouble is, I'm not sure how much that matters. Stalin wasn't going to surrender to Hitler no matter what. I don't have nearly so much confidence in our allies in Western Europe. If Russian soldiers start roaring over their frontiers, they're liable to decide they've been invaded often enough, thank you kindly, and cut a deal with dear old Uncle Joe."

Marshall weighed that with his usual deliberation—and with his usual poker face. He and Vyacheslav Molotov owned two of the deadest pans Truman had ever run into. Marshall knew the countries, and the people who ran them, too. He'd worn five stars on each shoulder during the last war. Before he ran the Defense Department, he'd been Secretary of State. The aid plan that had been helping Western Europe recover bore his name, and with good reason.

"There is that, Mr. President," he said at last, sounding reluctant to admit it but too honest by nature to deny it. "The Dutch and the Italians are as shaky as a big bowl of Jell-O right now."

Truman glanced toward the map again. The Dutch could

see—could practically smell—the Russians coming. The Italians were already up to their eyebrows with them. The Red Army held most of the Po Valley, the richest, most industrialized part of Italy. It wasn't pushing south, into the rest of the boot. No: it was heading west, to give a possible invasion of France two prongs, not just one.

"Too many Communists in Italy before the war started—even worse than France," the President said. George Marshall nodded somberly. Truman continued, "But West Germany is the big one. If Stalin takes all of it, he has the whole continent in a stranglehold."

"If he takes all of it, or looks like he's about to, whatever deals you cut with Konrad Adenauer don't seem so important," Marshall remarked.

"Yes, that's also crossed my mind," Truman said. The West German Chancellor had asked—begged—him not to use atom bombs on the fragile new almost-country Adenauer was in charge of. Truman understood the logic. He was supposed to be defending West Germany, not laying it waste. The Russians were, and needed to be seen as being, the ones responsible for that.

If, however, there was no free West Germany left to defend . . . If it turned into a matter of saving Western Europe rather than saving West Germany . . . In that case, didn't you do what needed doing and pick up the pieces afterwards?

If there were any pieces left to pick up. If it wasn't more like spilt milk. All you could do about spilt milk was cry. And even crying didn't help.

"The genie is out of the bottle, Mr. President," Marshall said quietly.

"Yeah, he is. And I let him out, and I can't put him back." Truman scowled. "If the Red Chinese weren't massacring our men in North Korea . . . MacArthur never dreamt they'd come over the border like that. Neither did I."

"Our best intelligence estimates insisted they wouldn't." Marshall paused, looking as unhappy as a man with a largely expressionless face was ever likely to. "Which only goes to show what are thought to be the best intelligence estimates are worth."

"Not even the paper they're printed on." Truman wasn't just unhappy. He was ticked off. "A lot of folks would say the smart boys who made those estimates and got us to believe them have blood—and plutonium—on their hands."

"Are you one of those people, sir?" Marshall asked.

"You know damn well I'm not, George," the President said. "They were responsible for making the estimates. I was—I am—responsible for acting on them. Whatever ends up happening, whether it's good, bad, or indifferent, it's my fault."

Marshall nodded. "Anyone would know at once that you used to be an officer, sir."

"FDR wasn't, and he stayed in the hot seat a lot longer than I have." Now it was Truman's turn to hold up a forefinger. "But he was a 'former naval person,' hey? Just like Churchill."

"Not quite like Churchill." Marshall was relentlessly precise. "Franklin Roosevelt was Assistant Secretary of the Navy. That is an important job. But Churchill was First Sea Lord. Especially during wartime, that's one of the two biggest jobs in the British government, right up there with Prime Minister."

"Churchill handled both of them pretty well, you'd have to say. Well, so did Roosevelt." Truman made a face. He was blathering on about this stuff so he wouldn't have to make the military decisions he'd come to Marshall's office to make. "If we are going to stop the Russians, we will have to apologize to Adenauer. That's how it looks to me. Using A-bombs in Germany—maybe in Italy, too—looks to me to be the only hope we have of containing them. The only way we have of keeping our other European allies in line, too."

"I was going to mention that if you didn't, Mr. President," Marshall said.

"I bet you were." Truman rolled his eyes. "I am really sick and tired of listening to Charlie goddamn de Gaulle going on about how soft the Germans have it. Germany got pulverized in the fighting. I don't call that soft, whether de Gaulle does or not."

"If you expect a Frenchman to stay rational after Paris gets hit, sir, you're expecting too much."

"Obviously. But the Russians have dropped atom bombs on Germany, too, not that the French remember that." Truman chuckled harshly. "De Gaulle doesn't care whether everything east of the Rhine turns into radioactive glass by day after tomorrow—not as long as the wind blows the fallout toward Russia and not toward him, he doesn't."

"That's about the size of it, Mr. President," Marshall said. "Shall I draft, for your review and revision, orders to use atom bombs against the forward Russian positions? If we do that, of course, we can't rule out the likelihood that they'll do the same to ours. We also can't rule out the chance that they'll strike cities and other targets behind the lines."

London. Amsterdam. Brussels. The names tolled like mournful bells inside Truman's head. "We can make them sorrier than they make us," he said. "I wish one of ours had caught Stalin. That would have solved a lot of our problems." He sighed and scowled and sighed again. Stalin animated the USSR the way Hitler'd animated Nazi Germany. Truman didn't believe there could be peace as long as the Soviet dictator lived.

"COME ON, you stupid lice!" the *Feldwebel* shouted, for all the world as if it were still 1943, still the *Führer*'s war, still the *Wehrmacht*. "Into the motherfucking trucks!"

That was a model Gustav Hozzel wasn't familiar with. But lack of familiarity wasn't what made him ask, "How come, *Feld*? We're holding the Ivans pretty good where we're at."

"How come? How *come*?" The sergeant acted as if he couldn't believe his ears. He probably couldn't; the *Wehrmacht* hadn't encouraged privates to question noncoms. "What are you, Hozzel, a goddamn American or something? We get into the trucks because we've got orders to get into the trucks. They give us the orders, and we follow 'em. That's how things work, see?"

Max Bachman saw the flaw in that, the same as Gustav did. "And then the war-crimes tribunal shoots us because we followed them," he said in a low voice.

Low, but not low enough. "You another troublemaking *Scheissekopf*, Bachman?" the *Feldwebel* growled.

"Not me." Max denied everything, as Gustav would have. He mooched toward one of the waiting American-built trucks. Gustav had hated those beasts in the last war. They let the Russians move up to and around the battlefield faster than his own poorly motorized side could. He headed for that truck, too. The plundered AK-47 was slung on his back.

"See what kind of shit you end up in for mouthing off?" Rolf said as he scrambled in behind Gustav.

"Wunderbar, Herr Gruppenführer," Gustav answered with sour relish. "Come on, General Staff guy. *You* tell me why we're retreating when the Reds can't knock us back."

The ex-*Leibstandarte Adolf Hitler* man opened his mouth. Then he closed it again without saying anything. After a couple of seconds, he took another stab at it: "I don't know, but I don't need to know. The officers who gave the orders must've had some good reason for 'em."

"You fought on the *Ostfront,* and you say that?" Gustav rolled his eyes. "I've seen Catholics with less faith in Pope fucking Pius than you. Stupid orders happen all the damn time, and you know it as well as I do."

"This *is* a stupid order, too," Max added. "We may pull out of Germany altogether if we retreat from here."

"That's another twenty-five, thirty kilometers," Gustav said. "We'd better not retreat that far."

"If we do," Rolf said darkly, "it's a sure sign the Americans aren't serious about staying in Germany and fighting it out with the damned Reds."

"They've had a hell of a lot of soldiers killed and maimed for people who're just playing around," Gustav pointed out.

Rolf gave him a dirty look. "You know what I mean."

"Half the time, Rolf, I don't think even you know what you mean," Gustav said.

The *Waffen*-SS veteran gave back a gesture that meant different things depending on who used it. When an Ami formed his thumb and forefinger into a circle and held up the other three fingers, Gustav had learned, he meant everything was fine. But when a German did that, he was calling you an asshole.

Guidebooks said the town of Wesel was surrounded by pleasant meadows and green forests. The sorry bastards who wrote guidebooks hadn't looked at the place and its environs since the Amis and Germans did their goddamnedest to hold the Red Army out of it. Gustav did look, out the back of the truck. The town, which had been smashed in the last war and then rebuilt, was leveled again. Wrecked vehicles and shell holes dotted the meadows, like carbuncles and smallpox scars on the face of a man with horrible skin. Shells and bombs and rockets and machine guns had chewed the forests to kindling and toothpicks.

"All we need now is a flight of Shturmoviks to come shoot us up," Rolf said. "That's still just as much fun as it was in Hungary back in '45."

"Or in Poland," Gustav said.

"Or in Czechoslovakia," Max agreed. They all chuckled, on nearly identical sour notes. Among the three of them, they'd done nearly everything German soldiers on the Eastern Front could do.

Nearly. None of them had been at Stalingrad. As far as Gustav knew, none of the *Landsers* who'd surrendered there had come home even yet. He wondered how many were still alive somewhere in Russia, and whether any still were. He and Max and Rolf hadn't got stuck in any of the smaller pockets the Ivans had cut off, either. Not many who had came out again.

"How far back *are* they taking us?" Max muttered discontentedly after the truck, and the others in the convoy, had jounced along for a while—the highway was in no better shape than the meadows and forests.

"A good long ways, looks like," Gustav said. "Here, have a knock of this." He drank from a little flask of schnapps he'd extracted from a trouser pocket.

"Don't mind if I do." Max also drank. After a moment's hesitation, he offered Rolf the flask.

"Danke schön." Rolf tilted his head back. His Adam's apple worked. He handed the flask back to Gustav. "Afraid I killed it. Pretty good hooch, though. I'm obliged."

Which meant that, next time he had some, he'd share . . . if he happened to feel like it. Gustav stowed the flask again. "Wasn't that much in there to begin with," he said, to let Rolf know he wasn't sore it came back empty.

"Fuck me!" Max said a little while later. "We *are* in Holland."

"Ja." Gustav had seen the sign announcing the border, too. He didn't like it any better than Max did, and not much better than Rolf. If that fat *Feldwebel* had been in this truck with them, they would have taken turns scorching him up one side and down the other. That wouldn't have been a *Wehrmacht* kind of thing to do, but it would have been a human kind of thing.

Rolf scorched him even though he wasn't here: "That stinking turd probably spent the war on garrison duty in Oslo, screwing the Norwegian girls. Pricks like him always have the luck."

As soon as the Germans got out of the truck, the *Feldwebel* and others like him started shouting, "Stay close to your transport! Stay close to your transport! Don't go wandering off!"

"Well, hell," Gustav said. "I was going to knock a Dutchman over the head, steal his bicycle, and take off for Amsterdam to see the sights."

Max wagged a finger at him. "You better watch out, funny boy, or they'll put you in the movies."

Rolf wagged a finger at him, too—a different finger. That gesture was American by origin, but there weren't many Europeans these days who didn't understand it. Laughing, Gustav gave it back.

A couple of Dutchmen on bicycles did ride up to look the newcomers over. When they realized the soldiers were Germans, not Americans, they spoke to each other in their own language. It was close enough to Gustav's that he could almost understand them. He thought the gist was something like *I hoped we were rid of these shitsacks for good.*

Under other circumstances, he might have been tempted to make something of that. As things were, he felt more like a refugee than the invaders the Dutchmen remembered. He smoked appetizing American cigarettes and ate unappetizing American rations and pretended he couldn't follow a word of Dutch.

Any artillery the Ivans aimed at the troops who'd pulled out of Wesel fell well short—another measure of how far back they'd gone. All the same, Gustav pulled his entrenching tool from his belt and dug himself a scrape to sleep in, piling up the dirt at the east side. The rest of the guys did the same thing. When you'd seen action, you dug in first and thought about it later.

And, in the middle of the night, a new sun woke him by rising, hideously bright, in the east. Then he saw it wasn't the sun at all, but a mushroom cloud like the ones the newsreels and the papers showed.

Shivering as he watched it tower high into the sky, he suddenly realized why they'd retreated as far as they had. A little closer and . . . No, he didn't want to think about that at all.

Istvan Szolovits curled up in a hole in the bottom of a battered trench as if he were a cat. Well, pretty much—cats didn't wrap themselves in blankets before they went to sleep. He was about as happy as a man could be while fighting in a war he wanted nothing to do with.

One of the reasons he was so happy was that the fighting today had been much lighter than usual. Most of the time, the

Americans and Germans in front of the forces in the vanguard of revolutionary socialism's advance (he was steeped in the jargon, no matter how silly most of him thought it was) fought as hard as they could for as long as they could. They might be heading for the ash-heap of history, but they took as many people's heroes with them as they could.

Today, though, only rear guards had held up the Hungarian People's Army—and the Red Army, and the Poles. The enemy soldiers still fought ferociously, but fewer of them were doing the fighting.

Sergeant Gergely seemed pleased, or as pleased as the sour sergeant ever let himself seem. "Maybe we've got 'em on the run at last," he said. "Took long enough, but maybe we have."

Istvan stuck his head out of the hole. "That'd be good," he said, meaning it in the sense of *I'm less likely to get blown to pieces if we do.*

Gergely's sneering grin told him the noncom knew just how he meant it. But Gergely said, "You think I want to slug toe-to-toe all the goddamn time, you're nuts. Easy's always better than hard, man. Christ, we must've come eight or ten kilometers past that fucking Wesel place that held us up for so long."

"Sounds about right." Istvan's weary legs and sore feet told how much marching he'd done. That was one of the many reasons he was glad to roll back up in that blanket and dive headfirst into sleep.

He dove into it headfirst—and was smashed out of it he never knew how much later. A light brighter than a hundred suns seared his eyes. He feared it seared his face, too. A few seconds later, a blast picked him up and slammed him into the trench wall like an angry child throwing away a rag doll. He tried to breathe. His lungs didn't want to find air.

For a second or two, he thought somebody's 155—American or Soviet, he had no idea, and what difference did it make, anyhow?—had gone off right above the trench. But if it had, where was the deadly shower of metal fragments? People were screaming (though he heard them as if from very far away), but it sounded more like terror than mortal anguish.

As a matter of fact, he was screaming himself. When he noticed he was, he stopped. Slowly, slowly, the green and purple glare faded from before his eyes. His face still felt burned. He was bleeding from his nose. His mouth tasted of blood, too. The overpressure from the blast must have come close to killing him from the inside out.

When he saw the swelling, glowing cloud in the sky above Wesel a few kilometers behind him, he realized his imagined 155 was like a fleabite alongside a great white shark.

"I can't see! Mother of God help me, I can't see!" That was Andras Orban, bawling like a baby—and who could blame him? He must not have covered his eyes as fast or as well as Istvan had. Istvan still couldn't see very well himself, but his eyes did work after a fashion.

He said so, adding, "Hang on, Andras. Pour water on them—that may help a little. Give it some time. With luck, it'll get better. My eyes are."

"Up your ass, you fucking kike!" Andras shrieked. "Don't you understand? I'm blind!"

"Good job, Szolovits. Do what you can." Sergeant Gergely raised his voice: "All you shithouse clowns who aren't too bad off, help the poor pussies who are." His laugh was harsh as a file. It still astonished Istvan till the noncom went on, "Well, now we know why the Americans didn't hit back harder, don't we?"

That hadn't occurred to Istvan. He wanted to admire anyone who could think straight at a time like this. Instead, he found himself wondering—and not for the first time—whether Gergely was human at all.

His face still hurt. "Anyone have any burn ointment?" he called. A moment later, half a dozen other voices echoed the question.

Istvan wondered how radioactive the air he breathed was. That, he might actually be able to do something about. He had a gas mask in a metal case hung from his belt, in case the Yanks threw poison around. A lot of the men in his company had "lost" their masks, but he still carried his.

He put it on. That hurt worse, enough to make him grind his teeth and swear. The air he drew in tasted of rubber. He didn't know whether the charcoal canisters could filter out the invisible but deadly atoms. He didn't see how using the mask could leave him any worse off, though.

Somebody clapped him on the shoulder. "You're a *smart* fucking Jew!" Sergeant Gergely said. He'd kept his gas mask, too. He would have. Now he donned it, fumbling less than Istvan had. Once it was in place, he yelled for others to follow his lead.

Istvan did what he could for injured men. In the face of what had happened, it seemed pointless. But you had to try. If you didn't do much good, it was still better than nothing. Wasn't it?

Up ahead—off to the west—American 105s opened fire. *We'll take care of whatever the A-bomb missed,* they seemed to be saying. Fresh screams rang out as the shells burst among the Hungarians. Yes, those damned guns were on the job.

"We will fall back!" a Magyar officer shouted. "We can't stay where we are, not when we're stuck between this and—that." *That* could only be the still rising, still fading dust cloud that had leveled Wesel—and Lord only know how many Soviet troops in or moving through the town. The officer didn't say *stuck between the Devil and the deep blue sea,* but Istvan guessed he would have if only he'd thought of it.

No one complained about falling back. Maybe the Russians would have, but they'd got hit harder than the Hungarians had. Yet the retreat soon swung south. Moving due east, the shortest route, would have taken them straight back through Wesel, and Wesel . . . wasn't there any more. The farther east they went, the more smashed-up the country through which they were traveling looked—which, considering that they were marching closer and closer to the spot where the A-bomb went off, was hardly a surprise.

How much radiation were they picking up as they marched? Istvan had no idea. He would have bet the men leading the retreat didn't, either. He wondered if radiation even crossed their minds. His flash burn hurt worse—he knew that.

He stumbled along with his head down, trying not to trip over whatever wreckage lay right under his feet. It was a black, moonless night. The glass eyepieces on his gas mask were none too clean. They also tended to steam up as he began sweating.

Here and there, people cried out in German and in Russian. He couldn't, and didn't much want to, see what had happened to Wesel. All he wanted to do was get away, to escape to a country where things like this never happened.

If there was such a country, anywhere on earth.

"I wonder how many of those bombs the Yankees dropped." The voice behind that pig-snouted mask could belong only to Sergeant Gergely. "I wonder how many healthy Russian soldiers are left around here."

Istvan nodded to himself. Those *were* interesting questions, weren't they?

Konstantin Morozov shoveled shchi and kasha from his mess kit into his chowlock. The cabbage soup was better than usual. The animal that had got chopped up and boiled in it had died recently, and was still pretty fresh. Konstantin suspected the animal was a horse, not, say, a cow or a sheep, but he knew better than to get picky about a field kitchen's shchi.

Hell, finding the field kitchen was a stroke of luck. Finding it next to a Red Army supply dump was a double stroke of luck. They could get bombed up and fill the T-54's thirsty tank with diesel fuel. They could, and Morozov intended to.

He nodded to Juris Eigims, who was also feeding his face as fast as he could. "I hope we can get topped up all the way," he said.

"It would be nice, *da.*" The gunner's accent turned the most ordinary thing he said into music. After swallowing, he went on, "You go into action light on ammo and fuel, sooner or later you end up paying for it."

"Usually sooner," Konstantin agreed. When it came to fighting, Eigims was fine. The Balt wanted to live, which meant he didn't try to undercut his tank commander while his neck was on the line.

"For now, we're driving the fucking imperialists hard," Vladislav Kalyakin said. *His* accent made Konstantin think of peasant dances and foolishness like that. Byelorussians were hard for Great Russians to take seriously. You didn't even have to keep an eye on them, the way you did with Ukrainians. They were just there to use, like a handy pair of pliers.

"About time," Morozov said. "We should have got to the Atlantic by now, not just to the other side of Germany. Things were different the last time around, I'll tell you that."

Kalyakin, Eigims, and Vazgen Sarkisyan all looked at one another. They did it in a way Konstantin wasn't supposed to catch, but he did, even if none of them was dumb enough to say anything. He could read their minds. They were thinking something like *You tell 'em, Grandpa.*

They hadn't fought their way through the Great Patriotic War. They didn't know what that war was like, not firsthand. That had been a fight where the only rule for both sides was to kill the other guy before he killed you. It had been that way from the start. When Konstantin was a new, green loader, the handful of veterans who'd been in it from the start told stories that showed it was always that way, right from the second the Nazis swarmed over the border. Hardly any of those guys lived to see the Hammer and Sickle flying over the Reichstag in Berlin.

To Konstantin the kid, those old sweats who'd worn the uniform on 22 June 1941 had seemed ancient by 1944. Now it was his turn to be a relic of bygone days. How had that boot ended up on the other foot? He didn't feel any older . . . except when he did.

"We'll just keep hitting them till they finally fold up and fall over," he said, in lieu of calling the youngsters he commanded a bunch of pussies. "With any luck, we'll be in Holland tomorrow."

"We luck has." No, Sarkisyan didn't speak much Russian. Using what he had, he went on, "We shells gets. We gasoline gets, too."

"This tank uses diesel, not gasoline, you dumb blackass," Eigims said. Konstantin wouldn't have wanted to call the squat, burly loader that. Juris was taller than Sarkisyan, but a lot skinnier. But the Armenian only laughed, so Eigims must have found the right tone of voice.

After supper, they dug themselves in under the T-54, the way they did in dry weather on hard ground. The front lay a few kilometers farther west. Konstantin figured they'd move up again tomorrow. If the company hadn't found the field kitchen and the dump, they might have gone up again before it got dark tonight.

Red Army guns banged away at the enemy troops in front of them. Not much artillery fire came back. Even with the tank's thirty-six tonnes of steel to shield him, Morozov wasn't a bit sorry about that. Every once in a while, a heavy, long-range gun—it had to be at least a 240—would throw a shell back this way. Those big bursts sounded like the end of the world, but none of them came very close.

The familiar smells of metal and diesel exhaust and hot lubricating oil and tobacco filling his nostrils, Morozov fell asleep as readily as he would have in a barracks. Other, earthier, odors would probably fill his nostrils later; cabbage soup gave everybody gas. That didn't worry him, though. It was nothing that hadn't happened before.

He wasn't so used to the screams of jet fighters' engines.

Those pried his eyelids apart, somewhere in the middle of the night. He would have gone straight back to sleep, anyway, only he noticed what sounded like every antiaircraft gun in the world going off. Were the Americans coming over? He didn't let it bother him. Unless a bomb hit right on top of his tank, he was safe. If one did, he'd be dead too fast to get bothered about anything.

Or so he thought, till the black cave under the T-54 suddenly filled with blinding, overwhelming, impossible light. Even more impossible, the massive tank heaved up on one side before crashing down again. For a mad moment, Konstantin feared it would get blown over like a wooden toy car in a high wind. Then he feared it would squash him coming down.

He did exactly the same thing as the other three men under the tank: he screamed and started gabbling prayers. His, like Kalyakin's, were in Old Church Slavonic. Eigims called on God in Latin, Sarkisyan in throaty Armenian. Jesus' name sounded very much alike in all three languages.

The blast that almost tipped the tank had been hot. How close was the A-bomb? That question translated into another one faster than Morozov would have wished. *Am I already dead?* he wondered.

If he was, if the radiation would roast him like a pork butt in the oven, he couldn't do anything about it. If he wasn't, he had to do everything he could to live. "Everybody into the tank!" he ordered. "Quick as we can. We'll close all the hatches and turn on the filtered blower."

The system hadn't been designed with radioactivity in mind. It was like a gas mask for the T-54. If the enemy started using poison gas on the battlefield, the tank could close down and keep going. It might protect the crew from fallout, too. Konstantin couldn't see how it would leave them any worse off, no matter what.

Warm rain spattered them as they scrambled into the T-54. A nearby tank was on fire. Maybe its paint had caught. What was left of a nearby wooden shed was burning, too. *How many men are burning?* flashed through Konstantin's mind. *How many are all burnt up?*

He slammed the cupola hatch behind him and dogged it tight. The other hatches clanged shut. Vladislav Kalyakin fired up the reliable V-54 engine. Then he hit the blower. The fan started sucking air—with luck, air cleansed of radioactivity—through the filters and into the fighting compartment.

As soon as Morozov got his helmet hooked up to the radio circuit, he heard Captain Lapshin shouting in his earphones: "All tanks, report in! All tanks, report in!"

"Morozov here. Over," Konstantin said, remembering to hit the SEND button.

"Good to hear from you, Kosta," the company commander said. "We have orders—I just now got them—to pull back for medical care and decontamination."

"I serve the Soviet Union, Comrade Captain!" Morozov said. Things were as lousy as he'd feared, then. If the brass thought they were likely to last even a little while, it would have sent them forward against the Americans. If they had to go back so the quacks could mess with them, they were really and truly fucked. He spoke to the driver: "You hear that, Genya?"

"*Da,* Comrade Sergeant," Kalyakin said. "How bad is it?"

"Well, it isn't good." Konstantin didn't know much about radiation sickness. Except that there was such a thing, he knew next to nothing, in fact. *Now* he knew next to nothing. He had the bad feeling he'd find out more than he'd ever wanted to learn.

The makeup girl clucked reproachfully. "*Please* turn your head more to the right, Mr. President!" she said: an order phrased as a request. A captain bossing a corporal couldn't have done it any better.

"Yes, ma'am," Harry Truman said. Making him look as good as he was ever likely to was her job. He let her get on with it. She smacked him with a powder puff, then, frowning in concentration, did some fine work with a skinny little brush.

None of the touches was unpleasant—if anything, the reverse. Truman hated the whole process, anyway. For one thing, he felt like a counterfeit sawbuck. And, for another, the process left his face smelling like makeup. He couldn't get away from the odor by moving away from it; it moved with him. And it drove him crazy. The first thing he did whenever he escaped the TV cameras was hop in the shower to wash it off.

When the girl drew back to survey her work, Truman asked her, "Will the bathing suit be green or orange this time, dear?"

She giggled. "You're a card, Mr. President!"

"I don't know about that, but people have been telling me for a long time I ought to be dealt with," Truman said, not without pride. When the makeup girl got it—she needed a couple of seconds—she made a horrible face. The President grinned.

An assistant director or director's assistant or whatever they called him said, "You're on in two minutes, sir!"

Getting ready for a speech or a press conference was always frantic. Truman gave a thumbs-up to show he'd heard. The makeup girl smacked him with the powder puff one more time. She studied her handiwork and nodded to show she was satisfied.

"Thanks, sweetie," Truman told her. He took his bifocals off the makeup table and set them on his nose. He didn't like the way his sight had lengthened after he turned fifty, but what could you do if you wanted to go on reading? You could wear glasses, that was what.

He looked through the mild, upper portion as he walked into the press room. A young forest of mikes sprouted from the front of his lectern. Radio and television were carrying this speech. Reporters waited for him to finish reading it so they could grill him afterwards.

The second hand on the wall clock was sweeping up toward eleven on the dot. The red lights under the TV camera lenses glowed, so they were filming or broadcasting or whatever the right word was. Truman took his place behind the lectern and glanced down at the papers. Yes, they said what they were supposed to say. If they hadn't, he could have given the gist without them. The gist was, the world was going to hell in a handbasket, and he'd just thrown some more gasoline on the fire.

"My fellow Americans, I come to you today with a heavy heart," he said. "To keep the Red Army from overrunning all of Western Europe and bringing it under Stalin's tyranny, we have had to use more atomic bombs in the fight. To destroy as many front-line Russian troops as we could, we dropped them on the territory of the Federal Republic of Germany."

Not *it has become necessary that we.* Truman said *we have had to.* He'd watched nonsense and bureaucratic drivel start to swallow the English language. He knew he'd never be a speaker in FDR's or Churchill's class—hell, nobody was in

Churchill's class—but by God he said what he meant without beating around the bush.

"I did not want to do this. The West German people are our allies in the fight against Communist oppression," he went on. "But with almost all West German territory under Russian occupation, and with the Low Countries and France threatened with invasion, I saw no other choice.

"We have also struck at Soviet troop concentrations deeper inside West Germany, and in Austria. And we have hit the Russian satellite nations in Eastern Europe. We will not let Russian soldiers cross their territory unpunished, and we will not let the petty tyrants who run them help Joseph Stalin snuff out freedom all across Europe.

"If Stalin wants peace, he can have it. I will not fight him as long as he is not fighting me. Let him pull his troops back behind the borders they held before the war started, let the North Koreans and Red Chinese move back north of the thirty-eighth parallel in Korea, and there will be no more reason to fight as far as I'm concerned. They've hurt us, and we've hurt them. The scales balance, near enough.

"But I warn the Russian leader: if he doubts our resolve, he's making a bigger mistake than the one he made by trusting Hitler. His puppets started the fight in Korea. He started the fight in Europe. We will finish them. On that, he has my solemn word."

He looked up again to show he'd finished his prepared remarks. The reporters all started yelling his name and waving. He pointed at one of them. "If we've used more A-bombs in Europe, Mr. President, how do we keep the Russians from doing the same thing?" the man asked.

"Chet, we will do the best we can with planes and radar and antiaircraft guns," Truman answered. "We will give their bombers the hottest time we know how to give them."

"Some of them will get through, though, won't they?" Chet persisted. "If enough do, won't the European countries grab at whatever kind of peace Stalin will give them?"

"They haven't shown any signs of that so far," said Truman, who had no idea what he and the United States would do if they did. He went on, "As a matter of fact, the French Committee of National Salvation seems more eager to get on with the war than the Fourth Republic did." There! He'd said something good about Charles de Gaulle! Who would have believed it? He pointed to another reporter. "Yes, Eric?"

"Mr. President, this set of bombs didn't hit Soviet territory?" Eric held his pipe in his left hand while he talked; smoke curled up from the bowl toward the press-room ceiling.

"That's right." Truman nodded.

"What will we do if they strike at us again, sir?"

Suffer. Bleed. Burn, the President thought. But, blunt-spoken as he was, he couldn't say that to a reporter. Sighing, he answered, "If that happens—and may God forbid it—I promise that we'll hurt the Russians much worse than they can hurt us."

Hitler'd made the same promise after English bombs started falling on Germany in reply to the ones the *Luftwaffe*'d dropped on London. The difference was, the *Führer* hadn't been able to make good on his promise. Truman knew damn well he could.

He aimed his left index finger at another reporter. "Walter?"

"Mr. President, what I want to know—what I think every American wants to know—is, will anything be left of the country and of the world by the time this war ends?"

"I think there will. I hope—I pray—there will. But I'm not the only one who has something to say about that. You also have to ask Joe Stalin. I'm sorry, Walter, but that's the way it is." He chose another gentleman of the Fourth Estate. "Yes, Howard?"

"Sir, how do you stand being one of the two men responsible for so much death and devastation?"

The question struck closer to home than Truman had expected. Slowly, he said, "I don't believe anyone who was in the White House would have been able to do anything much different from what I've done. What consolation I have, I take from that." This time, he didn't suggest that Howard ask Joe Stalin. Stalin, the President figured, simply didn't give a damn.

ALONG WITH HIS FLIGHT CREW, along with their new navigator, Boris Gribkov waited for orders. He was afraid he knew what kind of orders they would be—the kind of orders that had made Leonid Tsederbaum stick his automatic in his mouth and pull the trigger so he would never have to help carry out another set of orders like that again.

Radio Moscow (whose signal almost certainly didn't originate from Moscow these days) screamed about American atrocities. "Even the Germans the United States claims to protect now fall victim to the imperialists' insane blood lust!" Roman Amfiteatrov bellowed.

No one had ever heard, or heard of, Amfiteatrov before U.S. B-29s dropped three A-bombs on Moscow. By his accent, he'd done a local show in Stavropol or some other southern town till then. Yuri Levitan had been the chief radio newsreader for years—until, without warning and with no explanation, he wasn't. He had to be dead, with luck a quick and easy death, without it . . . not.

Gribkov didn't take the broadcaster's hysterics very seriously. He knew what war was—knew much too well, in fact. You killed the enemy's soldiers as best you could. And you smashed his cities behind the lines so his factories couldn't make what the soldiers needed to kill your men. If you also terrified his civilians—say, with an atom bomb—so they decided giving up made a better choice than going on with the fight, that was also all to the good.

Rumors swirled over the air base outside of Prague. Czechoslovakia was still a tricky place. It was the last satellite to fall into the Soviet orbit, only a bit more than three years before. Some of the locals might not be happy about that, so the Red Army had the country locked down tight. Klement

Gottwald, who ran it for the USSR, might be able to sneeze without asking permission from Stalin. But he sure couldn't wipe the snot off his upper lip unless Stalin told him that was all right.

"Know what I heard?" Vladimir Zorin said to Boris.

"No, Volodya. I don't know. What's the latest shithouse news?" Gribkov asked.

The copilot chuckled self-consciously. "That's about what it is, sure enough," he said. "But they say the east bank of the Rhine is nothing but glass from the Swiss border all the way to the North Sea. Glass from atom bombs going off, I mean."

"I understood you. You do know what a pile of crap that is, right?" Boris intended the question to be rhetorical. In case it wasn't, he went on to make the point: "How many bombs would the Yanks need to do something like that? If they had that many, wouldn't they have dropped them on us by now?"

"I suppose so, yeah," Zorin said. Talking about the resources the enemy enjoyed was always risky.

But Boris said, "I know so. I just wish they'd turn us loose to hit back at the imperialists." He said that partly to keep the MGB happy and partly because he did mean it—the odd double focus that suffused so much of Soviet life. It wasn't that he was eager to kill tens of thousands and roast tens of thousands more. He wasn't, even if it didn't weigh on his mind so much as it had on Tsederbaum's. But he'd been trained to fly the Tu-4, and he did want to hit back at the enemies who'd slaughtered so many Soviet fighting men.

"Some bombers have gone out of here," Zorin said. "I just thought so before, but I know for a fact now. I've talked with groundcrew men who serviced them."

"But not us," Gribkov said.

"No, not us," his fellow flyer agreed. "Damn that stupid motherfucking *Zhid,* anyhow. They don't trust us to do what they tell us to, not any more they don't. They think Tsederbaum's contagious."

"They ought to know better than that. They've questioned us hard enough," Gribkov said, sincerity and prudence once more mingling in his voice. "We serve the Soviet Union. We should get the chance to do it."

He listened to the news with special care that evening. Would Roman Amfiteatrov boast about the devastation visited on ancient cities in Western Europe? Amfiteatrov did nothing of the kind. He spent most of the broadcast talking about a Chinese attack in Korea. By the way he described it, if Mao's soldiers were any braver, they would have torn the Americans they killed to pieces with their bare hands.

Then he sang the praises of Stakhanovite shock workers shattering production norms in places like Magnitogorsk and Irkutsk. Boris believed at least some of that. Places like those were so far from anywhere, even B-29s would have a hard time hitting them.

But what had happened to the Tu-4s that set out from here? Had they carried ordinary bombs instead of the ones with atoms in them? Or had they flown west with the intent to avenge but gone down before they were able to?

He knew how possible that was. The B-29 had been a world-beating heavy bomber at the end of the Great Patriotic War. The ones that made emergency landings in Siberia so impressed the USSR, Stalin ordered Tupolev to make an exact copy within two years . . . or else. And Tupolev did—he'd already had one taste of the gulag, and didn't fancy another—and thus the Tu-4 was born.

The Tu-4 was every bit as marvelous as the B-29 had been and still was. The problem was, that soon proved not marvelous enough. Neither bomber had been designed to escape radar-guided, sometimes radar-carrying, night fighters or radar-guided antiaircraft guns. Neither bomber had the speed or the ceiling to get away from jets, and neither had a prayer of shooting them down.

Both were, if you wanted to get right down to it, obsolete. Both kept flying anyhow. They were the best tools their countries had for delivering atom bombs across thousands of kilometers of sea and land. If *best* didn't always mean *good enough,* well, in that case you went out and sent some more. Sooner or later, some would get through.

When sooner looked more like turning into never than later, Gribkov gathered his courage in both hands and called on Brigadier Yulian Olminsky, the air-base commandant. The visit took all the courage he had. He knew his own side could shoot him down far more easily than an American F-80 or F-86. The USSR didn't need radar to track him. The *rodina* already had him in its sights.

While he wanted to talk to Olminsky, the brigadier didn't want to talk to him. Boris cooled his heels for an afternoon while Olminsky dealt with a swarm of other people. He didn't get angry. He didn't give up. He went back early the next morning. This was how the game was played.

He sat there smoking, not looking bored, not twiddling his thumbs, for another hour and a half. At last, Olminsky stuck his head out of his office and rolled his eyes. "All right, Gribkov, I suppose I can give you five minutes."

"I serve the Soviet Union, sir!" Boris bounced to his feet.

He stood in front of the table that did duty for the brigadier's desk. He was not invited to sit. Olminsky wasn't round-faced, blunt-featured, and double-chinned like so many Soviet general officers. He looked more like a Scandinavian literature professor. He was tall and thin and craggy, and wore wire-framed spectacles.

Looks, of course, had nothing to do with anything. "Go ahead and spill it."

"Comrade General, I am a good pilot. I proudly wear the order of Hero of the Soviet Union." Boris tapped the ribbon and star on his tunic. He'd won the medal for bombing Seattle. (So had Tsederbaum. He tried not to think about that.) "All I want to do is go on serving the Soviet Union as I was trained. Please, sir, let my crew and me fly against her enemies."

Olminsky steepled his fingers. They were long and skinny, too. "If it were up to me, I would do that. For the moment, I can't. You are not judged reliable enough to be trusted with the country's ultimate weapons."

"By whom, sir? Point me at the son of a bitch and I'll punch him in the snoot!"

He got a small smile from the brigadier, but only a small one. "I'm afraid that isn't practical for you, considering the arm-of-service color of the men involved."

Olminsky meant the MGB; he couldn't very well mean anything else. "What am I supposed to do, then, sir?" Gribkov asked.

"Just wait. You're in what the Catholics call limbo. It may not be heaven, but it isn't hell, either." Yulian Olminsky paused. "Sooner or later, one door or the other will open. Believe me, if it's hell, you'll wish you were back in limbo. Now go away." Not even bothering to salute, Boris went away.

Ihor Shevchenko had his Kalashnikov. He had as many banana-shaped magazines full of the special cartridges it fired as he could carry. All things considered, he wished he were still toting his old PPD.

He'd picked up another wound. He was getting a collection of them from the wars he'd been through. This one was of the extraordinarily stupid kind. He'd sat down on a pile of freshly dug dirt that had come out of the side of a trench when Red Army men widened it. Unbeknownst to all of them—and especially to Ihor—a broken bottle lurked in that dirt, business end up.

When he sat down, it bit him right in the ass. Naturally, he sprang up swearing and clapping his hands to the wounded part. Just as naturally, the rest of the soldiers in the squad laughed themselves silly. That was the funniest thing they'd ever seen.

Even Ihor thought it was funny—till he saw that his left hand wasn't just red but dripping with blood. "Fuck me!" he said. "That got me bad!" He showed off the gory evidence.

Some of his mates turned sympathetic. Others kept giggling. "I bet it gave you a brain concussion," one would-be wit said.

Lieutenant Smushkevich came around a kink in the trench. "What's going on, guys?" he asked.

"Sir, I'm sorry, but I got hurt." Ihor showed off his red hand and his bloody trousers while explaining how he'd got them.

"That's dumb, all right, but you're sure as hell bleeding there," the company commander said. "Drop your pants so I can see what you did to yourself." Feeling more foolish than ever, Ihor obeyed. Smushkevich whistled softly. "*Bozhemoi!* You *did* tear yourself up." He turned to a nearby soldier. "Karsavin!"

"Sir!" Dmitri Karsavin said.

"Slap your wound bandage on his butt and take him back to an aid station," the lieutenant said. "He'll need stitches for sure, and probably a tetanus shot and whatever pills they give you to keep a wound from going bad."

"I'll do it, Comrade Lieutenant," Karsavin said. After he put on the bandage, Ihor pulled up his pants again. He was glad to have someone help him back behind the line. Moving started to hurt like a bastard.

The aid station had that butcher-shop smell that made your stomach want to turn over. A harried-looking doctor gave Karsavin a receipt for Ihor. Then he took a look at the wound. "What happened? Shell fragment?"

"Glass fragment. I parked my ass on a busted bottle."

"Well, you fucked yourself up pretty good. Let's get the stitches into you first off." He had some novocaine, so that wasn't too bad. Then he went off to get the tetanus antitoxin. When he came back, he was fuming. "We're out, dammit. You've got to have a dose. Sit on something filthy like that and you're lockjaw waiting to happen. That's a filthy way to go."

"What will you do with me, Comrade Physician?"

"Send you back to the second-level aid station. They'll have it, and with luck some sulfa or penicillin so you don't fester." He yelled for an orderly: "Hey, Borya!" When the man appeared, the doctor went on, "Stick this clown in the jeep and take him to the field hospital in Hörstel. Here, give them this so they know what to do with him."

"I'll take care of it, sir." The orderly stuck the note in his pocket. He eyed Ihor. "Can you walk?"

"As far as the jeep, yeah." Ihor did. It was a captured American one, with a red star painted over what had been a white one on the hood. He sat with a right-hand list. Hörstel was another town that had seen hard fighting. Red Cross flags were draped on the roof of the building that did hospital duty. Maybe they'd keep fighter-bombers away, maybe not. It was worth a try.

The people there took charge of Ihor as if he were a truck with a blown head gasket. He got the tetanus shot and a handful of pills that would have choked a mule. Under a doctor's stern and watchful gaze, he swallowed them.

When they put him in a cot, he lay on his stomach. He figured his right side might also work; his back and left side wouldn't. As the novocaine wore off, the wound and the stitches hurt more and more. They gave him aspirin, which did nothing much. He didn't have the gall to ask for morphine, though. Some of the men in there with him had their bellies torn open. Others were missing arms or legs. They needed the strong drug worse than he did.

He got better food, and more food, in the ward than he had at the front. They wanted wounded men to recover as fast as they could, and fed them so they would. He hadn't eaten so well back on the collective farm, either. No wonder he fell asleep right after supper.

Some time after midnight, the building shook as if in an earthquake. Horrid white light speared the wounded men's eyes. They were well behind the line. All the same, Ihor feared the building would fall down on him. "God, have mercy! Christ, have mercy!" he yipped. No one told him praying was antisocialist. Almost everyone in there who could talk at all prayed like a dying man—which most of them, like Ihor, had to think they were. The ward orderly called on the Trinity and the saints as readily as any of the injured men.

"Those atom things'll cook us even back here!" cried a man who had a bloody bandage over the stump of his right arm. Ihor wanted to call him a stupid fool. He couldn't very well, though, not when he was afraid the mutilated man might be right.

Only a moment later did he stop to think about the unit he'd left behind at the front. How many of them were still alive? Any at all?

In the last war, he would have been devastated, ravaged, had he been the sole survivor of his company. He supposed he still should be. And he still was, but only in an attenuated way. He hadn't wanted to go back to war to begin with. The whole regiment was hastily thrown together. None of the other guys wanted to fight, either. It was only that all their other choices looked worse.

Two doctors came into the ward as soon as morning twilight gave them enough light to see by. They divided the patients in half. The more badly wounded ones, they loaded into ambulances and jeeps and sent east.

"What about the rest of us?" Ihor asked an orderly.

"You guys'll be back on your pins in a few days," the man answered. "Either you'll be fighting again or the Americans'll roll forward and take you prisoner and get you off our hands. And we'll have Lord only knows how many more wounded coming in from the west."

He was right, of course. The atom bomb killed whatever lay directly under it. If you were a little farther away, it melted you or burned you or blinded you or simply knocked heavy things or sharp things down onto you without immediately doing you in. Or the radiation made your hair fall out and left you bleeding from every orifice you had, and from your eyeballs and the beds of your nails. Or . . .

Ihor saw more in the way of horror till they turned him loose three days later than he had in all his service before that time. When they told him to get out of there so they could deal with more of the desperately wounded, he said, "I haven't got a weapon."

"Well, pick one up off the ground," a doctor answered impatiently. "It's not like there won't be plenty to go around."

Yes, they'd told raw troops almost the same thing in the early days of the Great Patriotic War. Ihor couldn't very well doubt that the sawbones here was right. And, sure enough, that was how he got his AK-47 and plenty of ammo to fire from it. Whoever had owned the assault rifle didn't need it any more.

The way he got it was why he wished he still carried the PPD instead. He joined what was more a band than a section. No American infantry pushed forward right where they were. They'd stayed alive. For the moment, that was plenty.

Near the barbed wire that separated the men's and women's sides of the camp stood a wooden arrangement something like a small gallows. From the gibbet hung not a man but a 105mm shell casing with a hole drilled in the side so a rope could go through. When a guard whacked it with a hammer, the horrible clatter did duty for a wakeup call.

It was 0530. Since summer still ruled, the sun had been up for a while, and Luisa Hozzel's barracks had got light. That didn't matter; she would have slept till noon had she got the chance. But a slap in the face and a boot in the backside had quickly taught her she had to pay attention to those crow's-caw clanks. No matter how exhausted she was, they meant *get moving.*

She slid out of her bunk and put on her boots. She used them for a pillow and slept in the rest of her clothes. Then she staggered out onto the dirt courtyard in front of the barracks and took her place in one of the rows of ten. Guards—men with machine pistols—screamed curses at any female *zek* who didn't move fast enough to suit them.

Luisa was picking up Russian faster than she'd dreamt she could. She had to. Nobody with any authority would condescend to speak German while giving orders, not after that dreadful first day. *You're here,* was the guards' attitude. *You've got to figure out what we want.* She'd learned *zeks* were prisoners—like her.

Some of the Russian women seemed as dejected and stunned as the newly arrived Germans. They were the politicals. Falling foul of Stalin's henchmen here was as dangerous as irking the Nazis had been in Hitler's time. The rest of the women prisoners were what the guards called "socially friendly elements." They were ordinary criminals, in other words. They called themselves *blatnye,* which meant something like *thieves* or *bitches.*

They bossed the politicals around. They were used to this kind of life, where the women who'd thought of themselves as good Communists till the MGB grabbed them kept trying to believe it was all a ghastly mistake. The bitches bossed the foreigners around, too. Some of them were bull dykes, and as predatory as any man. Luisa didn't mind being bossed—they knew the ropes and she didn't. The other . . . She counted herself lucky no one had put a serious move on her yet.

When all the *zeks* were in place, the guards went up and down, making sure each row held ten women and counting the rows. That kind of arithmetic, even a camp guard could do. The Reds might not believe in God, but the count was sacred. Till the morning count came out right, nobody got breakfast. Till the evening count was right, no one ate supper or went into the barracks. At this season, that wasn't too bad. In winter, standing there in, say, half a meter of snow . . .

At last, after literally counting on their fingers to make sure they had everything straight, the guards decided no one had somehow escaped the camp for the dubious shelter of the pine forest that ran on for untold hundreds or thousands of kilometers in every direction. The top sergeant pointed toward the dining hall and yelled something that meant either *Go!* or *Eat!*—Luisa hadn't worked out which yet.

She went and she ate. Rations had been small and rotten—often literally—at the end of the war. They hadn't got better for a long time afterwards. Then, when they did, the Russians overran Fulda, and times turned tough all over again. Nothing, though, nothing had prepared her for what she got in the gulag.

She hadn't been to Dachau or Buchenwald, let alone Treblinka or Auschwitz. Maybe people there had got this kind of horrible slop. If they had, all the atrocity stories the Allies told were true. She didn't know how you were supposed to live. All she could do was try.

The stew the cook ladled into her bowl was so watery, it barely deserved the name. Bits of chopped cabbage and turnip or potato or parsnip or some other root gave most of what bulk it had. It was also vaguely briny; at some point or another, a salted herring or sardine must have swum past the cauldron it came out of.

Her parents, who'd lived through the Turnip Winter and the sawdust-stretched war bread of the Kaiser's time, would have turned up their noses at the black, badly baked brick she got with her stew. It was full of husks, and what grain there was was rye and oats.

In Fulda, she'd drunk coffee white with milk at breakfast. The wartime *ersatz* had been bad, but it beat the devil out of the weak tea the Russians grudgingly gave the *zeks*. They didn't even waste sugar on prisoners. The stuff's sole virtue was, it was hot.

No matter how bad the food was, she wolfed it. Partly, that was because she was hungry all the time. And they gave you only fifteen minutes to eat. Whatever you couldn't down in that time, you lost.

After breakfast . . . latrine call. Luisa had used some odorous outhouses in Germany, but nothing like these slit trenches. Everyone took care of her business—piss, shit, period, whatever—in front of everyone else. The setup was designed to humiliate. You tried not to breathe. You tried not to look. But Hercules, even if he'd cleaned out the Augean Stables, would have thrown up his hands and run away if he saw—and got a whiff of—this.

Then the women separated into work gangs and went out into those endless woods to fell trees. The Soviet Union proudly proclaimed equality between the sexes. It lived up to its claims by making the work norm for a gang of women the same as that for a gang of men. Guards cursed at *zeks* to keep them working. If that didn't work, they clouted them with the butts of their machine pistols.

Luisa and Trudl Bachman inexpertly used a two-person saw almost as tall as they were. This was what you got for having husbands who'd gone off to fight the Russians. Neither of them had any idea whether their man was alive or dead. They were both paying the price either way.

Back and forth, back and forth. Beavers as inept as they were would never have toppled enough trees to build a dam. Luisa's shoulders had the toothache. Sharper pain came from her hands. The blisters on her palms popped and bled, over and over. Some of the women who'd been here for years had calluses that let them stub out smokes without feeling a thing. Those were ugly, but Luisa craved them just the same.

Up in a pine tree no one was attacking, a jay called. Luisa could see it if she looked up. But it didn't sound like the jays back in Germany. It spoke a different dialect, the way a woman from Munich and one from up near the Dutch border would have.

When she looked up once too often, a guard yelled, *"Bistro!"* He wasn't looking for a French restaurant with a zinc bar. That was how you said *Hurry up!* in Russian.

After a while—it only seemed forever—the pine crashed to the ground. The jay flew off, screeching in fear. Luisa and Trudl traded the saw for two hatchets. They used them to trim the branches from the trunk. Bending to do that made Luisa ache in different ways in different places.

They put in twelve hours like that before the guards paraded them back to the camp. Luisa shambled along like a dead thing. They lined up for the evening count. As usual, the screws needed to try more than once before they were happy. Supper was breakfast over again.

Tomorrow would be the same as today. She had no idea how long they meant to keep her here. Till she was dead? Till Stalin was dead? Till the A-bombs made sure everybody was dead?

For now, she was too weary to care. After evening latrine call, she clambered into her bunk, took off her boots, and laid them under her head. When you got tired enough, any pillow felt great. She was tired enough and then some. She closed her eyes. She vanished.

Cade Curtis wore a clean uniform. His cheeks were freshly shaved. His hair was GI short, and smelled pleasantly of Vitalis. Except for the PPSh he carried, he might have been ready to appear in a Stateside review. It was nighttime, and blacked-out nighttime at that, so no one could get a good look at him, but he knew.

He clucked sadly as he slid into the jeep. "After you've spent a while in Pusan, you don't want to go back to the front," he said.

The corporal behind the wheel chuckled. "Sir, if I had a buck for every guy who told me that, I'd be rich like Rockefeller. A quarter, even."

"I believe you," Cade said. Pusan was almost as American as apple pie. When you got leave, you could go there to clean up. Cade had. You could eat American food that didn't come out of ration cans. Cade had. You could get crocked out of your skull. Cade had. He wasn't twenty-one yet, but nobody'd asked him about that, so he hadn't had to tell any lies.

And you could indulge in other pleasures. Korean women had quickly discovered that American men had more money than they knew what to do with. You didn't have to look very hard or very far to find joyhouses. Cade had. Buying his fun faintly embarrassed him. Buying it was better than going without, though. He'd been careful to use his pro kit right away every time.

The corporal started the jeep and put it in gear. Away it rolled, reliable as jeeps always were. It didn't roll very fast, though. Driving through darkness without headlights was suicidal if you hurried.

Driving through darkness in Korea with headlights was also suicidal. "Here's hoping Bedcheck Charlie takes the night off," Cade said.

"Amen to that!" the driver agreed. The Red Chinese and North Koreans flew night-harassment missions in ancient Russian wood-and-cloth-and-wire biplane trainers. They were slow and underpowered even by World War I standards. But they carried a machine gun and little bombs a pilot could lob from the cockpit as if all the years after 1915 had been canceled. They were damn nuisances, and they could kill you just as dead as more modern toys.

White-painted posts by the side of the road gave faint clues about where you were about to go off it. Nearer the front, North Korean infiltrators knocked them down or lied with them to lead traffic off the road and sometimes into an ambush. This close to the big American base on the southern coast, though, they were probably reliable.

Of course, the highway itself was in bad shape. The flimsy paving hadn't been made to support all the tanks and trucks and halftracks that used it. It also hadn't been made to get shelled. The potholes were of the tooth-rattling, kidney-crunching variety.

"Boy, this is a fun ride," Cade said after a jounce made him bite his tongue. "How much do I have to pay to get off?"

"Sir, you got to take that up with Uncle Sam, not with me," the corporal said. They both laughed for all the world as if it were funny.

They'd come ten or fifteen miles northwest when the formidable antiaircraft batteries around Pusan all started banging away at once. Cade peered back over his shoulder at the red and orange and yellow tracers scribing lines across the southern sky and the shells bursting in air.

"Looks like the Fourth of July there," he said.

"It does, yeah." The driver nodded. "I can see a skosh in my rear-view mirror. You don't mind, I ain't gonna turn around like you done." Like a lot of men in the Far East, the corporal used the Japanese for *a little bit* without even noticing it wasn't English.

And then Cade stopped caring about Japanese slang or any other kind, for a new sun blazed in the sky above Pusan. He crossed himself and whispered a Hail Mary before he even thought about it. Beside him, in the driver's seat, the corporal moved his lips in prayer, too.

Then the two-striper asked, "Sir, are we too far away for that fucker to, like, fry us?"

"I don't know for sure," Cade answered slowly. "I think we are, but I sure wouldn't swear to it or anything."

"Okay. Good." The corporal nodded. Behind them, the glow of riven atoms slowly faded. Cade stared, transfixed at the hellish beauty of the rising, swelling mushroom cloud. The corporal went on, "What do you want me to do now, sir? Go on taking you north or turn around so we can lend a hand to them poor sorry bastards back there?"

No one could possibly fault Cade for telling the driver to go on toward the front. That was what he was supposed to be doing. But his orders didn't take the A-bomb into account, and it struck him as more urgent than one more first lieutenant in the trenches. "I won't command you to turn around," he said after the briefest of pauses. "But if you're willing to do that, I'll thank you for it."

"Gotcha, sir. That's jake by me." The corporal made a neat Y-turn on the narrow road. They'd just started heading south again when wind from the atomic blast briefly buffeted the jeep. The driver let out a harsh chuckle. "We're a coupla goddamn fools, is what we are, y'know?"

"Now that you mention it, that did cross my mind, yes," Cade said, which made the corporal laugh again.

They hadn't gone very far south before there was another flash in the sky behind them, which meant that A-bomb blew to the northwest. It was much farther away than the one that had just incinerated Pusan. Somberly, the driver said, "The guys you was goin' back to, Lieutenant, they're liable not to be there no more."

"I know." Those were Cade's men, up there in the trenches near Chongju. Or they had been. Now they were part of a new mushroom cloud. *If I hadn't got leave and gone drinking and making a pig of myself and getting my ashes hauled, I'd be dead with them,* Cade thought. Guilt pierced him for no better reason than that he was still breathing and they weren't. The top part of his mind understood how ridiculous the feeling was, which didn't make it go away.

The other thing was, the Americans had just had a big hole bitten out of their line. Would the Red Chinese and the North Koreans swarm through it? He was all too sure they would. How much would they care if their soldiers got a little radioactive, or more than a little? That question answered itself as soon as it occurred to him.

There was light ahead, not just from the dissipating mushroom cloud above Pusan but also from the countless ordinary fires the bomb had set. "Fuck it," the driver said. "I'm gonna turn on my headlights. We got bigger things to worry about than Bedcheck Charlie an' gooks with Tommy guns."

"Fine by me." Cade wanted to see what he could, too. How often did you find yourself on the edge of an atomic explosion?

Once, he soon decided, was at least three times too often. The farther in they got, the worse things looked. Tents burned. Prefab buildings went over as if they'd been assembled from playing cards. They caught fire, too. Fighter planes that hadn't got off the ground blazed. So did the trucks that had fueled them.

Next to one of those trucks writhed a burning man. If you splashed kerosene on a cockroach and tossed in a match, the effect would have been similar but smaller. "Christ!" the corporal said. "Is he too far away for you to shoot him with that thing?"

Cade glanced down at the PPSh in his lap. "Afraid so. I sure would if I could, though."

"Oh, hell, yes. But Jesus God, sir, what are we gonna do? What *can* we do? What can anybody do? This goddamn thing is too big for people to do any good with."

Although Cade thought he was right, they did get stopped

and put to work before they'd gone much farther. They made up two links in the human chain of a bucket brigade that was trying without much luck to keep a barracks from going up in flames. Cade wondered how radioactive *he* was getting. Then another bucket came by. Passing it along was easier than thinking.

IT WAS A PARTY of sorts—a going-away party. It wasn't a big party. Marian Staley hadn't made or wanted to make friends at Camp Nowhere. Most of the people stuck there, and the people in charge of the people stuck there, weren't people she would have cared to have anything to do with in normal times.

But she'd known Fayvl Tabakman before, back when there still were such things as normal times. The two of them shared a bond, too, a bond of loss and disaster. It was a negative bond, yes, but no less real for that. And Fayvl's cronies, Yitzkhak and Moishe, also understood loss and disaster from the inside out.

Moishe produced what looked like a wine bottle. After he swigged from it, though, he passed it to Marian with the warning, "Drink—but go easy."

She did, with the caution he'd advised. She didn't worry about drinking from a bottle someone else had used the way she would have before normal times vanished in fire and destruction. Even so, when she swallowed she wondered if she'd downed a lit Bunsen burner.

"Wow!" she said once speech returned to her charred vocal cords. "That's—strong."

"Uh-huh." The middle-aged Jew from—from Minsk, that was where he'd grown up—nodded. "Pretty good *samogon.* How you say in English *samogon*?"

"Moonshine," Fayvl said. He had a knock himself, then passed the bottle to Yitzkhak. "Yes, not bad."

"Moonshine." Moishe thumped his forehead with the heel of his hand. He was one of those people who needed to be right all the time and got furious at himself when he wasn't.

Yitzkhak also drank. He raised the bottle in salute to Marian. "Here's to going from Camp Nowhere to somewhere that's *alevai* somewhere."

"Thanks." She took the bottle. She had to drink to that. She didn't think it was exactly moonshine—to her, that meant raw whiskey. This stuff was more like brandy, even if it had started life as Welch's grape juice. The second sip didn't burn so much. Maybe her gullet was stunned.

"We'll miss you. *I'll* miss you," Fayvl said as he also drank again.

Moishe and Yitzkhak nodded. She didn't think they meant it the same way the cobbler did. He was sweet on her. She would have laughed at that before Bill died. Now—who could say? People needed people, and not all the combinations that wound up working were the obvious ones.

"How come I don't get any of that?" Linda asked as the grown-ups passed the bottle back and forth.

Fayvl, Yitzkhak, and Moishe laughed. After a second, so did Marian. "It's booze, honey," she explained.

"Oh," Linda said, and then, "Yuck!"

"Before the war started, she kept after Bill to give her a sip of beer," Marian said. "Finally, he let her have some. She tasted it and she looked at him and asked, 'Am I poisoned?'"

The three survivors of the worst the Old World could do laughed again. "I been poisoned on beer sometimes," Fayvl said, miming a deadly headache.

"Yuck!" Linda said again, this time because of his expression.

Yitzkhak asked, "So what you will do, now you get out of this place?"

"Oh, Lord, I don't know. Pick up the pieces. Try to find a job." Marian didn't mention that she'd already had to spend money to get the Studebaker running again. Tires, battery, spark plugs, oil . . . Nothing came cheap. She did her best not to think about that. "Whatever it is, I'll be doing it out in freedom, not—here."

"Freedom," Fayvl echoed wistfully. "Freedom is wonderful."

"Freedom is hard to find, is what freedom is," Moishe said. "Used to be some here. How much is left in the middle of a stupid war? Well, who knows?"

Marian had heard stories that also made her wonder. After the A-bombs fell, the West Coast and some inland states where the governor and legislature got killed went under martial law, or something as close to it as made no difference.

In a way, it made sense. The military and the National Guard had lots of members. They had organization and discipline. And they had guns. If you needed to govern areas where civilian administration had literally gone up in smoke, where else would you turn?

That was fine for the short term. But as the short term grew longer, then what? How did you unfry and unscramble the egg? How did you get civilian government going again? How did you persuade the military to let go of the reins?

Those were all interesting questions. Marian had answers to none of them. "I'll just have to see what it's like and how things work out, that's all," she said.

Pretty soon, the bottle was empty. Marian's head spun; she was glad she wasn't leaving till tomorrow morning. Welcome to freedom! You're under arrest for driving drunk! That wouldn't be the way to celebrate getting away from the refugee camp, would it?

She'd drunk less than any of the men, too. Yitzkhak lit a cigarette. With all the potent booze he'd put down, she marveled he didn't burst into flames. "So long. Good luck," he said, and ambled away. It was also a wonder he didn't stagger or fall, but he didn't.

Neither did Moishe. "Keep your eyes open. Americans, they trust too much," he said. That struck her as making good sense. Whether it would when she was sober . . . she'd see. Moishe also went off, under his own power and steady enough for all practical purposes.

That left Fayvl. He fiddled with the skin at the end of a fingernail. "You take care of yourself and your little girl, your *oytser,* here," he said.

"I will," Marian answered quietly. "I'll do my best, anyway."

"All you can do is all you can do. I tell myself that a lot. Sometimes almost I believe it for a little while." Tabakman's eyes were a million miles and a million years away. He shook himself like a retriever coming out of a cold lake. "You need anything, you have any kind trouble, you get hold of me, hear? I help you any way I can, promise."

"Thank you." Marian didn't know what he could do. Maybe he didn't know himself. She did believe he would try.

"Well, I should ought to go." He touched a finger to his cloth cap, first at her, then at Linda. After that, he heaved himself to his feet. Like his friends, he moved better than he had any business doing. He looked back once, but only for a second.

"He's a funny man," Linda said.

"Is he?" To Marian, Fayvl Tabakman was about the least funny man she'd ever met. "Why do you think so?"

"Because he's sad all the time, only he doesn't want anybody to know," Linda answered.

Marian gaped at her daughter. *Out of the mouths of babes,* she thought. She couldn't have summed up Fayvl any better in one sentence herself if she'd tried for a week.

The next morning, she and Linda set out, going up the gravel road down which trucks brought supplies into Camp Nowhere. The camp had sprung up in what was a meadow. It was where people in Everett had clumped together after the Russian bomb went off.

Eventually, the gravel road ran into a real paved one. After a while, she came to Snohomish. It also showed damage from the bomb. She kept on driving south, sticking to roads that stayed well inland. If she veered back to the coast, she'd end up in Seattle, and Seattle was the last place she wanted to be.

She and Linda stopped for lunch at a roadside diner. She ordered a BLT. Linda had a kid's hamburger and French fries. "This is yummy!" she said. And so it was. Ordinary food in an ordinary place seemed wonderful when you'd got used to the slop they served up at the refugee camp. Marian did have to remind herself to pay before she left. She hadn't needed to think about that for a while. But you got what you paid for, sure as hell.

"This is Moscow speaking." The voice came out of a speaker mounted on a wooden pole in front of the government building in what passed for Smidovich's town square. Vasili Yasevich and a few other people paused to listen to the news.

"Moo!" one of the men said. Everybody who heard him chuckled. This broadcaster's southern accent did make him sound something like a cow. From things Vasili had heard, Radio Moscow no longer originated in the city it claimed as its own. And the newsreader had replaced another man who'd sat in that seat for a long time.

If you were a Russian, you already knew that—knew it and took it for granted. No, you did if you were a Soviet citizen. Vasili was as Russian as anybody in Smidovich—more Russian than the Jews and slant-eyed natives who shared the place with people like him. But he was having to learn how to be Soviet as he went along.

"In its valiant assistance to the forces of the People's Democratic Republic of Korea, the Chinese People's Liberation Army continues to storm forward against the American imperialists and their lackeys in Korea," the newsreader said. "Backing up its allies, the Soviet Long-Range Bomber Force, part of the ever-victorious Red Air Force, had previously punished the reactionary running dogs with doses of atomic fire."

"Good. That's very good," the fellow beside Vasili muttered, to himself but intending to be heard by others. Vasili was used to news with a lot of propaganda stirred in—both the Japanese who ran Manchukuo and the Red Chinese who took over from them had seasoned the stew that way. But Stalin's workers' paradise used more than even he could stomach.

After two coughs, Roman Amfiteatrov murmured, "Please excuse me." Then he went back to the news: "In Western Europe, progressive forces headed by that vanguard of proletarian triumph, the glorious Red Army, continue to regroup after the vicious and cruel onslaught staged by Truman's clique of rabid capitalist hyenas. The advance is expected to resume in short order."

When Stalin dropped A-bombs on Korea, that was patriotic and heroic. When Truman dropped them on Germany, that was vicious and cruel. Vasili was cynical enough to doubt that the American radio reporters saw things the same way. He did wonder how many of these Soviet citizens doubted as he did.

He wondered that for a little while, anyhow. Then he saw Grigory Papanin strutting along without a care in the world—and without any of his tough-guy henchmen. Vasili forgot about the mooing voice coming out of the speaker. As unobtrusively as he could, he followed Papanin. If the son of a bitch thought he could tell Vasili how to work, pretty soon he'd decide he could horn in on the money Vasili made, too.

Sure as the devil, Papanin figured he was the biggest turd in this little town. He might have been, till Vasili got here. Now he'd find out he wasn't any more. *Or I'll find out I'm in over my head,* Vasili thought. With a shrug, he pushed that aside. Such doubts, unlike the ones about newsreaders, did you no good.

Papanin didn't even look behind him as he took his one-man parade down a dirt street. He thought such arrogance was his by right. Vasili thought he was a jerk.

He gained ground on the bigger man as fast as he could while staying quiet. His right hand went into his jacket pocket—not for the straight razor, but for a knuckleduster he'd got from a white-bearded Jew as part payment when he put a new floor in the old man's house.

He tapped Grigory Papanin on the right shoulder from behind with his left hand. "Huh?" Papanin said as he turned to see who dared bother him. His face changed when he recognized Vasili. "You—" he began.

"Yeah, me, dickface," Vasili said, and hit him in the nose, as hard as he could, with the brass knuckles. Cartilage mashed under metal. Blood squirted. Grigory Papanin squealed like a bull calf when it was suddenly made into a steer. His hands flew to the wounded part.

Vasili did his best to turn Papanin into a steer, all right. His booted foot caught the other man square in the crotch. Papanin squealed again, on a higher note this time, and folded up like a concertina.

Another kick, this time in the pit of Papanin's stomach. Had Vasili had such footwork all the time, he might have played forward for ChSKA Moscow or Dinamo Kiev. Papanin sagged down to the dusty street.

Nobody sprinted out of the shops and cabins to either side, screaming for Vasili to stop beating up that poor man. Nobody yelled for the militia to come arrest him. That silence told him everything he needed to know about how popular Grigory Papanin was in Smidovich.

Once Papanin went down, Vasili booted him in the ribs three or four times. He hoped he broke some of them. He thought he did. He didn't believe in anything so stupid as a fair fight. He fought to win, and to teach a lesson the other guy would never forget.

Papanin was tough. Battered as he was, he tried to reach into his own jacket pocket for whatever equalizer he stashed there. Vasili stomped on his hand. Papanin screamed. Vasili plucked out the toy himself: a Tokarev automatic, Red Army issue.

"Naughty," he said mildly. "Mine now—spoil of war."

What Papanin called him then was a minor masterpiece of *mat.* Vasili gave him the critical acclaim it deserved: another kick in the ribs. He flipped his razor open and let the steel glitter.

"Now listen to me, you dumb pussy," he said. "You fuck with me again, you try telling me how to run my business, next time you're dead. Not just messed up—dead as your nose. I'll gut you like a hog, too, and use you for sausage casings. You hear what I'm telling you?"

When Papanin didn't answer fast enough, Vasili kicked him one more time. "I hear you," the local choked out, and was noisily sick.

"Khorosho," Vasili said, and then, "You're disgusting, you know that?" Shaking his head, he walked away.

Papanin wouldn't bother him for a while. He'd be weeks getting over what he'd walked into this morning. After that? He was tough, but how tough was he really? If he didn't kill Vasili, he'd be dead himself. He had to see as much. He might leave bad enough alone. Vasili could hope so. If not, he'd deal with it.

As he walked back toward the center of Smidovich, a plump man came out of a shop that sold fur hats and mittens. He looked at Grigory Papanin, who was up on his hands and knees but not making any effort to get back on his feet. His eyes were wide as millstones as they swung back to Vasili. "You—did *that*?" he asked.

"I sure did," Vasili answered. He hadn't expected to come away with a pistol, but he wasn't complaining.

"But—But—" The plump man groped for words. At last, he found some: "But he was the toughest guy in town."

"Maybe he used to be," Vasili said, "but he isn't any more. I don't like starting fights. If somebody else does, though, he'd better know I'll finish them."

"*Bozhemoi!* I guess so!" The man who sold fur hats looked at Papanin again. With puke and blood all over his face and with his nose mashed flat, he wasn't an appetizing sight. "He's lucky you didn't finish *him,* though I'm not so sure he'd call it that right now."

"If he leaves me alone, I'll leave him alone, same as I would anybody else," Vasili said. "If he doesn't, it's the last stupid stunt the fucker ever pulls."

"Are they all like you in Khabarovsk?" the hat-seller asked—like most of the townsfolk, he'd already heard about Vasili's story.

"Nah." Vasili shook his head. "I'm one of the soft ones. Why do you think the Yankees bombed us?" He laughed out loud when the plump man crossed himself.

* * *

Aaron Finch used plenty of Mum before he put on his Blue Front shirt. "It won't help," he said resignedly. "A day like this, I'll be *shvitzing* all over, not just under my arms."

"So I'll wash the shirt after you get home," Ruth said. "I still don't think this is as bad as St. Louis weather." With her brothers and sister, she'd come out to Los Angeles when her mother and father died within months of each other right after the war. Aaron understood that. Staying where they were would have been like living in a haunted house.

"St. Louis never gets this hot," he said, trying not to let her remember the bad times. "It's supposed to be 105 today. Just what I want to do—*shlep* stoves and iceboxes and washing machines around."

"But St. Louis is so muggy," Ruth said with a twisted civic pride. "This is dry heat. It doesn't feel as bad."

"It gets past 105, it's bad any which way," Aaron said. He'd been in the black gang aboard a Liberty ship in the South Pacific, so he wasn't a virgin when it came to heat and humidity. He did marvel that the L.A. area often got its hottest weather a week or two after fall officially started, but he'd seen before that that was how things worked around here.

"Well, come on to the kitchen and I'll fix you breakfast." Ruth didn't have the relentless Finch urge to grab the last word. Aaron sure did; his brother Marvin had an even worse case. She was easier to get along with the way she was. He did wonder now and then how she put up with him. Sometimes, though, you just had to count your blessings.

Breakfast was two eggs fried in the grease from sausages, with buttered toast and jam and coffee. If you were going to *shlep* appliances, you needed some ballast in there. And a cigarette was extra nice after food.

Leon came out of the bedroom right before Aaron took off for work. He was carrying his Teddy bear. He'd got Bounce for his second birthday, and ever since had had to be forcibly separated from the bear. He would have taken it into the bathtub if Ruth had let him get away with it.

Stooping to kiss him, Aaron said, "See you tonight, Leon. I've got to go to Blue Front."

Leon held out the Teddy bear. "Say bye-bye to Bounce."

"So long, Bounce." Aaron shook hands with the fuzzy plush toy. He was damned if he'd kiss it. Luckily, Leon seemed satisfied.

As soon as he went out the front door, Ruth locked it behind him. His hand went into the right front pocket of his gabardine work pants to pull out his keys. He was halfway down the concrete walk, the keys in his hand, before he looked up toward the old Nash parked in front of the house.

Except it wasn't parked in front of the house. It was gone.

He looked up the street and down the street, as if he could have left it in front of some other house by mistake. He hadn't, of course. Not only was it gone, it had had somebody else's help in going.

"Oh, for Christ's sake," he said. Glendale didn't have any refugee camps, but it was full of people who'd fled north after the A-bomb hit downtown L.A. Some filled cheap hotels and roominghouses. Others slept in their cars or on bus benches or in the bushes in parks.

Some of them peddled whatever they had. Some did such odd jobs as they could find. Aaron didn't look down his nose at those people; he'd lived that way himself during the Depression. Some of the women hustled, more because they had no other way to get money than because they wanted to.

And some people stole. Crime in town had zoomed up like a V-2 the past few months. If your choice was between going hungry or seeing your kids go hungry and lifting what didn't belong to you, you'd steal, all right.

Shaking his head, Aaron turned around and went back to the house. "Daddy!" Leon said when he opened the door. He was gladder to see Aaron than Aaron was to be seen.

"What did you forget, honey?" Ruth asked.

"Gurnisht," he answered. "Look out the front window. What don't you see?"

She looked. For a second, it didn't register, as it hadn't with him. Then her hands flew to her face. "The car!"

"Right the first time," he said. "You win sixteen dollars. Wanna try for thirty-two?"

"It's not funny!"

"No kidding, it's not."

"What are you going to do?"

Aaron had been working that out for himself. He ticked things off on his fingers. "Call the boss, tell him I'll be late. Call the cops. Get through the rest of the week somehow. If the car isn't back by Friday, go buy one Friday night or Saturday morning."

"We can't afford it," Ruth said, which was true.

"We can't afford to be without one," Aaron said, which was

also true. He feared he'd never see the Nash again. Odds were it already sat in some shady garage, getting butchered for spare parts. With a sigh, he went on, "I'll get something cheap, something where I can do a lot of the work myself."

"Okay." Ruth stopped. "No, it's *not* okay. The nerve of that SOB!" That was about as close as she ever came to really cussing.

"Uh-huh." Aaron went to the phone and dialed the Blue Front warehouse. He got the switchboard girl. "Hi, Lois, it's Aaron. Put me through to Mr. Weissman, will you?"

"Hang on a second," she said.

After a few clicks and pops, a man's voice came on the line: "Weissman here."

"Boss, it's Aaron. I'm sorry, but I'll be late today. Some *mamzer* went and swiped my car."

"Gevalt!" Herschel Weissman said, which was just what Aaron was thinking. "Okay. Try and get in as soon as you can, will you? Looks like things are finally picking up a little."

"*Alevai omayn.* I'll do my best. Thanks. 'Bye." Aaron reached for the phone book to find the number for the Glendale police. That one he didn't have memorized. He got transferred to a sergeant in the robbery detail.

That worthy took his name and address and the car's license number and description. Then he said, "Well, Mr. Finch, we'll do the best we can." His voice trailed away on the last few words.

"What do you think my chances are?" Aaron asked.

A pause. A sigh. "I'll tell you, they aren't great," the sergeant said. "These stolen cars, most of the time they don't get left on the street." He figured the Nash was in one of those garages, too.

"Okay," Aaron said, though it wasn't. "Let me know if you find it, that's all." He hung up, then checked the phone book for another number.

"Now who are you calling?" Ruth asked.

"Yellow Cab." Aaron didn't even think about Glendale's creaky bus system. It didn't deserve thinking about, either. Nor did walking, not in weather like this, not when he was going to be doing hard physical work all day. Maybe tomorrow, if it cooled down some.

"You could call Marvin and Sarah," Ruth suggested. "A cab's expensive."

"No, thanks. This won't be too bad—it isn't that far." He

dialed for the taxi. "Besides, a cab just costs me money. If I go and call Marvin, I guess he'll be there, yeah." Marvin often found himself "between projects," as he put it. But . . . "He'll cost me aggravation, though, and he never lets me forget when he does me a favor."

The cabbie showed up ten minutes later. "Yeah, I know where Blue Front's at," he said when Aaron told him where he needed to go. He eyed Aaron's shirt. "Looks like you know where it's at real good."

"You might say so," Aaron answered. "I would've gone there on my own this morning, only somebody took off with my car."

"Ouch! That stinks, buddy," the cab driver said as he put his Plymouth in gear. "It's all that riffraff from Los Angeles, is what it is. Them bums, they'd steal the paint off a stop sign if they could work out how to pry it loose."

Aaron had come to the same conclusion himself. It sounded uglier the way the cabbie put it. Well, he couldn't do anything about that. All he could do was lean back in the seat and let the other man get him to work.

Daisy Baxter found herself humming a silly love song as she cleaned the toilets after closing time at the Owl and Unicorn. She couldn't remember the last time she'd done that. After thinking for a moment, she couldn't remember ever doing it before.

She didn't need long to figure out why she was humming it, either. Before, she'd been getting through the days one after another. What else were you supposed to do—what else could you possibly do—when, with the war as good as won, they told you your husband would never come home again?

She'd pulled into a shell after they told her Tom was dead, pulled in and done her best to close off the opening between herself and the outside world, the world of feeling. If she didn't feel anything much at all, she wouldn't have to feel quite so empty.

"I didn't even know how empty I felt," she said, as if someone standing behind her in the small, smelly space had claimed she did. But after a while, you didn't just get used to something—or to nothing—you started taking it for granted without knowing you were.

One kiss from Bruce McNulty had changed all that. It had

suddenly given her a standard of comparison. Before, she'd had only the emptiness. Now, she could see that caring about somebody else, and having somebody else care about you, was better than not.

She laughed at herself as she washed her hands with strong soap under the hottest water she could stand, and then did it again. Like Lady Macbeth, if for different reasons, she never felt she could get them clean. As she dried them, she laughed again. It all sounded like something out of a soppy, sentimental film.

But why did soppy, sentimental films so often turn out to be hits? Surely because they showed something people wanted to find in their own lives, even if they didn't very often.

Daisy was walking up the stairs to the flat when the deep-throated rumble of bombers taking off from Sculthorpe made her stop and cock her head to listen. Even from two or three miles away, the noise could rattle her fillings. It surely woke some of the people in Fakenham lucky enough to have already gone to bed.

"Luck, Bruce," she whispered. She didn't *know* he was flying one of those Superfortresses, but that was the way to bet. And if he was, what kind of devastation did the big plane carry in its bomb bay? B-29s flying out of Sculthorpe had been striking targets in Eastern Europe—for all she knew, in Russia itself—since the early days of the war. She'd listened to McNulty and other pilots talking with a few, or more than a few, pints in them.

They talked more than they should have. Some of the stories they told chilled her blood. How could you do—that—to a city and sleep at night or look at yourself in a mirror afterwards? But then, most of these pilots had bombed Germany and Japan in the last war. They had bigger and more terrible bombs now, but how different was it in principle?

"Different enough," she said, there on the stairs. She'd seen what the Russian A-bomb did to the outskirts of Norwich. The army and police made sure nobody from outside got closer than the outskirts. That told her what she hadn't seen was bound to be worse than what she had.

One bomb. One city. That was all it took. One bomb had been plenty to rip the heart out of Paris. Norwich, smaller to begin with, was pretty much gone.

She cleaned her teeth and got into bed. It was still too early for her to need to huddle under blankets and quilts with a hot-water bottle at her feet. Her long flannel nightgown hadn't changed, though. She smiled to herself as she got comfortable. One of these times, with Bruce, she might lie down on this bed wearing nothing at all.

She took that thought into sleep. Her dreams were warm, warm enough to wake her for a little while. But she soon slept again. Minding the pub would have worn out a mechanical man, let alone a flesh-and-blood woman.

In the wee small hours, she woke once more, this time from a dream full of howling dogs. The howling didn't fade, though, after her eyes opened in the dark bedroom. It rose and fell, rose and fell, wailing like a damned soul.

"Oh, bloody hell! The air-raid siren!" Daisy said as she hopped out of bed and hurried for the stairs. The Russians had dropped that A-bomb on Norwich. And they'd struck Sculthorpe with ordinary high explosives—conventional bombs, people had taken to calling them, as if they were cozy and normal. Stalin's flyers knew where the planes that tormented them came from, all right.

Now they were hitting Sculthorpe again, or the air-raid wardens thought they were. Daisy tried not to break her neck on the pitch-black stairs. If the Russians missed, or had to dump their bombs in a hurry because fighters were on their tails, some might come down on Fakenham. You wanted to be down in the cellar in case that happened.

As she went down there, jet engines screamed, seemingly right above the roof. Ordinary airplane motors were loud. Jets were ridiculous.

That was the last thought Daisy had before the world ended.

She was in the cellar, in a building with all the windows covered over by blackout curtains. The sudden glare was so savage, she wailed and clapped her hands over her eyes just the same. A few seconds later, the bricks and plaster shook and groaned, as if in an earthquake. She'd never felt an earthquake in her life, but this didn't seem like anything else.

The Owl and Unicorn did more than shake. Things fell down and fell apart. Tinkling mixed with the rumble said the windows and the pint mugs and the mirror behind the bar were smashing themselves to hell and gone along with everything else in the place.

As soon as Daisy smelled the first whiff of smoke, she knew she had to get out of there *right now.* She'd bake if she stayed. She just prayed she wasn't already too late.

Up the stairs she scrambled. That was the word, all right, because chunks of the smashed pub had fallen down them. Her bare feet took a beating. She didn't care. A roof beam blocked the way up to the ground floor. She shoved it aside with panic-given strength. It wasn't quite a mother lifting the front end of a motorcar off a trapped child, but it came close.

The stumbling dash across the floor tore up her feet even worse. She fell once or twice, too, when she tripped on overturned tables and chairs she couldn't see—and on chunks of the ceiling and the first floor and the roof that had also come down. She was lucky (she supposed she was lucky) the whole thing hadn't collapsed and trapped her down below.

A glimmer of light showed her a way out. It wasn't the door; it was a rent in the front wall that ran from a corner of the window frame down to the ground. Afterwards, she never knew how she squeezed through it, but she did.

A brick fell down and smacked the sidewalk a few inches from her bleeding feet. She stumbled farther away from the shattered Owl and Unicorn. Would she ever be able to go back in there? Right this second, she didn't give a damn.

High into the sky towered a mushroom cloud—not just high but higher, highest. She'd seen the one above slaughtered Norwich, of course, but that had been well off to the east, a safe thirty miles away. Nothing about this one seemed safe. She guessed that the bomb had burst right over Sculthorpe. Had it gone off a little east of the air base, nothing would have been left of Fakenham.

Not much was left of the small town as things were. By the hellish light from the cloud, she saw that at least half the buildings had fallen down. Other people were crawling out of the ruins, all of them bloody and battered—she realized she had to look bloody and battered, too. Some had useless, probably broken, arms and legs. And how much radiation had they taken?

For the time being, none of that mattered. People were screaming for help. Not everyone had got out, and the fires grew. Daisy started digging through the rubble, doing what she could.

CADE CURTIS WASN'T USED to wearing a captain's bars on his shoulders. He knew damn well he hadn't done anything brave or clever to earn them. He'd got them because he was an officer who'd had the dumb luck not to be under either of the A-bombs Stalin dropped on South Korea.

They needed officers, needed them desperately. Even a captain had no real business commanding a regiment, but there you were. And here Cade was, giving it his best shot. He wondered if he was the first regimental CO still too young to vote. It might have happened, on one side or the other, during the War Between the States. He would have bet it hadn't since.

His men were holding, or anyway trying to hold, a ridge line about halfway between Chongju and vanished Pusan. The Red Chinese had poured through the gap the second Russian atom bomb tore in the American defenses. If this line didn't hold, the town of Kaeryong behind it wouldn't, either, and a bad situation would get worse. Shit would be out to lunch, if you wanted to get right down to it.

"Where's that air, dammit?" Cade asked a radioman hooked into the Navy network—most surviving U.S. planes in Korea flew off carriers these days.

"Inbound this way, sir," the sergeant with the earphones answered. "Suppose to be here in, like, five minutes." An 81mm mortar round thudded down in front of their trench, showering them both with dirt. Cade wondered whether they had five minutes left.

The Reds didn't have a lot of tanks. Stalin was using the ones he did have in Europe, not passing them along to Mao and Kim Il-sung. That meant machine guns counted for as much here as they had at places like Verdun and the Somme.

Nothing like a well-sited machine gun for making infantry wish it had never been born.

Several Brownings were stuttering bullets at the Red Chinese dug in farther down the slope. They were less eager to throw in human-wave assaults than they had been during the days just after they swarmed over the Yalu. They still did it now and then, but not all the time any more.

Then again, they used more mortars than they had then. They also had more mortars to use. Mortars were the poor man's artillery, and Mao's men were nothing if not poor. Sheet metal for the tube, loose tolerances . . . If you were a blacksmith, you could just about go into the mortar business in your back yard.

One of the bastardly little bombs burst in a kink of the trench, fifty yards down from Cade. Somebody over there started screaming for a medic. That wasn't good, but maybe wasn't so bad as if he were screaming for his mother.

Here came the Corsairs. Cade whooped when he saw the long-nosed fighter-bombers with the inverted gull wings. They were as obsolete as the rest of the prop jobs left over from World War II. Where there were no jets to claw them out of the sky, though, they could still do a fine job of turning human beings into raw—or sometimes burnt—meat.

Some of them carried rockets under those kinked wings. They ripple-fired them at the Red Chinese. Others had napalm bombs instead. Flame leaped and splashed when those went in. Next to the atomic fire the Russians had rained on Korea, it was puny and cold, but you sure wouldn't think so if you were luckless enough to have it come down on you.

Cade whooped again, and pumped his fist in the air. He knew that was an un-Christian thing to do. The Red Chinese were men, just like him. But they were also men trying their goddamnedest to kill him. Maybe he should have regretted their untimely demise, but he didn't.

The Corsairs banked and wheeled in the air for another attack run. They all had eight .50-caliber machine guns in their wings, so they could put a lot of lead in the air when they strafed trenches. If the rockets and the napalm didn't do for the Red Chinese, some good, old-fashioned slugs might turn the trick.

Waggling their wings in farewell, the Corsairs roared back toward the Sea of Japan. Cade cautiously stuck his head up over the parapet to see how they'd done. The napalm still blazed. Smoke rose from the rocket hits. And quite a few Chinamen in dun-colored uniforms legged it northward. They'd had more than flesh and blood could take.

Not all of them, though. A bullet cracked past Cade's ear, close enough so he thought he felt the wind of its passage. He ducked down in a hurry. He was just glad that wasn't a permanent reminder he hadn't come here to play tourist.

He was a captain in charge of a regiment. His company commanders were second lieutenants, except for a couple of sergeants. One of the lieutenants asked, "You want we should move forward and push out the rest of the Chinks, sir?"

"Howie, I just want to sit tight and make sure they can't push us out," Cade answered. "We've got to hold on to Kaeryong, and they won't be coming after us here right away, not after that pounding."

"Okay, sir." Howard Sturgis' tone said it really wasn't. He was in his thirties. He'd been a sergeant when the fighting here started, and won a battlefield commission for gallantry. He attacked first and worried about it later.

He did when you let him, anyhow. Cade wasn't about to. "Hey, look, eventually the States'll do a proper job of reinforcing us," he said. "Till then, we've just got to hang on so they'll have something *to* reinforce."

"Sir, they're way the hell over there. The ports on the West Coast are fucked up. The Panama Canal's fucked up. Now Pusan's fucked up, too, and that was the best harbor we had over here." Sturgis pointed north with heavy patience. "But all the Chinks in the world, they're right across the goddamn Yalu."

"I know about that, thanks," Cade said dryly. "I was up at the Chosin Reservoir."

For the first time, he got Sturgis' undivided attention. The older man stared at him. "But they killed just about all o' those guys," he said.

"I know about that, too." Curtis pointed at his own chest. "Just about all, but not quite. So if they give us too much trouble down here, who knows what happens? Maybe Peiping goes up in smoke, or Shanghai, or some other big cities."

"Wouldn't break my heart," Sturgis said.

"Only thing that worries me is, will anybody have anything left to rebuild with by the time this war is over?" Cade said. "In the meantime, we're gonna sit tight, let the enemy come to us, and slaughter him when he does. I can't think of any better way to keep our casualties down, so we'll do it like that."

"Got it," Howard Sturgis said reluctantly. "Uh, sir."

"Good."

"Sir?" Sturgis said. When Cade nodded, the veteran went on, "Sir, no shit, you made it back down from the reservoir?"

"Yeah," Cade said, in lieu of *Screw you if you think I'm lying.* He added, "I never would've if I didn't get help from the Korean Christians. They live up to the name better than a bunch of folks back home, and you can sing that in church."

"Huh." Sturgis sounded thoughtful: not a usual sound from him. "Guess they love Mao even better'n they love old Kim, then."

"That's about the size of it," Cade agreed.

He might have said something more, but all the American machine guns started going off at once. Airplane engines roared in at treetop height. Cade flung himself into a dugout. The Red Chinese couldn't call in Corsairs from carriers, but they had Shturmoviks. Those carried rockets and bombs and guns, too. The machine gunners on the ground were wasting ammo. The Russian attack planes laughed at that kind of fire. Only an F-80 or F-86 could make them say uncle, and not a whole lot of those were left over here.

Nothing came down too close to Cade, for which he thanked heaven. Of course, heaven had just decided to visit hell on some other sorry bastards instead, so how grateful should he have been, exactly? He shook his head. When you started asking yourself questions like that, where did you stop? Anywhere?

Konstantin Morozov climbed out of the bathtub. He took it slow and easy; he had about as much strength and endurance as a sand castle. He clucked sadly as he looked down at his naked body. He was a man. Ever since his beard came in, he'd been hairy like a man, with a mat on his chest, tufts at his armpits and crotch, and some pretty fair fuzz on his arms and legs.

Women liked men that way, dammit. It let them know they weren't lying down with another girl.

But, as far as Konstantin could tell, he had no more sprouting from his hide than a plucked chicken. It had all fallen out. And not just on his body. He hadn't had to shave since he came to the military hospital. He had no hair on his dome. He had no hair in his nose or ears, and no eyebrows or eyelashes, either.

"Will it ever grow back?" he'd asked a doc when he'd been a lot sicker than he was now, when he thought the tide was rolling in on that poor sand castle.

She'd only shrugged. "If you live, we think it will. Eventually." How long *eventually* was, she hadn't said. Maybe she didn't know, either.

He was still alive. He was pretty sure now he'd stay that way for a while, and he was even beginning to believe he might want to. All of his crewmen were still alive, too, though for Vladislav Kalyakin it was a close call. The driver wouldn't stop bleeding out his asshole, so they had to go in there and do . . . something. Konstantin was hazy on the details, but it seemed to have helped.

Even if it had, though, Kalyakin wouldn't be fit to fight again for a long time, if he ever was. Morozov, Eigims, and Sarkisyan were in better shape than that. Konstantin had puked blood only once, and not a whole lot of it. Food was starting to taste good to him again.

The Balt and Armenian were about where he was. They'd had their brush with the scythe-carrying skeleton in the black robe, but Old Man Death wasn't quite hungry enough to gnaw on them.

Yet. Konstantin knew too well it was always *yet.* He'd survived a near miss from an atom bomb? Okay, fine. As soon as he was healthy enough, the Red Army would throw him into another tank and try to expend him some other way. A mine, a bazooka rocket, a shell from an English tank he didn't spot soon enough . . . Any one of those would do to kill a man, even if they didn't murder by carload lots like the big son of a bitch full of atoms.

He made it back to his cot without getting too exhausted. Lying on the lumpy mattress couldn't have been much more boring. Even Konstantin had to admit it beat the hell out of lying at the bottom of a hole two meters deep with dirt shoveled in on top of him.

A doctor came by to check on him: an East German man who spoke Russian with the precision of a bright schoolboy. "You are feeling well?" he asked.

"Not too bad, Doc," Morozov answered. Then he opened

his mouth so the man in the white coat could stick a thermometer under his tongue.

"Oh, this is excellent!" the Fritz said when he looked at Konstantin's temperature. "You have no fever now for two days in a row. This shows your immunity to infection is recovering."

"Good." Konstantin supposed it was good. It sounded good, anyway. He asked, "How much can you do for radiation sickness, anyway?"

"Less than we would like, I am sorry to say," the fraternal socialist ally replied. (What had he done in the last war? Patched up guys for the *Wehrmacht*? Morozov wouldn't have been surprised—he was plenty old enough.) After a moment, he continued, "We treat the symptoms as they develop, to the best of our ability. We give supportive care—we keep patients comfortable and well-nourished, to help them recover from the dose of radiation they have received. But we cannot do anything about the radiation itself. If it is too much . . ." He let his voice trail off.

Konstantin held out his right hand, fingers in a fist, thumb pointing down. The German doctor nodded. Konstantin asked, "How close did my crew and me come to getting too much?"

"No one had a Geiger counter in your tank, so I cannot measure that exactly," the doctor replied. "I have seen people who were sicker than you men recover. I have not seen people who were much sicker than you recover."

"I get you." That marched pretty well with the way Konstantin had felt right after they brought him here. Then he asked, "How many other people with radiation sickness have you seen?"

"More than you think, perhaps. Remember, the Americans have used these horrible bombs against the German Democratic Republic. So my colleagues and I have had practice with our fellow citizens."

"Ah." Morozov left it there. As a matter of fact, he'd forgotten the Yankees had dropped A-bombs on this part of Germany. Like most Russians who'd lived through the Great Patriotic War, he had trouble working up much sympathy for Fritzes.

The doctor produced a lancet and a microscope slide. The slide had a label with Morozov's name and service number written on it. Well, actually the label said MOROZOW, not

МОРОЗОВ, but that was what the Latin alphabet and German language did to it.

"Give me your finger, please," the man said. With a small sigh, Konstantin did. He couldn't begin to remember how many times he'd got stuck since he came here. One more went on the list he wasn't keeping.

He'd taken more wounds, real wounds, than he could keep track of in this war and the last one. Gunshots, fragments, burns . . . He'd known some serious pain. Next to all that, a little poke with the lancet should have been as nothing. But it wasn't. It hurt, every single time.

As the doctor smeared his blood onto the slide and put a cover glass over it, Konstantin asked him about that. "Is it my imagination?" he wondered.

"Nyet," the doctor said, sounding very Russian indeed for one word. "For one thing, hands have more nerves than other parts of the body. For another, most wounds happen when you do not look for them. You know I shall stick you. You almost feel it before it happens."

"What do you know?" Konstantin said thoughtfully. Then he nodded. "That makes sense. Thanks, Doc." He wasn't in the habit of thanking Germans, but he did here.

"It is nothing." The doctor put the slide with Morozov's blood on it into the breast pocket of his white coat. One of the things radiation poisoning did to you was give you a fierce anemia. They took all the blood counts to see how people came back from it.

When the German came to the sick, bald artilleryman in the next bed, the fellow sang out: "Here's the vampire again!"

The Red Army soldiers in the ward laughed, Konstantin as loud as any of them. The doctor's smile was the kind you used when you wanted to clout the guy you were smiling at. "It is necessary so that we may help you regain your health again," he said primly.

"Sure, pal, but it's still no fun," the artilleryman said, echoing what Konstantin had been thinking.

Lunch was stewed liver. Liver stew, liver cooked with onions, chopped liver, liver dumplings, liver paste (that one had been a favorite German ration in the last war) . . . The cooks fed the men with radiation sickness every kind of liver dish they could come up with. They said it helped build blood. About the only things they didn't do were drip it in with a needle and serve it in suppository form.

Konstantin liked liver. Or rather, he had liked liver. He'd taken plenty of those tinfoil tubes of liver paste off dead Fritzes. He'd enjoyed them, too. They'd tasted like victory. Now . . . If they ever let him out of here, he didn't think he'd ever touch the stuff again. He'd had it up to there, and then some.

But at least he could think about escaping this place. Compared to how he'd felt when he got here, that was progress with a capital P.

Advancing! Gustav Hozzel wasn't used to advancing against the Russians. Last time around, he'd started fighting in the east just about when the Germans began their long, bitter, grinding withdrawal toward and then into the *Vaterland.* He'd lived through his first couple of scrapes as much by luck as anything else. After that, he'd started to see what he needed to do.

By the time the war ended, he was one of the hard-bitten veterans who kept the *Reich* on its feet for a year, maybe even a year and a half, after it should have fallen over. He'd retreated from somewhere near Rostov-on-Don to Germany, almost every centimeter of the way on foot.

He'd hardly ever gone forward. Oh, local counterattacks sometimes took back a few square kilometers of lost ground, but never for long. Things had worked the same way in this new war, too. There were just too many Russians. There were always too many Russians.

But if you blew a swarm of them to hell at once . . . Of course, the drawback to that was that the Amis had also blown a swarm of Gustav's countrymen to hell. They hadn't done that as long as they saw any chance of hanging on to West Germany. Once they didn't see that chance any more, they didn't hesitate, either.

Gustav's regiment moved east through the wreckage of Wesel two days after the bomb fell there. He had no idea whether that was safe. All his time in Russia had taught him not to ask inconvenient questions.

It was even worse than he'd expected. He knew what bombs did. He'd seen plenty of cities smashed flat from the air, and from the ground. He'd helped scorch Russian earth himself.

But the center of Wesel wasn't just knocked into ruins, the way ordinary bombs did. It wasn't just scorched, either, or even baked. It was incinerated, melted. The stump of the cathedral spire left after Russian guns bit off the top and the observers up there had flowed like candle wax. Stone wasn't supposed to do that, dammit.

In his pocket, Gustav carried a little piece of greenish glass—melted rock and concrete—he'd picked up near the doubly destroyed spire. He wanted something to remember Wesel by, and that seemed to fit. It was probably radioactive, but he hoped it wasn't *too* radioactive.

To his surprise, Rolf was all for the atom bombs. "You can't make an omelette without breaking eggs," said the ex-LAH man, who wasn't long on original thoughts. "As long as we kill Russians, what else matters?"

"You don't have any relatives in Wesel, do you?" Max Bachman asked, beating Gustav to the punch.

"If I did, I'd rather see them dead than living under the Bolsheviks," Rolf said. The really scary thing was, Gustav believed him.

Right under where the bomb went off, they found no dead at all. The A-bomb had simply erased them, as it had erased much of Wesel. As they moved farther east, they did come across corpses, but so charred and shrunken that Gustav had no idea whether they were men or women, Germans or Russians.

A little farther on yet, the bodies were burned and melted, but still recognizable as human beings. As far as Gustav was concerned, that was worse. A flamethrower might do such things, but to a few people at a time, not to hundreds or thousands at once. The smell was more of roasted meat than dead meat, though the latter was starting to gain.

They went past Russian tanks that could have blasted them to hell had anyone inside them remained alive. But the men in there were dead, and so were the tanks. The ones closer to the A-bomb had cannons that drooped like limp dicks. Farther away, they looked ready to go—but they weren't.

Then the advancing Germans came across people who weren't dead but who wished they were. Atomic fire could do things to bodies not even flamethrowers matched. Eyes seared and welded to cheeks . . . Several soldiers gave the *coup de grâce* to horribly burned men and women who thanked them for it.

Gustav had done that in Russia. He'd always hoped someone would do it for him if he needed it. This was worse, somehow. That line from the Poe story wouldn't get out of his mind. *And the Red Death held illimitable dominion over all.*

"If this is what winning looks like, I'm not sure I want anything to do with it," he said, hoping the last rations he'd eaten would stay down.

Rolf snorted. "Oh, come off it, man! Do you think the Ivans haven't done the same thing wherever they could?" Gustav couldn't answer that. He knew they had.

Here and there, Red Army men and units kept trying to fight back. But so much of what they'd had at the front was gone, gone forever. Also gone was the illusion they'd carried that atom bombs wouldn't come down on them but were just for cities behind the lines.

Along with the holdouts were plenty of Russians not just willing but eager to surrender. Some of them had doses of radiation sickness; the prevailing winds carried fallout from the bomb blasts into territory the Soviet Union occupied. Others had simply had enough fighting to last them for the rest of their lives.

Most of the Ivans in their late twenties and early thirties knew bits and pieces—sometimes more than bits and pieces—of German. They would have been the ones who'd fought their way into the *Reich* in 1945 and then settled down to occupy it after Hitler blew his brains out and everything he'd struggled for was *kaput.*

Gustav didn't think much about that one way or the other. To him, a prisoner who could understand what he said was easier to handle than one who couldn't, and that was about it.

Rolf had other notions. Whenever a Russian who spoke fair German gave himself up, the *Waffen*-SS veteran would ask, "And what did you do in the last war, you fucking *Arschloch*?"

One Ivan still had his pride. "Walloped the snot out of you Fritzes, that's what," he answered.

Two seconds later, he lay twitching on the grass, a bullet hole in his forehead, the back of his head blown out. "Any sack of shit who thinks he can give me sauce, it's the last stupid thing he'll ever do," Rolf said, chambering a fresh round in his rifle.

"No," Gustav told him. "Don't do that. It isn't 1945 any more. You can't get away with killing prisoners this time around."

"Says who?" Rolf's gray stare measured him for a coffin.

Gustav didn't care. If he hadn't long since quit worrying

about his own neck, he wouldn't have picked up a gun when the new fighting started. "Says me, dickface. You don't like it, we can settle things right now."

"It won't be a fair fight, either," Max Bachman added.

Rolf glared at him, too. But the ex-LAH man tried to defuse things with a joke: "Who's been feeding you two raw meat?"

"Not funny, Rolf," Gustav said. "They take war crimes a lot more seriously than they ever did in your old unit. And if you think the guys here won't squeal on you, you're the one who's *Scheissevoll.*"

"Kiss the Amis' asshole," Rolf jeered. "Go ahead."

"Crap," Max said. "War's bad enough any which way. But we fought cleaner against the Amis than we did against the Ivans last go-round. The Russians haven't murdered POWs for the fun of it this time around. We won't give them the excuse to start, either."

"Christ, I never figured I joined the motherfucking Salvation Army," Rolf said. "I supposed you clowns never found one of your buddies with his dick cut off and stuffed in his mouth."

"Who didn't?" Gustav said stonily. "But Max is right. They aren't doing that shit this time. We're not going to, either."

The finger Rolf gave him was borrowed from the Yanks he despised. Gustav ignored it. But he didn't like having friends who might be more dangerous than the enemy.

Cold rain drummed down on the tent where Daisy Baxter lay in a cot. She felt like hell. She had about as much hair left as a ninety-year-old granny, and more came out every time she dragged a comb across her scalp. She didn't do that as often as she should have; she didn't have the energy.

Seven other women from Fakenham lay in the tent with her. It was one from the British Army, made to hold eight cots. Some of the other ladies had burns, others had had things fall down on them when the A-bomb hit Sculthorpe. All of them had radiation sickness, some cases worse than Daisy's, one or two from the east end of town not quite so bad.

Most of the survivors were here, in this tent city that had sprouted on the sheep meadows like toadstools coming up after a rain. Toadstools would be coming up after this rain.

Daisy languidly wondered if she'd ever get the chance to see them.

One of the women held up her hand. A harried-looking sister got up off the folding chair where she'd been reading an Agatha Christie and came over to her. "Yes, Mrs. Simpkins? What is it?" *What is it now?* was what her tone said.

"I'm sorry, dear, but I need to use the bedpan," the middle-aged woman answered. None of the patients was strong enough to walk to the latrine trenches. Mrs. Simpkins couldn't have anyway; her left leg was splinted.

"Well, all right." The sister's brisk nod admitted that was an acceptable reason for summoning her. She slid it into place and used a sheet to give Mrs. Simpkins what privacy she could.

Like the other women in the tent, Daisy looked away. They all pretended nothing was happening. English politeness came as close to being reflexive as made no difference.

The sister, by contrast, peered into the bedpan as she took it away. "Oh, jolly good!" she said, sounding genuinely pleased. "Hardly any blood in your urine at all."

Daisy was pleased for Mrs. Simpkins, too. She hadn't had much bleeding of that sort herself, but the older woman had. If it was easing off, she might pull through after all.

An orderly in a rain slicker came by on the hour to take the bedpan away. Then another one fetched lunch for the patients and the sister: U.S. military rations, one more product of America's endless abundance. However abundant the rations were, they weren't very good. Daisy didn't eat much. But she wouldn't have eaten much if a fancy French chef from the Ritz were doing the cooking here. Her appetite was gone. She had to fight to keep food down.

It went on raining. The grass under the cots turned to mud. The sister squelched when she walked. There was nothing at all to do but lie there. Daisy wished for a wireless set or, that failing, a wind-up gramophone. Wish was all she could do.

After a while the raindrops drumming on canvas lulled her into a doze. That was good: she wasn't bored while she slept. But it was also bad: if she napped in the afternoon, she might lie awake at night.

Toward evening, a doctor who looked even more worn than the sister came to check on the tentful of women. "How are you feeling?" he asked Daisy.

"If this is a rest cure, I'd sooner be working," she said.

"It's no holiday, I know. We're at full stretch, dealing with a disaster like this. The little personal touches are right out, I'm afraid." But the man used a little personal touch a moment later. Instead of taking her temperature, he laid a hand on her forehead, nodded to himself, and started toward the next bed.

"It's all right?" she asked him.

"Oh, yes. Normal, or near enough." He nodded. So did she. A mother could gauge temperatures like that, and he was bound to have more practice than any mother in captivity. He added, "No sign of infections, is what that means. You people are vulnerable to them for a while."

By *you people,* he meant *you people who had an atom bomb smash your town to pieces.* But Daisy was glad she had no infections. One of the first things a doctor had done for her was pick bits of glass out of the cuts on her feet with tongs and then paint the wounds with merthiolate. It hurt like anything.

She did have trouble sleeping during the night. Lying there in the dark trying to stay quiet so as not to bother the other women snoring around her wasn't easy. She'd gone to bed alone ever since Tom took ship overseas for the last time. Having company gave her trouble any time. When she'd napped and didn't particularly need sleep . . . She passed a bad night.

Morning cuppas for everybody in the tent came in a big vacuum flask, with milk and sugar on the side. The tea was strong and bitter enough to open her eyes a bit. She wouldn't have minded American instant coffee that morning. It was foul, but she needed all the caffeine she could get.

At least the rain had stopped. That was good. The tents were leftovers from the last war, and they'd seen hard use. Daisy thanked heaven the one she was stuck in hadn't started leaking. She didn't know what anyone could have done if it had. Stuck a bowl under the drip and forgotten about it, probably.

Breakfast was more American food. Canned scrambled eggs, even with ham, made her think that, if you had to eat them all the time, you'd let the enemy capture you just to get a change of diet.

She kept feeling she ought to be dusting or sweeping or putting another cask of best bitter under the tap. The Owl and Unicorn was gone, though. Gone. She had no idea whether the insurance covered atom bombs. One more thing she'd worry about later.

At half past nine—an unexpected hour—the tent flap opened, showing muddy grass and watery sunshine outside. Daisy noticed them for only the shortest fragment of a split second. Into the tent ducked Bruce McNulty. He looked dashing in his dark blue U.S. Air Force uniform.

Daisy, on the other hand, looked like hell and knew it. She got a desultory sponge bath every other day. She hadn't had her hair, what there was of it, washed in much too long.

But all the other women in their cots, and even the much cleaner and healthier sister, stared as McNulty came over to stand by her. He took off his officer's cap and held it in both hands. "How are you, sweetie?" he asked.

"I feel better now you're here," she said, which was sappy but true.

"Yeah, well—" He left it there. Had he been at Sculthorpe when the Russian bomb fell, he would have been blasted to vapor. He had to know it, and to know she knew it, too. Instead, he was fine.

And why was he fine? Because he'd been up in his B-29, visiting the same hell that had fallen on her on untold thousands of people on the other side of the Iron Curtain. He was everything she admired in a man—and he was also a killer with more deaths on his shoulders than all but a few of the most heinous Nazi murderers.

Did the Russian who'd bombed Sculthorpe wonder about such things, assuming the fighters hadn't shot him down? How could he not? He was a man, wasn't he?

"I just came to see how you were doing," Bruce said.

"They think I'll get better," she answered. "I haven't the faintest notion what I'll do once that happens. Not much left of Fakenham, is there?"

"I drove past it on my way here. It got knocked around pretty good, yeah," McNulty said. "Anything you need that I can take care of, though, you just have to ask. Anything at all. You know that, right?"

"It's good to hear," Daisy said quietly. That was also true. She had no claim on him, none he was obliged to honor. "Thank you."

"Sure. Look, babe, I gotta go. But I'll come see you first chance I get, promise." He bent to kiss her cheek. Then he left. Daisy noticed the sunshine this time.

"FIRE AND FALL BACK!" Sergeant Gergely shouted.

Istvan Szolovits popped up out of his foxhole like a malevolent jack-in-the-box. He fired a couple of rounds at the advancing Americans—or maybe they were Englishmen or Germans—and then, satisfied he'd made them put their heads down, trotted east through the war-shattered Ruhr.

War-shattered or not, this town (whichever town it happened to be) still had people living in it. "Look at the Russian pigdogs run!" one of them said to her equally elderly friend.

I'm not a Russian, you ugly German twat, Istvan thought. He laughed. Anger, under the circumstances, seemed absurd. Well, war was nothing if not absurd. He'd already found that out, over and over again.

The other old lady scrounging with a stringbag clucked like a laying hen. She pointed right at Istvan as he loped by. "Look at that one, Ilse!" she shrilled. "His whole face is peeling. How did he get a sunburn this late in the year?" He counted himself lucky. That was the burn scar healing, not radiation sickness. His unit hadn't got it nearly so bad as others closer to the bomb.

Bullets were still cracking along the street, some from the Hungarians, others from the soldiers pushing forward against them. They bothered the two German crones no more than they did the men in uniform. Then again, it wasn't as if the old ladies weren't veterans at this kind of thing, too.

As for Istvan, he trotted around a corner and ducked into a recessed doorway. From there, he could shoot at anybody coming after him.

Some of the real Russians who'd come back from nearer to where the bomb went off had their noses and ears melted into their faces and the sides of their necks. He'd seen some things that gave him new nightmares. Just when you started to think you were hardened to horror, horror went and showed you you didn't know so much after all.

More boots thumped on the shattered pavement. Istvan leaned forward. He still didn't like shooting at Americans, but he'd seen they didn't mind shooting at him one bit. You did what you had to do to stay alive. Everything else, you could worry about later.

But these weren't Americans. They were comrades from the Hungarian People's Army. *My countrymen,* Istvan thought, not without bitterness. It was less than even money that they would think of him that way. They were Magyars. He was just a damned Jew who chanced to live in Hungary and to speak Magyar as if he'd learned it while he was a baby—which, of course, he had.

One of them trotted past the doorway without even noticing Istvan in its shadow. The other, more alert, started to swing his PPD that way. Then he recognized the uniform, if not the Jew wearing it. He lowered the machine pistol, waved, and ran on.

Istvan waved back. He didn't want the other man having doubts about what he was and which side he belonged to. From short range like this, there wasn't much that was deadlier than a PPD.

Then the door opened behind him. He whirled, sure he was dead. There stood Sergeant Gergely, a cigarette in his mouth, his own submachine gun cradled in his arms, a wicked grin on his face. "Hi, there," he said.

"Fuck you!" Istvan blurted, his heart still pounding like a runaway hippo.

"That's 'Fuck you, Sergeant!'" Gergely clucked in mock reproof. "You have to respect the rank."

"Fuck you, Sergeant! All right? Happy now?" After a ragged breath, Istvan managed to go on, "How the devil did you get there?"

"I was on the landing, one floor up, and I saw you coming. So I thought I'd bake you a cake." The sergeant was still grinning. He thought it was the funniest thing in the world.

It didn't seem that way to Istvan. Saying so, though, would only make Gergely laugh at him. What he did say was, "What are we supposed to do now?"

"Keep fighting. Slow the enemy down as much as we can.

Make him pay for everything he gets." Gergely would have listened to German officers talking that way in 1944 and 1945—talking that way about the Red Army, the army now on the same side he was. He went on, "And hope Stalin pulls some wonder weapons out of his back pocket, or maybe out of his asshole."

He spoke the key word in German: *Wunderwaffen.* There was irony, if you chanced to be looking for some. The Germans had talked about wonder weapons in the last war. They'd talked about them more than they'd produced them, as a matter of fact. The ones they did produce—the long-range rocket, the jet fighter—were too little and came too late.

Now the Americans and the Russians had the wonder weapons, with the atom bomb topping the list. And where did they trot out their fancy new toys? Why, on what was left of Germany. If Hitler had a grave, wasn't he bound to be spinning in it?

"Bet your balls he is, Jewboy," Gergely said when Istvan brought out that conceit. Somehow, the insulting name seemed like an endearment from him. He went on, "The guys who invented the fucking gyroscope got the idea by watching the way old Adolf spun."

Istvan gaped at him. "Bugger me blind if you aren't crazier than I am, Sergeant."

"I've seen way more shit than you have, kid," Gergely answered. "If that doesn't drive you round the bend, well, Christ, you ain't half trying." His eyes narrowed. In less than a heartbeat, he went from storyteller to wary soldier. No, he hadn't stayed alive to see all that shit by accident. "Something's coming," he said. "Sounds like trouble."

"Uh-huh." Istvan heard it, too: the rumbling clatter of a tracked vehicle. It was moving from west to east, which meant the people inside wouldn't be friendly. He ducked into the doorway Gergely'd come out of. The sergeant followed, closing the door after him. If those unfriendly people didn't see them, they wouldn't start shooting at them. Or Istvan hoped they wouldn't.

He and Gergely hotfooted it up to that landing and peered out through a glassless square that had been a window. An American self-propelled gun clanked around the corner. It carried a 105mm gun and a couple of machine guns. It didn't have as much armor as a tank, but it was fine for knocking down buildings or shooting up soldiers and trucks it caught in the open.

Or it would have been. It never got the chance. Istvan had seen less than Sergeant Gergely, but he knew armor inside a built-up area was hideously vulnerable. Somebody in a block of flats across the street had a rocket-propelled grenade launcher. A roar, a blast of fire, and that self-propelled gun turned into a blazing oven to cook its crew. It burned with savage ferocity. Flames and black, greasy smoke rose from the murdered machine.

"Stupid cocksuckers," Gergely said. "You send one of those babies up a street without an infantry screen, you're asking for something like that. It's blocked the road so nothing else can get through, too."

"They must have thought we'd thrown in the sponge," Istvan said. "After all, we're only Hungarians, right?"

The Americans would think he was a Hungarian. They'd kill him if they could because they thought he was a Hungarian. But how about Sergeant Gergely? What did *he* think? Somehow, the answer mattered very much to Istvan.

If Gergely had laughed and said something like *You, a Hungarian? You're a Hungarian like I shit angels,* Istvan might have shot him right there. But the sergeant just grunted and replied, "Yeah, well, in the last war the Russians got that kind of surprise a time or three, too. You have any smokes?" Istvan gave him a cigarette and lit one himself, feeling better about his small piece of the world.

In the country of the blind, the one-eyed man was king. A captain Ihor Shevchenko'd served under during the Great Patriotic War used to say that all the time. He'd said it all the time till a German bouncing mine blew off his balls, anyhow. If he still said it, he said it soprano.

Which might not have kept the Chekists from sucking him back into the Red Army. They might figure a guy who'd had balls once upon a time still did whether that was literally true or not. Or, if he helped them make their quota, they might not even care.

What brought the thought back to Ihor's mind now was the AK-47 he carried through northwestern Germany. As long as he had it, he could use it to get whatever he wanted. The front seemed to have broken down. No one gave him any orders after he got kicked out of the aid station. The docs there expected him to hook up with his old regiment again.

And so he would have, had he thought anything was left of it. But it had been in the trenches the Americans atom-bombed. He was one of the few people who'd watched two A-bombs delivered in anger go off and was still around to talk about it. A dubious distinction, yeah, but his own.

Only he didn't want to talk about it. He didn't want to rejoin the war, either. He went where he pleased. The A-bomb seemed to have blown up the MGB pukes behind the line, one of the few good things he could say about it. Nobody Soviet tried to dragoon him into the trenches.

And nobody German wanted to argue with him, not when he had Sergeant Kalashnikov's finest creation as a persuader. Using it and the bits of *Deutsch* he remembered from the last war, he had no trouble getting all the food and booze he wanted. Who would argue with an assault rifle?

He and the men he'd joined up with weren't the only Red Army soldiers roaming the countryside on their own. Soviet military discipline was stern, but not always stern enough to stand up to a good dose of radiation. Plenty of men who hadn't wanted to be in Germany to begin with had had all the war they wanted, thank you very much.

Loosely banded together as they were, they could pull off bigger heists than one man could on his own. Then they'd drink themselves into a stupor. Schnapps worked as well as vodka for that.

A corporal named Feofan hoisted a bottle and said, "Pretty soon the Americans will push forward and butcher all of us like hogs." He laughed till tears ran down his dirty face. He was very drunk.

Well, so was Ihor. So were all of them. And they all laughed. Ihor said, "We lived through the atom bomb. You think ordinary soldiers can do for the likes of us?"

"No fucking way!" Three Russians said the same thing at the same time. Or Ihor thought so. He was already drunk enough to be seeing double. Why shouldn't he be drunk enough to be hearing triple? That was the last thing he remembered before passing out.

He woke up the next morning feeling exactly like death. He lay under a blanket out in the open under chilly drizzle. And one thing about schnapps: it hurt you worse than vodka did. The only medicine Ihor could think of that might dent his jimjams was the hair of the wolfpack that had its teeth in him. Not all the bottles lying around the sodden soldiers could be empty . . . could they? Fate wouldn't be so cruel!

He found one with some life in it and swigged like a man in the desert who'd stumbled across an oasis. His stomach didn't like the dose, but the rest of him did.

The others were no happier as they came back to consciousness. They ran out of restorative before they ran out of men who needed it. Then, weapons at the ready, they descended on the nearest village to take more. Ihor feared his head would fall off if he had to fire his AK-47, but the Germans didn't know that.

What the Germans hereabouts did know was that Russians had done horrible things to their countrymen farther east. (Some were bound to know those horrible things were in revenge for what the Germans had done in the USSR, but that made them more nervous, not less.) When grimy, nasty Red Army men with assault rifles and machine pistols descended on them, they didn't do anything to try to provoke the invaders.

Schnapps? Food? Cigarettes? They were happy to cough those up, as long as the Russians didn't start shooting their men and gang-raping their women. Nothing could have stopped the Red Army soldiers from doing that, but they didn't. They'd get in trouble for it, either from their own officers if the USSR pulled itself together or from the enemy if their own country couldn't. However much he wanted to, Ihor couldn't get drunk enough to forget about the enemy.

Artillery fire said the Americans were moving forward not far south. The only reason Ihor could find that they weren't moving forward here, too, was that this wasn't the main axis of their advance. They'd push hard where they wanted to, and clean up backwaters later.

Backwaters like this one.

It wasn't till two days later that an American jeep nosed down the road to see what was going on. Like many jeeps, this one carried a pintle-mounted heavy machine gun: a lot of firepower for such a little vehicle.

The powerful machine gun did the Yankees in the jeep no good at all. They were gum-chewing teenagers, conscripts who had no idea what war was about. Since their very first lesson was the cruelest one possible, they never got the chance to learn.

They had no idea any Russians were within five kilometers

of them, either, when they drove into the village. Like Ihor, most of his pals had picked up their warcraft against the Fritzes the last time around. Setting ambushes was second nature to them. Guys who couldn't learn that stuff lay in unmarked graves all up and down the western USSR, when they weren't just bones under bushes somewhere.

Because he had the Kalashnikov, Ihor took out the man behind the machine gun with a single head shot. The range wasn't long for him, but it would have been for somebody with a submachine gun. The driver just had time to turn in alarm toward his stricken comrade when a burst from a PPD cut him down. He didn't die right away, so another burst finished him. The jeep rolled on till it hit a telephone pole. Then it stopped.

"Too easy!" Feofan said scornfully.

"They won't always be that blind," Ihor said. "We should grab the machine gun. That's one hell of a weapon for as long as we can keep it fed."

"Go ahead, if you've got a hard-on for it," Feofan told him.

So he did. It came off the pintle easily enough. But it weighed close to twenty kilos, not counting the box of bulky cartridges it fired. Using it without a tripod wouldn't be easy.

A sentry—Ihor had said he'd kick the man's ass if he didn't get over to the western edge of the village—sang out: "More Americans on the way!"

And there were, too many for the Red Army men to dispose of them all so easily. After an exchange of fire, the Yanks pulled back. Then they started lobbing mortar bombs into the village. That was no fun at all. By the local Germans' shrieks, they enjoyed it no more than Ihor did.

Before long, he and his friends had only two choices: stay where they were and get cut off and killed or pull out. Before he left, Ihor fired a belt of ammo from the heavy machine gun. He didn't aim, or need to. Not only was it loud fun, it made the Americans move up slower than they would have otherwise.

Three or four kilometers east of the village, the Red Army men ran into their own side's military police. "What are you slackers doing running around without orders?" a sergeant asked ominously.

"Slackers, my dick," Ihor retorted. "Didn't you hear the firefight? We were defending that village from the capitalist imperialists."

"Huh." The sergeant wasn't convinced, but he didn't try to arrest them all. Back under military control they went. Freedom had been fun while it lasted, but nothing lasted forever. Most things didn't even last very long.

Aaron Finch scowled at the 1946 Chevy that had replaced his stolen Nash. The car was okay. Whoever'd owned it before had taken decent care of it. The payments . . . He scowled again. He hated paying on time; interest sucked money the way leeches sucked blood. But if you couldn't afford to write a check, you did what you had to do.

He'd made the best deal he could. Almost the best deal—a pretty nice Ford a year newer had cost about the same. But Aaron was damned if he'd buy a Ford, even a secondhand one. Old Henry hated Jews and he hated union men. With two strikes like those, he didn't need a third one to be out in Aaron's book.

He unlocked the door and slid behind the wheel. He thought he'd locked the Nash the night before it disappeared, but he wasn't sure. He made sure all the time now. *Locking the barn door after the horse is gone,* he thought as he turned the key and pulled out the choke.

Off to Blue Front he went. At least he didn't have to bother people for a lift any more. He never would have been able to do that if he hadn't lived close to the warehouse. Still and all, he'd be buying the guys who'd gone out of their way for him lunch and cigarettes for weeks to show he was properly grateful. The scales had to balance. His father had knocked that into him with a heavy hand.

If only his old man had really been even half as smart as he thought he was. Back around the time of the First World War, Mendel Finch had run a moving and hauling business up in Oregon. In his wisdom, he'd decided that trucks were just a fad, while horses and wagons would stay around forever.

Not surprisingly, he'd gone broke about a year after the Armistice was signed. And, somehow, he'd avoided honest work ever since. Well, he was within two years of his ninetieth birthday now. But to this day he wouldn't admit he'd made a mistake with his business. He had to be right, always right, right no matter what.

There in the car with nobody else to laugh at him, Aaron laughed at himself. "Wonder where I got that from?" he said.

Yeah, Marvin had it worse, but neither of them was in the same league as their father.

Here was the intersection where that Russian came parachuting down from his bomber after it sent downtown Los Angeles up in smoke. Had Aaron cut his throat with a pocket knife or caved in his skull with a tire iron instead of capturing him, chances were he wouldn't have that letter from Harry Truman on his wall now.

He laughed again, mirthlessly this time. Whether he had it or not, Roxane and Howard would still think he got his kicks oppressing the proletariat. Aaron was a good union man and a good Democrat, and that was plenty for him. To some people in his wife's family—and to some in his own—that meant he might as well have worn a swastika button on his lapel.

When he pulled into the Blue Front parking lot, Jim Summers was just getting out of his Hudson. It was dirty. The paint was starting to peel. Jim didn't give a damn. He paused outside the car to light a Camel and blew a stream of smoke up into the air.

Aaron parked two spaces away. He nodded to his partner. "How's it going?" he asked.

"Not too bad," Summers said. "How about you?"

"I'm hanging in there." Aaron lit a Chesterfield of his own. Camels were too harsh for him—unless the choice was smoking Camels or not smoking at all. He couldn't imagine doing without coffin nails.

"You listen to Joe McCarthy on the radio last night?" Summers asked.

"Afraid I missed him." Aaron tried to keep that as diplomatic as he could. He thought the junior Senator from Wisconsin was a blowhard with delusions of grandeur, and he thought anybody who didn't think so was out of his tree. But he also thought fighting with the people you had to work with wasn't the smartest thing you could do.

Jim, by contrast, liked Senator McCarthy himself, and so couldn't imagine that any right-thinking American wouldn't. "You shoulda tuned him in," he said. "He ripped into old Harry Falseman somethin' fierce. If we'd smoked out all the damn Reds we got poisoning the country a lot sooner'n we did, we wouldn't be in the mess where we're at now. That's what he said—I boiled it down a little, y'understand, but there it is."

"Isn't that interesting?" That and *How about that?* were the only two phrases Aaron had ever found that you could drop in almost anywhere without making anybody want to grab for a broken bottle.

Or he'd always thought so, anyway. Jim's furry eyebrows zoomed up toward his hairline. "Interesting? It's important, is what it is! He says he'd got hisself a list as long as my arm of all the Commies and traitors we need to get rid of so's we can straighten up and fly right from now on."

Aaron wondered whether the list was real or a figment of McCarthy's imagination. If by some chance it was real, he wondered how many of Ruth's relatives, and of his own, were on it. To him, that seemed more an honor than a point against them.

He kept his mouth shut. It wasn't easy, but he did it. Glancing at his watch, he said, "We'd better go on in and punch the clock. I don't want to get docked for being late."

Jim Summers' mouth twisted. "Yeah, Weissman'd do that, sure as hell. Crummy Hebe squeezes ever penny till he can make flour out of the wheat on the back." He ground out the Camel under his heel as if wishing it were his boss' head. Then he said, "Plenty o' that kind on ol' Senator McCarthy's list, I betcha."

"Jim—" Aaron wondered whether going on was worth the *tsuris*. They'd worked side by side since not long after the end of World War II, and Jim had no idea he was Jewish. No one would ever accuse Summers of being the brightest bulb in Times Square.

"What?" he said as they walked to the door. "C'mon. You started to say somethin'. Spill, goddammit."

"Okay." Aaron didn't think it would be, but he spilled anyway: "What the devil do you think I am, a Chinaman?"

"You? You're—" Summers broke off. Maybe he *could* spell CAT if you spotted him the C and the A. He grinned a rather sickly grin. "Don't get your bowels in an uproar, Aaron. I didn't mean nothin' by it. Hey, some o' my best friends is Jews."

Bad grammar aside, Aaron had never heard that said when it wasn't a lie. Had Jim Summers been born a Bavarian, he would have been a brownshirt. Here, he was only a bigot—just the kind of guy Joe McCarthy was looking for.

They walked inside and punched their cards in the time clock. In spite of gabbing in the parking lot, they were on time. Jim stumped over to the big percolator in one corner and filled a waxed-cardboard cup with coffee. The java was still good now; it would be battery acid by the afternoon.

Still muttering and shaking his head, Jim went into the little cubicle he and Aaron shared while they were in the warehouse. The pinups and nudies decorating the walls were all his (which didn't mean Aaron didn't sometimes glance their way). He slammed the door behind him.

"What's his problem?" Herschel Weissman asked Aaron.

"Believe it or not, he just found out I'm a Jew," Aaron said.

His boss looked at him. Aaron knew what Weissman saw: the same very Jewish-looking mug that peered back from the bathroom mirror every morning. The older man raised an eyebrow. "Ripley wouldn't believe that," Weissman snorted, shaking his head.

"It's true, anyway. Now he has to figure out how much grief he'll get from Goebbels and Himmler for working with me." Not at all apropos of nothing, Aaron went on, "Did I ever tell you the guy we rent our house from has a number on his arm?"

"No. Well, at least he lived." Weissman set a hand on Aaron's shoulder. "And you can't expect a *shlemiel* not to be a *shlemiel*. It'd be a better world if you could, but you can't, dammit." Aaron nodded. He knew that, too, however much he wished he didn't.

Whenever Vasili Yasevich went to sleep, he wondered if he'd wake up smelling smoke. Grigory Papanin and his hooligan friends didn't seem to have the balls to challenge him openly. (That Vasili still carried Papanin's pistol was bound to be another reason they didn't want to mess with him when he could mess back.)

Asleep, though, he was vulnerable. He dossed in a long wooden building the people of Smidovich called a dormitory for single men not otherwise lodged. In Harbin, it would have been a flophouse. However you named it, it made even the shack he'd lived in after the Americans bombed Harbin seem a palace by comparison.

Compared to the Chinese, Russians were not a cleanly people. Vasili had seen that in nothing flat. Being more used to the Chinese way, he found Soviet grubbiness worse than someone accustomed to it would have. Living with other bachelors, some of them real refugees from Khabarovsk, didn't help.

Even young Chinese men with no women to keep them in line could be slobs. Young Russians . . .

Vasili wondered why the people who hired him to do their carpentry didn't have him make a pigpen for the men who shared the dormitory. It smelled of unwashed Russians—who stank worse than Chinese—and stale food. The other bachelors left their junk wherever it happened to fall. The only two besides him who made up their cots were veterans of the Great Patriotic War. Nobody changed his bed linen. Vasili's guess was, the dormitory had no spare sets.

People in the dormitory stole from one another whenever they saw the chance. They treated it as a game, something you did to amuse yourself or to make your life a little better. Vasili rapidly learned to keep everything that mattered to him in his pockets.

But if Papanin and his friends poured gasoline by the doors and windows and threw down three or four matches, what could he do? *Cook* was the first thing that occurred to him.

The second thing that occurred to him was *Do unto others before they do unto you.* If he roasted Grigory Papanin about medium-well, he wouldn't have to worry about him any more. How hard would the militia work to find out who did it? They might put in some effort to pin a medal on the right guy, but that was about it.

All he wanted to do was go on about his business in Smidovich without having anybody pay much attention to him. Drawing notice was dangerous. If the government officials decided to investigate him, they'd find that nobody who really was from Khabarovsk had ever set eyes on him. Then . . . Then he'd find out why his father and mother thought swallowing poison was a better bet than letting the Chekists get hold of them.

In the meantime, he wandered through the village, looking for things other people would pay him to do. After he shored up a cabin's sagging wall, the babushka who lived there said, "You did that faster than I thought you would, and it looks like a good job."

"Thanks very much, *Gospozha,*" he answered, and bit his tongue a split second later. *Ma'am* was one of those un-Soviet words people weren't supposed to use.

The old woman noticed, too. She wagged a blunt, work-roughened finger at him. "Where did you learn to talk, sonny?" she asked. "Not around here, that's for sure. Around here it's all *mat* and filth." But she seemed more pleased than affronted. Unlike people Vasili's age, when she was a girl *Gospozha* had been something you'd want to hear, not a slip that could land you in a gulag.

"I must have been raised by wolves," Vasili said with a wry grin.

"Very polite wolves." The babushka also grinned, showing off a mouthful of gold teeth. If she ever found herself in big trouble, she might bribe her way out of trouble by parting with them. She went on, "Heaven knows you've got better manners than that Papanin item. And you work harder than he ever did, not that that's hard."

"I'm just trying to get by, that's all," he replied. People here kept telling him how hard he worked. He'd never heard any such thing in Harbin. There, he'd felt like a man on a treadmill, running as hard as he could just to stay in one place. The Chinese had been desperately poor, but they'd all done everything they could to escape their poverty. If you didn't do the same, you'd go under.

"You seem to be doing pretty well for yourself." Her gray eyes, nested in a taiga of wrinkles, were disconcertingly shrewd. "And have you seen that Papanin lately?"

"Lately? No." There, Vasili told the truth. The less he saw of the fellow who had been Smidovich's handyman before he got here, the happier he was.

"You haven't missed much—I'll tell you that," the babushka said. "He never was what you'd call pretty, but these days he looks like somebody threw him into a stone wall face-first. His snoot leans to one side and it's flatter than a Chinaman's, the Devil's uncle grab me if I'm lying. And he walks like a truck ran over him."

"Well, what do you know?" Vasili said. Did she think he'd brag about ruining Papanin? He wasn't that dumb. He hoped he wasn't, anyway.

"What do I know? I know what I've seen, or I wouldn't've said anything about it." She knew, all right, whether he bragged or not. What he'd done wasn't a secret, however much he wished it would have been.

All the same, he gave back his most stolid, most Russian shrug. "I don't care a kopek for Papanin. I'll go my way, and he can go his."

"His almost took him to the undertaker," the old woman said. Vasili shrugged again. After a moment, so did she. She was twenty centimeters shorter than he was, but her shoulders might have been broader. "*Khorosho.* Those wolves who raised you must have known how to keep their mouths shut. Pretty smart wolves, hey? Don't you go away, now." She ducked back into the cabin for a moment.

When she came out, she was carrying two jars of pickled mushrooms. She handed them to Vasili. "Thanks very much," he stammered, caught by surprise. "You already paid me, you know. You don't have to do this."

She waved his words aside. "Enjoy them. I picked them myself, and I put them in the jars. They're good." She stuck out her chin, daring him to make something of it.

He didn't have the nerve. He knew he'd have to share them with the other guys at the dormitory, but that was all right. Without an icebox, they wouldn't keep after he opened the jars. He tapped one with his thumbnail and said, "I'll bring them back after they're empty."

"Thank you. Everything costs so much these days. I remember when . . ." She slowed to a stop and then laughed at herself. "That was years and years before you were born, so it wouldn't matter to you."

Vasili maintained a prudent silence. Prices in Smidovich were cheap compared to what he'd been used to in Harbin. China had too many people clamoring after not enough stuff. As soon as you crossed the Amur, all of that changed. There wasn't much stuff here, either, but there was hardly anybody around to go after it.

"Oh, and the next time you tangle with Grigory Papanin, hit him harder, why don't you?" the babushka said.

So much for making like I'm innocent, Vasili thought. "If I hit him any harder than I did before, I'll kill him."

"No loss." She might be a Russian, but no Chinese could have sounded more callous.

AS SHE HAD TO DO, Luisa Hozzel picked up bits of Russian: a word here, a clause there, a verb phrase somewhere else. One or two of the guards who took the women out to chop down trees had scraps of German. That made Luisa wonder what they'd done—and to whom they'd done it—during the last war, but she didn't ask. They might tell her. Or they might shoot her. Sometimes not knowing was better. They weren't even supposed to use their *Deutsch,* but they did. It let them get across what they wanted from the women.

One phrase the guards with some German all had down was "More work, cunts!" They yelled it at any excuse or none. They yelled it in Russian, too, which built Luisa's vocabulary.

She didn't need long to realize the Russian she was learning was filthy. If she'd used that kind of German, people would have stared at her, or possibly locked her up. But everybody in the gulag, guards and *zeks* alike, talked this way. Obscenity here was small change, not a big bill. When people really got mad, they could curse for ten minutes without repeating themselves once.

And the guards had other ways to make their prisoners unhappy. A flat-faced Tatar-looking fellow with a wispy black mustache pointed at Luisa and asked, "How you likes being in Jew country, bitch?"

"What do you mean, please, sir?" Luisa asked cautiously. She wasn't sure she'd understood. He hissed like a snake when he spoke. And what would he know about Jews?

But he did. "You German, *ja*? You Germans kill Jews last war, *ja*?" He waited for Luisa to respond.

"*I* never killed any Jews. I never hurt any, either," she said, which was true. True or not, it made the guard scowl and heft his machine pistol. Quickly, Luisa added, "I know that Germany killed Jews, though."

The guard nodded. "Germans kill Jews, *ja.* And now you in Birobidzhan Jewish Autonomous Region. How you like that?"

Her first thought was that, if Jews lived in this godforsaken stretch of Siberia, they were as much exiles as she was herself, whether or not they lived inside the barbed wire like her. Her second thought was that the guard—Uzbek? Tajik? Kalmuk? Mongol?—would clout her if she came out with her first thought. All she said was, "I'm here. I have to get through it if I can."

"Maybe you not so dumb, even if you is German," the guard said.

Luisa laughed bitterly. "If I'm so smart, what am I doing here?"

"Don't gots to be stupids to end up here. I seen that plenty," the Asiatic said. And he was bound to be right. Then he realized he'd been chinning with a *zek.* Guards weren't supposed to act human around prisoners; Luisa had seen as much. His face hardened. "Get to workings back. Plenties of branches to chopping."

Back to work, or even workings, Luisa got. The guards didn't push the *zeks* too hard. If you stayed anywhere close to the pace they demanded, chances were you'd stay out of trouble. Luisa had seen the same pace from Poles and Russians brought to Germany in the last war. She hadn't recognized it for what it was then. She'd just thought they were a pack of lazy foreigners. *Untermenschen,* if you wanted to get right down to it.

Now the shoe was on the other foot: her foot. She found out all the places it pinched. Here she was in a country where she didn't want to be, thousands of kilometers from home, doing work she didn't want to do because they'd rape her or kill her or rape her and then kill her if she didn't.

No wonder those Poles and Russians had moved in slow motion! She moved in slow motion herself, as slow as she could get away with. She picked up a little when the guards growled at her. When they turned and growled at somebody else, she slowed down again.

Yes, now she recognized the rhythm this unwanted labor called forth from the people who had to do it. It was a rhythm as ancient as the Pyramids and the Hanging Gardens of Babylon. It was the rhythm of the slave.

From things the bitches said, most Russians, even the ones who weren't in one gulag or another, worked at this pace whenever they could get by with it. Luisa hacked at a branch. She was better with a hatchet than she had been when she got here. She hacked again, then paused. Why not? The guard who might have ridden with Genghis Khan had gone off to shout at some other women. They worked harder . . . till he turned his back.

And no wonder even those Russians in what they called freedom worked like this. Wasn't the whole Soviet Union stuck behind barbed wire? It looked that way to Luisa. Stalin's tyranny might be grayer than Hitler's, but the only real difference between the MGB and the *Gestapo* was the name.

Stalin and his commissars recognized their problem. A couple of the first Russian phrases Luisa had learned were *shock worker* and *Stakhanovite.* As the Nazis had, the Communists tried to get people to work harder. By the gales of laughter the bitches went into whenever they heard those phrases, Soviet propaganda didn't work any better than its German equivalent had. It might have worked worse.

In Germany, someone who worked hard might possibly get rich doing it. In the workers' paradise, though? Here, they preached equality and the classless society at the top of their lungs. The idea of getting rich was like picking your nose and eating it or looking at filthy pictures in public.

The guard turned so he could see Luisa again. Down came the axe. The branch fell away from the trunk of the pine. Snow spurted up as it hit the ground. Luisa moved on a couple of paces and started on the next branch. Satisfied, the guard reached into a trouser pocket for his cigarettes.

Luisa laughed again, even less happily than before. Not even the gulag was a classless society, or anything close to it. The socially friendly bitches lorded it over the politicals and the Germans, who counted as political, too. The guards backed them up when they did it. You couldn't win.

For that matter, what would winning mean? If you won, you wouldn't be a *zek* any more. That, Luisa could see. But what would you be instead? If you weren't a prisoner here, wouldn't you be something a lot like a guard? What other choice was there?

She nodded to herself. That was what Russia was like, all

right. (And it was also what the Third *Reich* had been like, even if she didn't care so much to remember that.) Either you were a tasty sheep or a sheep-eating wolf. There was no middle ground.

There had been, in the Weimar Republic she remembered with a girl's memories. There was starting to be again, in the Federal Republic that was growing up from the ruins of the dead *Reich* like new, hopeful grass after a harsh winter. But the Ivans were taking care of that, not just for her and the others in the gulag, but also for those still in the west but now under Stalin's heavy yoke.

"Workings!" the flat-faced guard said. Luisa worked. It seemed to take less effort than thinking.

Along with the other women in the work gang, she trudged back to the camp when the sun drew near the trees. They gave up their tools outside. The guards counted saws and axes as carefully as they counted *zeks*. A prisoner with a weapon meant trouble.

Then the women lined up so they could be counted. Across the barbed wire, the male *zeks* were doing the same thing. They whistled and hooted at the women, and called to them in half a dozen languages. Their guards frowned, but that was all they did. They were men, too, the bastards.

Luisa wanted nothing to do with any of them. She was filthy, her hair matted with sweat. She could smell how she stank. They were just as grimy and smelly. How did they think anyone would be interested in them? How? They were men, the bastards.

All Luisa wanted was for the count to go smoothly and for the cooks to have turned out something almost worth eating. That was what her horizons had narrowed to, that and the chance for sleep Sleep! She couldn't imagine a word more delicious, in German or in Russian.

Brigadier Yulian Olminsky glowered at Boris Gribkov. His fierce black eyebrows gave him a good glower in spite of his skinny face; he looked like something that ought to live in a cave under a bridge. Gribkov didn't much care. He was past being intimidated.

After all, what could Olminsky do to him? Leave him here to rot? He was already rotting. Send him and his crew out in the Tu-4 on a suicide mission? The way things worked these days, almost any mission a heavy bomber flew could turn suicidal, but at least they'd be doing what the Soviet Union had trained them to do. Feed him to the MGB? That was just another suicide mission.

Olminsky scowled harder when he saw Boris wasn't turning to gelatin. "Well?" he rumbled.

"Well, what, Comrade Brigadier?" Gribkov asked. No, he really didn't care what happened to him next. That gave him an odd edge over the base commandant. A bully who didn't scare you wasn't a bully any more.

"Are you and your men loyal to the Soviet Union and to the revolution of the proletariat?" Olminsky demanded.

"Comrade Brigadier, I've been telling you at the top of my lungs that we are ever since we got here," Boris answered. "If you and the Chekists don't choose to believe me, how is that any sweat off my nuts?"

The senior officer turned the color of borscht. "What the devil makes you think you can talk to me like that?"

"My men have delivered three A-bombs, sir. We've flown conventional missions, too," Gribkov said. "And what thanks did we get for it? We got stuck on the back shelf like a sack of kasha your granny forgot about."

"I can have you court-martialed for your big mouth, you know, court-martialed or just put away for real."

"Yes, sir. But next to flying the Tu-4, a court-martial is a stroll through the grass," Gribkov replied. "If you want to kill us off, at least let us go after the Americans. Then we can go out trying to help the *rodina.*"

"All right," Olminsky said heavily. "*All right.* So you're ready to deliver the mail, are you?"

"I serve the Soviet Union, Comrade Brigadier. I've always served the Soviet Union," Boris said. "What is our next assignment?"

"You have been cleared by the security services to fly against Antwerp," the base commandant told him. "The Americans and the English are shipping men and tanks and shit into Europe through there like they're falling out of the Devil's asshole."

"I serve the Soviet Union!" Gribkov said one more time. If relief was in his voice, it was also in his heart. He'd feared Olminsky would order his Tu-4 to attack London. Even if they made it there and came back safely after ripping out the heart of England, he didn't know that he wanted two of the world's great capitals on his conscience. His grain was coarser than poor Leonid Tsederbaum's had been, but there were limits to everything.

"All right," Yulian Olminsky repeated. "This will be a low-level flight, over the sea as much of the way as you can. Fly so close to the water, the radar will have trouble telling your plane from the waves."

"We don't climb to deliver the bomb? Same kind of flight path as Paris?"

"That's right. There'll be a short delay on the fuse to let you get clear. More fallout that way, but it can't be helped. The enemy won't let you climb to eleven thousand meters to drop. We don't let them get away with that shit any more, either."

"I understand, sir," Gribkov said. "The whole crew will be glad to get airborne again. Only . . ." His voice trailed off as he visualized a map. "We can't stay over water the whole route. Denmark's in the way, and it's not on our side."

"It's not doing much to help the enemy, either." Olminsky gestured dismissively. "Just zoom across the peninsula. For a plane with the Tu-4's performance, not even ten minutes from east to west."

Just zoom across the peninsula. Yulian Olminsky made it sound easy. Making missions sound easy was one of the things base commandants were for. True, Denmark wasn't throwing divisions into the fight in Germany. But there were U.S. fighter bases and U.S. radar stations in the country.

"We'll have a better chance if the fighter-bombers hit them before we try the crossing," Boris said.

"It will be attended to." By the way Olminsky spoke, maybe it would and maybe it wouldn't. Well, if he wanted to get a plane with an A-bomb in its belly shot down, that was his problem. And the crew's.

Most of the men were eager to get back into action. "About time people quit treating us like we've got dogshit on our shoes," Vladimir Zorin said.

Yefim Arzhanov practically jumped up and down. "Comrade Pilot, I will take us to Antwerp! I will bring us home after we succeed in the mission!" the new navigator declared.

"Good. That's good." Gribkov did his best to sound enthusiastic, but half of his mind was figuring angles and ways and means. It might work. Of course, anything *might* work. If it did, it would hurt the imperialists. He could see that.

But they'd be alert, damn them. His plane would need new

IFF codes to fool the Americans. He and Zorin and Gennady Gamarnik, the flight engineer, went over the Tu-4 from the bombardier's station to the tail gunner's to see what else it might need. The engineer found and fixed some engine trouble that might have had them all sweating if it had cropped up while they were on the way.

Darkness was their best friend. Darkness was always the bomber's friend. They climbed into the sky after the sun went down. Boris looked right and grinned at Zorin when they did get airborne. The copilot grinned, too.

"Antwerp," Zorin said. "It's only Antwerp."

"You should go on the stage. You've got a terrific mind-reading act there," Boris answered. In the last war, the Germans had hung on to Antwerp tooth and toenail. After they got driven out, they clung to the Scheldt estuary weeks longer so shipping couldn't get into or out of the port. After the Anglo-Americans pushed them back there, too, Hitler had pounded it with V-2s. He had no A-bombs to put it out of action. Had he had A-bombs, he would have used them against the USSR first. There was a scary thought.

They flew north across Czechoslovakia and East Germany to the Baltic. Running out of sea and having to cross Denmark was another scary thought. All too soon, the low, flat land loomed up ahead of them. They were still flying close enough to the deck to scrape church steeples. The roar from the four big Shvetsov radials would wake the dead for kilometers around. But no one opened up on them. The radar operator didn't start screaming about fighters. Maybe the Soviet air raid had gone in after all. Maybe luck was still running their way.

And maybe some American at a radar screen was phoning units farther west, saying *Be ready—something juicy's heading your way!* Gribkov couldn't do anything about that . . . but worry.

Past the Danish peninsula. Out over the North Sea. Yefim Arzhanov told Boris to swing farther south. He obeyed, hoping Arzhanov knew what he was talking about. With Tsederbaum, he would have been sure. But Tsederbaum had chosen a longer road than this one.

"Everything ready for the drop, Sasha?" Boris asked the bombardier.

"Comrade Pilot, it is," Alexander Lavrov replied.

More ships sailed the North Sea than the Baltic. What

would their crews think when a bomber without lights zoomed past just above the waves? To whom would they report those thoughts?

"Getting close. Swing another couple of degrees south," Arzhanov said. Boris did. You had to trust your people. Land loomed up ahead. They'd fly over Holland for a little while before they let the city in northern Belgium have it.

Why wasn't flak going off like fireworks on Victory Day? Whatever the reason, here came the estuary of the Scheldt. "Let it go!" Boris told the bombardier. As soon as Lavrov pulled the lever and the bomb fell, the Tu-4 got lighter and friskier. Gribkov wheeled it out to sea, running the engines at the red line. He had to get clear before . . .

Hellfire seared the night behind. Blast tried to swat the bomber into the water. It didn't . . . quite. *Now to get back to the* rodina, Boris thought. He could paint another city on the Tu-4's flank after he did. His mouth twisted when that crossed his mind. Poor, damned Leonid!

"Antwerp? Antwerp!" Harry Truman didn't so much say the name as spit it. "How in holy hell did they get Antwerp?"

George Marshall looked unhappy, too. But then, as far as Truman could tell, the Secretary of Defense never looked happy. He sure had nothing to look happy about this morning. "As best we can piece together, sir, it was a great piece of flying. The only way they could have come in lower would have been to take their bomber through the moles' tunnels."

"Heh," Truman said. Every once in a while, Marshall showed that a dry wit did lurk beneath his somber exterior. He was almost as much a great stone face as Molotov or Gromyko, though Truman would never have insulted him by saying so. Dry wit or not, right this minute the President himself was more not amused than Queen Victoria had ever been.

"What really irks me is that we have no claims that anyone shot down that—that confounded Bull," Marshall said, using the NATO reporting name for the Russian B-29 copy. "It surprised us getting in? Okay. But how could our air defenses not catch it once they knew it was there?"

"Talent," Truman said bitterly. "Now I've got the Belgian Prime Minister and his Dutch opposite number screeching at me, one for each ear. Why can't we keep them safe? Well, why can't we, dammit?"

"Because war is like that, as you know perfectly well, sir," Marshall answered. "Things go wrong. Or the other fellow does something very well, or does something you didn't expect, and he hurts you. When he starts throwing atom bombs around, he can hurt you badly."

"Can't he, though?" Truman said. "Two in Korea, and now the one in Antwerp. What's next? New York City?"

"I don't believe so, Mr. President," Marshall said. "Bulls can't reach it from anywhere Stalin holds. If the Russians were to take Iceland away from us, that would be a different story, but there's a worry from a thriller writer's novel. It's nothing to lose sleep over in the real world. They don't have the navy to try it, let alone bring it off."

"Thank God for small favors. He sure hasn't doled out many big ones lately," Truman said. "What are we going to have to do to save Korea? More atom bombs? That's what got us into this mess to begin with."

"We've punished Stalin. We haven't really punished Mao yet," Marshall said in musing tones. "Yes, we bombed Manchuria, but to the Chinese that was an annoyance, something that slowed their move into Korea, not anything that hit home in the country as a whole. Manchuria is the back of beyond to them, the way Wyoming is with us."

"Peiping. Shanghai. Nanking. *That* would get their attention." The President grimaced. "How many people would we kill? I don't like blowing up cities and vaporizing civilians just to make Mao sit up and take notice, dammit."

"If he were one of the people we vaporized, that might do more than anything else to get Red China to go back to the *status quo ante bellum,*" Marshall observed.

"Yes, it might. But what are the chances?" Truman said. "Do we even know where he is?"

The Secretary of Defense shook his head. "If we did, a strike might be worthwhile. Most of our intelligence on him comes through Chiang in Formosa, you understand. From what the Nationalists hear, Mao moves from one town to the next every day or two to make it harder for us to rub him out like that."

"One more trick he picked up from Stalin." After a moment's thought, Harry Truman shook his head. "Mm, maybe not. You don't need to go to Harvard to see you're safer if you don't give the people who don't like you a sitting target."

"True enough, sir," Marshall agreed.

"I wish we could kill Mao, though," Truman said. "If we did, I bet Stalin would be willing to go back to the status quo and start picking up pieces. But if Mao wants to keep fighting, Stalin loses face for making peace. Who's the boss Communist then? It would be like the brawls after the Reformation, with each side saying it was more Christian than the other."

"And of course there are no arguments at all here about how we ought to deal with this war," Marshall said.

Yes, he was dry, all right. "Uh-*huh,*" Truman said tightly. "If Joe McCarthy knows what's good for him, he'd better keep moving like Stalin and Mao. I'd do everybody a favor if I dropped an A-bomb on his big, fat, hard head."

"That's not the kind of thing a sitting President is supposed to say," Marshal replied, voice prim as a schoolmarm's.

"Tough shit," Truman said. "It looks more and more like he'll run next year, and it looks more and more like he'll flush the Constitution straight down the crapper if he gets elected. Go on—tell me I'm wrong."

"Mr. President, one of the advantages of a long career as a soldier is that I let other people worry about politics," Marshall said.

"You're a sandbagger today, aren't you, Mister ex-Secretary of State?" Truman said. "And you may not worry about Tail Gunner Joe, but you can bet your bacon he worries about you. You're a Roosevelt crony, after all. Probably a Red in disguise."

"I hope that, if I were a Red in disguise, the United States wouldn't be doing so well in this war." George Marshall had his pride, sure as hell.

Maybe the USA was doing better than the USSR. Truman hoped so. But the country as it was reminded him of a battered pug on a stool pointing across the ring and going *Y'oughta see the other guy. Better* wasn't the same as *good.* It didn't come close to being the same.

After a moment's silence, Marshall coughed and said, "Mr. President, do you mind if I ask you something?"

"You can always ask," Truman said. "If I don't feel like answering, I won't, that's all."

"Fair enough, sir." The Secretary of Defense coughed again. "Whatever you do say, it will be in confidence."

Truman would have believed few men who made that

claim. George Marshall was one of the few. That he said it made Truman pretty sure he knew what Marshall would ask. He said "Go ahead," anyway.

"Thank you, sir. Have you, ah, decided on your own political plans for next year?" Yes, that was the question Truman had expected. Marshall couldn't have phrased it more delicately if he'd been testing clauses in his head the past week. For all Truman knew, he had. Marshall had never struck him as a man who did much off the cuff.

Most of the time, neither was Truman. Here, though . . . "I don't have to make up my mind just yet, so I haven't," he said. "What the war situation looks like when I have to will have a lot to do with it."

"Yes, sir. Of course I understand that," Marshall said. "One other thing you might take into account is doing whatever makes it less likely for Senator McCarthy to reach the White House."

"Why, George!" Truman wagged a finger at him. "For a soldier without politics, seems to me you just came out with something political."

"Yes, sir," Marshall repeated woodenly, and said not another word.

It wasn't as if he needed to. Sighing, Truman said, "Yeah, McCarthy scares the crap out of me, too. He doesn't give a damn about anything but himself, and he doesn't care how many lies he tells to get to the top."

"That last is what concerns me. Give him a toothbrush mustache and a floppy lock of hair—"

"And he'd be even uglier than he is, which ain't easy," Truman broke in. "But Adolf was a teetotaler, and dear Joe pours it down good. Maybe he'll torpedo himself while he's loaded." McCarthy hadn't yet, though. It was probably too much to hope for.

SLOW! a new-looking sign by the side of US 97 warned in big black letters. BORDER CHECKPOINT AHEAD!

"Can you read that, Linda?" Marian Staley asked as she dropped the Studebaker into second.

And damned if Linda didn't, even if she had to sound out *checkpoint* with exaggerated care. The Camp Nowhere kindergarten had taught her something after all.

"Will this be like the one we went through a couple of days ago?" Linda asked. "With the soldiers?"

"Probably. We'll see in a minute," Marian answered. She hadn't expected that National Guardsmen from Washington would check the car before it crossed into Oregon, and that National Guardsmen from Oregon would check it again after it crossed from Washington. The two states might as well have been two different countries. The soldiers on each side of the border were as suspicious of those on the other as if they were foreigners.

So it proved here, on the frontier between Oregon and California. Each state's National Guard was the main—almost the only—source of order that stretched all the way across it. With civilian authority only a memory, the military ruled the roost and feathered its nest.

"Show me your papers!" barked a gray-haired man with corporal's stripes and a Model 1903 Springfield. He might have been a plumber before the Guard called him up, but what did that have to do with anything? Now he could give people orders, and shoot them for not obeying. He knew it, too. It was all over his face.

"Here." Marian produced her Washington driver's license, her discharge paper from Camp Nowhere, and the document the Oregon National Guard had stamped and given her when she drove into the state.

Mr. Two Stripes examined those. "You've got a Washington exit permit, too, right?" he said, his tone suggesting she'd be heading for the calaboose if she didn't.

But she did. After rummaging in her handbag, she pulled out the permit and gave it to him. She had everything but a passport with a visa affixed. She didn't need that . . . yet.

"Hrmp." The National Guard corporal was visibly disappointed. "Lemme take this stuff to the lieutenant, have him check and see if it's legit."

"It is," Marian said, but she was talking to his Eisenhower-jacketed back.

The lieutenant examined the papers, added another one, and gave them back to the corporal. That worthy returned them to Marian. "I guess you're okay to pass on," he said, as if suspecting she had an A-bomb in the trunk rather than the couple of duffels of stuff that represented all her worldly goods.

Two privates swung the bar across the road parallel to it so she could head south. As soon as she did, she had to go through the same rigmarole with the California National Guard. They really did have her open the trunk so they could inspect her chattels.

"No contraband, no contagion—that's our motto," said the noncom who pawed through her dirty dungarees and the *Saturday Evening Post* she'd bought in Klamath Falls.

Marian kept her mouth shut. You couldn't tell these people off, no matter how much they deserved it. But if you didn't, wouldn't they just keep running things? What if somebody had told the Nazis where to go when they were just a bunch of barroom toughs? No Hitler?

Trouble was, if you just told people like that off with words, they'd give you a right to the chops or hit you over the head with a board. You needed to tell them off with machine guns. And doing that . . . Doing that was the reason Marian was a widow and a refugee.

Someone had once said people were the missing link between apes and human beings. By the way things looked, they still had a long way to go.

This particular uniformed anthropoid didn't find anything illegal or contagious in Marian's trunk. He slammed down the lid harder than he might have. He also plied a rubber stamp with might and main. "You are authorized to precede," he said as he handed her the papers.

Don't you mean proceed? she thought. Luckily, she didn't say it. Remind a lug he was a lug and he'd make you sorry.

"Enjoy your stay in California," he went on. *Oh, sure!* Marian swallowed that thought unvoiced, too. The National Guardsman went on, "What is your intended purpose here?"

None of your beeswax. No, that wouldn't work, either, not unless you had a machine gun to back it up. Since Marian didn't, she answered, "I want to find a place to settle down with my little girl."

"I see." The soldier didn't say *It's got to be cover for setting out course markers for the Reds' bombers,* but his attitude suggested it. Grudgingly, he added, "Well, I told you you could precede, so go ahead."

"Thanks." Marian put the Studebaker in gear and drove south down US 97. She'd rarely been so happy as when the border checkpoint vanished behind her.

"Mommy?" Linda asked.

"What is it, honey? You need to go potty?" Marian said.

Her daughter hadn't since well before they went through the third degree from both sets of National Guardsmen.

But Linda shook her head. "I can wait. What I want to know is, how will you find a good place to stop?"

"I don't know." Marian had hardly even thought about it. "When we come to a place that seems all right, we'll see how it is. If we like it, we'll stay. If we don't, after we decide we don't we'll go on. Does that sound okay?"

Linda considered with a gravity that didn't seem childlike. "I guess that's okay, yeah," she said, so seriously that she might have come out with a different answer.

They drove on down US 97. The two-lane blacktop ran south and a little west. Ahead, a mountain began to swell on the horizon. "That's Mount Shasta," Marian said. Her right index finger brushed the inside of the windshield as she pointed. "It's a volcano like Mount Rainier."

"That's good," Linda said. You couldn't always see Mt. Rainier from Everett; the way Washington weather worked, sometimes you couldn't see across the street. Mt. Shasta was still at least fifty miles away, but it seemed clearer than Mt. Rainier did except on the best and brightest of summer days.

US 97 and US 99 joined at Weed, a small town almost in Mt. Shasta's shadow. Marian stopped for lunch there. The diner she walked into was a step up from a greasy spoon. Both the cook behind the counter and the brassy, henna-haired waitress seemed friendly. Marian's chicken plate was pretty good. Linda made her kid-sized burger disappear.

"What are the chances of getting work around here?" Marian asked the waitress.

"You type and take shorthand?"

"Yeah." Type she could. Her Gregg was rusty as hell. People asked about it more than they made you use it. But if somebody did make her, she figured it would come back.

"Lumber companies need people for office work sometimes," the waitress aid. "You can try your luck with them."

"Maybe I will. Is there a motor court in town where the roaches and bedbugs won't jump us?"

"Try Roland's, right by the highway junction. Tell him Babs sent you, and he might give you a break on the rate."

Or give you a rakeoff, Marian thought. But she thanked Babs and left a fifty-cent tip. Roland's turned out to be okay. After Camp Nowhere, any halfway decent motor court was okay. Roland himself did knock six bits a day off the tab when she mentioned Babs' name—and when she said she'd stay awhile if she could land a job.

Weed itself . . . A small town in the middle of nowhere. That suited Marian fine. Better than fine, in fact. Nothing in the whole wide world could make the Russians want to drop an atom bomb on a no-account place like this.

KONSTANTIN MOROZOV RUBBED his chin. Whiskers rasped faintly under his fingertips. He'd got used to having skin as smooth as that of a boy who didn't need to shave yet.

No more. He'd grown some fine brown fuzz on top of his head, too. It wasn't enough yet for a Red Army barber to clip it down into a soldier's crop—a lot like a *zek*'s, when you got right down to it—but it was there. He could see it in the mirror every morning.

He was regrowing hair on the rest of his body, too. He itched in places where he hadn't even known he had places: the backs of his thighs, for instance. He scratched all the time. Sometimes he did it without even noticing. And sometimes he scratched himself raw.

Even so, the doctors seemed pleased. "This is a good recovery," one of them told him.

"I'm glad to hear it, Comrade Physician," Konstantin said. Like a lot of Soviet quacks, this one was a woman. Unlike a lot of the female doctors, she wasn't old or homely. He noticed that she wasn't, which seemed as novel to him as the fuzz on his scalp. When he was egg-bald, he wouldn't have cared if a gorgeous, naked nineteen-year-old plopped herself down on his cot. If that didn't say all that needed saying about how hard the radiation had bitten him, nothing ever would.

"Khorosho," she said once more, sounding . . . amused? Something of what he'd been thinking must have shown in his voice.

"How are my crewmates?" He realized she wouldn't remember offhand who they were, so he named them: "Eigims and Kalyakin and Sarkisyan."

"Kalyakin . . . still struggles." She picked her words with care. "He has needed blood transfusions, because his anemia persists in spite of everything we can do to combat it."

You don't know how to combat it. Morozov had no trouble reading between the lines. "The others?" he asked. Poor Vladislav would pull through on his own, or he wouldn't.

"They're in about the same shape you are," the doctor said. "You should all be ready to return to duty in ten days to two weeks. All of you but Kalyakin, I mean. He'll have to stay behind a bit longer."

"I hope it will be sooner," Konstantin said. "From what the radio says, the front's gone back since those damned bombs fell."

"Da," she agreed. "But we will not release you too soon. You're weaker than you think—and we've had bad results with radiation-sickness victims we sent back to duty before they could handle it."

What did *bad results* mean? He decided he didn't want to know badly enough to find out. He did say, "I'm tired of sitting on the shelf like a jar of pickled cabbage."

That got a smile out of her. But she said, "You're not sitting on the shelf, Comrade Sergeant. You're getting over a wound, a bad wound. Just because you don't have a hole in you and eighty stitches, that doesn't mean you weren't hurt. Radiation sickness is nothing to sneeze at. You're lucky you didn't get an infection, for instance. You might not have been able to fight it off."

One more cheerful thought. They hadn't said much about that when he was sickest. Probably they hadn't wanted to give him anything more to fret about. There was kindness, or as much as a Soviet military hospital was likely to show.

The doctor went on to the next patient. An orderly—by his bandaged left arm, one of the walking wounded—brought Konstantin a bowl of liver stewed with turnips and cabbage. He realized how sick of liver he was getting. It built blood, though. He remembered the East German doc talking about that.

How much liver were they feeding poor Vladislav? They might really be giving it to him up the other end, too. Transfusions? Konstantin shivered. He remembered the SS guys in the last war, with their blood group tattooed under one armpit. If they got captured, that tattoo usually bought them a bullet in the nape of the neck. But if they got hurt, it could keep them alive. They thought it was worth the risk.

In the last war, Morozov had never heard of Soviet doctors transfusing wounded men. They could do it now, plainly. Stalin had warned that the USSR had to catch up with Western Europe and America or go under. It had survived the Hitlerites—barely, but it had.

Now it was trading shattered atoms with the USA. America was rich and strong. Russia'd hit back hard, though. The *rodina* was still in there punching. Sometimes you'd win if you refused to admit you were beaten.

Sometimes.

He listened to Roman Amfiteatrov on Radio Moscow, going on about the victories the Soviet Union and the People's Republic of China and the Democratic People's Republic of Korea were winning over the forces of imperialism, capitalism, and reaction. Someone had brought a radio into the ward. The only way he could not listen was by jamming his fingers into his ears. The MGB would be curious about why he'd want to do something like that. And when the Chekists got curious, your story didn't have a happy ending.

Russian radios received only the frequencies on which the USSR broadcast. That made it harder for people with a counterrevolutionary cast of mind to hear what the BBC and the Voice of America and other lying, anti-Soviet subversive stations were saying about the world situation.

After you'd listened to Radio Moscow since you were in short pants, you learned what its claims were likely to mean in the real world. Konstantin worked out that the Chinese might still be advancing in Korea, but the Red Army had lost enough front-line forces so the Americans and their friends were moving forward, not back.

He'd damn near been part of the front-line forces the Red Army had lost. He wondered how radioactive his old T-54 was. He and what was left of his crew wouldn't get it back when they returned to action. He was sure of that. The men who gave orders would never let a runner sit idle so long. They would have had repair crews hose off the outside and scrub the inside and given it to some healthy foursome.

Or maybe they wouldn't have bothered with the hosing and the scrubbing. Maybe they would have just told the unsuspecting new guys *Here's your machine. Go out and smash some Americans for Stalin!*

He had the bad feeling it would have worked that way. You couldn't see radioactivity, or smell it or hear it or taste it or feel it . . . unless you got enough to make you sick, of course. If it wasn't at a level where it would fry a fresh crew right away, why not just slap them in?

Radiation might make them sick somewhere down the road? Comrade, that's down the road! They're a tank crew! We've got a war to fight! And chances are they won't live long enough for the radiation to bother them any which way!

Yes, that was how Red Army planners would use a tank that hadn't been quite close enough to an A-bomb for its cannon to sag. To be fair, those men used themselves as hard as any other soldiers they could get their hands on. It had worked against the Nazis. It might work again.

Konstantin went looking for Juris Eigims. He wasn't deathly tired all the time, the way he had been when he was sickest. Walking around, though, made him realize the nice-looking lady doctor had a point. He wasn't up to fighting a tank for a day and a half without sleep, or for keeping it in good running order.

The Balt looked pretty much the way he did, only with blond fuzz in place of brown. "Still want to shoot for me when we're good to go?" Morozov asked him.

"If they don't give me a beast of my own, yeah," Eigims answered. "I've had some real clowns give me orders just because they're Russians. You at least know what you're doing."

"Thanks," Konstantin said dryly. "Thanks a bunch."

"Any time." Eigims was unfazed. "You know what you're doing so well, we didn't *quite* get fried there at the front." Morozov found himself without a snappy comeback for that.

New recruits came up to the line. Cade Curtis watched them with more than a little skepticism. They wore American olive drab and U.S. pot helmets, and carried M-1s or grease guns. But their narrow eyes and yellow-brown hides said they were South Koreans, not Yanks.

"We need some bodies in the trenches," he said, trying to make the best of things.

Howard Sturgis, by contrast, eyed the ROK men with contempt if not loathing. "See how long they stay in the goddamn trenches, Captain," the older man said. "See how soon we send out the HA signal."

At the start of the Korean War, the Republic's soldiers were anything but eager to fight. They fell back from Seoul so fast, some people wondered whether those two divisions were riddled with North Korean fifth columnists. HA was the American radio signal that warned they were retreating again. The letters stood for *hauling ass*.

"They aren't as bad as they used to be," Cade said.

"They still ain't what you'd call good . . . sir," Sturgis said. "The North Koreans, say what you want about the fuckers, but they fight like they mean it. These clowns—they'll fight to the last drop of American blood, is what they'll do."

A South Korean lieutenant shouted at one of the men in his platoon. The soldier answered meekly. He wasn't meek enough to suit the officer, who hauled off and clouted him. It was no love tap. It might have flattened Ezzard Charles. The soldier staggered and tramped on.

"That kind of thing doesn't help," Cade said.

"No shit," Sturgis replied. "That looey, he was probably a corporal in a Jap labor brigade or something during the last war. The Japs, their sergeants and officers, knocked the crap out of the ordinary guys for the fun of it, you know?"

"I've heard that, yes." Cade knew he sounded troubled. He *was* troubled. The North Koreans were a bunch of Reds, sure. They cheerfully shot anybody whose ideology they didn't like. But their leaders had mostly resisted the Japanese occupation of Korea and Manchuria.

The South Korean leaders had mostly worked with the Japs. Collaborated with the Japs, the North Koreans said. In Europe, plenty of people in places like France and Holland and Czechoslovakia who'd collaborated with the Japs' Nazi allies wound up on the gallows or in front of a firing squad. Here, the collaborators were American allies now—and they also cheerfully shot anybody whose views they didn't like.

It made you wonder. It really did.

"I wonder if we ought to break them up, put one of their squads with one of ours," Cade said. "That way, we won't have a hole in the line with all of them together."

"We'd be less weak in any one place, but more over a longer stretch." Sturgis shrugged. "Six of one, half a dozen of the other, if you ask me. Other thing is, betcha the Chinks already know we've got gooks here. They'll poke us just to see how bad things are—you wait."

"Uh-huh." That had already occurred to Cade. Koreans

were gooks to him, too. Again, he did his damnedest to look on the bright side: "We've still got our artillery and air."

"Hot damn." No, Howard Sturgis wasn't a bright-side guy.

"They might perform better if they had more of that stuff themselves," Cade said.

"And rain makes applesauce," Sturgis retorted. "Sir, one reason they don't got it now is, they ran so fast they left it behind for the Commies to grab. If they didn't cough up ten divisions' worth o' shit in the retreat to Pusan, you can call me a nigger."

Cade had heard such stories, too. He hoped they were stretched—but he didn't know they were. Sighing, he said, "I'll go see if their company CO speaks English."

"Yeah, that'd be nice. What'll you do if he can't?"

"Try Latin," Cade said. Sturgis goggled, but he meant it. A surprising number of Koreans were Catholic, as was he. Bits and pieces of Latin had saved his bacon on the journey south from the Chosin Reservoir. Maybe they would again.

He turned out not to need to find out. The Korean captain knew enough English to get by. "We fight," he said. "We tough. We tigers."

"Good," Cade said. "You want to mix your men with ours? We can support each other better that way." He could have ordered the ROK officer to do that. They were both captains, but he headed the regiment. But he was willing—for now—to save the other man's face and leave it up to him.

And the Korean—his name was Pak Ho-san—shook his head and said, "Oh, no, no, no."

Koreans put the family name first; if Cade decided to get friendly, he'd call the other captain Ho-san. He wasn't feeling friendly. He was nervous. "You sure?" he asked.

"Oh, yes, yes, yes." Pak eyed him. He was close to Cade's six-one: big for an Oriental. "You no think we do. You think we *gooks*." He said the word as if he were upchucking. As Americans universally used it, so Koreans universally hated it. "You see. By God, we fight!" He didn't say *So fuck you, asshole,* but it was in his bearing.

"Okay." Cade still had his doubts about whether it was, but he didn't see how he could show them.

Damned if the Red Chinese didn't start lobbing mortars at the South Koreans within an hour. They yelled across no-man's-land. They didn't love Koreans, either. The people of the peninsula might not be niggers to them, but they sure as hell were poor yellow trash.

A few of the ROK guys took wounds. None of them HA'd, though. One of the wounded was that lieutenant who'd slugged the private. Cade wasn't sorry to see him carried moaning to the rear. Sometimes subtraction was addition in disguise.

He quietly told his men to can the use of *gook* while the Koreans were in the line. If the locals recognized any one word of English, that was too likely to be it. And he warned them to stay on their toes after the sun went down. If the Red Chinese decided to test the South Koreans, they'd do it when American air power had a harder time making them pay.

And they did. One American picket got off a burst with his grease gun before a wail said he was done. But, alerted, the dogfaces in the main line launched flares and started shooting for all they were worth. Machine guns, submachine guns, semiautomatic rifles . . .

Caught under that merciless white light, quite a few of the Red Chinese raiders who'd scragged the sentry quickly fell. The others fired back. A tracer snapped past Cade's head. A few of the enemy soldiers got into the trenches, but only a few. Then it was knives and entrenching tools and rifle butts: apes whacking away at one another with tree branches, as primitive and basic as combat got.

The Red Chinese didn't need long to realize it wouldn't be their night. They melted away toward their own positions, taking as many of their wounded as they could. A few men still whimpered and cried out north of the trenches. Machine guns swept the ground to make them shut up.

"I be damned," Howard Sturgis said as the gunfire slowed to spatters. "The, uh, ROK guys really did hang in there. Who woulda thunk it?"

"They did great," Cade agreed. "I should go tell Captain Pak they really are a bunch of tigers." They weren't, exactly, but they hadn't bugged out and they'd pulled their weight. It would do. He started up the trench.

Pak Ho-san met him halfway. The Korean officer carried something that wasn't a weapon in his right hand. "Here, Captain Curtis," he said, holding it up. "I have for you. We fight, hey?"

"You fight, you bet." Cade flicked his lighter to see what Pak was giving him. The Korean held a Red Chinese soldier's head by the hair. "Jesus!" Cade said. "I don't want that! Get rid of it!"

"I kill him my ownself, with bayonet." Captain Pak sounded sulky, as if he hadn't expected Curtis to be so soft. But, shrugging at the inscrutability of the Occidental, he threw the head back toward the enemy line. The thump it made hitting the mud sounded dreadfully final.

Istvan Szolovits crouched in a shell hole, using his left hand to jam his helmet down onto his head as hard as he could. The Americans were throwing artillery at his unit with positively Soviet abandon. Mortars, 105s, 155s, rockets . . . Everything but the kitchen sink seemed to be coming down on the Hungarians' heads. If some clever Yankee worked out how to fit a charge in the basin and a rocket motor instead of a drainpipe, they'd probably start firing sinks, too.

Fragments whined and snarled and screamed hatefully, not far enough overhead. Blast slammed Istvan around. The nearer near misses made him have trouble breathing. A shell didn't have to land on you to do you in. Close enough could be good enough.

In between the shell bursts, he heard people screaming. Some were wounded, more just frightened out of their minds. Half deafened and more than half stunned, he needed a little while to realize that one of those terrified voices belonged to him. He'd been through some hell since the Hungarian People's Army went into combat, but never anything like this. The atom bomb had scared him, too, but it didn't go on and on the way this bombardment did.

His father and a couple of uncles had fought for Franz Joseph during the First World War. They would have understood what he was going through. But they probably would have enjoyed better protection than he did.

He'd already dug a foxhole in the shell hole. He didn't have a proper dugout, though. You needed time in one place to dig those into the walls of your trenches and shore them up with whatever timber you could find.

"Watch out, you whistleass peckerheads!" No one but Sergeant Gergely would bellow a profane warning through the thunder of the shells. "When the Americans let up, that's when you better be ready, on account of that's when they'll come."

He made good sense. The enemy was trying to kill as many Magyars as they could (and even the occasional Jew who found himself in the same uniform), and to paralyze the ones they didn't kill. Then their advance would be a walkover.

But the Americans didn't let up, and didn't let up, and didn't let up some more. They sifted this field like a baker sifting cake flour. They didn't want any big lumps left in it before they stuck it in the oven.

At last, after a couple of hours that seemed like a couple of thousand years, the barrage moved past the Hungarians' position. That would make retreating hard for them and keep anybody else on their side from moving forward to give them a hand. Istvan stuck up his head to see what kind of prophet the sergeant made.

He wasn't surprised when Gergely could have matched himself against Elijah or Jeremiah. However big a bastard Gergely was, he knew his onions. Here came the Yankees. Their tanks were bedizened with white stars. Foot soldiers in olive drab loped along between them.

A Magyar popped out of his hole like a marmot—only marmots didn't carry rocket-propelled grenades. One of them took out a tank. All the ammo inside the Pershing went off at once. The turret flew through the air and squashed an infantryman ten meters away. Like a beetle under a boot, he died before he knew what hit him.

There were worse ways to go. Too many of them seemed to loom large across Istvan's future. The surviving American tanks pounded that Magyar with cannons and machine guns. The guy who'd fired would likely wind up too dead to try it again.

Rifle bullets cracked past Istvan. By the sound, some of them came from beside his hole, not in front of it. If he didn't fall back, he'd get cut off and surrounded and . . . *Killed,* he thought bleakly. Of course, he might also get killed trying to fall back. But the odds looked worse if he stayed where he was.

He scrambled out of the hole he'd worked so hard to improve and dashed eastward. He wasn't the only Hungarian doing the same thing. As his eyes darted this way and that, one of his countrymen let his rifle fall, threw his arms wide, and crumpled bonelessly to the shell-pocked turf.

A bullet kicked up dirt at Istvan's feet. *"Rukhi verkh, Russki!"* somebody yelled.

Istvan knew that meant *Hands up, Russian!* He'd heard Germans and Magyars shout it during the grim street fighting in Budapest at the end of the last war. But he needed an almost fatal second to realize that soldier was yelling it at *him.*

I'm no Russian! he thought with absurd indignation as he dropped his Mosin-Nagant and raised his hands. His captor was a pink-cheeked kid in an American uniform. He kept his own M-1 on Istvan. "You speak English?" he demanded, so he was a Yank and not a German.

Regretfully, Istvan shook his head. He'd never had the chance to learn it. *"Ich spreche Deutsch,"* he said. That was the one language they might share.

They didn't. For all the American could tell, he was using Russian. The kid gestured with his rifle—go back that way. Keeping his hands high, Istvan went back that way.

He'd often thought about giving himself up to the Americans. It wasn't as if this were his war, or Hungary's. But surrendering turned out not to be so simple. And he'd seen that the few minutes after you did surrender told the story of whether you'd live or die. If the guy who captured you was in a hurry or just feeling mean, he'd plug you and go on about his business instead of getting you back to where you might stay safe. To the soldiers who took them, prisoners were a damn nuisance.

Istvan tried not to tense as he walked west. If the American shot him in the back, he hoped it would all end in a hurry.

But the American didn't. Another Yank came up to him. They went back and forth in the language Istvan couldn't follow. He did hear the word *Russian* several times, though.

"Nicht russisch," he said, using one hand to point at himself. *"Ich bin ungarisch."*

More English. The soldier who was talking with his captor also pointed at him and said, "You're Hungarian?"

That was close enough to *ungarisch* for Istvan to get it. He nodded. *"Ja!"*

The Yanks held another palaver. The newcomer used his machine pistol to point down a muddy track. The man who'd captured Istvan trotted off to fight some more.

Along the track Istvan went. At last, under some trees the artillery had drastically abridged, he found half a dozen other Hungarians sitting and smoking. A couple of them were wounded, but the Americans had bandaged them and given them food and water. One of the Yanks guarding them spoke in German: "Use this language only. I need to be able to understand what you say."

"Zu Befehl, mein Herr!" Istvan said as he sagged to the ground with his fellow POWs. All his bones seemed to turn to water. He was going to live! You didn't usually shoot a bunch of prisoners behind the lines. If you were going to dispose of them, you did it right away.

"Hey!" one of the Magyars said in his own tongue. "How's it going?"

"Auf Deutsch, Scheissekopf!" the American barked. The other captive repeated the question in German. He had a country accent in Magyar, one that said he came from the southwest.

"Es geht ganz gut," Istvan said. *"Ich lebe noch." It's fine—I'm still alive.* What could be better than that?

Food could. The American guard tossed him a ration can. He opened it with his bayonet, which no one had bothered taking yet. Then he shoveled stew into his mouth with his fingers. It tasted richer, greasier, than Hungarian or Soviet supplies. He licked the can clean. He'd got lucky. He was out of the war.

Ivans with machine pistols had holed up inside a grocery store in Lippstadt. Gustav Hozzel cautiously peered round the corner at the strongpoint.

"They picked a hell of a place to dig in," Rolf grumbled from behind him. "They plug up the way forward but good. And with all the food in there, they can hang on for days."

"Could be," Gustav said. Like most Germans who'd fought in the east, he'd seen how Russians could keep fighting longer than anybody sensible would figure, and do it on next to no supplies.

Max Bachman shook his head. "Lippstadt's been under Russian control for a while now. What makes you guys think that store isn't bare as a stripper's chest?"

"Huh," Gustav said thoughtfully. "You've got something there."

"Yeah. Maybe sulfa drugs will cure it, though," Rolf put in.

"Funny. See? I'm laughing." But Max spoke without heat.

"I know what I'd like to use to pry those Ivans out of there. A *Flammenwerfer*'d do the job neat as you please," Rolf said.

"Go ahead. You first." Like most *Frontschweine,* Gustav

hated flamethrowers, his own side's hardly less than the Russians'. Yes, they could drive people out of places that would hold for a long time against other weapons. But he'd never seen or heard of anybody who carried one being taken prisoner.

"I'll do it," Rolf said. "Wouldn't be the first time."

Gustav lit a cigarette so his face wouldn't give away what he was thinking. He hadn't known that his comrade in arms had used a *Flammenwerfer* during the last go-round, but he would have been lying had he said the news amazed him. Rolf liked hurting things and killing things a little too much for even the guys on his side to be easy around him.

"Unless you feel like *fressing* a tonne of beans and lighting your farts, we haven't got a flamethrower," Max pointed out, which made even the *Leibstandarte Adolf Hitler* veteran laugh. Practical as usual, Max went on, "What can we do with what we have got?"

"Why don't we just shout for them to come out and give up?" Gustav said.

"Go ahead. You first," Rolf told him.

Which meant the *Waffen*-SS puke would think he was yellow unless he went ahead and did it. "Up yours, Rolf," Gustav muttered. Louder, he went on, "Let's see if I can find a white cloth bigger than my snotrag." The shop they crouched in front of proved to be a coffeehouse. Gustav yanked a cloth off a table. Before he showed himself, he told Rolf, "I get killed trying this, I'll fucking haunt you."

Rolf nodded. "You can join the club." He was tough to rattle.

Shaking the tablecloth around the corner before he went himself, Gustav gave the Red Army men a chance to see it. Still waving it, he stepped out where they could see him, too. "You Ivans!" he shouted—some of them were bound to know scraps of German. "Come out! Surrender! We won't hurt you if you do—soldiers' honor!"

You never could tell with Russians when things got strange. When they were proceeding according to plan, they'd keep going no matter what, as hard to divert or slow as a wrecking ball. But when they had to think for themselves or deal with the unexpected, you had no idea ahead of time what they'd do.

Nothing happened here for three or four minutes. The Ivans might have been holding their own little soviet inside the grocery. They didn't shoot him for the sport of it, the way they easily might have. He took that as a good sign. Standing there in the street waving his stupid tablecloth, he didn't know how else to take it.

And then, when he was getting antsy enough to want to dive back into cover, damned if the Russians didn't come out, one after another, their hands clasped on top of their heads. They came, and they came, and they came some more. It reminded him of swarms of clowns piling out of a little trick car in the circus. He'd figured four or five of them, tops, were defending the grocery. Dizzily, he counted seventeen men in Red Army khaki.

The Ivan in front came up to him. "No hurt us?" he said in broken German. "Soldiers' honor?"

"Soldiers' honor," Gustav promised, and raised his right hand with the first two fingers crooked as if swearing an oath in court. Then he pointed back around the corner. "You—all of you—come with me."

They came. Rolf stared at them, goggle-eyed. Max looked pretty well sandbagged, too. "Fuck me up the asshole," Rolf said. "I didn't think you'd bring back a whole division."

"Neither did I," Gustav said, "but here they are." He caught Max Bachman's eye. "How about the two of us take 'em back? I promised they'd get treated all right."

"Hey!" Rolf said. "What about me?"

"I promised they'd get treated all right," Gustav repeated. "You stay here and keep an eye on things. Or get some other guys and clean the weapons out of that grocery if you want."

He'd seen that the ex-LAH man was still atrocity-prone. It wasn't as if he had a snowy-white conscience himself. Nobody who'd lived through the war on the Eastern Front came away clean. But he aimed to keep the promise he'd made to those Russians. It might have been more for his own sake than for theirs, but he did. And that meant not letting Rolf have any more to do with them than he could help.

The quirk of Max's eyebrows said he got that. He climbed to his feet and hefted his American Springfield. When Gustav picked up his own AK-47, a couple of the Ivans nodded to themselves. They knew they made a good weapon there, one fine enough for even the other side to covet. One of them helpfully took three magazines off his belt and held them out to Gustav. He took them with a nod of thanks.

Gesturing with the assault rifle, he said, "Come on, you sorry sacks of shit—get moving." The Russian who spoke a little German translated that for his buddies. By the way some of them tried to keep from grinning, he translated it literally.

Off the prisoners went. Gustav and Max walked to either side of their column, guiding them through Lippstadt and out to the open country west of it like a couple of herdsmen's dogs keeping a flock of sheep going the way it was supposed to.

Pretty soon, three jeeps came up the road toward them. The Ivans stepped off onto the soft shoulder to let them by. Gustav couldn't tell by looking whether the men in the jeeps were Amis or Germans—they wore the same uniforms he and Max did.

Instead of passing the Red Army men and their captors, the lead jeep stopped, which meant the others did, too. "Jesus Christ!" the man in the passenger seat said in English. "What the hell have you got here?"

Gustav understood him the way that Russian POW understood German. He had fragments of English, but only fragments. Max knew a good bit more. He was the one who said, "Gustav, he capture them. Now we take them back."

"Goodgodalmightydamn!" the American said, running it together into one word the way a German might with *Himmeldonnerwetter!* Then he came out with some more English that Gustav couldn't catch.

Max translated for him: "He says there are some U.S. intelligence guys a kilometer or two down the road. They can question the Ivans."

"That should work out all right." Gustav wanted to get back to it. The fighting in Lippstadt hadn't stopped just because he'd cleared the grocery. He nodded to the Americans in the jeeps, then used his Kalashnikov to urge the POWs on again. *"Marschen!"*

March they did. The jeeps chugged on toward the town. Gustav opened a new pack of Old Golds and lit a cigarette. Seeing how hopeful the Ivans looked, he tossed one of them the pack. They all took a smoke. With American bounty at his disposal, he knew he could get more. Rolf would have called him a softy. *To hell with Rolf,* he thought, not for the first time.

BACK BEFORE SHE MET BILL, Marian Staley had worked as a clerk-typist for Boeing. That was a big company to begin with, and it had swollen like an inflating balloon under the pressure of World War II. The Shasta Lumber Corporation wasn't in the same league, or even in the one below.

But Shasta Lumber had hired her, so she wasn't about to complain. The pay—a buck thirty-five an hour—wouldn't let her run the Rockefellers out of business any time soon. Along with what she had left from the insurance policy, though, it meant she could get on with her life.

The local school was full of loggers' kids. It was full, period. Lots of couples with men back from the war had had babies about the time she'd had Linda. Quite a few of those little kids had littler brothers and sisters who'd fill the classrooms over the next few years. And half the women Marian saw on the streets of Weed seemed to be expecting.

As soon as she had the job, she moved from the motor court to a rented house close enough to the school so Linda could walk back and forth. It was a small place, only about half the size of the one the A-bomb had wrecked up in Everett. It did seem extra roomy at first, because she had such scanty furnishings. Thanks to that atom bomb and her stay at Camp Nowhere, she was starting from scratch.

She bought the undowithoutables—beds for her and Linda, a table and a couple of chairs, a dresser—new, and a little fridge and basic kitchen stuff to go with them. The stove was already in place, for which she was duly grateful. Everything else she got secondhand . . . except for the end table that sat on somebody's front lawn waiting for the garbage men, which she'd rescued before they could take it away.

If you wanted wild living, Weed wasn't the place to come.

Well, there was one kind of wild living, but not one that appealed to Marian. After the loggers got paid, they filled the bars and drank and brawled and chased the kind of women who didn't need much chasing till they ran out of money. That seldom took long.

Marian quickly learned to stay away from the small downtown on those days. Having to do that annoyed her when she wanted to bring Linda to a cartoon at the one local movie house, but you had to take a place as you found it, not as you wished it were.

One of the secondhand purchases was a tinny Philco radio with a dark brown Bakelite case. Or maybe the radio wasn't so very tinny; maybe it was just that all the stations she could pick up came from far away, and she heard them through veils of static.

At night, she could get KFI all the way from Los Angeles. It reached Weed as clearly, or as fuzzily, as the smaller stations in places like Redding and Red Bluff and Klamath Falls. She missed television, but the nearest station was down in Sacramento, too far away for even the tallest antenna to bring in a signal. TV might come to Weed one of these days, but it wouldn't be tomorrow.

Work was . . . work. She filed papers and typed letters and reports and inventories and whatever else the people who paid her put on her desk when they emerged from their fancy offices far down the hall. She ran a mimeograph machine, cranking out copies of forms. She did all the other things they told her to do.

Since she was the newest hire, she also inherited the percolator that sat on a hot plate all day long. The gal who had been in charge of it turned it over to her with nothing but relief. Marian didn't mind. It gave her an excuse to stand up and stretch and take a short break every so often. Nobody groused about the coffee she turned out.

Like the other office workers, she brown-bagged lunch most of the time. It was cheaper. Once or twice a week, though, she would visit the diner where she'd stopped when she first came into Weed. For some reason she couldn't fathom, Babs had taken a shine to her.

"You see? This ain't such a bad place," the waitress said, setting a bowl of beef stew in front of Marian. "You find yourself a fella here, you'll have all the comforts of home." She winked. Her heavily mascaraed eyelashes flapped like a crow's wing.

"You may be right," said Marian, for whom the thought of a fella was the last thing on her mind.

"Oh, you bet I am," Babs said. "A man keeps you warm better'n a hot-water bottle every day of the week, and twice on Sundays. Twice on Sundays if he's young enough, anyways." She leered and laughed a filthy laugh.

"You're awful," Marian said.

"You can say whatever you want, sweetie. *He* told me I was pretty darn good." Babs laughed again. This time, so did Marian. If you couldn't lick 'em, you might as well join 'em.

A couple of days later, after picking up Linda from the school playground where she hung around till her mother got off work, Marian drove to the Rexall that was Weed's one and only drugstore. She bought Band-Aids and Kotex. As she was getting ready to pay the druggist, she plucked a color postcard of Mt. Shasta from a little revolving rack on the counter and bought that, too.

"What do you need that for, Mommy?" Linda asked. "All you have to do is go outside and you can see the mountain."

"I know," Marian said. "But if I send the card to somebody who doesn't live here, that person can see it, too."

"Who would you send it to?"

"I don't know. I'll think of somebody. Or if I don't, I'll just keep it." Marian gave the druggist a five-dollar bill. She put the change in her wallet and coin purse, stuck them back in her handbag, and went out to the car with her daughter.

Dinner that night was liver and onions. Marian liked it. She would have made it more often, but Linda didn't. She'd got pickier after their stretch—and that was what it felt like: a jail term—in Camp Nowhere. The food there was as bland as the cooks could make it, when it wasn't military rations that were born bland. Now strong flavors seemed all the stronger.

After pushing her share around her plate for a while, Linda said, "May I be excused, Mommy?"

Marian told herself she should make her daughter eat more. No matter what she told herself, tonight she didn't have the energy. "Yes, go ahead," she said. "You can play for a while, then we'll get you ready for bed."

"Okay!" Linda escaped while the escaping was good.

Moving more slowly, Marian cleaned off the table and the stovetop. She washed the dishes and put them in the drainer.

She looked at the dish towels, then looked away. She didn't have the energy to use them, either. The dishes would be dry in the morning any which way.

The postcard sat on the kitchen counter. She had the feeling it was eyeing her. She picked it up, found a pen, and started to write. *This is where we've ended up,* she said, and added her newly memorized address. *It's not too bad. It's a long way from anything big. Times like this, that's good. Hope you and your friends are doing well.*

After she signed her name, she wrote out the address where the card needed to go: *Fayvl Tabakman, Seattle-Everett Refugee Encampment Number Three.* She could have written *Camp Nowhere,* but for all she knew half the refugee camps in the country carried the same nickname.

She found a three-cent stamp and stuck it on the card. That was wasting a penny, but she couldn't lay her hand on two one-centers. To help raise money to fight the war, the penny postcard was now a thing of the past.

Next morning, she tossed the card into the wire basket for outgoing mail at Shasta Lumber. That was easier than using some of her lunch hour to find a mailbox or to walk to the post office. It was right by the bars and the pawnshop where she'd picked up some of the small things for the house.

Having got rid of the card, she forgot about it. She had a financial statement to type up, and those were always a nuisance: lots of tabs, complicated centering, and everything had to be perfect. She was still new enough in the job that she took special care to make sure it was.

Boris Gribkov didn't think he'd ever seen Brigadier Olminsky smile. The man was either scowling or looking as if his stomach pained him. Right now, he combined the two expressions. "Comrade Pilot, a problem has presented itself," he said.

"I serve the Soviet Union, sir!" Gribkov said.

"Good. Excellent, in fact. That is what I wanted to hear," Yulian Olminsky said, and Boris wondered what he'd just bigmouthed his way into. The senior officer wasted no time letting him know: "There has been a reactionary uprising in the Slovak region of the Czechoslovak Socialist Republic."

"Has there?" Gribkov said tonelessly. Czechoslovakia had been the Czechoslovak Socialist Republic for only about three years. It was the last satellite to fall into orbit around the

USSR. There were probably still some people left who didn't care for their country's new orientation.

Sure enough, Olminsky said, "Elements believed to be affiliated with Father Tiso's Slovak Fascist regime have seized Bratislava. A disloyal military clique is cooperating with them. If they succeed in detaching Slovakia from its affiliation to the cause of class struggle and world revolution, it will damage Red Army logistics and worldwide socialist solidarity."

"I see," Gribkov said. Father Tiso had run Slovakia as a Nazi puppet state after the Germans grabbed Bohemia and Moravia in the aftermath of the Munich sellout. Even before committing to Marxism-Leninism-Stalinism, Czechoslovakia executed him and a good many of his henchmen and tagged more of them with corrective-labor or jail terms.

As if plucking that thought from his ear, the brigadier said, "The regime here in Prague must have been too soft, or we wouldn't have to put up with this pestilential nonsense now. They should have done a better job of eliminating that faction. Now we have to pay the price for it."

"What does this have to do with me, sir?" Boris asked.

Olminsky's frown said he was slower on the uptake than the senior man had hoped. "We can't let the fucking Slovaks get away with this horseshit," he answered. "Do you want the Hungarians and the Poles to start playing games, too? That would screw us in the mouth for real. And so we are going to wipe Bratislava off the face of the earth."

"With an A-bomb?" Gribkov's heart sank. Leonid Tsederbaum might have known what he was doing, all right.

But, reluctantly, Olminsky shook his head. "We have none to spare for the Slovaks, I'm sorry to say. So instead we will send many Tu-4s against the reactionaries with conventional bombs. Bratislava will still be destroyed."

"Yes, sir." Gribkov knew better than to show how relieved he was. The ten tonnes of bombs his plane carried might still kill hundreds of people. All the Tu-4s the USSR could afford to despatch would drop a couple of hundred tonnes of bombs and might kill thousands. One A-bomb was worth fifteen or twenty thousand tonnes of high explosives, and would surely kill tens of thousands.

This was war. It wasn't quite wholesale slaughter. Boris wouldn't want to add Bratislava to the nose art of murdered cities that the bomber in his mind carried.

Something else occurred to the pilot. "Excuse me, Comrade Brigadier, but will these revolting reactionaries—"

"That's just what they are, damn them," Olminsky broke in.

"Yes, sir," Gribkov said patiently. "Do they have any air defenses? Flak? Fighters? What are we getting into?" He didn't remind Yulian Olminsky that the Tu-4 was easy meat even for the leftover Soviet fighters the Czechoslovakian Air Force flew. Olminsky had to know it already. Or if he didn't, he didn't deserve the stars on his shoulder boards.

"There may be some flak under their control," he answered now, sounding as if he didn't like to admit it. "As far as we know, socially friendly forces are still in charge of the warplanes in Czechoslovakia. No one's attacked the airstrip here, you'll notice. Any more questions?" The way his eyebrows drew down and came together warned Boris had better not have any.

"No, sir!" he said, and saluted crisply. "I serve the Soviet Union!"

"Khorosho," Olminsky said. "Now beat it. You'll fly tonight."

Gribkov tried not to let his face show what he was thinking as he walked back to brief his crew. That was a good idea for any Soviet citizen at any time, and all the more so when trying to digest news like this. He supposed the satellites were going to try to get out of the war their tutor had dragged them into. Germany's less than eager allies had done their best to escape when things stopped going Hitler's way.

As he told the men what the next mission would be, he watched their expressions freeze up the way his had when Olminsky told him. Dropping bombs on the enemy was one thing. Dropping them where a lot of people were your friends was another . . . wasn't it?

Vladimir Zorin went through a cigarette in a few quick, harsh, deep puffs. "Well, this is something different, isn't it?" he said. Not many questions could pack more possible meanings into them.

"Oh, maybe a little," Gribkov answered: another handful of words with more than a handful of meanings.

The copilot ground the butt under his boot and lit a new smoke. "Shame Leonid isn't here," he said. "He could read the angles better than anybody else I ever knew." Boris feared that Zorin was right. And what did that say about what the former navigator had done?

"We'll deal with the rebels' treason the way it deserves," Yefim Arzhanov declared. The quick navigator, unlike the dead one, didn't seem afflicted by doubts. Did that make him a lucky man or a fool? How much difference was there, when you got down to it?

They took off a little before midnight. Boris' grip on the yoke eased off when he was sure the Tu-4 would stay airborne. Full of high-octane avgas and TNT, the bomber was itself a bomb that, if not quite of atomic proportions, would take out a big chunk of the landscape if one—or two—of the overstrained engines failed trying to lift it off the ground.

The plane circled up to bombing altitude while still over the Czech half of Czechoslovakia. Then it flew southeast. Gribkov wasn't used to going in that direction on the way to a mission. It was the kind of route he might have to fly if unrest ever broke out inside the *rodina.* He didn't even want to think about such a thing, much less do it.

As Olminsky had promised, no fighters rose up inside Czechoslovakia to assail the Tu-4 and its companions. Radar made finding Bratislava in the darkness far easier than it would have been during the last war. Then, on a long-range flight (which this, of course, wasn't), you were lucky if your bombs came down within ten kilometers of their intended target. Destruction was more efficient now.

So was flak. The Slovak rebels did have guns down there on the ground. For all Boris knew, they were 88s the Nazis had given to Tiso's men. Whatever they were, they had excellent direction. Shells started bursting below the incoming bombers, and then among them. A Tu-4 spun out of the sky, fire all up and down the wings.

"Drop the bombs!" Gribkov called to Alexander Lavrov as near misses buffeted the plane.

Away they went. Not thirty seconds later, a direct hit knocked out both starboard engines and killed the bomber's pressurization. Gribkov had an oxygen mask on, or he would have slid straight into unconsciousness and death.

"Get out!" he screamed over the intercom. "Get out while you can!"

The hatch was by the main engineer's station. The engineer and radio operator were already gone before Boris got back there. He jumped into the blackness. When he yanked the rip cord, his parachute opened. Shivering, he slid down, down, down toward whatever waited on the ground.

* * *

Ihor Shevchenko's sergeant sent him a suspicious stare. Anatoly Prishvin had been doing that ever since Ihor wound up in his section. "I've got my eye on you, Ukrainian," he said for the third time that day.

Rolling tobacco in a torn chunk of newspaper and lighting it seemed a better idea than answering. Ihor had heard cracks like that during the Great Patriotic War, too. Most of the time, ignoring them was the smartest thing you could do.

Most of the time, but not always. The sergeant did his best impersonation of a poisonous snake. He hissed angrily. His beady little eyes didn't even blink. "I've got my eye on you," he said yet again. "You hear what I'm telling you?"

"Oh, yes, Comrade Sergeant," Ihor said after a deliberate puff. "I hear you real good."

"Then act like it, you worthless fucker," Prishvin said. "I know your kind. You were the traitors who went out and said hello to the Nazis with bread and salt."

Some Ukrainians *had* done that when the Germans invaded in 1941. There had been a Ukrainian *Waffen*-SS division, though more of its men came from Poland than from the Soviet Union. Glancing at Prishvin out of the corner of his eye, Ihor could see why so many of his people had thought Hitler a better bet than Stalin. Hitler hadn't starved millions of Ukrainians to death.

He hadn't yet. But he started in as soon as he got the chance. Ihor said, "Comrade Sergeant, I fought the Fascists in the partisans and then in the Red Army. I was wounded in the service of the Soviet Union."

"Da, da, da," Prishvin said, by which he meant *Nyet, nyet, nyet.* "All you cocksuckers who can't say *G* talk about what heroes you were. It's all bullshit, too."

"Would you like to see my scar?" Ihor asked, making as if to unroll his puttees and hike up his trouser leg.

"I don't give a shit about your scar, on account of it won't tell me whose gun gave it to you," the sergeant said. "And you were screwing around in front of our lines just now. For all I know, you were screwing around with the Americans. If I could prove it, I'd shoot you myself. I know how to shoot my own dog."

Any son of a bitch would, Ihor thought. He didn't come out with it. He had no interest in cutting his own throat. All he wanted to do was get through the war in one piece and make it back to Anya at the collective farm outside of smashed Kiev.

It was funny. He'd been eager to fight the Hitlerites. He'd seen what they'd done to the Ukraine. They'd treated it even worse than Stalin had, and that wasn't easy. But the Americans? As far as he knew, there were no Americans within a thousand kilometers of the Ukraine. Yes, they'd bombed it. But Stalin had also bombed America.

Rain started coming down on the field somewhere west of Paderborn. Sergeant Prishvin sent Ihor one more glare, then ambled off to spread joy and good tidings to some of the other soldiers in his charge. Ihor pulled his shelter half out of his pack and stuck his head through the slit. It was an old one, hauled from a storehouse where it had sat since the Great Patriotic War. The rubberized fabric had cracks and bald spots. It still did a better job of keeping the water off him than anything else would have.

He got a cigarette going, leaning forward so the brim of his helmet shielded the coal from the rain. Another man—a blackass from the Caucasus—also decked out in a rain cape spoke to him in halting Russian: "What you do to make sergeant love you so big, uh, so much?"

"I don't know, Aram." Ihor shrugged. "He likes my face, I guess. Or maybe I'm just lucky."

"Ha! Some luck!" Aram Demirchyan snorted. Then he asked, "You got more smokes?"

"Sure." Ihor gave him one. He'd taken the pack off a dead German civilian. One thing about the Red Army hadn't changed a bit since the last war: the higher-ups expected you to do your own scrounging. They'd give you ammo, vodka, and a little food. For everything else, you were on your own.

"Spasibo." Demirchyan's stubbly cheeks hollowed as he took a drag. Some of the stubble was gray; he had to be four or five years older than Ihor. He'd also been through the mill the last time around. After blowing out a gray stream, he muttered, "Something should ought to happening to that cunt."

"Who knows? Maybe something will," Ihor answered. Noncoms and company-grade officers who made their men hate them sometimes had accidents. All the men who served under them said they were accidents, anyhow. Other people sometimes wondered, but war was war. Even good people wound up hurt or dead when they came to the front. Even good people occasionally caught a bullet or a grenade fragment from their own side, too. If that happened to the fuckers a little more often, well, proving such things wasn't easy.

Demirchyan did some more muttering, this time in his own throaty language. Ihor thought he heard Sergeant Prishvin's name in there. He didn't think the Armenian was reciting love poetry.

"He give you a hard time, too?" Ihor asked.

Aram Demirchyan's big, heavy-featured head bobbed up and down. "He give everybody hards times," he said. "Even Russians. Russians don't act Russian enough to happy him."

A machine gun stuttered out a burst, a few hundred meters to the south. That was a Red Army Maxim. Ihor knew the sound as well as he knew that of his own voice. He was still getting used to the reports and deadly rhythms of the Yankees' automatic weapons.

But the machine gun that replied wasn't American at all. The rounds came back one after another, so close together that the shots merged into a single, horrible ripping roar.

"Ah, fuck 'em!" he exclaimed. "They've yanked one of Hitler's saws out of storage."

"MG-42 scare shit out of I," Demirchyan said matter-of-factly.

"They scare the shit out of everybody on the wrong end of them," Ihor said. The German machine gun with the ridiculous rate of fire and the quick-change barrel was still the finest piece of its kind, and kilometers ahead of whatever ran second. It had turned *Wehrmacht* squads into machine-gun crews and a few other guys to protect them with rifles and Schmeissers.

The Nazis made a fair number of weapons that were better than anything their foes used. In the end, they didn't make enough of them, or have enough bastards in *Feldgrau* to use them. A T-34/85 might not be so fine a tank as a Panther, but when there were six or eight or ten Soviet machines for every German one. . . .

In that case, you waited five or six years and then you fought another war.

"Listen to me! Listen hard, you drippy pricks!" Sergeant Prishvin yelled. "We're going forward! We're going to push back the men north of that fucking Nazi gun, we're going to fire on it from a flanking position, and we're going to put it out of action or make it retreat. Forward! *Za rodina!*"

Whether it was for the motherland or not, Ihor didn't want to go forward. The machine gun might get him. Other enemy weapons might, too. Of course, the MGB *would* give him a bullet in the nape of the neck if he hung back. Out of his hole he came, chambering a round in his Kalashnikov.

The Red Army men moved by groups and rushes, each attack party covering the other's advance. They'd learned from the Great Patriotic War's suicidal charges. The ones who lived had, anyhow.

Anatoly Prishvin was a dickhead, but a brave dickhead. He led from the front, cursing his section on. Somebody in an American helmet popped up and aimed a rifle at him. Ihor shot the enemy soldier before he realized what he was doing.

"Wasting of good bullets," Aram Demirchyan said when they flopped down behind a fallen chimney.

"I know," Ihor agreed mournfully. To his surprise, they did make the machine-gun crew fall back. Prishvin didn't thank him for dropping the American. That suited Ihor. The less he had to do with the sergeant, the better.

"Bedtime, Leon," Aaron Finch said.

"No," Leon told him. He wasn't saying that because he said *no* all the time. He was getting over that. He was saying it because he didn't want to go to bed. Uncle Marvin and Aunt Sarah and Cousin Olivia were over, which made the living room even more interesting than usual.

"Bedtime," Aaron repeated, a little more firmly this time, so Leon could see he wasn't kidding.

"Bounce is waiting," Ruth added. The kid loved the bear so much, Aaron wondered if it was normal. Ruth and Dr. Spock assured him it was, so he let it go. Two-year-old and bear had all kinds of imaginary adventures. They were often noisy, so Aaron hoped like blazes they were imaginary, anyhow.

His wife's ploy worked. Leon's face lit up. "Bounce!" he said.

"Give everybody a good-night kiss," Aaron said. Usually, that just meant him and Ruth, but now Leon had a whole round to make. Aaron's younger brother took the pipe out of his mouth so his kiss would work better. Sarah moved her drink to keep Leon from knocking it off the coffee table. Olivia, who was fourteen, gave her cousin a big, smacking smooch. Leon squealed with laughter.

Ruth took him back to the bathroom—he was getting potty-trained, but he hadn't got all the way there yet—and to his bedroom.

"He's a good kid," Marvin said. "Must come from his mother's side of the family."

"Heh," Aaron said. All the Finches had barbed wits. The barbs on Marvin's were longer and more rebarbative than most. That crack would have been nothing in some tones of voice. Not in the one Marvin used.

Aaron glanced over at Sarah Finch. *Is it her fault that Olivia's a good kid?* he wondered. But, though he did wonder, he didn't come out and say it. That showed at least some of the difference between himself and his brother.

Ruth walked back into the living room. "He's in there talking with Bounce," she reported. "I think he'll settle down."

"It's when the bear starts answering that you've got to worry," Marvin said.

Sarah and Olivia laughed. Even Aaron chuckled. But Ruth said, "The bear does answer sometimes. Leon starts with this high, squeaky voice, and it's Bounce talking. Leon's smart. I just hope like anything he's smart enough to stay out of trouble."

"He'd better take after you, in that case. His father wasn't." Marvin pointed to the letter from Harry Truman that Aaron had framed.

"Do I have to get *tsuris* about that from you, too?" Aaron said. "Roxane and Howard already told me I should have bought that Russian a ticket to Vladivostok. First class, too."

"Why don't you get me another scotch, Aaron?" Sarah did her best to defuse things when Marvin started sniping. The trouble was, her best wasn't good enough. Marvin didn't pay attention to her most of the time.

If Aaron had been in her shoes, he would have bopped Marvin in the nose. But Sarah seemed resigned to being Marvin's punching bag. Or maybe she even liked it. Some people did. How could you know for sure?

You couldn't. He could fix Sarah another scotch. He got out of the rocking chair, plucked her glass from the coffee table, and took it into the kitchen, where he built her a reload. He took another Burgie out of the icebox for himself, too. Sometimes Marvin was easier to stand after a couple of beers.

By that logic, Sarah would never draw a sober breath if she

had any sense. But if she was a lush, she was a quiet, discreet lush. Plenty of people went on like that for years and years.

Ruth raised an eyebrow when she saw him come back with the fresh beer as well as the scotch. To his relief, that was all she did.

Not at all to his relief, Marvin pointed to the letter again. "You know, you never should have got that," he said.

"Daddy!" Olivia could sound indignant where Sarah didn't dare. "Uncle Aaron did a brave thing, catching that Russian."

"I suppose." Marvin sounded as if he didn't believe it for a minute. "But if Truman wasn't a dumb *shmo,* there wouldn't have been any Russians parachuting down into Glendale."

"If pigs had wings, we'd all carry umbrellas." Aaron didn't feel like getting into it with his brother tonight. He lit a cigarette, even though he'd stubbed one out just a few minutes earlier. Tobacco lent a little calm—not a lot, but a little.

Or so people said. Marvin's pipe didn't seem to lend him any. "Truman never should have dropped those A-bombs on Red China," he declared, as if Aaron claimed Truman should have done exactly that. "Stalin couldn't just sit there after he did that. So of course he started dropping bombs of his own."

"You may be right," Aaron said. Ruth blinked—he seldom came even so close to agreeing with his brother. He didn't intend to come that close tonight, either. He went on, "But don't you think it's close to a year too late to *kvetch* about it now? He did what he did, not what he might have done. We have to roll with the punches, not say he shouldn't have thrown that left hook."

"But anybody with the sense God gave a camel could have seen it had to mean trouble." Marvin stuck out his chin. Yes, he was always ready to argue.

"I didn't hear you complaining about it then," Aaron said.

"That's because you weren't listening." Marvin didn't like it when anyone called him on anything. He never had. And he'd skated on thin ice often enough that he'd been called more often than he should have.

"No, it's because you weren't talking—for once," Aaron retorted. His younger brother turned red. Once they got going, they might have been back in their folks' home in Portland during the First World War. The years since then fell away like magic. Aaron added, "Hindsight makes you look smarter now than you did then."

"Geh kak afen yam!" Marvin said furiously. When he—

or Aaron—dropped into Yiddish like that, they were well and truly steamed. "You were an ass then, and you're still an ass now."

"Ass? I'll tell you about ass! *Tukhus* means *ass,* and I'll kick yours for you if you want!"

Both men jumped to their feet. Before they could go for each other, Ruth and Sarah and even Olivia jumped between them. It didn't come to punches. It hadn't for years, even if the potential was always there. Sarah said, "I think we'd better head for home," which would do for an understatement till a bigger one burst like an atom bomb.

Ruth said most of the good-byes. Aaron managed a nod or two. The urge to smash in his brother's capped front teeth ebbed even faster than it had swelled. And the emptiness it left behind made him feel stupid, almost sick.

"The two of you!" Ruth said after Marvin's De Soto purred away. "You ought to be ashamed of yourself."

"I am ashamed of myself—now." Aaron might have been a hung-over drunk mourning his fall from the wagon. "But he always gets my goat."

"You had nothing to do with getting his, of course," his wife said.

"Who, me?" Aaron sounded more innocent than he knew he was. "Marvin gets everybody's goat, though. Did I ever tell you he came to our older brother Sam's wedding in black-face?"

"*Vey iz mir,* no!" Ruth said. "How old was he?"

"Thirteen, maybe fourteen," Aaron answered. "He's always been a piece of work. Sam's wife still hasn't forgiven him, not to this day."

"And you have?" Ruth said—fondly, Aaron hoped. In another week or two, they'd see Marvin again. Things might go pow again, or they might not. How could you know till you knew?

"OH, THAT'S EXCELLENT!" The sister beamed at Daisy Baxter. "We've eaten all of our custard, haven't we?"

Daisy didn't beam back. She glared. "It's bad enough, getting treated like a three-year-old. When people start treating me like *two* three-year-olds, that's a bit much."

"I'm sorry." The sister didn't mean it; Daisy could hear that. Why should she mean it? She hadn't been at Fakenham when the A-bomb leveled the airfield at Sculthorpe next door. She still had all the health she'd been born with. Daisy knew too well the same didn't apply to her.

She was still here to glare at obnoxious, well-meaning fools. Too many people from Fakenham couldn't any more. Some of the women who'd been in the tent with her had their last plot of earth these days, six feet by three feet by six deep.

That she didn't meant she wasn't on the road to recovery. So the overworked doctors assured her whenever they stole a moment to spend on reassurances during the gallop that did duty for their rounds. Sometimes she believed them. At least as often, when she was feeling about as sturdy as the custard she'd just spooned up, she thought wasting away seemed more likely.

Sometimes she felt as if it would be a relief, too. Her hair had fallen out—all of it. It was trying to grow back, but it wasn't trying very hard. She had no appetite and no strength.

The one thing she could say was that she wasn't in a tent any more. As the weather worsened, the survivors from Fakenham who weren't able to return to the outside world got hauled down to East Dereham. This building had been a school. Where the pupils were these days, Daisy had no idea. The classrooms made fair wards. The sisters even used the blackboards to write notes to themselves and to one another.

“I feel like I should be working,” Daisy said fretfully. “I’ve worked hard my whole life. I’m not supposed to be lying on my backside all the time.”

“You don’t lie on your backside all the time.” The sister radiated prim disapproval. “You’d get bedsores if you did. We make sure you turn onto your side and stomach.”

They rotated her like a set of tires, was what they did. Daisy didn’t say that; she knew too well the sister wouldn’t think it was funny. She did say, “You know what I mean.”

“Yes, dear, of course,” the sister answered.

That might have been the most insincere *dear* Daisy had ever heard. She asked, “When will I be well enough to get out of here and do . . . something?” She didn’t know what she’d do, or what she’d be able to do. Did the Owl and Unicorn’s insurance policy cover damage from an atom bomb? If she ever got back on her feet again, she’d have to find out.

“When you are, dear,” the sister said. “You *are* getting better. You’re doing better than some of the other patients I see, not quite so well as others. It’s all a matter of time, and you need to be patient.”

Daisy was impatient with patience, and with being a patient. She put it differently: “I’m sick and tired of being sick and tired all the bloody time.”

“Language,” the sister clucked. “Thank heaven you’re alive, that’s all. So many poor souls from Fakenham aren’t. I pray they’re in a better place now.” Her conversation abruptly switched from the next world back to this one: “Before I go on to the next bed, do you need the bedpan?”

“Not right now, thanks.”

On to the next bed the sister went. The woman there was in worse shape than Daisy. Along with her radiation sickness, she had an arm and a leg encased in plaster. Half her chimney had fallen on her as she was getting out of her smashed house.

“How are we today, dear?” the sister asked her—again, the delusion that her charges were twins.

“I’ll tell you how I am,” she answered. “If one of those stones had dashed out my brains, I wouldn’t be in such pain now. And I wish I weren’t.”

“That’s not a Christian thing to say.”

“I don’t care. See how Christian you feel when you’re all broken in pieces and your poor carcass doesn’t want to fix itself.”

The complaint hit too close to home. Though Daisy didn’t

have all the broken bones the other woman did, her body didn't want to get well. That was the radiation sickness, still poisoning her. Not wanting to think about it, she picked up a Penguin mystery and started reading. The small, light paperback was easy to handle even for her.

Next morning, a different sister watched the room, one who came closer to being a real human being. A messenger stuck his head in, beckoned to her, and whispered something. The sister came back to Daisy's bed with a smile on her well-scrubbed face. "Your Yank is here to see you again."

Daisy nodded. "I'd like to see him. Shame I can't do any proper primping."

"He doesn't seem to mind. I'll let Joe know it's all right." She hurried over to the messenger.

My Yank, Daisy thought. Bruce McNulty was that, sure enough. But now Daisy understood just what he did when he climbed into his B-29. He went out and incinerated cities. He killed people like her neighbors. He left others with radiation sickness, like her. And then he flew back to Britain—not to Sculthorpe any more—and got ready to do it all over again.

And he liked her. He might well love her. She liked him, too, and wondered if she loved him. He made her come alive in a way she hadn't since she found out Tom was dead.

But he did . . . what he did.

All the same, she thought his smile did more for the way she felt than all the doctors' fumblings. "How are they treating you, kiddo?" he said. The lower-middle-class accents she heard all the time carried whiffs of familiarity and mediocrity. His sharp American tones? Those put her in mind of Hollywood. He talked the way people in films did.

"I'm not too bad," she answered, and smiled back as brightly as she could. "They do keep telling me I'm gaining. Every so often, I even think I believe them." *Mostly when I see you* went through her mind. She didn't say that. She didn't want him to think she was throwing herself at him, or would have been if she were in any shape to do it.

"Good. That's good." He had to know all the women in the ward were basking in his health, in his good looks, in his simple ability to walk in and walk out whenever he pleased. He went on, "I did some poking around up in Fakenham."

"How did you get them to let you anywhere near it?" she exclaimed. Soldiers had turned her away before she got close to hammered Norwich.

"Remember what my job is," he said, and his smile stopped reaching his eyes. "I told 'em I wanted a look at what I do on the far side of the Iron Curtain."

"And they said you could?" she asked, astonished.

"They grumbled. They told me I wasn't supposed to worry about stuff like that. Then they kind of looked the other way while I went ahead." He chuckled, not in real amusement, not if Daisy was any judge, but trying to make her feel better. The smile fell off his face altogether. "It was . . . pretty bad. I've seen pictures, but it's not the same as being there. And Fakenham was a miss—a near miss, but a miss. Sculthorpe . . . The sun stomped all over Sculthorpe."

"Now you know," Daisy said.

"Yeah. Now I know." Bruce McNulty's mouth twisted. "Like I said, I did some poking around. I knew about where your place was. I found this. Is it yours? You said your husband was a tankman."

He pulled a photo out of his pocket. It was creased and torn and the worse for rain and weather, but there were Tom and his crewmates grinning in front of their Cromwell. None of them got out when the Germans brewed it up a few weeks later. Tears stung her eyes. "Yes, that's mine. Thanks. I thought it was gone forever."

"Hang on to it, then." He leaned over and kissed her on the cheek. "And hang in there. I'll be back." He nodded. Then he was gone.

"You're wiggling again, Mr. President," the new makeup girl said.

"Well, what do you expect me to do when you keep whacking me in the chops with that stupid powder puff?" Harry Truman said.

That might not have been the only reason he was fidgeting. The girl who'd made him presentable for television before had been cute. This one was drop-dead gorgeous, with a shape to match. He was very married to Bess, but nobody'd ever accused him of being blind. It wasn't fair to imagine such things with a girl almost young enough to be your granddaughter. The only excuse he could find for himself was that most other men who got to his age found themselves with similar imaginings. As long as he didn't do anything about them, he was okay.

And as long as he didn't tell Bess.

"If you hold still, it'll be over sooner," the makeup girl said. Truman did his best. He closed his eyes so he wouldn't have to keep staring at her from close range. It didn't help. His memory was too good. After what seemed like forever but couldn't have been longer than a minute, she told him, "We're all through, sir. Do you want to see?"

"Sure." Truman opened his eyes. The girl held up a mirror so he could admire her handiwork. "Doggone!" he said. "It still looks like me. I thought I'd end up with Clark Gable's mug there."

As soon as the words came out of his mouth, he hoped he hadn't hurt her feelings. She was too pretty for him to want to do that. But she sassed him right back: "The mustache and the ears take a while to grow in."

He threw back his head and laughed. "I bet they do!" Then he had to fight his features back to sobriety. One thing he hadn't expected was going in front of the cameras with a case of the giggles.

That assistant director stuck his head into the dressing room. "Two minutes, Mr. President! You just about ready?"

"You betcha, Eddie," Truman answered, and the makeup girl nodded. Eddie stared at her, too, so Truman wasn't the only one with an active imagination. She took it all in stride. Her manner said she was used to it, and might even be offended if you didn't notice her.

Into the press room Truman went. There were the cameras. There was the lectern, with mikes for TV and for radio as well. Here was the typescript for the speech, in a manila folder in his left hand. He knew what he was going to say. So did Bess, and their daughter Margaret. So did George Marshall and Dean Acheson. The Secretaries of Defense and State needed to be apprised ahead of time.

As far as the President could tell, no one else knew. Well, Marshall wouldn't have told his mother his own name if she hadn't tagged him with it. And Dean Acheson was also pretty good at keeping his mouth shut. People in the press wondered why Truman had asked for radio and television time, but no enterprising reporter had put the substance of his speech in the paper before he could deliver it. In Washington's incestuous world, that was tight security.

He took his place behind the lectern and opened the manila folder. The lectern would hide his turning pages. He looked into the cameras and waited for the red lights to go on. Bit by bit, he was getting used to the rituals of television.

There they were! Most of the United States could see him. In a moment, the whole world would hear him. Maybe his crack about Clark Gable wasn't altogether silly. He had an audience even a movie star would envy.

"Ladies and gentlemen," he said, "I am sorry to have to tell you that the war goes on. Our offer to our foes of peace with the borders in place before North Korea invaded South Korea has been ignored. The United States cannot and will not accept anything less than that.

"Now, some have claimed that I am fighting the war the way I am to make my chances for reelection look better. For a long time, I thought that notion was too stupid for anyone with an ounce of sense, or even for Senator McCarthy, to take seriously. But we are getting close to 1952, and 1952, like it or not, is an election year.

"Since it is, I aim to make my political plans for the coming year as clear as I possibly can. I can do no better than General Sherman did in 1884, and so I will repeat what he had to say: 'I will not accept if nominated and will not serve if elected.' That *is* what he really said. You usually hear it as 'If nominated I will not run; if elected I will not serve.' They mean the same thing.

"And, because I will not run for reelection next year, I am free to carry on the war for freedom as seems best to me until my successor, whoever he may be, takes the oath of office. I do not want my own political career to become an obstacle to victory or to peace. Thank you, and good night."

The red lights went out. No reporters tonight to shout questions. He'd wanted to speak directly to the people who'd sent him back to the White House after he had to set up shop here when Roosevelt died. Now that he'd done it, he felt . . . He tried to decide what he felt.

It was over. That was all there was to it. He'd worked very hard for a very long time. Everyone, without exception, had to step aside sooner or later. Better to do it on your own terms than to get tossed out on your ear. Much better to do it that way than to have the Grim Reaper set the terms for you.

Wasn't it?

Part of him, and not such a small part, wanted to stay in the saddle as long as he could. A very big part of him wanted to stay in the saddle till he mounted Joe Stalin's head on the

Oval Office wall, with Mao's on one side and Kim Il-sung's on the other to keep it company. Well, he still might manage that. He'd be here till January 1953.

If he couldn't do it by then . . . Maybe Uncle Joe would have nailed his head to the Kremlin wall instead. Except there were no Kremlin walls any more. American B-29s had taken care of that.

His press secretary burst into the press room. Joseph Short bore an astonished, goggle-eyed expression, as if someone had slapped him in the chops with a big dead salmon. "You're— You're not going to run?" he choked out.

"Nope. I'm not gonna run." Saying it again made it seem realer to Truman.

"You could have told me," Short said reproachfully. "You should have told me."

"Sorry, Joe." Truman more or less meant it. He would have told Charlie Ross, who'd died the year before. But then, he'd gone to high school with Charlie, while Joe Short was a long-time Washington press-man. Charlie, characteristically, had had a heart attack or a stroke while holding a press conference, and from what the docs said was gone before he hit the floor.

Truman hadn't told Joe Short because he didn't trust him the way he'd trusted poor Charlie. It was that simple. Most of the time, you wanted somebody like him for your press secretary. But a press secretary naturally spent much of his time chinning with the press. Truman wasn't a hundred percent sure Short wouldn't blab, the way he had been with Charlie Ross.

"What will the country do without you?" Short exclaimed.

"The country will do fine. If it did okay after FDR died, it won't miss me even one little bit," Truman said. "I'm not Stalin, thank God, and this isn't Russia. We have a government here, not a dictator."

"That may not last if the Republicans pick McCarthy," Short said.

He'd hit Truman's biggest fear, too, but the President said, "If they're dumb enough to pick him, and if the people are dumb enough to elect him, they almost deserve what happens to them after that. I don't think it'll happen." He didn't tell Short he worried that McCarthy was likelier to beat him than some other Democrat.

"It's the end of an era," the press secretary said.

"Eras end. That's what makes them eras," Truman said. "Pretty damn quick, whoever comes after me will start looking like a dinosaur, too."

As usual, the speaker in Smidovich's sorry little square blared out reports from Radio Moscow. Vasili Yasevich paused to listen. Snow crunched under his felt boots. He'd already seen that it got colder here than it did in Harbin, which was really saying something.

"American President Truman has taken the coward's way out by refusing to stand behind his war of capitalist aggression," Roman Amfiteatrov declared in his cowlike southern accent. "By contrast, the great and beloved Stalin will persevere until victory is won and true Communism established, as the historical dialectic assures us it must be."

Vasili nodded. He wanted to be seen to nod, so people believed he believed all the nonsense that came out of that speaker. Three or four others were also nodding. For the same reason? He wouldn't have been surprised.

Someone set a hand on his shoulder. He spun around, ready for anything. If it was Papanin or one of the pricks who followed him . . . But it wasn't. It was one of the handful of town militiamen. The guy looked startled and alarmed at the speed of Vasili's reaction.

"You're Yasevich, right?" The militiaman's voice shook as he asked the question.

"What if I am?" Vasili answered cautiously. "Who wants to know, and how come?"

"Gleb Sukhanov, that's who." The militiaman straightened his fur cap. The motion seemed to lend him courage. "And he's the one who asks you things. You don't ask him. So come along with me, hey?"

After a long pause, Vasili nodded. "All right." He could have plugged the militiaman with the pistol he'd taken from Grigory Papanin. But then what? He'd have to run off into the taiga. Either they'd catch him or he'd starve. He didn't want anything to do with Sukhanov or any other Chekist, but you didn't always get what you wanted. Sometimes you got what you got, and you had to make the best of it.

The militiaman took him into the log-walled town hall. By himself, the man was nothing. He had the Soviet state behind him, though, and his strut said he knew it.

"Here's the Yasevich item, Comrade," he said to Gleb Sukhanov.

"Thanks." The MGB man eyed Vasili with a more-in-sorrow-than-in-anger air. "What did I tell you when I gave you your replacement documents?"

"You told me to keep my nose clean, Comrade Sukhanov." Vasili made sure he didn't come out with *Gospodin* again. He didn't want to piss off the Chekist. His tone still quiet, he went on, "That's what I've done."

"You say so, but I've heard different," Sukhanov said.

"From who?" A split second later, Vasili saw the answer to what he'd said: "From Grigory Papanin? What kind of lies did that motherfucker tell about me?"

"He said you were a violent hooligan. The way he looks these days doesn't make him seem like a liar."

"You can say that again!" The militiaman eyed Vasili as if he were a Siberian tiger.

"You know what that was about, Comrade?" Vasili said to Sukhanov. "He didn't like it that I work harder than he does. He and his punks tried to shake me down. A little while later, I got him by himself and I made him see that that wasn't such a hot idea."

"I'm not sure he can see anything out of one eye," Gleb Sukhanov murmured. "He's been here for years. Why should I believe somebody the wind blew in with the fallout?"

"Comrade, if Papanin's been in Smidovich for years, then for years you've known what kind of a son of a bitch he is. Am I right or am I wrong?" Vasili knew he was rolling the dice, but he thought the odds were with him. He couldn't imagine Papanin being smart enough to play the choirboy.

Sukhanov pursed his lips and blew air out through them. The militiaman looked up at the roughly trimmed boards of the ceiling. That told Vasili everything he needed to know.

"Well," the Chekist began. Then he stopped, as if he'd come out with a complete sentence. He tried again: "That is . . ." Vasili waited, doing his best to play the respectful subject. At last, the official managed, "His behavior may not always be exemplary, but he is a socially friendly element."

Vasili had been in the Soviet Union long enough to understand what that meant. Papanin was a thief, with connections to other thieves. "I'm no political myself, Comrade!" Vasili said. "I'm not a *zek* at all!"

"Yes, we know that," Gleb Sukhanov replied. "After you . . .

dealt with Papanin, we made inquiries. The corrective-labor system has no record of you."

"You see?" Vasili said happily.

But Sukhanov held up a hand to show he hadn't finished. "As far as I can tell, the Red Army has no record of you, either. Given your age, that seems, well, unusual." He clicked his tongue between his teeth to show how unusual it seemed.

All of a sudden, Vasili wasn't so happy any more. "I served the Soviet Union," he said. "My records would be in Khabarovsk."

"Some of them would. Most of them would, probably. But not all of them," the MGB man said. "A copy of your service record ought to be on file in Moscow." He shrugged. "If it is, they haven't found it."

"Comrade, I don't know what to tell you," Vasili said, fearing anything he did tell Sukhanov would only get him in deeper. He went on, "I've done my part ever since I washed up here after the bomb fell. I haven't had trouble with anybody but that Papanin turd, and he started it."

"So you say, anyhow." Out of the blue, Sukhanov switched to Mandarin almost as fluent as Vasili's: "Do you understand me when I speak this language?"

Vasili was glad he'd wasted time in gambling halls. His face stayed blank in spite of his surprise. "That's Chinese, isn't it?" he said. "Traders would come over the Amur and jabber like that. I learned a little of the stuff they'd yell when they got mad. *You stupid turtle,* that kind of thing." He put on a Russian accent thicker than the Chekist's. Still playing dumb, he added, "It's like *mat,* isn't it?"

"It's not filthy the same way *mat* is. It's filthy a different way." Sukhanov shook his head in annoyance, like a bear batting at a hive when the bees went for his nose and ears. He scowled at Vasili. "You can go. I can't pin anything on you. You aren't wrong—Grigory Papanin is a dick with the gleets. But you haven't got all your cards on the table, either. Not even close."

"Comrade Sukhanov, who but a fool ever puts any more of his cards on the table than he has to?" Vasili was a great many things. Not even the arrogant Chinese had ever accused him of being a fool.

He won a chuckle from the militiaman, who'd been watching him and the Chekist go back and forth like a spectator at a tennis match. "He's got you there, Gleb Ivanovich," the fellow said.

"And who asked you?" Sukhanov snapped.

The militiaman deflated like a balloon in a rose bush. Vasili could practically see the poor guy's balls crawl up into his belly. "Nobody, Comrade. Sorry," he muttered, staring at the spot on the floor between his shoes.

Everywhere you went, there were important people, and then there was everybody else. There sure had been in Harbin. And there were in Smidovich, too, even if someone important here would have been a nobody anywhere else. An MGB man here was one of the people who gave orders. The town militiaman was one of those who had to take them.

Sukhanov's gaze didn't seem so mild and friendly as it had while he was arranging Vasili's documents. "Yes, you can go," he said. "But I've got my eye on you now."

Vasili and the militiaman left together. Which was less happy with the world would have been hard to say. Vasili was unhappy with one part of the world in particular: the part named Grigory Papanin.

Luisa Hozzel and Trudl Bachman worked a two-man—well, here a two-woman—saw. Back and forth, back and forth. Sooner or later, the damned pine would fall. Luisa hoped it fell sooner. Camp work norms stayed the same no matter how hard it snowed.

And it snowed . . . more than Luisa had imagined it could snow anywhere. The camp lay at somewhere not far from the same latitude as Fulda. The days here had grown shorter about the same way they did in the town where she'd lived her whole life till the Russians grabbed her.

To her way of thinking, that meant the camp should have had the same kind of weather as Fulda. And it had, during the summer. It got about as hot as Fulda ever did, and about as muggy. There were more mosquitoes here in the course of a day than Fulda saw in a hundred years, but mosquitoes weren't *exactly* a part of the weather.

The trouble was, summer here didn't last. Snow started in October, and kept piling up and piling up. Luisa was convinced this was how the last Ice Age must have started.

As she learned more Russian, and as the woman prisoners from the USSR picked up scraps of German, she got to indulge in the ancient human pleasure of complaining about the weather. Almost without exception, the Russians and other Soviet folk thought that was hysterically funny. Some of them came from places with climates worse than this. All of them knew of such places.

"You hear of Kolyma?" one of the bitches asked in a mish-mash of Russian and German.

Luisa'd shaken her head. "What Kolyma? Where Kolyma?"

The woman—her name was Nadezhda Chukovskaya—pointed north. "On edge of Arctic Ocean. Lots of camps around Kolyma. All bad, some worser, some worstest. In winter, you know what they give you for punishment for not making norms?"

"Chto?" Luisa asked. *What?* was a handy question in any language.

"They put you in tent without heat." The bitch mimed shivering. She was a pretty good mime—and she glanced at Luisa sidelong, to see the impression she was making. Luisa ignored that, wondering how much colder it would be up there than it was here.

"How do you keep from freezing?" She couldn't imagine any way.

"Chekists kind people," Nadezhda said. "They let you run around tent to stay warm. They don't shoot you for doing."

What really alarmed Luisa about that was how the Russian woman sounded as if she meant it. As far as she was concerned, the camp guards might have put people in those tents without giving them any chance at all not to die. *Why not?* Luisa thought. *Hitler's men did such things. Everyone knew it, even if nobody talked about it.*

When the tree she and Trudl were felling started to sway, snow fell off a branch and hit her in the face. Brushing it out of her mouth and nose and eyes, she shouted, *"Yob tvoyu mat'!"*

Snow fell near Trudl, too, but didn't get her the way it got Luisa. Gustav's boss' wife clucked. "Going native, are you?" she asked in German.

"It doesn't seem quite so bad in Russian," Luisa said sheepishly.

"I don't know. If you ask me, it's worse," Trudl Bachman said. "All the Russians swear like sailors or whores. They swear so much, they don't even notice they're doing it. It's nothing but the foulest language every minute of every day."

It wasn't as if she were wrong. Luisa had noticed the same thing. You couldn't very well not notice it. She said, "I think it's like it was in the Weimar inflation, when you needed a wheelbarrow full of marks to buy a paper or a can of beans."

Trudl frowned. "What do you mean? I don't follow." Neither one of them stopped working as they talked, though they did slow down. The pine would crash to the ground soon enough to keep the guard quiet either way.

"When one mark isn't worth anything, you need a stack of marks to get something," Luisa said. "When you swear all the time, one cuss word doesn't mean anything. You've got to string a bunch of them together to let off any steam at all."

"Oh. Now I get you," Trudl said. "Yes, you may be right. My Aunt Käthe was one of those people who went to church every Sunday and tithed for the poor and that kind of thing. The hardest word I ever heard her say was 'Shucks,' and she only said that a couple of times. But she got more from it when she did than Max would if he cussed for a week."

"There you are." Luisa nodded. "And here we are, too." The tree tottered and started to come down. Both women shouted warnings to the others in the work gang and skipped out of the way. The pine dropped within a meter or so of where Luisa'd thought it would, kicking up a flying white veil of snow. Not without a certain pride, Luisa said, "We're getting good at this."

"We are, *ja,*" Trudl said as a hooded crow flapped away cawing in fright. "For as long as we live, though, is this all the Russians will let us get good at?"

Luisa had no answer to that. She couldn't imagine any *zek* who did have an answer to it. If they made you do something over and over and over again, you could hardly help getting good at it. Practice would make you good whether you wanted it to or not.

And then you starve to death, and they throw you into a hole in the ground, and some other poor soul gets good at whatever it was you used to do, she thought.

Trudl's mind wend down a different track, or perhaps not so different after all. "I think I'd kiss a pig to keep from going out here every day. This is death, nothing else."

"If that's how you feel, Lord knows you've got plenty of pigs to choose from," Luisa said tartly.

As if to prove her point, one of the guards ambled over to the downed tree. He had a flat, Asiatic face, and didn't speak a whole lot of Russian himself. What he did speak was even more full of obscenity than most people's here. "You knock that fucker over, hey?"

"Da." Luisa was still proud of how precisely the pine had fallen.

"Khorosho." The guard hefted his submachine gun. "Now you cunts trim that prick. Got work norm to meet. Get your ugly asses walloped, you no meet him."

"Da," Luisa said again, this time on a lower note. How could you take pride in what you did if the people you did it for, the people who made you do it, wouldn't let you?

She and Trudl went to work with one-man saws and hatchets, hacking the branches off the trunk. Then they cut the trunk into chunks small enough for two people to haul them. Luisa stopped caring how cold it was. She worked up a sweat under her quilted jacket and trousers. She'd be chilled and clammy when she eased up, but she couldn't do anything about that now.

There was less than half as much daylight at this season as there was in high summer. The sadistic oafs who set norms did take that into account. Even if they couldn't tell the difference between men and women, they could understand that guards had trouble stopping escapes if *zeks* disappeared into the darkness. As twilight lowered like a candle-snuffer, the work gang trudged through the snow back to the encampment.

Evening lineup was the usual botch. Luisa stood there and stood there, getting hungrier and hungrier, while the guards shouted at the *zeks* and at one another. At last they decided no one had run away. Supper was a stew of cabbage and salt fish and a brick of black bread. Luisa had had worse. She wouldn't have believed that was possible when she first got here, but she knew better now. As in all things, there were degrees of misery.

There certainly were degrees of exhaustion. When Luisa tumbled into slumber, she hoped she wouldn't come out.

"RAIN, RAIN, RAIN!" Leon said happily from the back seat.

"Well, kiddo-shmiddo, you got that right." Aaron Finch was less delighted than his son. He was driving, and Leon wasn't. He was also more than two and a half. Rain to him wasn't something exciting. It was a nuisance, and a dangerous nuisance at that.

It drummed down on the roof of the newly acquired Chevy and splashed from the windows and windshield. The Chevy's wipers were lazier than Aaron would have liked. He hadn't checked that when he bought the car, and grumbled to himself for not thinking of it. *Next time,* he told himself. *When I buy my Rolls.* That was ridiculous enough for him to stop giving himself a hard time.

The traffic light ahead changed. "It's red, dear," Ruth said.

"I know, dear," Aaron said with heavy patience. He hit the brake. On the other side of the transmission hump, Ruth's foot pressed down on an imaginary brake pedal. He thought that was funny . . . up to a point. As the Chevy smoothly stopped—he had checked the brakes—he glanced over at her and added, "This car drives from the left front seat only."

"I'm not a backseat driver," his wife said.

"Only 'cause you're sitting in the front seat with me," he answered. She made a face at him. He laughed. She didn't drive at all, but she thought she could tell him how to do it. This wasn't the first time he'd trotted out his left-front-seat maxim—nowhere close.

Anybody else who did that kind of thing would have driven him straight up the wall. That he could laugh about it when Ruth did it showed how much in love he was. Either that or it showed how many of his marbles had already dribbled out his ears. Senility didn't run in his family, but maybe he'd prove an exception.

He put the car in gear just as Ruth opened her mouth to go, *It's green.* She closed it again. If he called her on that one, she'd deny everything. Well, he would have denied it, too, if she tried to gig him for something he hadn't actually said.

After a moment, she did speak up again: "I'm glad you're burying the hatchet with Marvin."

"You mean, and not in Marvin?" he asked, about three-quarters kidding. The remaining quarter was enough to make her look worried, or maybe scared. He took a hand off the wheel and waggled it to let her know she could relax. "I won't start anything if he doesn't, promise."

"Okay." She sounded relieved. If she knew one thing about her husband, she knew he kept his promises.

He was trying to get Leon to be as serious about them as he was. So far, the results were mixed. He kept reminding himself Leon was just a little kid. Not many his age were smarter, but his age wasn't very big. He was still working out where his imagination stopped and the real world started.

Up into the hills Aaron drove. The way it looked to him, Marvin was still working out the same thing. The difference was, Aaron's brother didn't have the excuse of being a toddler.

When they got to Marvin's house, Aaron and Ruth both popped open umbrellas. Leon paid no attention, but started to charge up the walk on his own. Then he discovered that raindrops were more fun when they were on the outside of something and you were on the inside. He came charging back to Daddy and Mommy and the shelter of their bumbershoots.

Aaron knocked on the front door. His brother opened it. "Look what washed up on our shore," Marvin said. "Nice weather for ducks, hey?"

"Yeah, it's not all it's quacked up to be," Aaron said. Marvin sent him a reproachful look. So did Ruth. She'd known Finches made bad puns before she met him, but she hadn't known how bad they could get.

Marvin stuck the umbrellas in a brass boot. He was the kind of person who put a brass boot in the front hall in case of umbrellas. "Come on in," he said, gesturing toward the living room. In Aaron and Ruth and Leon came.

"Surprise!" everybody yelled. Actually, Caesar the German

shepherd barked, but he barked twice, so even that worked out.

There were Sarah and Olivia and Sarah's mother, who lived with them. There were Ruth's two brothers, Chaim and Ben—alike as two balding peas in a pod, except one was thin and the other chunky—and her sister Bernice, all in from the wilds of Reseda in the Valley. Bernice looked the way Ruth would have if she dyed her hair red and weren't so pretty. There were Roxane and Howard and Roxane's mother, Fanny Seraph. And there was Herschel Weissman, a martini in his hand.

Everybody but Caesar started singing "Happy Birthday." By the way Ruth joined in, Aaron knew she'd been part of the plot. His actual birthday had been the Sunday before. Ruth had fixed a big mess of chicken *pippiks* and hearts, which he loved. And she'd got him a copy of *The Caine Mutiny.* He really wanted to read that one. He hadn't been a Navy man, but he'd seen shipboard action himself. He'd figured that was as much of a celebration as he'd get. It was as much as he wanted. But he'd figured wrong.

"Happy fiftieth, you *alter kacker,*" Marvin said, clapping him on the back.

"Good God!" Aaron said. "I think the last time I had a birthday party, I was turning nine." Everyone laughed.

Bernice kissed him on the cheek. Her breath smelled of whiskey. It often did. Aaron thought she was holding the bottle and not the other way around, but he wasn't sure. She sold shoes at a store on Sherman Way, the Valley's main drag. Chaim wrote bulletins and manuals at the General Motors plant in Van Nuys. Ben . . . Ben had come back from the South Pacific with malaria, and maybe with combat fatigue, too. He was bright, but he was also damaged. He had trouble finding a job and more trouble holding one.

People pressed presents on Aaron. He found himself awash in booze, which was nice, and in ties, which he could have lived without. No way in hell he would ever wear the gaudy one Howard Bauman gave him—he thought blue dress shirts were loud. He made grateful noises, anyway.

Dinner was an enormous ham with candied yams—they were Sarah's specialty. Marvin raised a glass. "Here's to *treyf*!" he said. Almost all the Jews at the table drank. Leon didn't, but his only drinking was a taste of Manischewitz at Passover. He ate ham and yams with great enthusiasm. And neither did Fanny Seraph, who clung to Old Country ways. There was chicken for her.

Two apple pies served as dessert. When Sarah's mother brought them out of the kitchen, Aaron said, "What will the rest of you eat?" He got another laugh.

After dinner, the talk turned to politics. Everybody had an idea about who would run for the Democrats now that Truman had bowed out. Roxane and Howard, predictably, liked Hubert Humphrey, who stood farthest to the left. So did Sarah and Ben. Marvin was for Averell Harriman, and seemed offended that his wife dared have an opinion of her own. Aaron and Ruth and Bernice and Chaim spoke up for Adlai Stevenson.

"I'd like to like him," Herschel Weissman said. "I *do* like him—as a man. But he's not in touch with the people. He thinks too much. He doesn't feel enough. He'd make a better professor than a President."

That was more sensible than Aaron wished it were. Not caring to argue with his boss, he said, "Any of them would be okay. The real question is, Who will the Republicans run against our guy?"

"Before the war started, I would have bet on Taft or Eisenhower," Weissman said. "Now . . . Now that McCarthy *mamzer* is making so much noise, he may grab it in spite of everything. Everything sane, I mean."

"God forbid!" Aaron exclaimed, at the same time as his wife said the same thing in Yiddish.

"He's a Nazi," Roxane said. Howard nodded vigorously. He would, having made the acquaintance of the Un-American Activities Committee. But Aaron had trouble arguing with his wife's cousin himself.

"*Alevai* it won't happen!" Chaim said.

"Alevai omayn!" half a dozen people chorused.

"Alevai omayn!" Leon echoed. Sometimes you were lucky, not having any idea of what was going on.

"Here you go, Comrade Captain," the Hungarian secret policeman said in German, the only tongue he shared with Boris Gribkov. "Drink this. It will put hair on your chest."

This was a tumbler of strong red wine. Gribkov had never been much of a wine drinker. He chose beer for a little buzz, vodka when he was serious about pouring it down. Declining here, though, didn't seem like a good idea, so he drank.

"Very tasty," he said, putting the tumbler down half-empty. "Yes, very tasty." His German wasn't as good as the Hungarian's. "What do you call it?"

"That, my friend, that is the famous Bull's Blood of Eger," the secret policeman replied. "It is a wine to send men roaring into battle. Then, after they have won the victory, they celebrate with sweet Tokay."

When the Red Army wanted to send men roaring into battle, it fed them a hundred grams of vodka. That did the trick just fine, as any number of dead Germans—and Hungarians—might have testified. More vodka helped men descend from the peak of fighting madness.

Again, Boris kept his thoughts to himself. He took another swig of Bull's Blood and said, "I thank you and your countrymen for your kindness."

"It is our pleasure. It is our privilege," the secret policeman said. His name was Geza Latos or Latos Geza; Gribkov wasn't sure which. The Hungarians seemed to put surname first, which struck him as an odd thing to do. The man went on, "The Slovaks deserve everything you can drop on their heads. They're nothing but rubes with shit on their boots, and we don't want their trouble spilling over into the Hungarian People's Republic."

He talked about the Slovaks as a Russian would have talked about Uzbeks or Kazakhs. Socialist solidarity seemed moderately thin on the ground here. Gribkov drained the tumbler. The wine wasn't vodka, but you could feel it when you drank enough. With a lopsided grin, the pilot said, "Instead, you got me spilling over into your country."

"I'm just glad the militiamen found you before . . . anyone else did," said Geza Latos or Latos Geza.

"So am I," Boris said. Some of the troubles he'd tried to bomb away in Bratislava plainly *had* spilled over into northwestern Hungary. The secret policeman's comment wasn't what brought them to the Russian's notice. The way the militiamen kept close together, as if against a hostile world, and pointed their machine pistols every which way spoke volumes about how nervous they were.

"Traitors. Traitors and Fascists. We're hunting them down. When we catch them, they're sorry they ever had anything to do with the decadent, reactionary West." The secret policeman poured Gribkov's tumbler full again. This time, he poured wine for himself, too. He raised his glass. "To the triumph of the world proletarian revolution!" He drank.

So did Boris. No Soviet fighting man could possibly fail to drink that toast. As he savored the Bull's Blood, the Russian eyed the secret policeman. The Hungarian seemed more zealous than most Soviet Communists Gribkov knew. Maybe he had to be. Hungary was newly Marxist-Leninist-Stalinist. If you weren't a zealot here, people were liable to take you for a backslider.

Gribkov's head started to buzz. The wine wasn't so strong as vodka, of course, but drink enough and you'd know it was there, all right. As inconspicuously as he could, he touched the tip of his nose. It was numb. That was a sure sign he was on his way to getting smashed.

He had to work harder to remember German. "How will I go back to the Soviet Union?" he asked, knowing he made a hash of the verb and the syntax. Well, Geza Latos or Latos Geza or whatever the hell his name was didn't talk exactly like a Fritz, either. He had his own funny accent and turns of phrase.

"We've notified the Soviet embassy and the Soviet occupying forces that we recovered you," the Magyar answered. "They are sending a convoy to bring you to the airport outside of Budapest. As far as I know, nothing has gone wrong with the convoy. It should come here to Magyarovar quite soon."

"I see." Boris wondered if he did. Magyarovar lay in the far northwest of Hungary, where a chunk of it stuck up between Austria and Czechoslovakia. "Why do they need a convoy? Wouldn't a car do? Aren't the roads safe?"

The secret policeman stared down into his half-empty glass of Bull's Blood as if the crimson liquid held the secrets of the universe. After a long hesitation, he said, "Not . . . perfectly. Because of your value, Comrade Pilot, your countrymen don't wish to take any chances with you. As I say, some trouble has spilled into the Hungarian People's Republic from Slovakia. They want to be sure they can frighten off or beat back any bandits they may meet."

"I see," Gribkov said again. What he saw was anti-Soviet rebellion in Hungary as well as Czechoslovakia. Was there more in Poland? He wouldn't have been surprised. Poles and Russians had always fought like cats and dogs. The Russian dog was bigger, so it won most of the brawls, but not without picking up scratches on its nose and ears.

"We will triumph in the end. True Communism will arrive. The dialectic shows how inevitable that is," said Geza Latos or Latos Geza. He was about forty, with narrow green eyes and a cleft chin. Not quite idly, Boris wondered what he'd done and which slogans he'd mouthed during the last war.

It didn't matter, really. As long as his bosses were happy with the man, Boris couldn't complain. When you gave a country a whole new government, as the USSR had done all over Eastern and Central Europe, you used the tools that came to hand. You couldn't do anything else. The ones who hadn't been true believers before the Red Army thundered in were at least smart enough to see which side of their bread held the butter.

The convoy didn't come when the secret policeman thought it would. He tried to telephone Budapest, but had trouble getting through. "I'm sorry," he told Gribkov. "It can't be helped."

"Nichevo," Boris replied, which meant the same thing in Russian.

They gave him a bowl of pork stewed in cream and peppers hot enough to make sweat burst out on his forehead. To cool his scorched mouth, they gave him more Bull's Blood, enough so he stopped caring about the convoy.

It was dark by the time his escort did reach Magyarovar. Boris blinked when he saw it: it consisted of four tanks shepherding a BTR-152 armored personnel carrier. The tanks were only T-34/85s, but even so. . . .

"Sorry we took so long, sir," said the first lieutenant in charge of things. "We lost one tank to a mine in the roadway."

"Bozehmoi!" Gribkov wondered how much lethal hardware left over from the last war was squirreled away here and there in countries like this. He also wondered who was taking it out of the hoards and using it against the USSR now that his country had bigger worries.

They loaded him into the armored personnel carrier and headed east, toward Budapest. Unlike the tanks, the BTR-152 was new. Though the Germans and Americans had, the Red Army hadn't fielded a vehicle of this class in the last war. They'd made up for it since. The rear compartment could hold seventeen soldiers. Gribkov had it all to himself. He realized that his superiors really must have believed him valuable to the *rodina*.

An hour and a half out of Magyarovar, several bullets clattered off the BTR-152's armor. Boris almost jumped out of his skin. He jumped again when the carrier's machine gun fired back. One of the tanks' cannons thundered. The convoy didn't stop, or even slow.

That was the sole trouble they had on the way to Budapest. Gribkov saw only the stretch of ground between the personnel carrier and the Li-2 (a Soviet copy of the DC-3) that waited for him at the airfield. The plane took off, flying east. The little Boris *had* seen of Hungary was . . . interesting.

The POW camp where they stashed Istvan Szolovits was not far outside of Lyon. It held captured soldiers from Hungary, Poland, Czechoslovakia, and East Germany, plus a few Bulgarians and Romanians who had trouble talking with anybody else.

A colonel named Bela Medgyessy was the senior Hungarian officer in the camp. "Ah," he said when they brought Istvan to him. As such things went, that was polite, but Istvan understood what it meant. *Here's a damned Jew.* The colonel didn't look like an old-fashioned Magyar aristocrat; he looked like a plumber. But he had the same prejudices as the men the new Communist regime had purged.

"Here I am, sir," Istvan said resignedly. The soldiers who'd captured him had treated him better than his alleged countrymen were in the habit of doing.

"Here you are, yes." Medgyessy showed a little more distaste than one of those smooth aristos would have, but only a little. "Since you're here, tell me where you were and what you were doing when they caught you."

"Yes, sir." Istvan did, finishing, "They took me for a Russian at first, the stupid clodhoppers."

No Magyar would have taken kindly to that. Of course, in Bela Medgyessy's eyes a Hungarian Jew *was* no Magyar. The colonel looked him over. "You're good-sized, anyhow. Do you play football?"

"Oh, yes, sir," Istvan answered at once.

"A back, I'd guess," Medgyessy said, and he was a good guesser. Istvan wasn't quick or nimble enough for midfield or forward, but he wasn't afraid to bang in the penalty area, either. The officer went on, "We've got a league going with the Czechs and the Fritzes and the Polacks. We'll see what you can do."

"That should be, uh, interesting, sir." Istvan wondered whether he'd got into a fiercer war than the one he'd got out of. Magyars and Czechs got along like water and sodium. Magyars and Poles weren't a match made in heaven, either.

"They used to keep Russians here, too," Medgyessy said. "They had to put them in a camp of their own. Too many fracases with everybody else."

"Fraternal socialist allies united against the capitalist world," Istvan said dryly.

"That's right. They aren't far away, though. And the International Red Cross has officially notified the Soviet Union that the two camps are very close." The colonel paused expectantly.

Back before Istvan was conscripted, his trig teacher had had a mannerism like that when he was waiting to see whether the class got it. And, like a flash of lightning, Istvan did: "If we're close to the Russians, they won't drop an atom bomb around here!"

Bela Medgyessy eyed him with the same fond contempt he'd known from Sergeant Gergely. It was as close as Magyars of a certain stripe could come to liking people like him. "You *are* a smart Jewboy," the officer murmured.

What did he expect? All over Eastern Europe, stupid Jews had been weeded out for centuries. Darwin could have used them to illustrate natural selection. Medgyessy was waiting. Istvan managed to murmur, "Thanks—uh, sir."

The colonel took the deference as if he were an old-time aristocrat, too. "Go on and find yourself a bunk. Chow call pretty soon. The food's shitty, but there's plenty of it."

Istvan found a bunk. The mattress was thicker and the blanket warmer and softer than the ones he'd used in basic training. But as soon as he looked at the blond guy across from him, he knew he'd found the wrong bunk. The Magyar was in his late twenties, with a scar on one cheek. He had an Arrow Cross tattooed on the back of his right hand and a Turul, a legendary bird of prey also beloved of Hungarian Fascists, on the back of his left. The Hungarian People's Army had issued him a rifle anyway, probably because the recruiters knew an attack dog when they saw one.

He was looking at Istvan, too. He didn't need long to add up what he saw. "Are you what I think you are?" he growled.

"Me? No, I'm a plate of stuffed cabbage," Istvan answered. In the middle of the sentence, he threw himself at the tough guy. This fight *was* going to happen. He'd had plenty of brawls like this before. Better to get it over with now, and to enjoy the advantage of a tiny bit of surprise.

It wasn't pretty. It wasn't stylish. The bastard with the Fascist tattoos was no coward. During the fight for Budapest, Istvan had seen that being a Fascist son of a bitch and being brave had nothing to do with each other. For that matter, there were plenty of Communist sons of bitches, too, and not all of them were cowards, either.

Pretty soon, Istvan couldn't see out of his left eye. He tried to gouge out the Arrow Cross man's right eye. The guy jerked his head away and did his best to bite off Istvan's thumb. It was that kind of fight.

Fittingly for that kind of fight, it ended when Istvan brought up his knee, as hard as he could, into the blond guy's crotch. The Fascist let out a shriek and folded up like a concertina. Istvan gave him a right and a left that made his nose lean to one side and fountain blood.

Then, painfully, he climbed to his feet. He booted the Arrow Cross POW in the ribs. "Well, you stinking sack of shit, am I what you think I am?" he choked out. His cut tongue found a broken front tooth. For that, he kicked the Magyar again.

Like him, the man with the tattoos could see out of only one eye. He peered blearily up at Istvan. "You're a kike, all right," he said in a thick voice—his mouth had taken damage, too. "But you're sure as hell one motherfucking tough kike."

Istvan glanced at the other Hungarian prisoners, who'd gathered to watch the free entertainment. Battered as he was, any one of them could have knocked him to pieces without breathing hard. If they mobbed him, he was dead.

One of them, a lance-corporal, nodded to him. "Miklos is right—you *are* a tough Jew," the man said. "He should've found out sooner."

"Does everybody get this kind of hello?" Istvan asked. He spat blood on the floor near Miklos, but not on him. The Arrow Cross man wasn't close to trying to stand yet.

The lance-corporal shrugged. "Some people do, some people don't. Miklos must've thought he needed to see if you could take care of yourself. Well, you gave him the old horse's cock up the ass."

A thousand years after the Magyars had settled in Hungary, their curses still showed that their ancestors once roamed the steppe as mounted warriors. *My ancestors roamed the desert even longer ago,* Istvan thought. He didn't know any Hebrew curses, though. He hardly knew any Hebrew at all. His family had been secular, not that the Nazis and their Arrow Cross stooges gave a damn.

When he went to the kitchen to get lunch, he wondered whether the guards—he thought they were French, though they wore mostly U.S.–style gear—would notice his battered face. If they did, they didn't care. They ignored Miklos, too, and he was even more banged up. Their attitude was, whatever the POWs did to each other was their own business as long as it didn't involve firearms.

With his broken tooth and a wounded tongue, chewing hurt. The food came from American ration packs. Colonel Medgyessy had it right: none of it was anything a Hungarian really wanted to eat. But it did fill you up. Istvan had been hungry all the time as a conscript in training. He'd guessed a prisoner of war would have it even worse. Evidently not. The USA was so rich, it fed POWs better than his country fed its soldiers. How did the Hungarian People's Republic—or Russia, for that matter—hope to win against such wealth and production?

Vasili Yasevich looked at the old Jew. "Yes, that's opium, all right." It was more than a hundred grams of opium, in fact. "Are you sure you want to get rid of it, David Samuelovich?" He couldn't imagine anyone who used opium wanting to sell any. If you sold it, you couldn't smoke it or eat it yourself.

But David Samuelovich Berman nodded. "I have no use for it," he answered. "I bought it for Natasha when she was sick and in a lot of pain. It eased her better than anything else I could give her. But now she's gone, so"—he spread his mittened hands—"I'll get rid of what's left."

"I'm sorry," Vasili said. He wore mittens, too, and a padded jacket and trousers, and a rabbit-fur cap with the earflaps down. Their breath smoked. It was almost as cold inside Berman's little log hut as it was outside. It also looked as if he hadn't cleaned in there for a long time. With Natasha—

who must have been his wife—dead, he must have stopped caring about himself, too.

"So am I. She was . . ." Berman paused to think. "She was everything, is what she was." After a moment, he seemed to recall why Vasili was there. "So what will you give me for the drug?"

"Two rubles a gram?" Vasili said tentatively. He still wasn't sure about prices here. In Harbin, he would have known just what to pay, only he would have been afraid to pay it. Opium was illegal in Smidovich, too, but they wouldn't shoot you for having some. This kind of chance, he was willing to take.

David Berman eyed him in surprise. At first, Vasili thought he'd been too low. He knew he could come up. But then the skinny man with the scraggly white beard murmured, "That's more than I paid for it."

"You'll never make a haggler," Vasili said.

"Shows what you know, pup," the Jew replied. "But this, this I just want to get rid of. It reminds me of the bad times. So two rubles a gram is fine. I might have given it to you for nothing if you'd sung me a sad song."

"Believe me, you don't want to hear me sing." Vasili had the small satisfaction of making David Berman smile. He took three hundred-ruble notes from his jacket pocket. Each bore Lenin's fierce, scowling face on one side and the onion domes of the A-bombed Kremlin on the other.

"It's too much. I'll give you fifty back." Berman started to dig into his own pocket.

"Don't worry about it," Vasili told him. "You need the cash worse than I do. Buy yourself something good to eat or some nice vodka."

"I'm cheating you," Berman said fretfully. "That's not why I asked you to stop by. I heard you bought and sold things and didn't steal too much, and so. . . ."

"And so," Vasili agreed. "I'm not stealing from you, either, and you aren't cheating me. Go on, take the cabbage, for God's sake!" He wished he could tell Berman to spend some on a pretty girl who'd make him forget his troubles for a little while. But he could tell the old man wouldn't listen to him if he did.

He put the opium in the pocket from which he'd taken the money. Little by little, he was adding apothecary to carpenter and bricklayer and odd-job man. As David Berman knew, poppy juice was good for more than keeping addicts happy. It cut pain where nothing else would: a blessing in this world if ever there was one.

It occurred to Vasili that Marx hadn't been joking when he called religion the opiate of the masses. Like opium, religion gave solace and took pain away. And not everybody could afford opium.

Wind bit his nose as soon as he stepped outside. His *valenki* sank into the soft, newly fallen snow. Walking was awkward, almost as if he were slogging through mud.

Slog he did, as did the others who lived in Smidovich. A few of them had snowshoes, and moved awkwardly in a different way. Everyone seemed resigned to the weather. It wasn't as if people came to Siberia from the Riviera. If they weren't born here, then, like Vasili, they already knew all they needed to know about hard winters. He lowered his head and turned away from the wind. It didn't help much, but it might have done a little.

A woman came by with a wool scarf wrapped around her face so only her eyes showed. That was a good idea. Vasili had a wool scarf—who didn't? He'd have to try her trick himself.

And there was Grigory Papanin. His smashed nose left him instantly recognizable. He moved with hunched-over care; he still wasn't back to the swaggering cock-o'-the-walk he'd been before he made the mistake of messing with Vasili.

In the snowy cold, with everyone bundled up, he didn't see that he was nearing his nemesis till they almost bumped into each other. His eyes widened a little. If that wasn't from fear, Vasili had never seen it. Papanin owned some new reasons to fear him, as a matter of fact.

"Don't just clump on by, smegma-lips," Vasili said. "I need to talk to you."

Papanin's eyes went wide again. "I don't want to talk to you," he mumbled.

"I bet you don't," Vasili said. "Who tried to sell me to the Chekists? Was that a piece of shit who smelled like you?"

"I don't know what you're talking about."

"Fuck your mother in the mouth if you don't. They told me it was you."

That brought Papanin up short. "They . . . told you?" he said, something not far from existential despair in his voice.

"Sure they did. Why wouldn't they?" Vasili realized he'd struck a nerve. Like a dentist doing a root canal, he probed deeper: "You never did figure out what you were screwing with, did you? You aren't just ugly. You're stupid to go with it. If I have to have anything to do with you again, bet your balls it's the last time you'll be sorry."

"I didn't know you were—" Papanin broke off. He couldn't make himself come out with it.

"I never said I was." Vasili made sure he said that. He might imply he belonged to the MGB, but if he just went and claimed it they'd land on him with hobnailed jackboots as soon as they found out. "But do you want to have another go like the last one? We can take care of that right now."

A younger, more innocent Papanin would have sailed into a fight without a thought in his thick head. A man who'd already taken one bad beating, though, wasn't so anxious to risk another. Papanin seemed to shrink into himself. "Just leave me the fuck alone, why don't you?" he whined.

"This time, cunt. Not the next." Vasili went on his way. He didn't look back. Had Papanin had the nerve, he could have jumped him. Vasili had got him that way.

All he did was mooch off through the blowing snow. He knew he was facing a beast meaner than himself. Vasili hadn't thought of himself that way in China. There, he'd been an ordinary fellow getting along as best he could. He'd looked funny, but he'd known how things worked.

Here in Smidovich, he looked ordinary. But he still felt much more out of place than he ever had in Harbin. If he worked hard, these people suspected him. How was anybody supposed to guess that might happen? Why would anybody sneer at someone who tried to get ahead?

For a moment, he thought the question had no possible answer. Then he realized that, in Soviet terms, it did. Working hard for your own benefit was un-Communistic. Stalin and his henchmen wanted people to work hard for the state, to be what they called Stakhanovites and shock workers. The state and the state alone deserved such slavish devotion . . . or so you thought if you were Stalin or one of his henchmen.

Peasants who worked hard for themselves and didn't want to give up to the state what they produced were called kulaks. Stalin had liquidated them when Vasili was still a kid. Reports leaked out of the USSR and into northern China. A few refugees got out. Their tales didn't shrink in the telling.

And was the Soviet Union better off for the way it operated? Looking around Smidovich, Vasili had a hard time seeing how.

THE MORE CADE CURTIS saw of Captain Pak Hosan, the less he liked him. True, the ROK officer wasn't a bugout artist. Since too many of his countrymen were, that counted for something. In every other way, though, Pak made Cade wonder why the United States wanted anything to do with a country that produced the likes of him.

He vented his spleen with Howard Sturgis. "It's the Lord's own miracle one of those Korean privates doesn't toss a grenade onto his sleeping bag. What happens to those sorry SOBs is a shame and a disgrace. The sergeants beat on 'em like drums, and old Pak, he just watches and smiles. What kind of noncoms are those? What kind of officer is he?"

"Japanese," Lieutenant Sturgis said. "Remember, I told you that the day the ROK, uh, guys"—he didn't quite say *gooks*—"came into the line."

"Shit, that's right," Cade said. "You did."

"Uh-huh." Sturgis nodded. "Remember, the Japs ran the show here for forty years. Assholes like Pak, when they saw soldiers, what kind of soldiers did they see? They saw the fuckin' Japs. And the way the Japs treated their enlisted men, if I did that to a dog, the SPCA'd take him away from me."

"Yeah," Cade said thoughtfully, and then, "I didn't know they let Koreans be real soldiers."

"That's right—labor gangs were pretty much it," Sturgis said. "I don't think there were any Korean officers, just noncoms. But we were an English colony, and our army still does a lot of things the way England did. Korea was a Japanese colony. Who were the Koreans gonna copy?"

That made more sense than anything Cade had thought of on his own. All the same, he said, "We don't do that kind of crap, and we beat the hell out of the Japs. Next time I see Pak or anybody under him knocking some poor damned draftee around, I'm not gonna put up with it."

"You'll piss off the brass if you mess with our allies," Sturgis warned.

Cade threw back his head and guffawed. "What's the worst thing they can do to me? They can put me in the line in Korea! I'm already in the line in goddamn Korea. Why should I worry?"

"They can bust your ass down to private if they feel like it."

"Big deal. I'd be a private in the line in Korea."

"Okay, sir." By Howard Sturgis' tone of voice, it wasn't. Sure enough, he added, "Don't say I didn't warn you."

Once Cade made up his mind and decided to do something about the way Captain Pak and the men he led treated the ordinary South Korean soldiers, he figured he wouldn't have long to wait before they gave him a gold-plated chance. He wasn't wrong, either. The very next day, Pak Ho-san screamed at a private for having mud on his uniform. The whole trench was muddy. When it wasn't, that was because the mud had frozen or was covered in snow. Cade didn't speak Korean, but the way the captain kept jabbing at the spot on the poor private's tunic with his index finger left him in no doubt about what was going on. Then Pak smacked the private across the face, hard enough to draw blood at the corner of his mouth.

Cade squelched down the trench. His own uniform was muddy, too. So were most of his men's. He didn't get his bowels in an uproar about it. There was a war on, dammit.

"Hey!" he said sharply. "Yeah, you, Captain Pak! Knock that off!" His voice went louder and deeper than he usually made it. It was, though he didn't quite realize it, the voice of an angry, fully mature man, the kind of man other men didn't care to trifle with.

Pak Ho-san didn't quite realize that yet, either. "What you say?" he asked, as if he couldn't believe his ears. He went on poking the ROK private.

"I said, knock that off. Leave that man alone. He hasn't done anything worth screaming at him like that or slugging him. So leave him alone."

"He my man," Pak said. "He not your man. None of your fucking business."

"He's *a* man," Cade said. "That makes him my business. Cut out your crap, you hear me? Or you'll be sorry."

Plainly, no American officer had ever talked to Pak Ho-san

like that before. He didn't laugh in Cade's face, but he might as well have. "Oh?" he jeered. "Who make me?"

Cade carried his PPSh. He carried it everywhere, all the time, except when he was sleeping or eating or taking a crap. Then it lay right beside him. He swung it so it bore on Pak Ho-san's belly button. "I'll make you," he said. "It'd be a pleasure."

Arguing with a submachine gun took more in the way of intestinal fortitude than arguing with a kid captain. Pak opened his mouth. Then he closed it and stormed away. He got mud on his own trousers. Would he gig himself for it? Cade didn't think so.

The ROK private stared at him. It wasn't gratitude. It was more like terror. What would happen to him as soon as his protector went away? Nothing pretty, that was for sure. Cade realized he'd just adopted a puppy. He gestured toward his own men with the PPSh. A smile broke out on the Korean's face like sunshine through clouds. He hustled to join the grimy dogfaces.

Cade dug into a can of chili and beans. He grinned at Howard Sturgis. "The condemned man ate a hearty meal."

"You're gonna catch it," Sturgis predicted dolefully.

"If I do, somebody else can run this madhouse." Cade was still grinning. He felt great. "Maybe it'll be you."

"They won't give a lieutenant a battalion," Sturgis said.

"I had one for a little while with only one bar." The great feeling went away. "Those guys are dead now. I would be, too, only I was on a pass when the Russians dropped that bomb."

He got summoned to Division HQ, back in Kaeryong, that very afternoon. The summons included a jeep ride, so he could get in trouble faster. "What did you do, sir?" the driver asked. "They usually let you guys walk."

"I believed in democracy and the rights of the little man," Cade replied.

"Hoo-boy!" The driver clapped a hand to his forehead. "No wonder you're in deep!"

"No wonder at all," Cade said.

When he told the clerk-typist in the headquarters prefab who he was, he found himself escorted forthwith into the august presence of Brigadier General Randolph Hackworth, who was commanding the division. Hackworth sported a cigar, a chestful of medals from the last war, and a steely glare, which he fixed on Cade. "Captain, what the hell do you mean by interfering in the way our ally conducts his military business?" he rasped.

By then, Cade didn't care what happened to him any more. "Sir, what the hell does our ally mean by treating his soldiers like peasants out of the War of the Roses?"

The Havana jerked in Hackworth's mouth. "You are insubordinate, young man."

"No, sir," Cade said. "If Captain Pak Ho-san were an American, you'd court-martial him so fast it'd make his head swim . . . sir."

"You *are* an American," Hackworth said. "I can do that to you."

"Go ahead, sir. After what I've seen, it's no wonder Kim Il-sung's men fight harder than the Koreans on our side. The guys who give them orders weren't taking orders from the Japs ten years ago." Cade silently thanked Howard Sturgis for that bit of intelligence.

"How does Leavenworth sound, Captain?" Hackworth asked.

"Sir, after better than a year here, it sounds like a vacation," Cade said. "But I wouldn't go, not once my Congressman got my letter."

The brigadier general went so dusky a red, Cade wondered if he had heart trouble. "You don't have the proper attitude," he said.

"I guess I don't, sir. If we aren't fighting for the idea that every man is just as good as every other man whether he's rich and connected or not, why don't we just jump into our boats and let the Reds have this stinking place?" As it did with Pak Ho-san, his voice took on its mature timbre. Even Cade had no idea how intimidating he sounded.

Hackworth stared at him. "Get the hell out of here," he said at last.

"Am I under arrest, sir?"

"No. Just get out. I'll fix things with the ROK mucky-mucks. Beat it!" Out Cade went. He didn't know if he'd won, but he didn't think he'd lost.

Konstantin Morozov stared at his "new" tank. He stared at the sergeant in the tank park who'd led him to the machine. "You're tying my dick in knots," he said.

"Comrade Sergeant, it's a runner," the tank-park sergeant answered. "Half the machines I've got here are just like it. Somebody's going to take it. Your turn happened to come up."

Behind Konstantin, Juris Eigims and Vazgen Sarkisyan looked as appalled as he felt. So did Demyan Belitsky, the driver they'd added to their crew, and Ilya Goledod, the bow gunner. Seeing the dismay in their eyes stiffened his spine.

"Give it to the Devil's nephew. It's bound to be older than he is," he said. "I know fucking well it's older than you are."

Even though the tank-park sergeant was a fresh-faced kid, the T-34/85 wasn't older than he was. They hadn't started making them till the end of 1943. He wasn't wrong that he had a lot of them in the tank park, either. None of that had anything to do with anything.

"I don't care if that piece of shit is a runner or not," Morozov continued furiously. "It's a coffin, is what it is. Put it up against a Pershing or a Centurion and we're all chopped to sausage meat and burned to charcoal ten seconds later."

"We use what we have, Comrade Sergeant." The guy at the tank park tried to stay reasonable. He could afford to. His balls weren't on the line. He went on, "The Americans are using Shermans, I've heard. The English are using Cromwells and Churchills. Any tank is better than no tank."

"Even the Nazis killed these things last time. I ought to know—I was in a couple of them. My men and I didn't recover from radiation sickness to go back to duty in a horse and buggy!"

"I'll bring the lieutenant over here if you want," the tank-park sergeant said.

As soon as Konstantin heard that, he knew he and his crew were stuck with the T-34/85. When an officer poked his beak into something like this, what would he do? Back the guy he worked with, of course. And he would order the crew into the obsolescent tank instead of just giving it to them.

"Fuck you. Fuck your mother. Fuck both your ugly old grannies, one in the mouth and one up the ass. Fuck your father up the ass," Konstantin said wearily. "You're sending us out there to get us killed."

The tank-park sergeant only shrugged. "You aren't the only ones in machines like this one. I told you that before." How many other tank commanders who got an ancient rustbucket had cussed him up one side and down the other? How many of them were still alive?

"Come on, boys," Morozov said to his crew. "Let's see what we can do with this pile of garbage." He'd feared this would happen as soon as he saw they'd given him a bow gunner. The T-34/85 had a machine gun at the right front of the hull and one coaxial with the cannon. The T-54 carried only the coaxial machine gun.

As soon as he climbed into the tank, the faint smell of kerosene filled his nostrils. He knew what that meant. They'd swabbed out the fighting compartment with it to get rid of the stench of death. How many crews had already bought a plot in here? Better *not* to wonder about that.

"Crowded in here," Juris Eigims remarked.

"You think this is bad, you should've seen the first T-34, the one with the 76mm gun," Konstantin said. "Really small turret, and the commander had to aim the gun along with everything else. The Germans could shoot three times as fast as those babies could."

"This sight is junk, too," the Balt said, as if he hadn't spoken. "The one on the T-54 isn't great, but this. . . . How are you supposed to hit anything with it?"

"Do your best, please." Morozov tried the intercom to the forward part of the tank and discovered it didn't work. He only wished that surprised him more. He shouted into the speaking tube instead: "Start the motor, Demyan."

"Right, Comrade Sergeant." Demyan Belitsky's voice came back brassily. The diesel farted to life, belching black smoke. Konstantin swore under his breath. If it had refused to go, he could have claimed another tank. But that would have been a T-34/85, too, unless they had something older. You couldn't expect favors after you proposed fucking somebody's father in the ass.

"Take us up to the regimental tank depot," Morozov said. "They'll tell us what to do when we get there."

"I serve the Soviet Union!" Belitsky said, and put the tank in gear.

Konstantin stuck his head out of the cupola to look around. It was safe enough; they were still a good ways behind the front. The shape of the tank, so much more angular than the turtle-topped T-54, was as familiar to him as the look of an old lover's body after he hadn't slept with her for several years. She might have got long in the tooth, but he still understood her moods.

Whether that would do anything at all to keep him breathing was liable to be a different question.

Tank tracks had chewed up the paving on the road Belitsky was using. Most of the buildings Konstantin saw had been blown up or burned or blown up *and* burned. In one T-54 or another, he might well have helped to knock some of them down. Now he was going over the same ground again for another round of destruction. The Americans' A-bombs had let the enemy retake a big chunk of western Germany.

He shuddered. He knew he still wasn't a hundred percent himself. Somewhere not far away, someone fired a ripping burst from a PPD or a PPSh. Konstantin ducked down into the turret and closed the cupola hatch. It was cold out there, and starting to rain.

The major in charge of the tank regiment was a veteran named Kliment Todorsky. He actually seemed glad to see Morozov's crew join his unit. "I'm using T-34s as point vehicles in my platoons," he said. "They develop the opposition, and the T-54s behind them deal with it."

"I serve the Soviet Union!" Konstantin said, because he couldn't tell a major to go fuck his father in the ass. By *develop the opposition,* Todorsky meant *draw enemy fire.* Any enemy fire a T-34/85 drew in this day and age was all too likely to leave it a smoldering hulk, and the men inside it mangled or dead.

Had he commanded the regiment, though, he knew he would have been as ruthless. One of these tanks could still make any infantry around run. It just wasn't up for a fight against another tank.

"We have to be quick, and we have to stay lucky," Morozov told his men. "I went through this the last time. I was always scared of Tigers and Panthers. They could kill me easier than I could kill them. It's the same thing now, only more so."

They pushed on toward Paderborn. The rain came down harder, with snow mixed in. Visibility dropped to a couple of hundred meters, even though Konstantin stuck his head out of the hatch again. He wouldn't spot trouble till it was on top of him. Then again, the T-34/85 couldn't hurt a more modern tank at anything but point-blank range.

When trouble came, it didn't come from an enemy tank. A man with a rocket launcher popped up from behind the corpse of a Volkswagen by the side of the road. The intercom didn't work, dammit. Konstantin had to duck inside to scream to the bow gunner: "Ahead and a little to the right! Fire! Now!"

Ilya Goledod spat death in that direction. Konstantin popped out again, just in time to watch the enemy soldier launch his rocket. But the machine-gun rounds were enough to spoil his aim. The deadly missile flew past the T-34/85 instead of burning through its frontal armor. A moment later, Juris Eigims put an HE round into the dead VW. The guy with the bazooka tumbled away. *He* wouldn't cause any more trouble. But how many more like him were still around?

Weed, California, was up near 3,500 feet above sea level. That wasn't enough to make Marian Staley notice the altitude when she breathed or anything. Winters were colder and harsher than they would have been lower down, though. As soon as summer ended, she'd found out about that. She and Linda had no clothes to suit the weather.

Thick jackets. Wool watch caps. Wool socks. Long johns. Waterproof boots. She didn't like spending the money, but she liked shivering even less.

Logging slowed down in the wintertime. It didn't stop, but the men with the axes and saws had a harder time getting to the trees they were supposed to fell and a harder time getting them away from where they'd fallen once they did go down.

Big, snorting trucks hauled trunks secured with chains to long trailers. When the snow started falling and when rain turned to ice after hitting the ground, the trucks and trailers got chains on their tires, too.

And sometimes that helped, and sometimes it didn't. The men who ran Shasta Lumber wanted to do as much cutting and as much hauling as they could, so they made as much money as they could. The other lumber bosses in and around the town felt the same way. If their men had accidents, that was part of the cost of producing the most board-feet possible.

It was to the men who ran the outfits, anyhow. To the ones who sawed away in the snow or drove the steep, twisting, icy roads . . .

Marian was typing one chilly afternoon when the front door flew open. A logger in a dark green plaid Pendleton shirt and Levi's staggered into the office. Everyone gasped or squawked when he did—he had a bloody nose and a gash over one eye.

He seemed unaware he'd been hurt. "Tom put truck number three down a scree slope," he gasped. "Threw me clear, so I'm okay"—he was anything but—"but he's still back there, and he's tore up pretty good. I made it back to the road an' flagged down a car. Somebody call Doc Toohey to go up there and give poor Tom a hand."

Glancing down at the list of telephone numbers she might be expected to use fairly often, Marian saw one for Dr. Christopher Toohey among them. Before she could dial it, one of the other secretaries beat her to the punch. "Yes, come here first," she told the doctor. "Billy Hurley's here, and he'll show you where the accident's at." She hung up and nodded to the logger. "Doc's on the way."

"Swell," he said, as if time had stopped in 1928.

Marian pulled tissues from the box on her desk and went over to Billy Hurley. "Here," she said, dabbing gently at the cut. "Let me clean this up if I can. You may need stitches—I don't know. Hold some of these to your nose, too."

"What're you talking about?" He sounded irritable. "*I'm* okay. It's poor Tom who got crunched up."

"You're *not* okay." She showed him the bloody Kleenexes.

He gaped. "Well, swap me pink and call me Bluey. No wonder I got a headache!"

"No wonder at all," Marian agreed. "Dolores, get me some more of these, will you please?"

"Sure thing," the other secretary said, and did.

Dr. Toohey rushed in no more than a minute later; nowhere in Weed was very far from anywhere else. He had his black bag in his hand. "Let me patch up that cut first of all," he said.

"Never mind me, Doc. Slap a Band-Aid on it or somethin'. Tom Andersen's the one who needs you bad," Hurley said.

"If he's worse off than you, then he must," Toohey said. They hurried out together. Two car doors slammed. An engine roared.

Marian stared at the handful of soggy, bloody tissues she was holding. With a small, disgusted noise, she threw them in the nearest wastebasket, then went into the ladies' room and washed off Billy Hurley's blood. None of the high mucky-mucks down the hall had even noticed the commotion out front.

"That was fun," she said after she came out. "Does this kind of thing happen all the time during the winter?"

"Not all the time, but it happens, yeah," Dolores answered. "You did all you could for Billy there. That was great." The other office workers nodded.

"I was closest to him, that's all. Anybody else would've done the same." Marian looked down. "We've got blood on the rug."

"Cold water. Lots of cold water," Dolores said. "That's not the kind of reminder we need."

Billy Hurley came back to the office a couple of hours later. He wasn't bleeding any more. His nose had stopped, and he had a bandage wrapped around his head—so much for *slap a Band-Aid on it.* "Doc dropped me off. He's taking Tom down to the hospital in Redding," he reported. "Says he's got some busted bones he can't deal with here."

"How far is it to Redding?" Marian asked.

"Eighty miles—something like that," Dolores said.

"Poor Tom!" Marian wouldn't have wanted to spend all that time in a car jouncing down US 99. She'd known Weed had no hospital, but she hadn't thought about what that meant till now. If something went badly wrong . . . "There's not even an ambulance that could take him?"

"Nope," the logger said. "Doc's it, pretty much."

"You ought to—we ought to—be able to do better. Logging's dangerous work. People get hurt." Marian glanced down the hall. The bosses were still busy doing whatever bosses did.

"Stuff like that costs money, though," Billy Hurley said. "Who's gonna fork it over? Lord only knows how Tom'll come up with the cash for whatever they got to do to him down in Redding."

The lumber companies ought to pay, Marian thought. *They're the ones whose people go off the roads in the snow or have trees fall on them or get hit in the leg by an axe that goes wrong.*

But even though she thought it, she didn't say it. She knew what would happen if she did say it. Shasta Lumber would fire her. They might not open the door before they kicked her through it, either. They'd call her a Red and a radical. No one else in town would hire her after they canned her. She and Linda would have to move away. The way things were these days, that kind of reputation, deserved or not, was liable to follow her, too. Political arguments made everybody insanely suspicious.

She got less done the rest of the day than she would have liked, even if nobody else complained. Weed wasn't a bad place. It had reasonably nice people and a breathtaking view. After Camp Nowhere, it had seemed like heaven on earth. But it wasn't.

Had it been just her, she might have packed up and left from sheer annoyance at the lumber barons. Linda was settling in pretty well, though. She'd already had her life torn up by the roots twice this year—three times if you counted finding out that her father was dead. Little kids shouldn't have that happen to them. Sometimes they did, in spite of everything, but they shouldn't.

On the way home from work, she stopped at the office of the *Weed Press-Herald,* the town's weekly. The editor was a tall man named Dale Dropo. "Yeah, I heard Tom got hurt," he said. "It's a shame, but logging's a tough business."

"I'll tell you what's a shame," Marian said. "It's a shame the town doesn't have an ambulance, much less a hospital."

Dale Dropo couldn't have been more than thirty-five. He wasn't more than a few years older than Marian, in other words. He might never have worried about the lack of such things before. Till today, she hadn't. He scratched at one ear. "You know what?" he said. "You're right."

"Would an editorial light a fire under anybody?" she asked.

His grin was sour. "I only wish it were that easy. Weed would have a lot of things it doesn't if people paid any attention to my editorials. But I was wondering what I'd put in the one for next Friday's paper. Now I know. I'll give 'em something else to ignore me about. Thanks."

"Any time," Marian said. "Any time at all."

Ihor Shevchenko was an old soldier. He was also an old soldier who acted like an old soldier: he did no more than he had to do to get by. The way he looked at it, he'd done everything he needed to do to serve the Soviet Union during the Great Patriotic War. He had the scar and the limp to prove it. If the Soviet Union wanted more from him now, that was the *rodina*'s hard luck.

His attitude did not endear him to Sergeant Prishvin. Of course, he could have been a Stakhanovite for extra duties and worn a Hero of the Soviet Union's star on his chest, and that wouldn't have endeared him to Anatoly Prishvin, either.

Since he was a Ukrainian, dying was the only thing that would have endeared him to Prishvin.

"You're a lazy, worthless cunt," the sergeant said. Ihor stood mute. He was willing to cop to lazy, but not the rest of the abuse. Prishvin went on, "They should stick you in a penal battalion. See how you'd like being lazy then."

Penal battalions were for getting rid of soldiers and officers who'd screwed up in a major way. If you lived, your sins were expiated. But the whole point to penal battalions was using the bodies of the men in them to smother the fires the enemy started. Men went in where things were hottest. Most of them, by the nature of things, didn't come out again.

Prishvin went right on glaring. "Well? What have you got to say about that?"

"Nothing, Comrade Sergeant," Ihor answered. Anything he did say would only inflame the Russian more.

Saying nothing didn't help, either. "You're too lazy to even talk to me, huh? No wonder you and that cocksucking black-ass hang around together. I bet he smokes hashish to make him like he is. What's your excuse?"

Ihor made a small production of starting to clean his AK-47. He'd always kept his weapons in good shape. That helped you stay alive, which he approved of. He hadn't trained on the Kalashnikov, but you hardly needed training to take care of it. The mechanism was about as simple as it could get and still work. It was so simple, it would go on working even if you didn't bother cleaning it.

Not quite idly, Ihor swung the muzzle toward Anatoly Prishvin. That was just to take the edge off his own feelings. He couldn't reassemble the rifle, release the safety, and pull the trigger here and make it seem like an accident. When they went into action against the Americans, though . . . A corpse shot by an AK-47 looked the same as one shot by an M-1, especially after it had a few days to swell up and change colors and stink.

He did wonder how many stupid, vicious officers and fuck-headed noncoms had died at their own men's hands during the Great Patriotic War. The tally wouldn't include only the fuckheads who served the Soviet Union badly. Plenty of Fritzes who gave orders were vicious and stupid, too. Ihor had developed a healthy respect for the ordinary German soldier. Here and there, *Landsers* would have weeded out their assholes, too.

He supposed even Americans could see it might be better to arrange an untimely demise for a captain before the bastard got his whole company killed.

Eventually, Prishvin went off to make the other men in the section love him even more than they already did. Aram Demirchyan ambled over to where Ihor was sitting and said, "Here. Have of these some." He held out his canteen.

"Thanks." Ihor took a cautious sip. It wasn't hashish, but it was pretty good schnapps. Aram might speak only mangled Russian and no German at all, but he had a scrounger's gift for coming up with useful things.

"Sergeant, he big *metyeryebyets.*" No matter how mangled Demirchyan's Russian was, he had no trouble with the obscenity.

"Think so, do you?" Ihor said dryly. The Armenian thought that was funny. After the schnapps mounted to Ihor's head, he did, too. How could anyone *not* think Prishvin was exactly what Aram had called him?

A couple of days later, they went into action outside of Paderborn. The enemy hadn't wasted any time retaking a large stretch of northwestern Germany after the A-bomb kicked the Red Army in the teeth. Ihor crouched behind the burnt-out hulk of a T-34/85, a survivor from the last war that hadn't made it through this one.

He didn't want his head to end up like the killed tank's turret, which lay upside down ten meters away from the hull. He thought he smelled charred meat along with all the other battlefield stenches, but it might have been his imagination. He could hope so, anyhow.

Soviet artillery slammed the American lines on the eastern outskirts of the German town. "Forward!" Sergeant Prishvin shouted. "Forward for the great Stalin!"

"For Stalin!" the men yelled as they ran toward the Yanks' foxholes and trenches. Even Ihor yelled, though he'd somehow lived through what the great Stalin had done to the Ukraine.

An American heavy machine gun in a house with an east-facing window opened up. Ihor did a swan dive behind a rock and started digging in. All around him, other Red Army men flopped to the ground and slithered toward whatever cover they could find. A couple of luckless fellows got hit before they could hit the dirt. They went down, too, bonelessly, as if they'd taken one on the button from a heavyweight. A round from that baby could punch through a couple of centimeters of hardened steel. What it did to mere flesh and blood hardly bore thinking about.

The USSR had fielded large-caliber machine guns during the last war. The Hitlerites hadn't, so this was Ihor's first time on the wrong end of one. He could have done without the honor.

Red Army men popped up every now and again to take shots at the house. But the heavy machine gun could kill them out past a kilometer, and they couldn't hit back at that range. A couple of guys in the section carried rocket-propelled grenade launchers, but they didn't have a prayer of getting in close enough to use them. So Ihor thought, anyway.

Sergeant Prishvin had a different view of things. He called "Forward!" again, adding, "We can get that fucker!"

He wasn't a coward. That wasn't what was wrong with him. He ran toward the house with flame and death spitting from the shattered window. So did some of the men he led. Ihor got up and gained thirty or forty meters; the bare-branched bushes he chose for shelter didn't conceal him as well as he would have liked, but they were ever so much better than nothing.

One of the RPG men launched an optimistic round. It fell far short, blowing a hole in the muddy ground. Ihor fired a few times himself, though he knew he was only wasting ammo. The AK-47 wasn't made for long-range combat. Even a sniper with a scope-sighted Mosin-Nagant would have had trouble hitting the American machine gunners from where he was.

"Forward!" Prishvin roared. "Everybody forward! Come on, you cunts, you whores, you needle dicks! We *will* take out that gun! For Stalin!"

Forward he went. Forward the other soldiers went, too, some of them firing from the hip as they ran to try to make the Yankees keep their heads down. Ihor bent to stick on a new magazine. One of those big, fat bullets from the machine gun cracked over his head.

And one of them hit Aram Demirchyan and knocked him to one side as if he were a crumpled sheet of newspaper. Crimson blood soaked his dun-colored tunic. He thrashed feebly for a second or two, then lay still.

Ihor yanked back the charging handle and chambered the first round. He fired several shots, first high, then lower.

"The sergeant's down!" someone yelled. "*Bozhemoi!* He won't get up again, either!"

"We better fall back!" someone else said. "We need a mortar to shift that goddamn machine gun!"

Nobody argued with him. Retreat was almost as dangerous as advancing had been. Ihor hoped no one else knew how Sergeant Prishvin had fallen. One more chance he'd have to take.

LUISA HOZZEL SHOOK HER HEAD. "Not for me," she said in a mixture of German and bad Russian. "I have a man back in Germany."

"In Germany?" Nadezhda Chukovskaya tossed her head. She was short and stocky and tough. Laughing, she went on, "Germany is the other side of the moon. You don't have anybody here. Everybody needs somebody."

Yes, but you aren't the somebody I need. Luisa didn't say it. Nadezhda was one of the two or three women with the most pull in her barracks. If she got mad at somebody, she could make that person sorry. Telling her off was a last resort.

Another soft answer, then: "Not for me. I am woman for men, not woman for other women."

"Men!" Nadezhda laughed again, scornfully this time. "Men don't know anything! Wait till somebody loves you who can make you feel good because she understands what makes you feel good."

The only polite answer Luisa found to that was a shrug. She hadn't been lying. Women didn't stoke her fires. They never had, and she didn't think they ever would.

The Weimar Republic might have taken lesbianism in stride, along with so much else. But by the time Luisa was old enough to notice such things and to have such feelings herself, Germany had turned away from the Weimar Republic—about as far away as it could turn. Hitler and the Nazis? To them, anything that had to do with homosexuality was degenerate and disgusting. Homosexuals didn't reproduce, after all, and that made them unnatural and not worth keeping alive (unless, she'd heard, they happened to belong to the SS).

Teachings from the Third *Reich* might still linger inside her. Or her natural bent might simply be the more common one. Whatever it was, past wishing she had Gustav back she seemed immune to the lure of romance here.

Nadezhda Chukovskaya might have seen as much in her eyes. They sat side by side on Luisa's bunk in the brief, tired interlude between supper and lights-out. Nadezhda laughed once more, this time more nastily than the first two put together.

"You want a man so much?" she said. "You want a dick in you? Go to the fence between our half of the camp and theirs. Bend over and stick your ass in the air like a washerwoman. You'll get a dick in you, all right, dog-fashion. And nobody breaks a rule because you both stay on your own side of the wire."

"No!" Luisa had seen that happen once or twice. She thought it was unimaginably depraved. She'd looked away as soon as she realized what was going on. Most of the time, so did other people. Once, guards had whooped and hollered and cheered the couplers on.

"Why not? You'd sooner have a man than me? That's how you get a man here."

That might have been one of the ways. It wasn't the only one. She remembered all too well the barber groping her while he trimmed her bush. If she'd said yes to him, she could have had soft work inside the barbed wire, not hard labor out in the taiga. But she wanted him no more than she wanted Nadezhda. Less, if anything.

"It's not about *a* man. It's about *my* man," she said.

"Your man is in Germany." Nadezhda spoke as if to an idiot child. "Germany is I don't know how many thousand kilometers away. Lots of thousands—I know that. You'll never see him again. Might as well grab what fun you can here."

Luisa only shrugged again. She had no idea whether her husband was alive or dead, either. She hadn't told that to Nadezhda, though the Russian woman might already know it. The reason the MGB had seized so many German women in this camp was no secret. It would just have strengthened the other woman's argument.

Nadezhda stood up, her face set in angry lines. She strode away. Her stiff back and long strides made her more mannish than ever. That didn't add to her attractiveness, not so far as Luisa was concerned.

She would have had things easier if she'd given in to the barber. She was sure she would have things easier if she gave in to Nadezhda, too. But her body was the only thing in the camp that still belonged to her. Other *zeks* had slept in this bunk before her. She was sure others would after her, too. Even her clothes, with Г963 replacing some older number, were hand-me-downs that belonged to the Soviet state.

She lay down on the hard, lumpy mattress. Maybe she could claim the bedbugs that bit her as her own, too. Other bugs also called the camp home. Sometimes Luisa felt more like a stray schnauzer than a human being.

Right this minute, she felt like a worn-out stray schnauzer. As soon as she lay flat, her eyes closed. She couldn't have stayed awake more than a minute after that. As she often did, she dreamt she was back in Fulda.

No matter what she'd been talking about with Nadezhda, her dreams had nothing to do with Gustav. They revolved around food. A chocolate cake smothered in whipped cream her mother had made when she was small. A roast duck with cherry sauce. Goose-liver sausages. A giant pork roast she'd fixed for Christmas one year, with potatoes and sauerkraut on the side. Malty beer, its foam thick enough to give you a white mustache.

You could live without a man, and even without taking a woman as a substitute for him. You couldn't live without food. When you did hard work without enough of it, your body reminded you of that every chance it got. When you slept, it played pictures—and tastes, and smells! oh, smells!—inside your head of all the good things it wanted.

Luisa was just bringing a spoonful of fragrant beef-and-barley soup to her mouth when the raucous clang of hammer on shell casing thrust her eyes open and rudely dropped her back into the real world. Her stomach growled in anger and frustration. Whenever she listened to it, that was all it ever reported.

She had no time to listen to it now. She had to get outside as soon as she could, to stand out there in the predawn cold for the morning count. The guards had to be satisfied before the *zeks* ate.

Outside she went, still yawning. Cold slapped her in the face. Electric lights blazed, making the assembly area noon-time bright. A bright star—would that be Venus?—shone in the east. The lights drowned out the rest of those feeble little gleams.

"Line up!" the guard shouted. "Line up, you dumb cunts!"

Across the wire, the Chekists who kept an eye on the men greeted them with the same insults.

Trudl Bachman slid into place next to Luisa. "Another wonderful day here in paradise," she murmured out of the side of her mouth, her lips scarcely moving. Talking during the count was *verboten,* which didn't mean people didn't do it anyhow.

"Aber natürlich," Luisa answered the same way. The two women smiled at each other. If you didn't smile, if you didn't joke, wouldn't you start screaming instead?

Up and down the ranks prowled the guards. Counting the women should have been easy. It would have been easy, if the men with the machine pistols had had the brains God gave a tsetse fly. As things were, they needed four tries before they were sure that the number they got matched the number they thought they were supposed to have.

Only then could the women head for breakfast, which they did at a dead run. To be so eager, so desperate, for thin cabbage soup, a lump of black bread, and weak tea only went to show what the camp was like. It would have been a starvation ration even in the worst days of the war. When it was all you had, though . . .

Luisa ate with an animal intensity that left her frightened. So did her fellow *zeks.* She was surprised when Trudl asked her, "Was that *Leckschwester* after you again?" Talk at breakfast seemed a rare luxury.

She managed a nod. "Nadezhda? *Ja.* I told her again I wasn't interested, but she doesn't want to listen."

Then they hurried to the stinking latrines: a necessary part of the day, but Luisa's least favorite. And then it was out into the snow, out into the woods, once more.

Gustav Hozzel turned over a Russian's corpse. The stink that came from the dead Ivan said he'd lain there for a while. So did the way he'd swollen enough to split his tunic and his trouser legs. Normally, Gustav wouldn't have wanted to come within a hundred meters of him.

Normally, here, meant before he'd taken that AK-47 from the other dead Russian, the one in Wesel—before the American A-bomb flattened and melted Wesel and all the Ivans in it. Now he checked every Russian's body he came across. He had to, if he was going to keep the assault rifle in cartridges.

The enemy was the only source for them. They weren't like 7.62mm and 9mm pistol rounds, the standard calibers for machine pistols, which were made all over the world.

He made sure he turned the dead soldier by the tunic, not by his bare skin. The corpse made horrible squashing noises just the same.

Rolf laughed. "Ain't you got fun? That piece is more trouble than it's worth."

"They said the same thing about your last girlfriend, right?" Gustav returned. By the way Rolf scowled, maybe they *had* said something like that about his latest flame. Gustav didn't care. He pointed happily. "Will you look at that?" The Ivan had several of the distinctive curved magazine pouches for the Kalashnikov hooked to his belt. Gustav took the magazines out of them. One went into a pouch he'd lifted from another Russian. The rest he stowed in his pockets and pack.

Max Bachman pointed to a roadside sign that tilted but hadn't got knocked flat. "Look. Next stop is outer space."

"You'd know all about that, wouldn't you?" Rolf jeered.

"*I* think it's funny," Gustav told Max. The sign announced that Marsberg was five kilometers away. The Germans were somewhere south of Paderborn, trying to take as much land back from the Russians as they could before the Red Army recovered from getting atom-bombed . . . if it did, if it could.

"Of course you two laugh at the same shit," the ex-LAH veteran said. "You've been asshole buddies for God knows how long."

"Only *Arschloch* I see around here is you, Rolf," Gustav said. He figured he and Rolf would have it out one of these days. One of them would knock the crap out of the other, and they'd go on from there. Or maybe they'd rack each other up, and then they'd both get some time off from the war.

But a sputter of gunfire broke out from the direction of Marsberg. Whatever he and Rolf did to each other would have to wait. They both trotted toward the trouble, as did Max.

Russian generals spent men the way a drunk tycoon spent money on dancing girls. They kept throwing them into the fight, on the notion that whatever they were facing was bound to fall over sooner or later. It had worked for them against the *Wehrmacht*. They thought it would again.

"Urra!" the Red Army men shouted. The war cry always made the hair at the back of Gustav's neck stand up in alarm. To him, it meant a swarm of drunken Ivans rolling forward

like the tide, careless of whether they lived or died, and no King Canute anywhere to hold them back.

Gustav skidded down behind a jeep that would never go anywhere again. He rose to one knee and started banging away with the Kalashnikov. He could hit what he aimed at out to three or four hundred meters, twice as far as he would have been able to with the PPSh. The bullets had more stopping power when they hit something—somebody—too.

This Russian steamroller had less steam behind it than attacks Gustav had faced in bygone days. When the Ivans saw they wouldn't smash the forces in front of them, they didn't keep trying to break through in spite of casualties. They went to earth and started digging scrapes, the way any sensible soldiers would have.

Back in Marsberg, some potbellied Soviet lieutenant colonel had to be on the brink of apoplexy. How could you fight a proper war if soldiers kept trying to stay alive? Mortar bombs started whistling down on German and Russian positions with little discrimination between the two.

Blasts, screaming fragments . . . Gustav tried to scramble under the dead jeep. But its tires had burned, and on the iron wheels it sat too low to let him. A clang announced that a fragment had ripped into the back fender. A few centimeters farther to the right and it would have ripped into him instead. You went into a stupid little fight like this, you rolled dice with your life as the stake.

And if you went into enough stupid little fights like this, you *would* crap out. The odds made it a certainty.

Lieutenant Fiebig got up and dashed toward the Russians, firing his U.S.–issue grease gun from the hip as he ran. "Come on, boys!" the company CO shouted. "Follow me!"

Those had been the magic words in the last war, and they still were. Officers and sergeants who led from the front got better results than the ones who just ordered their men forward while they stayed safe in the rear, the way so many World War I commanders had. Of course, officers and sergeants who led from the front also took more casualties than the other kind. Bravery could be its own punishment.

Gustav got up, too. He slapped a full magazine onto the AK-47 and ran after the lieutenant. Fire and rush, fire and rush . . . No one needed to tell the Germans how to advance. It wasn't as if most of them hadn't learned in a school that buried you if you flunked an exam.

Some of the Russians knew how to fall back the same way. But they had more kids in their ranks than Gustav's countrymen did. The Germans in this fight were all volunteers. The Ivans put any warm bodies they could find into uniform. Even in the last war, Gustav had been fighting sixteen- and seventeen-year-olds. Hitler kept screaming how Stalin was scraping the bottom of the barrel. Stalin was, too. But Hitler's barrel had no bottom left to scrape after a while.

A terrified guy with a broad Slavic face threw down his rifle and threw his hands in the air. *"Kamerad!"* he bleated. *"Freund!"*

Gustav pulled the ammo pouches and grenades off the Russian's belt so he couldn't change his mind, then gestured with the Soviet assault rifle. "Go on back," he said. "Somebody'll take care of you."

Blubbering palatal gratitude that Gustav couldn't understand, the Red Army man headed west, hands still high above his head. And maybe some German would get him off to a POW camp, or maybe somebody like Rolf would decide he wasn't worth wasting time over and plug him. Surrendering could be the riskiest thing you tried on the battlefield.

Marsberg was another town whose church had a tall steeple. The Russians didn't put an artillery spotter up there—they had a couple of snipers banging away at the advancing German soldiers. But the Red Army wasn't the only force that issued its men mortars. Bombs began bursting around the church. Then two in a row slammed into the steeple and sent it crashing down.

If the Ivans had tanks in town, taking it wouldn't be easy and might be impossible. As Gustav knew too well, any tank, no matter how old-fashioned, was death on infantry without armor support. The Germans still relied on the Amis for that. Memories of panzers and blitzkrieg left the USA skittish even yet about a West German army with tanks and planes of its own.

But no tracked behemoths started flinging murder at the advancing foot soldiers. Nor did the Red Army men in Marsberg seem determined to fight to the death to hold every laundry and secondhand bookstore. A couple of machine guns slowed the Germans, but not for long. The Russians pulled back, leaving behind a stench of strong tobacco and sour sweat.

Cautiously, locals started coming out of their cellars and

looking around their battered town. A woman burst into tears at seeing the shattered church. "What are you blaming us for, you stupid bitch? It's Stalin's fault!" Rolf shouted at her. For some reason, that didn't make her stop crying.

It was over, but then again it wasn't. In thirteen months, Harry Truman wouldn't be President of the United States any more. He and Bess would go home to Independence. The reporters would write about him. Then, as soon as he'd settled into the obscurity that was all an ex-President merited, they'd forget about him. After that, the historians would get their licks.

In the meantime, though, he had a war to fight, and with luck to win. He didn't want to burden his successor, whether Donkey or Elephant, with cleaning up the mess he'd made. He was a proud man, and a tidy one. He wanted to clean up his own messes.

The Oval Office telephone rang. He picked it up. "Truman here. Yes?"

"Mr. Kennan is here to see you, sir," Rose Conway said.

"Send him in," Truman answered.

That he was conferring with George Kennan showed how much he wanted to clean up his own messes. Kennan was a Soviet expert. He'd been assistant chief of mission at the U.S. embassy in Moscow till after the end of the last war. He'd helped shape the policy of containing the Russians that Truman had carried out. As the Russians blockaded Berlin, set off their own first atom bomb, and let their stooges start the fight in Korea, containing them didn't seem such a hot idea any more. Pushing them back looked ever more necessary.

Kennan had opposed letting Douglas MacArthur take American troops north of the thirty-eighth parallel in Korea. He'd said it was dangerous. No one else had thought so. MacArthur sure hadn't. Neither had Truman himself. And neither had Dean Rusk, the Assistant Secretary of State for the Far East. And they'd all proved wrong, and George Kennan much too right.

In he came. He was in his late forties, with a patrician bearing, or maybe just one that said he was used to being the smartest man in the room. He was tall and slim and dressed well. His strong-chinned face probably wowed the ladies even if his hairline was in full retreat.

"Mr. President," he said, and held out his hand. Something in his voice shouted Ivy League.

Truman shook with him. Kennan had a good, firm grip. "Thanks for coming in," the President said, more conscious than usual of his own Missouri twang. He waved the diplomat to a chair. A colored steward followed Kennan in with coffee.

After the steward disappeared again, Kennan remarked, "I wasn't sure you'd want to talk to me any more after our earlier . . . disagreements, sir."

"I'm not fool enough to think I'm right all the damn time," Truman said. "That's for Hitler and Stalin and Mao and people of their stripe. When I sit down on the pot, I know what comes out, and it ain't angels."

He got a thin smile from Kennan, who said, "That's a healthy attitude."

"Well, I hope so. Healthy or not, it's *my* attitude. And you *were* right, much too right, about what would come of MacArthur's push north," Truman said. "So now I want to pick your brain about something else."

"I'll do whatever I can for you, Mr. President," Kennan said, "but I know that, even if I happened to be right the last time, that doesn't necessarily mean I will be this time."

"Fair enough," Truman said. "Don't worry. Whatever happens, you won't get the blame. I will. That comes with sitting on this side of the desk."

"Oh, yes." George Kennan nodded. "I wouldn't trade places with you for all the money in the world."

"I don't particularly like this seat myself, but I've got it. I have to do the best I can in it," Truman said. "Stalin has made it plain as day that he won't settle for the *status quo ante bellum.* Do you think the other Russian Communists will show better sense if he isn't there any more to stop them?"

"If he's deceased, do you mean?"

Truman nodded. "That's just what I mean. As long as Hitler stayed alive, the Germans wouldn't surrender. He scared them worse than we did. Christ, he scared 'em worse than the Russians did, and that's really saying something. But it wasn't much more than a week after he blew his brains out that they decided to throw in the towel."

"It's an interesting question, sir." Kennan, who probably looked thoughtful all the time, looked more thoughtful now. "It would depend on who took power after he, ah, died, of course."

"Well, sure." The President nodded. "With luck, some of his higher-ups would go to the Devil along with him. I'm talking about landing an A-bomb on his head, you understand."

"Yes, I thought you had to be," Kennan replied. "I assume you haven't tried to do this before—"

"Oh, we did, when we hit Moscow," Truman broke in. "It didn't work, but not for lack of effort."

"I see. I wondered if that might be so. I might have tried harder to find out if some of my acquaintances in the Defense Department hadn't got nervous about talking to me." Kennan brought out the implied accusation with no particular rancor.

"I never told anyone not to talk to you," Truman said truthfully.

"I didn't say you did, sir. People there did understand, though, that I was no longer in good odor here or at the State Department." Kennan had got on fine with George Marshall when Marshall was Secretary of State. He and Dean Acheson, though, struck sparks off each other.

Marshall, of course, was one of the few men perhaps even smarter than Kennan. Acheson, while nobody's dope, wasn't in that lofty league. Chances were he'd disliked being looked down upon from on high, as it were. Few human beings didn't. Truman himself had the unpleasant suspicion that he was being measured by Kennan's mental calipers.

"Suppose we do send some of Stalin's button men to hell with him," Truman said. "Will the ones who're left make peace?"

"If they see that their national survival, or maybe their personal survival, is at stake, I think they will," Kennan said. "But I gather that finding where Stalin is isn't easy. If I were in his shoes, I wouldn't sleep in the same bed twice in a row."

"We're working on that," the President said. It was, in fact, something of an understatement. The less he said, the better the chance nothing would leak. No one had told him about the atom bomb till he moved into the White house, and he'd been Vice President. He'd been mad about that at first, but only at first. Till the weight of the world landed on his shoulders, he hadn't needed to know.

George Kennan was only—only!—a diplomat out of work at the moment. There were plenty of things he didn't need to know. Truman was no Joe McCarthy, to distrust an out-of-work diplomat's loyalty. But he understood that the fewer chances you took, the better off you were likely to end up.

"I do thank you very much for your help," the President said.

That was dismissal. George Kennan recognized it as such. He rose from his chair. Truman also stood. As they shook hands again, Kennan said, "I'm pleased to do whatever I can, sir, as I told you before. But I shouldn't be the only man whose views you seek. Get as many opinions as you can, judge the value of the people who give them, and make your own choices accordingly."

"I'm trying to do that, yes," Truman said. "I called you in because I wanted to hear from someone who wasn't connected to the State Department."

"Oh, I'm still connected to it," Kennan said. "It doesn't pay my salary any more, but I'll always bear its mark."

"Its scars," Truman suggested with a grin.

"Well, yes, there is that," Kennan agreed with a wry grin. "We all have them here and there, don't we? At least I know where those came from."

"True enough." In his late sixties, Truman had plenty of scars of his own. But he also had the satisfaction of knowing he'd dealt out even more of them than he'd taken.

Bruce McNulty swept off his officer's cap and bowed from the waist. "Madame, your humble chariot awaits," he said in what an American fondly imagined to be an English accent.

The accent wasn't what gave Daisy Baxter a fit of the giggles. Neither was the humble chariot: a jeep from some U.S. Air Force motor pool. The uncovering and the bow, though . . . "You act like somebody out of a movie about Henry VIII or Shakespeare or something," Daisy said.

He took off the cap again and looked at it with regret. "No feather, darn it," he said in his usual American tones. "But I can buckle a mean swash without one. What's Errol Flynn got that I don't? I mean, besides money, looks, and talent?"

"I like the way you look just fine," Daisy said.

"That's nice," he answered blandly. "I notice you didn't talk about the other two."

"You're impossible," she said, wagging her finger at him.

His grin was pure impudence. "Hey, I do my best. C'mon, toots—hop in. You've got yourself a pass from the hospital. I've got one from my base. Let's go cut a rug. Tomorrow morning it'll be 1952."

Daisy was glad to slide into the jeep's passenger seat—which, since it was on the right, to her way of thinking should have been the driving seat (or, if you were a Yank, the driver's seat). Even though it hadn't been built for comfort, sitting down was a relief. She still didn't have all her strength, or all her hair, back. But they'd let her go out on New Year's Eve once she promised not to get too crazy or wild.

Bruce got in beside her. "You warm enough?" he asked.

"I'm fine," she said. "I won't break if you look at me sidewise." She was also bundled into a thick lamb's-fleece coat one of the sisters had lent her. It would have kept a giraffe cozy at the South Pole.

"Okey-doke." He turned the key and put the jeep in gear.

"Are you all right driving on the left?" She had frets of her own.

"I've done it enough by now that I've got the hang of it," he answered. "I have to remember not to look the wrong way, that's all. But nobody's going to be moving real fast even if we do bump fenders."

"Mudguards," Daisy corrected automatically.

"Yeah, mudguards." Bruce's agreement was sarcastic. "And the boot, and a spanner to change the tires—you don't say those funny, you just spell 'em wrong—and the hood is the bonnet. Can you imagine a jeep with a bonnet? Makes me think it ought to have curly hair."

"Impossible," she said again, but she couldn't help laughing.

He did drive slowly and carefully. The blackout was as stern as it had been during the Blitz. Starlight was what he had to steer by, and the clouds scudding across the sky robbed him of much of that.

The dance was in Yaxham, a tiny village a few miles south of East Dereham. Daisy wondered how Bruce had heard about it, and how he intended to find the hall where it was being held once he managed to find Yaxham.

That, she turned out not to need to worry about. Once they got into Yaxham, they could play it by ear. The hall might be blacked out, but music spilled into the street even if light didn't.

"Let's see if I can park this critter without leaving it in the middle of the road," Bruce said.

"That would be good." Daisy nodded, though he might not be able to see her.

He did a splendid job, possibly by Braille. Then he said, "Shall we go make fools of ourselves?"

"Let's," she replied. She wasn't sure how much dancing she was up for, not when she'd spent so long flat on her back. Even a little would be fun, though. She reached for his hand in the darkness as he was reaching for hers. They squeezed each other. The firm pressure felt good.

Two sets of blackout curtains kept lights in the dance hall from leaking out. Daisy wore a cloche straight out of the Roaring Twenties to hide as best she could how much hair she'd lost. *As best she could* wasn't all that good; she'd been nervous about showing herself in public. She needn't have been. Several other men and women were about as bald as she was. She recognized a man who lived only a few blocks from the Owl and Unicorn. They smiled and waved to each other.

Bruce didn't get jealous, the way he had once before. He just asked, "Somebody you know?"

"Stuart? Only my whole life. I went through school with his kid sister," Daisy answered. She looked around. "I don't see Kitty here. I hope she's all right."

"Me, too," Bruce said. "Well, if old Stuart cuts in on me, you can ask him. C'mon."

Out on the dance floor they went. The combo on the bandstand played hot jazz, or what a provincial combo imagined hot jazz to be. Their front man had a trumpet, a sloping belly, and a balding pate with nothing to do with radiation sickness. Other than that, he resembled Louis Armstrong much less than he wished he did.

"He'd better be careful with that thing," Bruce said, nodding toward the trumpet. "He's liable to hurt somebody with it."

"You're a horrible man," Daisy told him.

"Yeah, but I have fun. I try, anyway," the American answered. On the other side of the Iron Curtain, people would also be gathering for New Year's. They'd also be looking around to see who was there and who had died under atomic fire. And he would have been the one who'd visited it upon them.

Daisy wondered if he thought about that. How could you help it? Then again, how could you live with yourself if you did?

She didn't want to think about it. She danced two quick numbers and a slow one, then felt herself drooping. Bruce noticed as soon as she did. "Want to take a break and grab a pint?" he asked.

"That sounds marvelous," she said. They had to queue up for the beer. Standing wasn't too bad. Bruce shoved money across the bar. The red-faced man behind it returned two pint mugs. One sip told Daisy she'd served better bitter. She wasn't about to complain, though.

Bruce liked what they had here. From the things Daisy had heard about American beer, this was bound to improve on that.

They danced some more, then took another break. She did get to talk to Stuart. Kitty *had* come through the bombing. She was up in Wells-next-the-Sea, waiting tables at a café. That was good news.

The trumpeter with delusions of Satchmo counted down the seconds to midnight on his wristwatch. "Happy New Year!" he shouted when there were no seconds left to count. "Happy 1952!"

Everyone cheered. Men and women embraced. Bruce bent his head to kiss Daisy. She clutched at him greedily.

Not too much later, they slipped out of the hall. Bruce found the jeep without even lighting a match. There was more starlight now. It had cleared up, though it was colder than before.

"That was wonderful!" Daisy said as he started the motor. "Thank you so much! I had the best time."

"It was fun, yeah." She could just about see him nod. "Now . . . Can I work out how to make it back to good old East Dereham?"

"If you need to stop along the way to get your bearings, I won't mind," Daisy said. She felt flame on her face. Had she really been that brazen?

She must have been, because somewhere north of Yaxham he pulled off onto the shoulder. The brakes squeaked as the jeep stopped. They were as much alone as if they'd booked a hotel room.

"I don't want to worry about a baby," Daisy said, somewhere in the midst of the kisses and caresses. Not just her cheeks were on fire now. She burned all over.

"Then we'll try some other things instead," Bruce answered. And they did. The jeep's seats were awkward. So was the steering wheel. They managed. His fingers and tongue were knowing and skilled.

She discovered he was circumcised, which Tom hadn't been. He came before she quite expected him to, so she choked a little. She managed to laugh about it when she pulled away. She was still laughing as he started the jeep again.

BORIS GRIBKOV GAVE the Tu-4 more throttle. The air base lay between Odessa and the Romanian border. It was winter here, as it was winter everywhere in the Soviet Union, but it wasn't the kind of winter that piled snow in drifts a couple of meters high. You could fly here without worrying about clearing the runway first. Most of the time, anyhow.

"Everything all right?" he asked the copilot.

"All my instruments are where they're supposed to be, sir," First Lieutenant Anton Presnyakov replied. He was short and blond and seemed bright.

Seemed! Boris was having to get used to a whole new flight crew. He didn't know how many men had got out of the Tu-4 that was hit above Bratislava. He did know he was the only one back in Soviet service.

He sent the engineer the same question over the intercom. "All good," First Lieutenant Lev Vaksman said. Having another Jew in the crew faintly unnerved Gribkov, but what could you do? They were smart fellows—sometimes too smart for their own good—and often wound up in slots that took technical knowledge and skill.

"*Khorosho.* Up we go, then." Boris pulled back on the yoke. The Tu-4 left the runway and climbed for the sky. It was an easy takeoff, not nearly so nervous-making as a lot of them. The bomb bays were empty, and the plane carried only half a load of fuel. All that meant the Shvetsov radials didn't have to strain nearly so hard as usual to get airborne.

Presnyakov must have felt the same relief, for he said, "They should all be this smooth."

"Da," Boris agreed through the clunking noises of the retracting landing gear. He flipped on the intercom again to ask the radioman, "Are you in touch with the milch cow?"

"Comrade Pilot, I am," First Lieutenant Faizulla Ikramov answered. He was an Uzbek, from somewhere beyond the Urals. His Russian held a slight hissing accent, but it was fluent enough. It would have to be, for him to sit in the seat he had. Not many from his folk reached officer's rank. He was uncommonly able, he had connections, or more likely both.

"Milch cow," Presnyakov echoed as they droned up toward their assigned altitude of 9,000 meters. "That's funny, if you like."

"So it is," Boris said. It might be funny in ways the copilot, who was a youngster, didn't suspect. During the last war, the Hitlerites had sent special submarines out into the North Atlantic loaded with food and fuel and fresh torpedoes for the U-boats that were trying to sever the lifeline between England and America. They'd called those supply subs milch cows. The Germans failed, but it was still a clever idea.

It was also an idea that tied in with what Gribkov and the men in the bomber with him were doing on this training flight. Some Soviet higher-up must have thought so, too, or he wouldn't have tagged the other plane with the handle he'd given it.

Boris stared through the not quite perfect Plexiglas of the Tu-4, looking for the circling milch cow. He also kept an eye peeled for fighters. He didn't really expect any—it was a long haul from even the closest American bases. But P-51s with drop tanks *could* come this far, and the Tu-4 would be in a world of trouble if a few did.

Anton Presnyakov pointed ahead and to the right. "There it is, Comrade Pilot!"

"You're right." Gribkov nodded. "That's very good. Now we can just finish our climb and take station with it." He asked the radioman, "Can you patch me through to them?"

"Hold on one moment, Comrade Pilot," Lieutenant Ikramov said. Boris listened to him talk with the other Tu-4's radio operator for a few seconds. Then Ikramov came back to him: "Go ahead, sir."

"Milch Cow, this is Calf One. Milch Cow, this is Calf One. Do you read me, Milch Cow?" Gribkov said.

"Calf One, this is Milch Cow. Reading you loud and clear. How do you read me, Calf One?" The new voice in Boris' earphones was calm and unflustered. The other pilot made him think he was dealing with someone experienced, someone who wouldn't panic if anything unexpected happened.

"Also reading you loud and clear, Milch Cow," Gribkov said. "Do you have us visually? We are climbing up to take our position."

"I see you, yes," the other pilot replied. "I will continue to cruise at 330—I say again, three-three-oh—kilometers an hour."

"I understand. As I approach, I will also slow to 330—I say again, three-three-oh."

"I hear you, Calf One," Milch Cow's pilot said. "We'll talk some more when you get into position. Out for now."

"Out," Boris echoed.

Up he climbed, and took his place behind the milch cow. The other bomber's pilot came back on the radio: "Deploy your cable. I am deploying ours."

"Deploy the cable," Gribkov told Lev Vaksman.

"I am deploying the cable, Comrade Pilot," the engineer replied.

That other cable descended from the milch cow. It met the one from Gribkov's calf, which guided the nozzle at the end to a fitting at the end of Gribkov's Tu-4's right wing. From his station on the starboard side of the fuselage, Vaksman could see when contact was made.

"We have a join, sir!" he said, his voice rising in excitement.

"Milch Cow, this is Calf One. We have a join." Boris relayed the news.

"I see it, Calf One. I was waiting for you to confirm," Milch Cow's pilot said. "Shall I commence fueling?"

"Yes, Milch Cow. Commence fueling." Gribkov went through all the repetition without the least fuss. Everything had to be right.

The Soviet Union had started working on in-flight refueling as early as 1948. It was the obvious way to extend the Tu-4's range and let the heavy bomber hit targets it couldn't reach with what it carried in its own tanks. Till the war started, not much progress got made. Now . . . Now they had to learn how to do it right. American planes could reach most of the important places within the USSR. Without in-flight refueling, Soviet bombers couldn't do the same to the USA. America's heavily populated, highly productive East had been safe, shielded by distance.

Just because it had been, though, didn't mean it would stay that way.

"I see the fuel gauge moving," Gribkov said to Vaksman. "We *are* taking in fuel?"

"Comrade Pilot, that's what the instruments show. This is really something, isn't it?" the engineer said. "It's like long-distance screwing."

One more Zhid *with a half-baked sense of humor,* Boris thought. But the milch cow's pilot guffawed when he passed along the comment. "I've got a long dick, all right," the man said.

Boris' bomber took on several hundred liters of fuel in fifteen minutes. The milch cow had a pump to speed things along. Early Soviet efforts at in-flight refueling had used gravity feed. It worked well enough to show the brass that the idea was possible, not well enough to make the possible practical. The pump made an enormous difference.

As the milch cow refueled the other Tu-4, the pilot flew in a wide circle. Part of the practice session was to get Boris used to keeping station with the milch cow. Bombers didn't usually fly in such close formation, for obvious reasons. It turned out not to be difficult, only to require constant close attention. The milch cow's pilot was as smooth as his voice and manner suggested he might be. He made no sudden, jerky, or unlooked-for maneuvers.

When the fueling was done, he said, "Release the nozzle."

"I am releasing the nozzle," Lev Vaksman replied, and then, a moment later, "The nozzle is released. I say again, the nozzle is released."

"Thank you. I see that the nozzle is released." The milch cow's pilot, or more likely his engineer, reeled in the refueling cable. Vaksman did the same with the catching cable. The two big planes separated. A different pilot would come up to have a go with the milch cow. Boris' next chance would come tomorrow afternoon.

A lieutenant handed Ihor Shevchenko new shoulder boards. Instead of being plain khaki like the ones on his tunic now, these had a dull-red horizontal stripe. "Congratulations, Shevchenko! You're a corporal now. You've done well, and we've noticed," he said, speaking Russian with a Ukrainian accent not much different from Ihor's own.

Ihor saluted stiffly. "Thank you, Lieutenant Kosior, sir! I serve the Soviet Union!"

"We all serve the Soviet Union, and the great Stalin," Stanislav Kosior replied. He might come from the Ukraine, but he talked like the New Soviet Man you always heard about on the radio but hardly ever met. "We will drive back the forces of reaction, imperialism, and capitalism. True Communism *will* come to the entire world, I expect even in our lifetimes. It will be wonderful!"

"It will, Comrade Lieutenant!" Ihor sounded as enthusiastic as he could. He knew how to mask what went through his head. You didn't dare let people like this know you thought they'd been putting hashish in their *papirosi.* They'd make you sorry if you slipped like that.

"Carry on, then, Corporal, and congratulations again!" Kosior looked like a New Soviet Man, too. He kept himself clean and well groomed, even in the field during winter. He was taller and slimmer and handsomer than most. If you wanted to get rude about it, he looked the way a Russian who'd turned halfway into a German might.

No matter what he looked like, he wasn't so smart as he thought he was. Had he been, he wouldn't have promoted a man who'd just scragged a sergeant from his own side. *If I'd known it would get me promoted, I'd've started shooting the bastards a long time ago,* Ihor thought. He remembered plenty of noncoms and junior officers from the Great Patriotic War whom nobody would have missed.

The promotion also convinced him none of his squadmates had seen him shoot Sergeant Prishvin. Or, if someone had, he also thought the son of a bitch had it coming. That would do.

Ihor unbuttoned his plain shoulder boards and replaced them with the striped ones. He was still a corporal even if he didn't; he'd seen majors wearing a second lieutenant's rank markings because no one had bothered to issue them new ones. In the fight against the Nazis, things often got too busy to worry about details like that.

Now he wouldn't have to chop firewood or fill canteens at a stream or dig latrine trenches any more—well, not so much, anyhow. The Russian word for corporal, *yefreitor,* was borrowed from the German *Gefreiter,* a junior noncom who was freed from fatigue duties.

One of the other veterans in Ihor's section, Pyotr Boky, clapped a hand to his forehead when he saw the new shoulder boards. "They promoted *you*?" he exclaimed in mock, or maybe not so very mock, horror. "Christ have mercy! The Red Army's going to pot!"

"Fuck you, too, Petya, right up the poop chute," Ihor answered sweetly. "I can order you out on forward guard duty for the next hundred years."

"Sure you can, if you're the right kind of prick," Pyotr said. "Everybody knows you're a prick, yeah, but I thought you were a different kind of prick."

They jawed back and forth, neither man taking any of it seriously. It was the kind of thing soldiers did when there was a lull in the fighting. Ihor didn't think the lull would last long. Not only had the Red Army failed to break into Paderborn, the enemy had pushed several kilometers east of the city. Something had to give. Either the Americans were going to try to move up again or his own side would mount another drive to the west.

When Soviet tanks clattered up under cover of darkness, Ihor realized which of those was about to happen. The chemical-factory stink of diesel exhaust made him cough.

And the armored vehicles made him stare. They were a motley mix of T-54s, modern as day after tomorrow; SU-100s, hard-hitting assault guns that still packed a punch; and T-34/85s, which, as far as he was concerned, might just as well have stayed in the tank parks where they'd gathered cobwebs since the Nazis surrendered.

Pointing to one of those familiar silhouettes—more angular than the turtle-topped T-54—Ihor said, "They're sweeping out the antiques shop pretty hard, aren't they?"

"We both know too damn well they are," Pyotr Boky replied. "Why else d'you think they made you corporal?"

"Yob tvoyu mat'," Ihor replied, more amiably than not. He knew full well that Boky had at least part of a point. It wasn't just in throwing the T-34/85s into the fight that the Soviet Union was sweeping out the antiques shop. He wouldn't have been hauled back into the Red Army, much less promoted corporal, unless the commissars were desperate for whatever they could lay their hands on. Like the obsolescent tanks, he and most of the men in his regiment were at least better than nothing.

Lieutenant Kosior summoned his noncoms to discuss what the company would do in the upcoming attack. This was Ihor's first such gathering. If he'd expected strategy that would make Marshal Zhukov jealous, he would have been doomed to disappointment. Since he had enough experience of the Red Army to expect very little, he wasn't.

"We go in before dawn tomorrow," Kosior sad, "as soon as our shelling lets up. Keep the men moving. Keep them close to the armor. They'll stay safer that way, and they'll take out the Yankees with bazookas and keep the tanks safer, too. Any questions?" He waited. None of the corporals and sergeants said anything. He nodded. "All right. Good luck to all of you. We serve the Soviet Union!"

"We serve the Soviet Union!" the noncoms echoed, Ihor loud among them.

As soon as the guns left off pounding the enemy positions ahead, the tanks and assault guns rolled forward through mud and chilly rain. Along with everybody else, Ihor gulped his hundred-gram vodka ration. It was enough to make you not care so much about what might happen to you, not enough to leave you too stupid or clumsy to fight.

Stanislav Kosior blew a loud blast on his brass officer's whistle. "Forward! Forward for the Soviet Union and the great Stalin!"

He believed it, or he'd acted well enough to convince Ihor he did. "For the great Stalin!" Ihor roared at the top of his lungs. If you were going to be a liar, best to be a loud liar.

He didn't need long to decide it wouldn't be the Red Army's day. The artillerymen hadn't done enough to stun the Americans or knock out their machine-gun positions. Red tracers spat through the predawn gloom, red foretelling blood and pain.

And the shelling hadn't taken out the enemy's rockets, either. A lance of fire slammed into a T-34/85. The tank twisted sideways and stopped. Flames burst from every hatch. A T-54's armor might have deflected the bazooka round. No way to know for sure. The only thing Ihor knew for sure was that the bazooka killed the older tank. More to the point, it killed the tank's five-man crew. All he could hope was that they died before they suffered.

The tanks and self-propelled guns tried to do what the artillery hadn't. They poured HE rounds into what they could see of the Yanks' defenses. They couldn't see enough. More bazookas struck at them. The machine guns went on chewing up the infantry. And U.S. artillery shells started screaming down on the Red Army soldiers.

"Dig in!" Ihor yelled—the first order he'd given as a noncom that might actually mean something. He followed it himself. One of the things he'd learned in the Great Patriotic War was how to dig in while lying flat as a crushed serpent. Like riding a bicycle, it was a skill that never went away. Unlike riding a bicycle, it could save his neck.

One of the big wheels at the Shasta Lumber Company emerged from Mahogany Row—no plebeian pine for him—and set three checks on Marian Staley's desk. "Make out a deposit slip for these and bring them back to me with it," he said. "I'll endorse them and sign the slip, and you can take them to the bank."

"Sure, Mr. Cummings," she said. What else was she going to say? She was a flunky and he was a boss, so *Sure* was the only sensible thing. But why didn't he endorse them beforehand? Why didn't he sign the deposit slip beforehand? God forbid he should try to add the three numbers himself, but the other steps would have saved time and weren't beyond even a boss' abilities.

She supposed Carl Cummings had no idea where the peons who worked for him kept the Bank of America deposit slips. Asking someone would have been beneath his dignity. Let her take care of it.

Take care of it she did. She walked down the hallway and knocked on the closed door before entering his wood-paneled sanctum. The door was so thick and solid, she barely heard him bid her come in. He affixed his John Hancock to the checks and the slip. He didn't tell her not to goof off on the way to and from the bank. He assumed she'd never dare do anything so wicked on company time.

The biggest thing he had going for him was that Weed, California, didn't offer even the most dedicated goof-off many chances to waste time. The shops weren't interesting enough to attract her.

She did light a cigarette as soon as she stepped outside. She'd largely lost the habit while she was stuck in Camp Nowhere. Now she had it back. A cigarette was one of the best excuses for wasting a little time God ever invented. She even had to stop and fiddle to get this one going. It was chilly and breezy and drizzly: wonderful weather for a boss to send a flunky out in. Let her walk the four blocks to the bank. He'd stay right where he was, where it was warm and dry.

It was Tuesday, not Friday, so the bank wasn't full of loggers cashing their checks. She went in, did what she had to do, and walked out again. "To hell with you, Mr. Cummings, sir," she muttered, pausing to light another Pall Mall. If he didn't like it, too damn bad.

After blowing out smoke, she started back to the office as slowly and reluctantly as Linda headed for school. Her eyes traveled up the street. They traveled down the street. If she saw anything even the least little bit interesting in one of the shop windows, she intended to walk in and have a look around. And if his High and Mightiness Mr. Carl Cummings didn't like it, too goddamn bad.

There *was* something interesting. A storefront that had been dark and empty behind a plate-glass window since before she came to Weed now had a light on inside. The new place, whatever it was, must have opened in the past few days. Otherwise, she would have noticed it earlier. She was sure she *would* have noticed, too; any changes in downtown Weed stood out.

She walked half a block to the new business. She hoped it would be a place that sold children's clothes and not, say, another gun shop. Weed already had two of those. The business they did was so brisk, the town might have room for a third. If Russian invaders ever came as far as Weed, local hunters and plinkers might be able to drive them back without waiting for help from the U.S. Army.

It turned out to be neither. Large Old English gold letters on the plate glass proclaimed **Shoes Repaired**. Smaller ones said **Half Soles, Heels, Steel Toes, Ripped Uppers.** Another line added **Custom shoes made to order**.

Marian nodded to herself. Weed hadn't had a cobbler's shop. With all the loggers who lived in and around the little town, she could see that one might well make good money. Someone else must have seen the same thing. That thought had just crossed her mind when she reached the last, smallest, and most modest line of gold lettering. It said **Fayvl Tabakman, proprietor.**

She blinked. She rubbed her eyes. The lettering still said the same thing, even if it was hard to read. *See what happens when you send a postcard?* she thought dizzily. She hadn't heard back from Tabakman after she mailed the photo of Mt. Shasta. She hadn't even been sure it got to him. The postal service at all the refugee camps ranged from erratic to worse.

But she couldn't imagine any other reason Fayvl Tabakman would suddenly wind up in Weed. She'd been looking for an excuse to waste a little time. Now she had a better one than she'd dreamt of finding.

She looked in the window. There he stood, behind the counter, in his old-fashioned cloth cap. He didn't look up at her; he was tapping away at a shoe on a last with a little cobbler's hammer. His face was a mask of concentration. Back in Everett, back before the world turned upside down and inside out, she'd appreciated the fine, precise work he did. That plainly hadn't changed.

Of itself, her hand closed on the latch. It clicked under the pressure of her thumb. The door opened. A bell above it jingled, just as one had in the now-ruined shop in Everett.

The bell made him look up from what he was doing. "Hallo, what can I—?" he began automatically. Then he did a double take that would have set the whole country laughing fit to burst had Sid Caesar or Milton Berle pulled it on TV. The smile that followed would have been pretty damn funny, too. "Marian!"

"Hello, Fayvl," she said. Here as in Camp Nowhere, a face and a voice she knew were welcome. Was it anything more than that? She'd left the camp before she'd really had to make up her mind. "Welcome to beautiful, scenic Weed."

She didn't say *beautiful, romantic Weed.* For one thing, Weed was about as romantic as the mashed potatoes from dehydrated spuds the Camp Nowhere cooks turned out by the enormous vat. For another, she *hadn't* made up her mind about *romantic.* Till she did, if she did, careful was better.

"Scenic it is, yes. The real mountain even more than your card. Beautiful? The town?" He shrugged. "Not so much."

"You know what? You're right," Marian said. "How *did* you end up here? I guess the card had something to do with it?" That, she figured, was one of the safer guesses she'd ever made.

He nodded. "That's right. I was thinking, it is time I got out of the camp. Your card, it told me where I should ought to go."

"You got down here, though," Marian said. "You have the shop. How . . . ?" Her own access to money had gone up in smoke, along with the bank she and Bill used. She'd assumed the same held true for Fayvl. If it didn't, why would he have stayed at Camp Nowhere? Why would anybody stay at Camp Nowhere who didn't have to?

"I got down here." The cobbler nodded. "Buses run. Buses, they are cheap. The shop was not such a lot, because the man who owns the building, he wants someone in here. Anyone, almost, will do. And in the camp, there are ways to get money. You stayed in your car with your little Linda. You don't know what it was like in the big tents."

Marian made a questioning noise. She not only didn't know what it had been like in the big tents, she didn't know what Tabakman was talking about. The first thing that occurred to her was the world's oldest profession. Somehow, she couldn't imagine him prospering in it.

But he didn't mean the world's oldest profession. He meant the world's oldest pastimes. "Always card games, always dice games, going on," he said. "If you gamble with your head, not with your heart, you can make money. Not always, but enough. And they played chess for money. Some of them was pretty decent. Me, in Poland I was not too bad. So I got for mineself a stake. You call it in English a stake, yes?"

"That's the word," Marian agreed.

Me, in Poland I was not too bad. What did he mean? He wouldn't have been a world champion or anything like that. Otherwise, he wouldn't have needed to keep on fixing shoes. But he was good enough to win money from players he called pretty decent. As she'd thought before, there was more to him than met the eye.

"Listen, I have to get back to work," she said. "But I'll see you again. I'm—I'm glad you're here." She could say that much without lying. How much she meant by it . . . they'd both find out.

Cade Curtis clumped through the trenches on the ridge line in front of Kaeryong. His felt overboots crunched on the snow. His breath smoked even when he didn't have a Camel in his mouth. It was cold—it was bloody cold—but he'd known worse. He wasn't cut off and a long, long way from anybody friendly, either. He could cope with this.

He'd done better than deal with it, in fact. They'd given him this regiment and told him to hold the ridge and keep Kaeryong out of Red Chinese hands. And, rather to his own surprise, he'd damn well done it. He was modestly (well, perhaps not so modestly) proud of that.

Here came Howard Sturgis, who did have a cigarette dangling from the corner of his mouth. He gave the barest sketch of a salute and said, "Mornin'."

"Good morning, Howie!" Cade threw his arms wide, as if to embrace the second lieutenant. "You can kiss me now."

Sturgis recoiled. "I'd sooner kiss a pig," he said. "Uh, sir."

"Is that any way to talk on Valentine's Day?" Cade sounded much more hurt than he really was.

"Valentine's Day? Already?" Sturgis made as if to count off days on his fingers. Since, like Cade, he was wearing thick wool mittens with a slit to let him pull a trigger when he had to, he quickly gave that up as a bad job. Instead, with a sheepish smile, he said, "Time flies when you're having fun."

"Right," Cade said. "It flies so fast that the year and a half I've been here seems like forever."

"I believe that." Now Sturgis' smile turned crooked. "And how's democracy coming along, sir?"

"Oh, shut up," Cade said. "Hard to imagine how our enemies could like it a whole lot less than our so-called friends do."

"Yeah, but if you shoot the Commie gooks our brass pins more medals on you," Sturgis said. "If you make like you're gonna shoot the ROK gooks, the brass rakes you over the coals. You already went back to Division once. How come they didn't bust you down to PFC?"

"Because they saw I didn't care if they did." That was the only explanation that made any sense to Cade.

He discovered it also made sense to Howard Sturgis. "There you go!" the older man said. "I'd shake their hands and thank 'em if they made me a sergeant again. Trouble is, the fuckers know it, so they never will. You think I *want* to run a company? Christ!"

"You might be running one even if you were a sergeant," Cade said. All the companies save one in his outfit had officers in charge of them, but that one was still under a veteran three-striper. It seemed to run as well as any of the others, which was . . . interesting, anyhow. Cade wagged a finger at Sturgis. "And don't call 'em gooks, dammit, especially not where there's even a little chance they can hear you."

"What do you want I should call 'em? Niggers?"

That opened a different can of worms. As a little kid, Cade had heard the word all the time. Some Southern whites used it to revile people with dark skins, others simply to describe them. It all depended on how you said it, and on how the people who were listening to you took it.

As World War II wore on, as Americans began to see what the Nazis had done to Jews in lands they ruled, and as people with dark skins began to insist they were people like anybody else, *nigger* started to be used less and less. Cade had said it only a handful of times, if that, since the war ended.

Things in the South had gone on the same way, more or less, from the end of Reconstruction to Pearl Harbor. Strange to think that, but for Hitler, they might have kept on that way for another generation or two. They wouldn't here and now. Cade could see as much.

With an effort, he wrenched himself away from the American South and back to South Korea. "Gook, to them, is as bad as nigger is to a Negro," he said. "Even when they don't savvy any English at all, they know what that means. So just forget you ever heard it, okay?"

That was an order, though he might not phrase it as one. Sturgis had been in the Army too long to mistake it for anything else. "Okay, sir. I'll watch it," he replied. His face told what he thought of the order, but that had nothing to do with anything. This wouldn't be the first order he'd disliked that he had to follow, or the last.

"Thanks, Howie." Cade tried to soften things as much as he could.

"Sure." Mischief glinted in Sturgis' eyes. "How's about I just call 'em kikes? That's one they probably won't know."

Cade started to ream him out. Luckily, he saw the glint before he said anything. He made do with a dry chuckle and one word: "Cute."

"Phooey on you, sir," Sturgis said. "You're taking my fun away."

"Besides," Cade said, "you don't want to get Jimmy ticked at you, right?"

"Well, no, there is that," Howard Sturgis allowed. Jimmy was the ROK private Cade had rescued from Captain Pak Hosan. Now that he'd been rescued, he was doing his best to turn into a GI. His real name was Chun Won-ung. Americans thought learning Korean was a waste of time. Chun became Jim and Jim became Jimmy, a handle they could wrap their tongues around. Sturgis said, "Only thing is, he's liable to start calling the ROK chumps gooks himself."

He was, too. The more he stuck with the Americans, the

more scorn he had for the folk he'd come from. But before Cade could reply, a voice blared perfect English from the Red Chinese loudspeakers: "Happy Valentine's Day, Yankees!" A POW with a gun at his head? An American Red who'd fled his country one jump ahead of J. Edgar Hoover's G-men? Whoever he was, he went on, "Want to see your squeeze back home? Don't want to go back in a box, or missing an arm or a leg, or blind? Come on over to the people's side, the side of the workers' revolution! We'll treat you right! We'll feed you and we'll send you home as soon as this stupid capitalist war is over. Don't fight your class allies!"

"I wish those noisy bastards'd stick to leaflets," Howard Sturgis said.

"How come?" Cade asked.

"On account of I can't wipe my ass with noise from a loudspeaker."

"Well, okay." Cade laughed. He didn't know what he'd expected. Whatever it was, that wasn't it.

Getting yelled at by the enemy was better than getting shot at, but it wore thin in a hurry. The Red Chinese kept playing the same message over and over, always at top volume. They probably had a bored corporal standing by the phonograph and smoking a cigarette while he waited for the record to get to the end. Then he'd grab the tone arm, put the needle back at the beginning, and send the lies out one more time.

When one side's snipers scored a couple of hits, the other side would deploy more sharpshooters with scope-sighted rifles to pay them back. When one side's machine gunners kept raking the other's forward positions, their foes' machine guns soon made life miserable for their front-line troops. Mortars begat more mortars; artillery, more artillery.

And a propaganda bombardment quickly brought on a propaganda counterbombardment. The loudspeakers behind the American lines started bellowing at the Red Chinese in their own language. Cade had always thought a Chinese conversation sounded like cats in a sack right after you'd kicked the sack. Listening to it hideously amplified did nothing to improve it.

There, he found Howard Sturgis in complete agreement with him. "Jesus H. Christ!" Sturgis said, wincing. "That shit'd drive anybody Asiatic. Makes me want to grab a Tommy gun like yours and shoot up those goddamn speakers."

Cade held out the PPSh. "Here. Be my guest, man. No

court-martial would convict you. Hell, they'd probably promote you."

"Don't tempt me, sir." Sturgis made pushing-away motions. "Y'know, even if they did convict me, I could probably get out of it on a Section Eight."

"A psych discharge? I wouldn't be surprised." Cade shook his head. "No, I take it back—I would. You have to be crazy to be in Korea, right? Everybody says so, and when everybody says something it's gotta be true. So if they gave Section Eights to everyone who deserved it, nobody'd be left to fight the war."

"Shit. You're right. We're fucked coming and going." Sturgis lit a fresh cigarette. Loudspeakers roared Chinese at loudspeakers roaring English. Cade began to wish for a Section Eight himself.

ISTVAN SZOLOVITS PULLED OFF his uniform. The barracks in the POW compound had a stove in it, but it wasn't what anybody would have called warm. As if to prove he'd lost his mind, he pulled on red socks, white shorts, and a short-sleeved green shirt with the number 3 on the front and back.

As he was tying on his football boots—they had longer cleats than army boots, although that might not matter much if the pitch was frozen—Miklos told him, "Go get 'em, Jew-boy!"

"You're fucking crazy, you know that?" Istvan said.

"Like hell I am," said the Magyar ornamented with the Arrow Cross and the Turul. "You may be a fucking clipcock, but you're a clipcock on the Hungarian team. And if you give those Czech dipshits a quarter of what you gave me, they'll run from you the way they ran in World War I."

If Istvan gave anybody on the football pitch a quarter of what he'd given Miklos, the man in black would eject him from the match and probably ban him from playing in any more. Miklos had to know it, too. But center-back wasn't a position for ballet dancers. As much as you could be in a game, you were in the trenches there.

Since the war, Hungarian football had been some of the best in the world. The national team might well be favored at the upcoming World Cup . . . if the team members stayed alive, and if there was enough of a world left to hold a World Cup when 1954 came around.

This match wouldn't be like that. Istvan hadn't been sure he could make the team when he tried out. He really hadn't been sure because the coach, a captain named Viktor Czurka, had Colonel Medgyessy's attitude toward Jews. But the captain cared more about football than he did about Istvan's missing foreskin. Seeing Istvan could do the job better than the man he had in there, he said, "We'll see how you play Saturday."

Istvan had practiced as much as he could with the other backs. A good back line was a unit. Like an army, they advanced and retreated together. If they didn't, the other side would get in behind them and then the keeper would be screaming at them as he went to the back of the net to pick up the ball that had just tallied a goal.

"Let's go get 'em," said the captain. He was the team's number 9, the striker. Geza was small and quick and dangerous, like an adder. Off the pitch, he was a lance-corporal, a nobody. On it, he ran the show.

Footballers and ordinary POWs headed for the pitch. The Czechoslovakians—red shirts, blue shorts, white socks—and their supporters came out of their barracks at the same time. The Poles and East Germans didn't have a dog in this fight, but they were eager to watch and bet.

"Arschlochen!" Miklos yelled at the Czechoslovakians.

"Schweinehunde!" a Czech or Slovak shouted back. Yes, it might still have been the days of the Austro-Hungarian Empire. The only way Magyars and Czechoslovakians could insult one another and make sure they got the message across was to use German. Chances were the Poles could manage in it, too.

The referee was a French sergeant. He must have come from Alsace, because he spoke German himself, with an accent that made Istvan have a devil of a time following him. Well, he had an accent himself when he spoke German. The guys from Prague and Bratislava had a different one. The way they all talked would have appalled someone from Cologne or Leipzig.

An aluminum-bronze ten-franc coin spun in the chilly air. Geza won the toss. He chose to play against the breeze in the first half. The Czechoslovakians would kick off to start the game, then.

And they did, as soon as the referee's whistle gave the signal. They were big men, mostly beefier of face and feature than the Magyars. The teammates who'd been here long enough to have played them before said that they were also slower, and that they weren't shy about throwing elbows.

Well, Istvan wasn't shy about throwing elbows, either. You couldn't be, if you were going to play back. And everybody on both sides was a soldier. They'd all seen, and many of them had done, things far worse than any that happened on the pitch.

Here came one of the Czechoslovakian midfielders, dribbling with decent skill. Istvan moved up to cut off his path. The guy in the red shirt tried a dummy, pretending to go right but then really cutting left. His eyes telegraphed the move. Before he could bring it off, Istvan stole the ball with his left foot.

He quickly sent it up to a Hungarian midfielder. "Yeah! There you go!" the other center-back called.

"Thanks, Gyula." Istvan wanted to do well. Doing well would help him fit in, make him less the man on the outside looking in.

A halfway-promising Hungarian attack developed. A linesman aborted it, raising his flag to show that a Magyar had been offside.

"You're blind, you *Dummkopf*!" Istvan yelled. He was fifty meters away from the play, but he assumed the referee's assistant must have got it wrong. He knew how football worked. What were linesmen good for but botching calls when your side was on the move?

The Czechoslovakian goalkeeper, a mountain of a man, booted the ball down to the Magyars' end. Istvan sprang into the air to head it away. A foe also leaped, to flick it on toward the goal. They crashed together and knocked each other sprawling. The ball flew over them both.

"You good?" Istvan asked as he scrambled to his feet. The ground was hard and cold.

"I'll live," the Czechoslovakian said.

They went back and forth, as evenly matched sides will. The Hungarians scored. Less than two minutes later, the Czechoslovakians equalized. Then they went ahead. Just before halftime, one of the men in red broke through the Magyars' midfielders and charged toward Istvan. One other man was still behind him, but he took no chances. He leveled the Czechoslovakian.

As he'd known it would, the referee's whistle screamed. The man he'd fouled swore at him in German, which he understood, and then in Czech, which he didn't. When the ref ran up to position the ball for the free kick, he said, "You do that again and I'll throw your sorry ass out of the match. You hear me?"

"I hear you." Istvan did his best to sound sorry. The Frenchman put him in mind of Sergeant Gergely. He wouldn't listen to excuses or nonsense.

He grudged a nod. "All right. Once, all right—not twice. That was a professional foul, and this isn't a professional game."

But the Czechoslovakian who tried the free kick put the ball a meter over the crossbar. So the professional foul did what it was supposed to do: it took his team out of danger.

At halftime, Captain Czurka smacked Istvan on the back. "That's how you do it!" he said. "Don't back away from the bastards. Never back away from the bastards. If they beat us, they beat us. But we'll still be going forward when that frog fucker blows the whistle to end things."

Halfway through the second period, a burly Czechoslovakian knocked Istvan head over heels. He was nowhere near the ball, but that had nothing to do with anything. It was payback for the professional foul. He reassembled himself, got up, and went on with the game. A few minutes later, when the referee was looking somewhere else, he flattened the red-shirt who'd got him.

"Don't fuck with me, turdnose," he said as he trotted away.

Geza scored twice in the match, once on a header from a corner kick, the other time with a half-volley any professional would have been proud to claim as his own to give the Hungarian side the lead once more. But the Czechoslovakians leveled things again five minutes before full time, and the match ended 3–3.

The draw left everybody imperfectly satisfied. The weary Hungarian footballers shook hands with their opponents. As Istvan came off the pitch, Miklos folded him into a bear hug. Istvan would have laughed if he hadn't been so tired. Like a surprising number of Fascists, Miklos had found himself his very own pet Jew.

Daisy Baxter had her strength back, or most of it. She was getting her hair back. She was out of hospital in East Dereham (Bruce said *out of* the *hospital,* as if it were something special, which it surely wasn't), and living in a furnished room above a chemist's shop.

She had the rent covered because of what had happened to Fakenham, and got a couple of quid a week to keep her going.

She was on the dole, was what she was. It should have been humiliating, but living through an atom bomb took away a lot of smaller stings.

She might have dwelt on it more if she hadn't been happy. Happiness was something she wasn't used to. It felt faintly illicit, or more than faintly, like a drug that made you think you were God or at least Superman but that could send you to gaol if the coppers caught you with it.

She'd had happiness wiped off her map the moment she learned Tom was dead. Since then . . . every day had been gray and cold and drizzly. She'd got used to gray and cold and drizzly; she'd come to think that was the way things were meant to be.

Now she'd changed her mind. It wasn't what Bruce made her feel, not in the physical sense of the word. Yes, he knew how to please a woman. But he couldn't make the lights go on behind her eyes any better than her own hand could. Every so often, after Tom died, her body had felt the need for that. Quietly and without any fuss, she'd taken care of it. Then the need went away . . . till the next time.

Your hand could scratch that particular itch, certainly. What your hand couldn't do, though, was make you not feel lonely afterwards. More often than not, you felt lonelier than before, because as the brief pleasure faded you remembered that once upon a time you'd enjoyed it in the company of someone you loved, not all by yourself.

That was what had gone missing. That was the absence that turned her life drizzly and cold and gray. Now she had it back again. It was like going from Kansas to Oz. Suddenly, the world's film ran in glorious Technicolor.

Of course, with a man you always worried that he was just out for whatever he could get, that he cared more about what you were doing to him than about you as you. Till Bruce came along, Daisy'd ignored every would-be ladykiller who walked into the Owl and Unicorn. That worry was the biggest reason why.

As he'd given her joy, there in the jeep stopped between Yaxham and East Dereham, so she'd returned it. If that was all he'd been after, or if he'd decided she was a slut and he didn't want anything more to do with her now that he'd had his fun, she never would have heard from him again.

She also wouldn't have heard from him if the Russians had shot down his B-29. She had no formal ties to him, not yet. If he'd stopped coming to see her, would she ever have known why? Would some other American flyer have hunted her up to let her know Bruce's luck had run out? Or would she have spent the rest of her life wondering?

There was something she didn't need to worry about. He came to see her as often as duty let him, sometimes in a jeep (she couldn't look at one now without feeling warmth between her legs), sometimes in a hired car. "Isn't that terribly dear?" she asked him the first time he showed up in a Vauxhall.

"You mean expensive, dear?" He grinned at her, and at two countries separated by the same language. "I can spend my money on booze. I can spend it on pretty girls." He blew her a kiss. "Or I can waste it."

She made a face at him. "You're impossible! I've told you that before, haven't I?"

"Now that you mention it, toots, yeah." Bruce was still grinning. "But you know what else? I don't give a darn."

And that, she realized, had to be an understatement. Every time he climbed into a B-29, he walked through the valley of the shadow of death. Yes, he visited death and destruction on city dwellers luckless enough to live where Stalin's whim was law.

But he visited death and destruction himself with each mission he flew. She didn't know how many he'd flown, in this war and the last. All she knew was, the number wasn't small, and kept getting bigger. No wonder he seemed to live as if each moment might be his last. He knew too well that it might in truth.

So they went out drinking and dancing, and afterwards the auto would stop on some pitch-black, secluded lane. If it was a hired car and not a jeep, the windows would steam up so no one could have seen what was going on inside even if it had been noon and not midnight.

"It's warmer in an enclosed car than it is with a jeep," Daisy said during one of those nocturnal encounters.

"Yeah, it is," he agreed, his mouth no more than an inch from her ear. "But sometimes I can get a jeep from the motor pool without going through all the paperwork and stuff I need to rent a beast like this."

Which was all well and good when it wasn't pouring rain. In an English winter—or, for that matter, an English summer—the sky could turn on the tap whenever it decided to. Daisy didn't worry about that. Right this minute, Daisy wasn't worrying about anything at all.

A few minutes later, when the Vauxhall's windows had got well and truly steamed, she heard a small ripping noise, as of paper being torn. "What's that?" she asked.

"That, sweetie, is a rubber," Bruce answered. "I know you don't like taking chances, and I don't blame you a bit, but sometimes the real McCoy is better than anything else you can do."

"Oh, yes." Daisy shifted to give him room. The Vauxhall was less roomy than a jeep would have been, even if it was enclosed. Her breath sighed out. "*Oh,* yes!"

As he drove her back to East Dereham, he said, "This would all be simpler if I could just come to your room."

"It would, yes." She nodded, though she wasn't sure he could see her do it. "But you've met Mr. Perkins. He wouldn't be happy, I'm afraid."

"He'd be jealous, is what he'd be." Bruce McNulty paused. "Or maybe not—who knows? I wouldn't be surprised if he was a queer."

"Neither would I," Daisy said. Simon Perkins, the chemist above whose shop she lodged, was past fifty, and a lifelong bachelor. He was more precise than prissy, but she wondered whether any normal man could possibly have been so neat.

If he was a pansy, he was a discreet pansy. And well he might have been, when relations between men remained as illegal and scandalous as they had been in Oscar Wilde's day, and when a good many sodomites who didn't write nearly so well or so wittily as Wilde sat in prison for their crimes.

Since Bruce wasn't going much above ten miles an hour, the hired car's motor made next to no noise. When two jet fighters roared by overhead, Daisy wanted to clap her hands to her ears at the noise of their engines. "That will wake up everybody for miles around," she said.

"It sure will," Bruce agreed. "They don't scramble like that unless they're after something."

"If they are, I hope to heaven they get it!" she said.

"Doesn't have to be a Bull with an A-bomb in its belly," Bruce said. "Those rotten twin-jet Beagles are a lot harder to catch."

"Whatever it is, I want them to shoot it down before it can unload," Daisy said. "This poor country's been bombed too much already."

"Honey, the way things are right now, there aren't a whole lot of countries that haven't been bombed too much already. Take it from somebody who knows," Bruce said. "And the ones that haven't, like Venezuela or Liberia or Pakistan, you wouldn't want to live in 'em, anyway."

He was bound to be right. But those weren't Daisy's countries. England was. She went right on rooting for the fighters.

"Show me an A, Leon," Aaron Finch said.

Without hesitation, Leon chose the A from his set of wooden letters. Aaron had made and painted them himself, using patterns he'd got from *Popular Mechanics.* He'd taken special care to sand them smooth so he wouldn't give his son splinters.

"Good job!" he said. It was, too, considering that Leon was still more than two months shy of his third birthday. The kid was smart, no two ways about it. Now the real worry was whether he'd turn out too smart for his own good, the way Marvin had. Aaron shrugged. In a kid not quite three, that was a worry for another day. "Now can you show me a V?"

The A was easy. It was the first letter of the alphabet, and one of the most used. Ruth had bought a Scrabble set not too long before, which underlined that. V was at the back of the line and in narrower use. Leon didn't hesitate, though. He grabbed it and said, "Vee!"

"That's what that is," Aaron said. "You *are* getting good at this stuff, kiddo."

"Vee!" Leon squealed, and threw it as far as he could. He didn't throw far or straight. Not only was he still a little guy, but his brain ran ahead of his body. He wasn't what anybody would call graceful. Aaron wondered if he ever would be. Himself, he'd always had arms and legs that did just what he told them to. His son might not.

None of which had anything to do with anything. "Go pick that up and put it back with the rest of the letters," Aaron said.

Leon pooched out his lower lip. "I don't wanna!" he declared.

"You made the mess. You police it up," Aaron told him. You couldn't expect a kid his age to clean up after himself all the time. Little kids and messes went together like coffee and cream. But Leon had to understand he couldn't get away with chucking his toys around for the fun of it.

"Don't wanna!" he repeated. No, he didn't get that yet.

"I didn't ask you what you wanted. I told you what you needed to do." Aaron waited. When Leon showed no signs of going after the red V, his father wheeled out the heavy artillery: "I guess you don't feel like sleeping with Bounce tonight."

That turned the trick. Aaron had thought it would. Leon was as attached to the Teddy bear as if it had grown out of his hip. As far as he was concerned, going to bed without it was a tragedy beside which the A-bomb that smashed downtown L.A. was as nothing. He talked to it while he was awake, and answered for it, too. He halfway made Aaron believe it was alive.

Now he scurried over to the wooden letter and made a small production of bringing it back to the rest of the set. "Okay?" he asked.

"You did it, so that's good," Aaron said. "But do you know why you did it?"

Leon looked at him as if he were an imbecile. "So Bounce will sleep with me." He wasn't good at lying yet. Whatever went through his head came out of his mouth.

"You did it because leaving it lying out there is sloppy," Aaron said. "And you did it so nobody would step on the V. It might get broken, or it might hurt Daddy or Mommy's foot."

The summer before, crazy Bill Veeck had brought a midget to the plate to start a game for the St. Louis Browns against the Tigers. From what the papers said, the Tigers' hurler tried to pitch to him, but was laughing so hard that all his offerings went way high. Aaron could see that his explanation flew over Leon's head by at least as much.

He didn't give up. Leon was growing every single day. An explanation that flew over his head today wouldn't tomorrow, or maybe the day after. And he remembered things, even when he didn't fully understand them. Aaron's older brother Sam had a memory like that. He didn't himself, but he'd seen how useful it could be.

Ruth walked in from the kitchen after finishing the dinner dishes. Leon picked up the letter he'd just retrieved. "Look, Mommy! It's a V!"

"You're right. It *is* a V," his mother said. "Can you show me an A?"

Leon's face clouded. "I already did that one."

"Mommy didn't see you do it," Aaron reminded him. "Find the A again, and then she'll give you a new letter."

"Oh, okay." Leon might have reached a deal for the price of a secondhand car. He picked up the A and held it over his head, as if to show this was really too easy for someone of his talents.

"That's the A, all right," Ruth said. "Now show me the Q."

"Ten points!" Leon sang out. Aaron and Ruth looked at each other. Yes, they played Scrabble, but Aaron had never expected Leon to pick that up. His son had no trouble finding the wooden letter. "It's got a little tail, like a piggy," he said. That was how Aaron had told him to know which was the Q and which the O.

Aaron had made the blocks only a couple of months earlier. He hadn't thought Leon would be ready for them yet, but the kid kept surprising him. By now, Leon could reliably pick out almost all the letters. E and F sometimes confused him, and every so often he'd use an upside-down W for an M or vice versa. Other than that, he had them straight.

"One of these days before too long," Aaron said, "I'm going to dig out my old reader." He and Marvin had both learned to read from it. It was made, and made well, to show little kids how to put letters together to make words. Marvin had used it to help teach Olivia how to read. When Aaron had a son, he'd passed it along.

"He's not ready to read yet," Ruth said, but then she softened it by adding, "I don't think."

"Well, I don't think he is, either, not yet," Aaron admitted. "I said before not too long, not right this minute."

"Okay." His wife nodded, perhaps with relief.

Oblivious to them both, Leon built a tower out of the letters. They were also good for that. Then he finished reenacting Babel from the Bible by knocking the tower over like an angry Jehovah. "Kaboom!" he yelled as the letters flew and bounced and cartwheeled every which way.

Destruction complete, Leon started to head off to some new mayhem. "Hang on a second, sport," Aaron said, holding up a hand like a traffic cop. "What do you do after you make a mess? We were just talking about that, remember?"

If Aaron hadn't asked if he remembered, Leon would have been all the more tempted to forget. But he couldn't resist showing off how much he knew. "You police it up." He even got the word right.

"Why don't you do that, then? Put the letters back in the box I made for them," Aaron said.

That wasn't Leon's idea of fun. You always had a better time making your mess than cleaning it up afterwards—a great human truth not enough people thought about ahead of time. But Leon must also have remembered the dreadful prospect of a night without Bounce. He started retrieving letters and returned them to the ABC box.

"You still need to get the G and the N," Ruth said when Leon looked as if he thought he was done. "They're over there by the coffee table."

"Hoo, boy," Leon said.

Aaron laughed so hard, he started coughing. Words and intonation were a perfect imitation of Ruth when she had to do something else on top of everything she'd already done. The world might have been too much with Leon, but he went over and got the last two letters.

"Anybody would think he listens to us or something," Ruth said.

"Little pitchers have big ears, yeah," Aaron said. "Wait till he turns sixteen, though. See if he hears a word we tell him then."

He'd be in his mid-sixties himself when Leon hit sixteen. He wondered whether he'd be able to keep up with a boy who imagined himself a man. That worry was still years away, though. For now, he lit another Chesterfield.

It was late in the year for snow. The stuff drifted down over north-central Germany, thick and wet. The sky was gray. The land was white. Color seemed to have washed out of the world.

"Christ, you'd hardly think this was Germany," Gustav Hozzel said. "Reminds me of the Ukraine in 1943."

"Me, I was thinking of Spring Awakening in Hungary in '45," Rolf said. "Except it was more rain and less snow then. When we got the move order, I watched the Tigers bog down in the mud and I thought, *Shit, this won't work the way they planned it.*"

"Well, you were right about that." Max Bachman said it before Gustav could. They looked at each other. Neither of them was in the habit of saying such a thing to Rolf.

"Hey, we drove the Ivans back in spite of the shitty weather,"

Rolf said. "We pushed 'em for a solid week, made 'em retreat, thirty, forty, some places even fifty kilometers. Even in March of 1945, we were better soldiers than they ever dreamt of being."

He was a *Waffen*-SS veteran, all right. He remained proud of everything the LAH and the other SS panzer divisions had accomplished. He ignored everything they'd done that made almost all the other countries in the world ally with Stalin against the Nazis. And he ignored the bitter crack from Sepp Dietrich, who'd commanded the Sixth SS Panzer Army during Operation Spring Awakening—*They call us the Sixth Panzer Army because we've only got six panzers.*

"Rolf . . ." Gustav put things as gently as he could: "How much good did driving the Russians back fifty kilometers do for the war? Didn't we lose just as fast as if you'd stayed in the barracks and played skat? It was March of 1945, for God's sake. The *Reich* was screwed coming, going, and sideways."

"We fought hard, anyway," Rolf said. "We didn't know how messed up things were all over."

"You didn't? You weren't looking real hard, were you?" Max said. "Why did you think we were in Hungary instead of in Russia, the way we were a year earlier? Did we fall back so the Magyars could teach us to dance the fucking mazurka?"

"You know what you've got, Bachman? You've got a goddamn big mouth." Rolf tapped a Lucky from an American ration pack against the back of his hand before he stuck it in his own mouth.

You know what you've got, Rolf? You've got a goddamn small brain. Gustav was tempted to come out with it, but he didn't. There were things over which he and Max would never agree with Rolf. Agree with him or not, though, the ex-LAH man was somebody good to have on your side. Next to that, the arguments about what had been, what might have been, and what should have been were nothing serious.

The three Germans and their countrymen sat in the wreckage on the east side of Warberg, a small town ten or fifteen kilometers east of Marsberg. The front south of Paderborn hadn't moved much lately. The Ivans weren't giving ground the way they had right after the A-bombs smashed them farther west. They fought hard when the Germans came at them, and hit back hard whenever they saw a chance.

"Hello!" Rolf pointed east. "What the devil's that about?" Hard suspicion filled his voice.

Flares flew into the low-ceilinged sky: red and green and white together. The Russians didn't normally use that kind of signal. Here, Gustav found himself agreeing with Rolf once more. Any time the Ivans did something unfamiliar, you found yourself wondering and worrying about what was up.

Gustav didn't have to wonder long. Drawn by those flares, a squadron of Shturmoviks zoomed in from the east to shoot up Warberg and pound it with bombs and rockets. The Germans on the ground fired at the Il-10s with rifles and submachine guns and machine guns.

Even as Gustav emptied his assault rifle into the air, he knew he was wasting ammo. Two of the nicknames *Landsers* had given the Shturmovik in the last war were Flying Tank and Iron Gustav. Engine and cockpit were both heavily armored, making the attack plane invulnerable to small arms.

But the Ivans got a nasty surprise of their own. Three American jet fighters swooped down on the Shturmoviks from above. They were straight-winged F-80s, planes hardly better than the *Luftwaffe*'s Me-262 (as Rolf would have been sure to point out had Gustav said anything about them). They far outclassed the prop-driven attack aircraft, though. In less than two minutes, three Shturmoviks were burning wrecks, their corpses sending pillars of greasy black smoke up to the clouds. The rest of the Il-10s raced east as fast as they could, hoping to find a country where such things didn't happen.

When Russians had a plan, they stuck to it even if parts of it didn't work the way they wanted. Even though the Shturmoviks hadn't hit the Germans in Warberg as hard as they would have wanted, they followed up the air assault with a brief mortar barrage. Then the infantry came forward.

Some of the Red Army men had snow smocks and white trousers over their uniforms. Others wore khaki, and stood out against the background almost like running lumps of coal.

Regardless of whether he thought they had any chance of breaking through, Russian attacks always scared the whey out of Gustav. The Ivans advanced as if they didn't care whether they lived or died. That probably meant they feared the secret policemen behind them more than the enemy soldiers ahead. They kept coming till they took their objective or till they all fell trying.

Sometimes they did that. Not always. They showed they were human after all at the oddest times. Anything they weren't looking for could turn them from stoic heroes to fear-mad fugitives in seconds.

That was what happened this morning. The Germans had a well-hidden machine gun farther forward than the Ivans realized. And it wasn't just any old machine gun. It was an MG-42, a *Wehrmacht* leftover that still outdid any other country's murder mill.

The crew played it cool, too. They let the Russians hurry past them, then opened up from what was now a flank. The Red Army men started falling from bullets that seemed to come out of nowhere. And one MG-42 could put out as much fire as a company's worth of riflemen.

Quite suddenly, the Russians weren't running toward Warberg any more. They were running away as fast as they could, those still able to. Before he joined the *Wehrmacht,* Gustav had thought it wasn't sporting to shoot a man in the back. That attitude didn't last long on the Eastern Front. You did whatever you could to stay alive.

Dead men's greatcoats were blots on the snow. Splashes and drizzles of scarlet seemed an artist's embellishments . . . if the artist worked with pain and suffering. Gustav clicked a fresh magazine onto his AK-47. He had only a couple more left, but he could scavenge plenty from the dead Russians.

He lit a Lucky of his own. After a deep drag, he said, "They ought to pin gongs on those machine gunners."

"Amen!" Max agreed.

"You bet." Rolf nodded, too. "Hit the Ivans from the side when they don't expect it and it's two to one they go to pieces. They're as sensitive about their flanks as a virgin."

"They aren't virgins any more," Gustav said. "We fucked 'em pretty hard here." He got a dirty laugh from Rolf and a smile from Max.

Not all the men lying in front of Warberg were dead. Some still thrashed and cried out to the uncaring heavens. An Ivan carrying a white flag came forward. "Permission to pick up our wounded?" he shouted in good German. "An hour's truce?"

"An hour," a German officer agreed. "Starting *now.*" The Russian waved. Stretcher-bearers hurried forward. Gustav swore under his breath. The nerve of them, taking ammo away from him like that!

HARRY TRUMAN TURNED ON the radio in the Oval Office. After it warmed up, music came out. It wasn't music he particularly enjoyed, but it didn't make him want to heave the set through the window and watch it smash on the White House lawn.

Fewer and fewer comedies and dramas were on the radio these days. Some of them had migrated to TV; others had simply disappeared. For more than a few of them, disappearing was the best thing they could have done. Now if only something interesting had taken their place.

Whoever this singer was, he wouldn't make Sinatra go back to hustling pool and shooting craps in Hoboken. The President endured him because it was almost the top of the hour. Like the papers, radio news helped him keep a finger on the country's pulse.

The song stopped. The singing commercials that followed it made Truman think Beethoven had done its music and Caruso the singing. It wasn't that good. They were that bad. He thought only residents of a home for the feebleminded would want to buy the cleanser and soap and margarine they plugged, but some ad man out there was in a high tax bracket because he'd perpetrated them.

Then an announcer said, "This is WRC radio, Washington, D.C., 980 on your dial." NBC's familiar chimes followed. The announcer went on, "The National Broadcasting Corporation brings you the news."

"Good evening," the newscaster said. "Here is the news. In the war, Red jet bombers have staged nuisance raids against France, Italy, and southern England. Damage is said to be light, and American and English night fighters have claimed several Russian planes as destroyed or damaged. No fighters are known to have been lost."

Just because they'd claimed them didn't mean they'd hit them. Those Russian Beagles were pests. They got in, they dropped their bombs, and they got out. They didn't hang around waiting to get shot down the way the lumbering Soviet Bulls (and identically lumbering American Superfortresses) did. The only thing they couldn't do was carry atom bombs. *Thank God for small favors,* thought Truman, who didn't have many large favors to thank Him for.

"Italian defense authorities have officially denied that Bologna is under Russian control," the newscaster went on. "They insist that their forces, stiffened by American soldiers and tanks, still hold the important city."

And that was a bunch of bologna, or Bologna, or plain old baloney, too. Truman knew it was only too well. No matter what the Italians denied, the Red Army was in Bologna. Italy was a backwater in this war, as it had been in the last. Had Stalin wanted to, he could have grabbed much more of it. But his generals were mostly using it as a road to southern France.

American troops waited to try to stop the Russians if they got past the mountains on the border between Italy and France. They waited here and there, scattered across Provence and Savoy. You couldn't concentrate men the way marshals had all through history. One A-bomb and they would be history themselves. Everybody was having to learn how to fight all over again.

"In Korea, the UN High Command has admitted the fall of the town of Kaeryong to the Red Chinese and North Koreans. Strong defensive positions south of Kaeryong will make it impossible for the enemy to advance any farther."

Truman wished he had a knock of bourbon. The whiskey might wash the taste of all these lies out of his mouth. The strong defenses had been on the high ground north of Kaeryong. They'd kept back the flood for a long time, but here it was.

"In domestic politics, Senator McCarthy has won the allegiance of two convention delegates from Ohio, which is Senator Taft's home state," the broadcaster said.

Truman said something he was glad Bess couldn't overhear. Her reproachful cluck would have hurt him worse than a smack in the face from someone he cared about less. Even George Marshall would have raised an eyebrow at Truman's choice of words. The men who'd served the battery of 75s he'd commanded in 1918, though, would have laughed till they had to hold their ribs—not at what he'd said, for they all talked that way Over There, but at the idea that a little cussing could embarrass him.

Well, Joe McCarthy embarrassed him. That the United States could think Joe McCarthy made a good President did more than embarrass him. It scared the crap out of him.

Not that anyone political paid the least attention to a word he said these days. Since announcing he wouldn't run again, he was a lame duck, a ruptured duck, a dead duck. He'd known he would be. He'd put it off as long as he could.

His fellow Democrats thought he'd put it off too damn long. Alben Barkley wanted to be President, but no one else seemed to want him in the White House. When you were the Vice President in an administration that pulled the country into an atomic war, that was liable to happen to you. Averell Harriman, who was Truman's fix-it man in Europe and the Middle East, also wanted to be President. He had the same problem on a smaller scale, because fewer people had heard of him. Estes Kefauver wanted to be President, too. Whether the country felt like electing anyone, even a capable Senator, from the wrong side of the Mason-Dixon line was anybody's guess.

And Adlai Stevenson wanted to be President. He was from Illinois, a good state to be from if you had that particular craving. He was smart. He was witty. He had everything a good politician needed except any real connection with the little man.

That would hurt him against McCarthy, who was nothing if not an ordinary Joe. It would hurt him against Dwight Eisenhower, too. Eisenhower had presided over a war America won cheaply and easily. That also gave him a leg up on any Democratic foe.

If the Republicans ran Taft . . . But Robert Taft was their Stevenson. He had brains. He had integrity. His main reason for wanting to sit in the White House, though, seemed to be that his father had sat there before him, so now it was his turn. Turn or not, he was about as warm as an ice cube.

Put it all together and it spelled a mess. Truman wished the new President would have been inaugurated on March 4 instead of January 20, as he had been starting in 1936. In case

McCarthy got nominated and elected, that would have given the outbound Truman six extra weeks to try to set things right.

He didn't have those six extra weeks. Maybe he didn't deserve them. Again, he wished he did stash a bottle of bourbon in the desk here. He really wanted a good, stiff knock. He'd done everything with the best intentions—and he'd gone straight down the road paved with good intentions to its appointed destination.

Western Europe smashed even worse than it had been during the last war? Who would have dreamt that was even possible? The West Coast laid waste? Oh, and Russia and Manchuria and Korea? And the Suez Canal and the Panama Canal?

"That's one hell of a bumpy ride, all right," Truman muttered. Mercifully, a slick-voiced huckster told him which brand of cigarettes doctors preferred because its smoke was so smooth. That, at least, he could ignore. He wished he could do the same with the news.

He'd done what he'd done. He hadn't thought Stalin would do what *he'd* done. How many million people were dead because he'd miscalculated? How many million twenty-first-century schoolkids would learn to curse his name along with Benedict Arnold's and Aaron Burr's because he'd miscalculated?

When you looked at it that way, how could Joe McCarthy possibly do worse than he had?

The radio went back to music. It was trying to get on with normal life. So were people all over the world. They didn't want war to interrupt important things like getting enough to eat and having a warm place to sleep, like falling in love and watching their children.

Too many children wouldn't grow up now. With a sharp twist of the wrist, Truman turned off the radio.

A road led from Smidovich to Birobidzhan. The capital of the Jewish Autonomous Region lay about eighty kilometers to the west. The road paralleled the Trans-Siberian Railway. With Khabarovsk to the east and Blagoveshchensk to the west both hit by atom bombs, the railway was eerily quiet.

Vasili Yasevich walked along the road. His *valenki* crunched in the snow. The endless pines of the taiga ran close to the road, which was no more than a dirt track hacked through them. The pines were snow-dappled, too. They looked like overgrown Christmas trees in a children's book.

That thought made Vasili laugh. From what people in Smidovich said, corrective-labor camps were scattered through the taiga. Every day, *zeks* went out and chopped down more pines. Did the Communists send them forth on that particular kind of corrective labor to attack the trees for being symbols of religion?

He had no answers. From what he'd seen, the Communists had no answers, either. If they thought you thought that, though, you would learn more about corrective labor than you'd ever wanted to know.

His breath smoked as he walked along. His own footfalls were the only human sounds he heard. He might have been the sole person for a thousand kilometers in every direction.

He wasn't, of course. Smidovich lay only three or four kilometers behind him. Still, the odd feeling lingered. In China, separating yourself from all the other people who swarmed around you was next to impossible. It was the easiest thing in the world on this side of the Amur.

A hooded crow on a snow-covered branch cawed rustily. Nice warm feathers covered its body, but its feet were bare and scaly, like a lizard's. Why didn't they freeze? Maybe scientists knew, but Vasili didn't.

He walked on. A red squirrel chittered, warning whatever else lived in the forest that a dangerous human was running around loose. Its tail made a momentary splash of color as it darted around to the far side of the pine. A moment later, it peered around the trunk to see where he was, showing only its nose and its beady black eyes.

Vasili lit a Belomor cigarette and let the lit match fall into the snow. He got his reward—a tiny hiss he could hear clearly as the flame went out. The squirrel heard it, too, and chittered again. When Vasili blew smoke its way, it vanished to the far side of the pine once more.

He stood there smoking till the coal from the Belomor almost scorched his lips. Then he spat the butt out into the snow. No hiss this time: just a sudden extinguishing.

With a sigh, he started back to Smidovich. He hadn't felt like working today, so he damn well hadn't. He had no boss to threaten to sack him for taking the day off. Enough rubles padded his pockets to keep him in food and tobacco for a while. If he wanted to buy a magazine—and if he could find one to buy—he could do that, too.

He didn't have a big, fancy house or an expensive motorcar, a Cadillac or a Rolls-Royce. He'd soon seen that, as long as he lived in the Soviet Union, he never would. But neither would any of the other *tovarishchi* who lived here with him. No point mooning after what wasn't available.

When he got into town again, the first person he saw was Gleb Sukhanov. He waved. He didn't want the MGB man annoyed at him. But Sukhanov looked like someone with other things on his mind. His face could have doubled for the Mask of Tragedy carved on the façade of the biggest Russian theater in Harbin.

"Gleb Ivanovich!" Vasili said as he drew near the Chekist. "What's troubling you?" By the way Sukhanov's mittened left hand kept going to the side of his face, Vasili could make a shrewd guess, but he knew he might be wrong.

He wasn't. "This stupid tooth is killing me," Sukhanov answered. "It blew up last night, and I've got little men driving spikes into my jaw. I've swallowed so many aspirins, my ears are ringing like cathedral bells. Stinking thing still hurts like a kick in the balls. I see the dentist tomorrow morning so he can yank the goddamn bastard, but it feels like a million years between now and then."

"Maybe I can do something for you, Comrade." Vasili dug in his jacket pocket. He pulled out a dirty handkerchief wrapped around a lump of dark, sticky stuff. After shedding his own mittens, he pinched off about half a walnut's worth and offered it to Sukhanov. "Here. Chew half of this now and the rest tonight. That should keep you going till the dentist can do his dirty work."

"What is it?" the Chekist asked.

"Somebody paid me with poppy juice for some work I did," Vasili answered, which was true enough.

"How much do you want for it, though?" Sukhanov asked. "I know that stuff's not cheap on the left." He meant the unofficial buying and selling that went on in spite of Soviet disapproval. He wasn't wrong, either.

But Vasili said, "For you, Gleb Ivanovich, it's free. You're my friend, and you're hurting. You don't just want poppy juice. You need it."

"Thanks very much! I won't forget that," Sukhanov said.

That was exactly what Vasili hoped. Having an MGB man

in his corner was worth more than a little opium ever could be. It could prove worth its weight in gold and then some. "I hope it helps, that's all," he said.

"So do I!" Sukhanov shed his mittens, too, so he could divide the lump. He popped half into his mouth and put the rest in his pocket. As he gingerly chewed, he made a new face. "Tastes like a mountain of poppy seeds boiled down to half a liter," he said.

"That's close—it's the juice from the seed pods," Vasili said. "My father was a druggist. I never wanted to do that myself, but I know a little bit about it."

"How long does the stuff take to work?" By the way Sukhanov said it, the sooner the better.

"Twenty minutes, maybe half an hour," Vasili answered. "You'll get light-headed and sleepy. It's not just like being drunk, but it's more like being drunk than anything else."

"I was going to get drunk tonight," the Chekist said. "Anything to dull this fucker even a little bit."

"If you drink some now, that won't be too bad. But don't get smashed," Vasili told him. "That wouldn't be smart, not with the booze and the poppy juice in you at the same time. If the poppy does the job, you won't need so much vodka anyway."

"Here's hoping!" Gleb Sukhanov looked at his wristwatch. Wearing one marked him as a prominent man in Smidovich, as it would have in Harbin. There weren't enough in China or in Russia for all the men who wanted them. You had to have connections to get hold of one. "*Bozhemoi!* Why is the second hand moving so slow?"

"I hope the poppy juice helps, Comrade," Vasili said again, "and I hope the dentist isn't too awful."

"This won't be the first time I've visited Yakov Benyaminovich," Sukhanov answered glumly. "He has ether to knock you out before he does his worst."

"That's good, anyhow."

"Da." Sukhanov nodded. "It'll still be sore after I wake up, but it won't be sore like this." The rotten tooth must have twinged, because he pulled another horrible face.

Vasili thought about saying the Chekist could have some more opium then. He kept quiet, though. If Sukhanov came looking for it, he'd give him some. If not, not, and he'd have more to sell or trade. He'd already done his good deed for the day.

He did say, "Good luck, Gleb Ivanovich."

"Thanks. I can use some."

"Can't we all?" Vasili patted him on the shoulder. They went their separate ways.

Juris Eigims sat by the T-34/85, cutting up sausage with a bayonet he wasn't likely to use for anything more bloodthirsty. He reached back and set a hand on one of the tank's big steel road wheels. "She's an old whore, Comrade Sergeant," he said, "but she's *our* old whore."

"Too right, she is. Who else would want the ancient bitch?" Konstantin Morozov returned. "Hack me off about twenty centimeters of that, will you?"

"Here you go." The gunner tossed him a length.

"Thanks." Konstantin took a bite. It was stale—not surprising, when it was plunder from an abandoned butcher's shop. But it had enough salt and garlic and pepper in it to keep the ground-up pork from being too nasty. He alternated bites of chewy sausage and chunks of black bread.

"I never thought I'd get inside one of these beasts." Eigims paused to light a cigarette, then went on, "I sure watched plenty of them go by when I was a little kid."

"I bet you did," Morozov said. Latvia and Lithuania had seen heavy fighting during the last war. The Balt knew better than to say that he hadn't welcomed the T-34s he'd watched then. He would have been cheering on the Panzer IVs and Panthers that tried to hold them back. Well, too bad for him. All the Baltic lands were back under Russian rule, where they belonged. Morozov added, "When you were a little kid, I was in one of them, learning to be a tankman."

Juris Eigims grinned crookedly. "Tell me more, Grandpa."

What Konstantin told him was *"Yob tvoyu mat'."* Had the Balt taken him the wrong way, the bayonet might have got blood on it along with sausage grease. As with most things, though, what you said mattered less than how you said it.

"It's still a decent tank. It's better than I thought it was going to be." Eigims patted the road wheel again. "No wonder the Germans hated them so much. The only thing I still don't like about it is the sight. That really needs to be better."

"The suspension's good. The engine's good. The armor . . . It's sloped well, but it won't stop an AP round or a bazooka," Konstantin said.

"Neither will a T-54's," Eigims said.

"Well, you aren't wrong, no matter how much I wish you were. But with a T-54, we have as good a chance of killing the other guy as he does against us. The gun we've got now won't put a round through a Pershing's frontal armor, or a Centurion's. Not a chance."

"Mm, there is that," the Balt allowed. "We're still here, though."

"I noticed that, yes," Konstantin said dryly. Eigims chuckled. The tank commander continued, "We haven't had to do any tank-against-tank fighting lately. That has a lot to do with why we're still here."

"Why *are* we here?" Juris Eigims spoke in musing tones. "Why is anybody here? Why is there a *here* to be in? What's the point to any of it? Does any of it have a point?"

"You think *I've* got answers to shit like that?" Konstantin stared at his gunner. "What I've got is some schnapps, if you want it. You can use it to wash the taste of questions like those out of your mouth."

"Do you have enough so everybody gets a slug?" Eigims asked. "I don't want to make a pig of myself."

" 'From each according to his abilities, to each according to his needs.' Karl Marx knew what he was talking about there, fuck me in the mouth if he didn't," Morozov said. Eigims didn't try to tell him he was wrong, or that Marx was. For anybody in the Red Army to reject the preachings of the founder of the world Communist movement would have been like a Crusader bound for Jerusalem denying the Virgin Birth.

Konstantin opened one of the storage bins some enterprising mechanic or repairman had welded onto the T-34/85 during the last war. They weren't standard issue on the Soviet tank, as they had been on German machines. He took out a nearly full bottle of golden schnapps and tossed it to Eigims. The gunner caught it and yanked out the stopper. He tilted his head back. His Adam's apple worked.

After a couple of coughs, he shook his head and said, "Whew! Well, if hooch like that doesn't cure me of the constipation of philosophy, nothing ever will."

"There you go!" Konstantin said. Eigims held out the bottle to him. He drank. He liked vodka better than schnapps, but schnapps beat the crap out of nothing.

And talking about schnapps drew the rest of the crew. Konstantin gave Demyan Belitsky the bottle. "Thank you, Comrade Sergeant," the driver said politely. After his own swig, he passed it to Ilya Goledod. The bow gunner also guzzled. Goledod, from what Konstantin had seen, owned a thirst respectable even by Russian standards.

"Me? What about me?" Vazgen Sarkisyan said, watching in alarm as the schnapps level fell.

"What, you mean you want some, too?" Goledod sounded as if he couldn't believe his ears. Konstantin wouldn't have tested the loader like that. Sarkisyan was twice as thick through the shoulders as the man holding the bottle. Goledod handed it to him in the nick of time.

Though not a Russian, Sarkisyan could also put it away. He upended the bottle, drained it, and chucked it into the bushes. "Good shit," he said.

"We'll all sleep hard tonight," Konstantin said. Of course, they all would have slept hard without the schnapps, too. When war gave you a chance, you curled up and hibernated like a wintering bear. He also knew he still didn't have the full strength and energy he'd enjoyed before his bout with radiation sickness. Neither did Eigims or Sarkisyan. They functioned, but they were still damaged. In that, they were much like the army of which they made up a tiny part.

Next morning, Konstantin dry-swallowed aspirins. Schnapps hurt him worse than vodka did. His headache was in retreat when Captain Lezkov, the regimental CO, summoned his tank commanders. "We are ordered to make another attack in the direction of Paderborn," he said.

None of the sergeants said anything. Most of them were men Konstantin's age, men who'd put in their share of attacks in this fight and more than their share during the Great Patriotic War. When the brass told you attack in the direction of Somewhere-or-other, they didn't think you'd get there. From the way the fighting had been going, Morozov didn't think they'd get to Paderborn, either. The enemy had their tails up. They also had more bazookas than they knew what to do with.

"I will be in the lead tank," Captain Lezkov said. "I promise you, no one will get ahead of me. We will do what we are commanded to do. How do you like that, comrades?"

"We serve the Soviet Union!" the sergeants chorused. *And the Soviet Union serves us, too—medium-rare,* Konstantin thought.

He delivered the news to his crew. "And we'll be the point

tank for our platoon?" Demyan Belitsky asked, sounding gloomily sure he already knew the answer.

And he did. Konstantin nodded. "That's how they're going to do it."

"Maybe we'll stay lucky one more time," the driver said.

"Or maybe something will break down and they'll have to leave us behind. That would be a shame, wouldn't it?" Ilya Goledod said.

Morozov eyed the bow gunner. "That won't happen. Not a chance. And if you try to make it happen, I'll tie you to a post so the MGB firing squad can finish you off. Is that clear enough, or shall I draw you a picture, too?"

The bow gunner licked his lips. "That's very clear, Comrade Sergeant."

Nothing broke down. They clattered forward with the rest of the regiment. They'd got about a kilometer and a half closer to Paderborn when a bazooka round slammed into the engine compartment. The T-34/85 slewed sideways and stopped.

"Out!" Konstantin yelled. "Out as quick as you can! The next one blows us all to the Devil!" He scrambled out the cupola and jumped to the mud below. By what would do for a miracle, everyone escaped. Maybe that was the last round the bastard with the stovepipe had. But they wouldn't see the inside of Paderborn, not without a new tank, or even a new old tank, they wouldn't.

"Come on, you stupid pussies!" the camp guard shouted. "Come on, you sheep! Baaa! Time to get washed! Time to get sheared!"

Luisa Hozzel and Trudl Bachman made identical revolted faces at each other. They both hated this part of camp routine worse than anything else, even standing in ranks waiting for the morons counting them to be sure they had their numbers straight.

"It could be worse," Trudl said resignedly.

"How?" Luisa demanded.

"He could have yelled, 'To the showers!'"

"Oh." Luisa had no comeback to that. Who possibly could? When SS guards sent Jews to the showers after they stumbled out of cattle cars at the camps in Poland, they got cyanide instead of hot water. The only way they left those camps was through the crematorium chimneys.

These Soviet gulags weren't designed to murder you as

soon as you arrived. Had they been, Luisa and her countrywomen would have been long dead. The Russians weren't just out to murder people. They wanted to get work out of them, too. If they didn't feed them enough or give them enough rest for the work they did, if *zeks* broke down and died in large numbers because they didn't, that was a by-product of their system, not its planned result, as it had been with the Nazis.

The people who died were just as dead either way, of course.

"You'd better hurry up, cunts!" the guard said. "Or else I'll kick your skinny asses all the way to the bathhouse!"

He meant it. He'd do it. He'd laugh while he did it, too. Luisa had seen him and his pals in action before. She'd felt his boot, or that of one of his comrades. And if her behind was skinnier now than it had been before she got to this awful place, that was the Reds' fault, not hers. Gustav had always liked how she gave him plenty to grab.

"Maybe it won't be so bad this time," Trudl said as she and Luisa and the rest of the women from their barracks shambled toward the baths.

"And then you wake up!" Luisa didn't believe it for a minute. The baths and the clipping were always bad. Sometimes they were horrible.

Guards leered and whooped as the *zeks* peeled off their clothes and climbed into the tubs of water and harsh disinfectant. So did the bitches who took their pleasure from other women. As usual, Luisa tried to imagine everything was happening to someone else, not to her. As usual, she failed. However much she longed for that kind of detachment, she didn't have it.

Despite the antiseptic reek and the guards' relentless eyes, she enjoyed the bath. Hot water was a precious rarity in the camp. She wished she could soak in there, but the guards didn't let you get away with that. You climbed in, you scrubbed, and they herded you out.

It did make sense. That way, they could funnel all the *zeks* through the baths as quickly as possible. Time wasted on maintaining their bodily well-being was time when they weren't working. And what was a corrective-labor camp for, after all, if not corrective labor?

Naked, dripping, and rapidly getting cold, Luisa walked to the waiting barbers. Again, she did her best to pretend that none of this was happening to her. Again, that failed. It failed all the more completely because she found herself walking up to the man who'd clipped and fondled her when she first came, bewildered, into the camp.

"How do you like logging?" he asked in his accented German as he set to work.

"Not very much," Luisa answered: such an obvious truth that she saw no point in wasting time lying about it.

The way his eyes traveled her body made her want to hit him. Only fear of what would happen to her if she did held her back. "You're scrawnier than you were," he said, as if that were her fault.

Luisa shrugged. "And so?"

"Lift your arms," he said. Hating him, she obeyed. While he worked the clippers, he went on, "And so you don't have to be, if you stay inside the wire with somebody who takes care of you."

"Somebody like you, you mean?"

He nodded. "*Ja.* You take care of me, I take care of you, you don't go to sleep with an empty belly every night." He sheared away her pubic hair. As he had before, he felt her there while he did.

As it had before, it roused disgust and rage in her, not the lust he hoped for. "I'd sooner starve than give myself to you," she said in tones that should have shriveled him to a raisin.

He only laughed. "Well, you're on your way," he said. "You're lucky I still even notice you, that's all I've got to tell you. Pretty soon, there won't be enough of you left to bother with."

"Are you finished, you—thing, you?"

He didn't swat her on the backside, the way he had before. He patted her two or three times instead, as if he had every right to rest his hand there. That was worse. "I'm finished, all right," he answered. "You'll be finished yourself before long if you don't get some sense."

She walked off, her back stiff with fury she had no other way to show. As she started down the hall to retrieve her clothes, she saw Trudl Bachman laughing at something the man clipping her had said. Laughing!

Trudl wouldn't forget Max so casually . . . would she? When she'd said she would kiss a pig to escape from the outside work gang, she'd been joking . . . hadn't she?

The guards baked jackets and trousers and underwear and shoes to kill bugs and eggs. It was hard on the clothes, but it worked—for a few days, anyhow. But they couldn't bake all the bedding. They couldn't bake the whole barracks, which was what they really needed to do. Inevitably, she'd start itching and scratching again soon.

Coming out of the oven, the clothes were still hot when she put them back on. That had felt wonderful when winter was at its worst. Now, with the weather warming again, it wasn't quite so great, but plenty of other women besides her sighed with pleasure as they got dressed.

Trudl came up. She found the clothes with her number painted on them. She sighed, too, when she put them on. In the gulag, enjoyment was where you found it, only you couldn't find it in very many places.

Then again, you could find it if you went looking for it. "Is that barber a friend of yours?" Luisa asked, as casually as she could.

That wasn't casually enough. "No, not really," Trudl answered, her voice much colder than her jacket and trousers. "And even if he were, how does that make it your business?"

"I didn't say it was my business. I just asked," Luisa said. "It's only that our husbands are friends if they're still alive, and I hope to heaven that they are."

"So do I, *aber natürlich,*" Trudl said. "But do you think we'll ever see them again? We're halfway around the world, we're in this prison camp, and we're behind the Iron Curtain. This is the only life we've got, Luisa. If it doesn't get any better than it is now, is it worth living?"

Is getting a full stomach and a soft job worth prostituting yourself for? Is your life worth living after you do? Luisa knew that, if she asked that of Trudl, the husbands might still be friends, but the wives wouldn't. And it wasn't as if she hadn't asked the same questions of herself. Up till now, she'd answered them both with a no.

Up till now. How long in this camp before she changed her mind? That was the real question, the scary question, because Trudl wasn't wrong.

A TANK CLANKED PAST Gustav Hozzel. He looked at it with faint, or not so faint, contempt. He hadn't seen many Shermans on the Eastern Front. The Ivans got some as Lend-Lease from America, but German panzer crews worried about them much less than about the far more common T-34s. They *did* make trouble for German ground-pounders when no *Wehrmacht* panzers were around to knock them out. As the *Ostfront* slowly came to pieces, that happened ever more often.

His first thought on seeing this one was that it stood an even worse chance against modern Russian armor than it would have against a Panzer IV or a Panther. His second thought . . . "I'll be fucked!" he exclaimed.

"I wouldn't mind that myself about now," Rolf said with a lewd grin.

"Oh, shut up," Gustav told him. He pointed at the Sherman. "What do you see?"

"When I was in the Battle of the Bulge, we called them Tommy cookers," Rolf answered. "One good hit and they'd burn like blazes." His chuckle showed he meant that for a joke. It was as much of a sense of humor as he ever showed.

"Ja, ja," Gustav said impatiently. "But look at the recognition mark on the side of the turret."

Rolf looked. His jaw dropped. *"Donnerwetter,"* he muttered. Had he been a Catholic, he might have crossed himself.

"Uh-huh." Gustav nodded. The mark wasn't the white American star or the blue-and-white roundel the English were using these days. It was a white-edged black cross, as familiar to Gustav as the scar on the back of his left hand. "We've got our own panzers again! Panzers with Germans in them! See how the Russians like that!"

Max Bachman had less nationalistic fervor than Gustav (to say nothing of Rolf), and more hard common sense. "They're only Shermans," he said. "Ivan will like it fine. The Germans in those Shermans? Maybe not so much. It's murder to send them out against T-54s."

"Probably just what the Americans have in mind," Rolf said. "What do you want to bet? Plenty of us have been yelling to get a chance in panzers again. So they give us what we say we want—and they get rid of our panzer crews as fast as we can train 'em. *These are what we've got left,* they'll say. *Take 'em or leave 'em.* Of course we take 'em. And of course we pay the price."

That was the most ridiculous thing Gustav had ever heard . . . till he thought about it for a little while. The more he did, the more of a certain kind of sense it made. Germans these days, like children growing away from the dark times of the Third *Reich,* did want to do as much for themselves as they could. How could the Americans help but worry that their allies would get too big for their britches and see that they were the strongest power in Western Europe even now?

Panzers? You need panzers? Here, we'll give you some Shermans. They weren't much good in the last war. They wouldn't have been any good at all if we hadn't made a million of 'em. But we did, and so we've still got a bunch in storage. Go ahead, use 'em. And if your crews die like ants at an anteaters' picnic, well, just remember, you asked for it.

Max's face said he was going through similar mental contortions. After a few seconds, he said, "I don't believe it."

"Why the hell not?" Rolf demanded. "The *Führer* would have done it. Stalin would do it. Christ, Stalin *is* doing it. The Poles and the Czechs and the Hungarians, their shit isn't near as good as what the Russians use. You think that's an accident?"

"No. But I spent five years in Fulda dealing with the Amis," Max answered. "They don't play that kind of deep game. It's hard to get them to worry about day after tomorrow, let alone about what they do now will mean ten years down the road."

"What about the Marshall Plan?" Gustav said.

"Mm, there is that," Max admitted. "The Marshall Plan's about as long-term as anything a good Communist would do. Most of the time, though, the Yankees are plenty good at tactics and not so hot with strategy."

Another German Sherman rattled by the shell hole the soldiers shared. The commander rode head and shoulders out of the cupola, the way the man in charge of a panzer should have. He looked no more than twenty years old, and as proud of himself as if he'd invented the machine he rode in.

Nodding in his direction, Gustav said, "Max, I'd find it easier to go along with you if that guy were an old sweat like us. But a *Feld* who was in charge of a Panzer IV the last time would know better than to climb into that motorized herring tin now."

"You're right," Rolf said. That wasn't the kind of encouragement Gustav wanted, but he had it whether he wanted it or not.

A sergeant trotted along with the panzers. He scowled at the soldiers sitting in the hole in the ground with cigarettes in their mouths. "Come on, darlings!" he called shrilly, and blew them a kiss. "You're invited to the dance, too."

"If somebody hadn't invited his mother to the dance, she wouldn't've got knocked up and had him," Gustav muttered. But he didn't pitch his voice loud enough for the noncom to hear. Instead, he yanked back the AK-47's charging handle to chamber the first round from a fresh magazine. Then he climbed out of the shell hole and moved forward.

Max and Rolf came, too. Not much went on for a little while. They moved forward several hundred meters. There was only light fire, and none of it close enough to tempt them to hit the deck. Gustav saw a couple of dead Russians, but no live ones. He approved. If he never saw another live Russian as long as he lived, he wouldn't be sorry.

Rolf pointed toward a bump behind a swell of ground up in front of them. "Watch out! That's a—"

Before he could say *panzer turret,* the T-54 hiding back there showed exactly what it was. Its 100mm gun spat fire. There was a horrible rending crash, a noise somewhere between an accident on the *Autobahn* and one in a factory. A Sherman ahead of Gustav and to his right brewed up. Smoke and flame belched from every hatch. None of the crewmen got out. Machine-gun ammo made cheerful popping noises as it cooked off.

The Shermans all started shooting at the T-54. The American panzer came in two flavors. One carried a 75mm gun useful only as a door-knocker. The other came with a longer 76mm gun that fired a heavier shell with better muzzle velocity. That weapon was about as good as the long 75mm gun

Panzer IVs had mounted: pretty much adequate for the last war, pretty much hopeless in this one.

For all Gustav knew, some of the rounds the Shermans fired hit their target. If they did, they surely scared the men inside the T-54. But scaring them wasn't the name of the game. Killing them was, and the Shermans couldn't begin to do it.

The T-54 found another target. Its big, nasty gun fired again. This AP round caught a Sherman in the turret. All the shells in there went off at once. Still burning, the turret slid back over the engine compartment and fell to the ground behind the chassis.

"Christ have mercy on their souls," Max said. Gustav nodded.

Another Sherman went up in flames before the surviving crews realized this wouldn't be their day. They used the smoke mortars on their turret roofs to make a screen behind which they could escape. Maybe they'd run into Russian infantry without armor support somewhere else.

To discourage the German infantry from moving up under cover of the smoke, the T-54 lobbed HE shells almost at random. Gustav hit the ground when one kicked up a dirt fountain a hundred meters off to his left. He was just reaching for his entrenching tool when another shell screamed in. This one seemed as if it would burst right on top.

An American walked into the Hungarian POWs' barracks. Istvan Szolovits couldn't have said how he knew at once that the newcomer *was* an American. He wore the same uniform as the French camp guards. He could have been a Frenchman as far as looks went. He had a thin, dark, intelligent face, with brown hair beginning to fall back at the temples.

But he wasn't French. Maybe it was the way he carried himself: as if nothing could possibly go wrong. He had German confidence, but not the same arrogance.

Miklos spotted him, too. "Here comes trouble," the ex-Arrow Cross man said.

He didn't bother keeping his voice down. Like most Magyars, he assumed no foreigners spoke or understood his language. That wasn't chauvinism; it was what experience taught. Istvan assumed the same thing.

Which only went to show you couldn't always trust your assumptions. The American came over to Miklos and Istvan.

"Why do you think I'm trouble?" he asked in Magyar as clear as theirs. He didn't even have the old-timey, backwoods accent Istvan had heard from other Magyar-speaking Yanks. He might have left Budapest week before last.

Whatever he was, he didn't faze Miklos, who answered, "You wouldn't be here if you weren't trouble."

"I love you, too," the American said. "I'm Imre Kovacs. Who're you?" He waited while Miklos rattled off his name and pay number. Then he nodded to Istvan. "How about you?" Istvan did the same as Miklos had. Kovacs gave him a once-over. "Rootless cosmopolite, are you?"

"He doesn't have to answer that," Miklos said before Istvan could even open his mouth.

"You, sticking up for *him*?" The American hoisted an eyebrow. "Don't get your bowels in an uproar, though. I'm one myself."

"Maybe I should stick up for Miklos, in that case," Istvan said.

"Nobody's got to stick up for anybody. Nothing horrible will happen to either one of you. I'm just going to take you back to the administrative building. I'll talk with one of you. Another guy who knows your lingo will talk to the other one."

"We don't have to answer *any* questions," Miklos said. How many times had he been interrogated? By whom? And for what? Istvan suspected he might be better off not knowing the answers to those questions.

"The only things you have to do is come with me to the administrative building," Imre Kovacs said. "After that, we'll play it by ear, all right?"

By the look on Miklos' scarred face, it was a long way from all right. But Kovacs didn't give him anything on which to hang an objection. The Hungarian-American Jew was too obliging.

"It'll be fine," Istvan said.

"Szar az élet," Miklos answered morosely. Istvan had no good reply to that. Since he'd got dragooned into the Hungarian People's Army, he'd seen that all too often life *was* shit.

Maybe it wasn't if you were American. "C'mon," Kovacs said, as if inviting them to the corner eatery for a plate of stewed pork and Vienna-style coffee with whipped cream.

They came. Istvan saw no other choice. Miklos looked as if he would rather have fought, but even he could work out that

that wasn't a great plan. If Miklos could work it out, it had to be true.

The Polish football side was practicing on one side of the pitch, the East Germans on the other. Istvan would rather have stopped to watch them than gone on. The Poles had a match against the Hungarian side come Saturday. The East Germans would play the Czechoslovakians on Sunday. Neither encounter was likely to be what the sporting papers called a friendly.

"Here we are," Kovacs said, as if the POWs didn't know what the prefab building with the guards out front was.

As promised, another American who spoke Magyar waited inside. He was fluent, but he'd plainly learned it as a foreign language. That made him far more unusual than someone like Kovacs, who'd grown up with it. The other fellow led Miklos into a small room and closed the door behind them. Kovacs took Istvan into another one on the opposite side of the hallway.

His first question was "How'd you get an Arrow Cross thug for a buddy?"

"About the way you'd expect," Istvan said. "I beat the crap out of him." He explained how he and Miklos had become acquainted.

"Well, that's one way to do it, I guess," Kovacs said. "Other interesting thing is, how come the Reds didn't purge him?"

"He's a weapon, the same as a rifle is," Istvan answered. "Point him at something and he'll kill it for you. Szalasi's boys saw that. So did the ones the Russians give orders to. Armies need that kind of people."

"You're right. They do." Imre Kovacs nodded. "What's your rank, by the way? Even the Geneva Convention says I can ask you that."

"Me? I'm just a private. My sergeant said he'd make me a lance-corporal when he had the chance, but I got captured before he did it. Can I ask you what yours is?"

Kovacs tapped the two joined silver bars on his collar. "These show I'm a captain." He eyed Istvan. "You're smarter than most privates."

Istvan shrugged. "What about it? It doesn't mean anything. It doesn't even keep you alive, or not very much. It just leaves you scared all the damn time." He hesitated. "Can I ask *you* something?"

"Sure. Go ahead."

"Thanks. Are you smarter than most American captains? I bet you are."

"I won't even try to answer that. You had it straight—it doesn't matter any which way," Kovacs said. "So tell me, how do you feel about the proletarian world revolution and the victory of the masses over their capitalist oppressors?"

Had a Russian officer asked him that, Istvan would have known what to say. But would an American captain really believe himself to be fighting on behalf of those capitalist oppressors? Istvan didn't know enough about America to be sure. Cautiously, he answered with something close to the truth: "I don't know. It wasn't my fight, you understand. But when they give you a uniform and a rifle and throw you at the guys on the other side, what are you gonna do? If you don't shoot at them, you get killed even quicker."

Imre Kovacs scribbled in a notebook. Was he writing in Magyar or in English? That didn't matter, either. He'd have to know English, or he wouldn't be a captain. Closing the book, he said, "If I had a forint for every Magyar POW who told me a story like that, I'd be one of those capitalist oppressors myself."

"I think you just called me something I'm not, or not exactly," Istvan said.

"Oh, a Magyar?" Captain Kovacs didn't pretend to misunderstand him. "If I said 'every POW from Hungary,' would you be happier?"

"Happier? Nah, not so you'd notice. I can't do anything about what I am. But you'd be more, mm, accurate." Istvan hesitated. "Can I ask you something else?"

"Be my guest."

"What's it like for Jews in America?"

Kovacs pursed his lips. "It isn't perfect. It isn't perfect for us anywhere, even in Israel. I'm sure of that. But it's not so bad. There are people who don't like us, but there aren't any laws against us." He smiled a sardonic smile. "It's not like we're niggers, after all."

The key word came out in English. "Like we're what?" Istvan asked.

"Colored people," the captain explained. "What Europeans do to Jews, Americans do to them. Everybody does it to somebody, believe me."

Istvan did, too. He found a different question: "What's going to happen to me here?"

"You'll play football on Saturday," Kovacs answered. "After that, who knows? We may talk some more. Or we may not." And with that Istvan had to be not especially content.

Red Chinese 105s howled in. Cade Curtis crouched in his dugout and hoped one of them wouldn't come down right where he happened to be. He'd begun to hate just about everything that had anything to do with war, but he hated getting shelled worse than most things. No matter what Einstein said, this was God rolling dice with the universe. Whether you lived or died had nothing to do with you. Luck ruled, luck good or bad.

You were just as dead if you stopped a rifle bullet with your ear. You were just as maimed if you stopped one with your leg. At least someone had aimed the rifle at you, though. Shells came down like rain or snow.

If you lived through a bombardment, you really had to worry when the shells stopped falling. That was when the enemy would try to take advantage while he had you discombobulated.

Better to discombobu late than never, Cade thought vaguely. He wondered if he had combat fatigue. He was sure as hell tired of fighting. The brass insisted that wasn't the same thing, but when in the whole history of the world had the brass known its ass from third base?

Somebody down the trench was screaming for a medic. Cade bit his lip till he tasted blood. Luck, good or bad.

Then, except for the screams, it was quiet. "Out!" Cade yelled. "Out and up onto the firing step! Be ready!"

He hoped he was giving the right order. The Chinks were sneaky bastards. Sometimes they'd stop the artillery fire, wait till you emerged to repel infantry, and then start shelling you again. They had more tricks than a trained circus monkey.

They weren't trying that particular one today. Even before Cade got to the firing step, two American machine guns had started raking the ground in front of the trenches. There had been three sandbagged machine-gun positions that should have been banging away, but one was silent. Cade feared he knew what that meant. One of those 105mm rounds, or maybe more than one, had smashed through the protection. There'd be casualties besides the poor guy who was still screaming his head off.

Here came the Reds. It wasn't a human wave like the ones that had swamped the UN forces by the Chosin Reservoir. Mao's commanders understood they had to spend men to advance, because they had less matériel to spend than the Americans did. But they wasted fewer soldiers than they had at the end of 1950. They'd learned how to do fire-and-move rather than thundering forward in a mob to get chopped down.

Cade fired a short burst from his PPSh. The diagonally cut end of the barrel jacket made a compensator of sorts, so the submachine gun didn't pull up and to the right as much as it would have otherwise. But it still would if you went through a magazine at a time, so Cade tried not to. When he remembered. When panic didn't jam his finger to the trigger. Fire discipline, they called that. Like a lot of disciplines, it was more easily preached than practiced.

He ducked down behind the parapet and came up again a few feet away for another quick burst. The Red Chinese soldiers shrieked just like white men when bullets slammed into them.

Howard Sturgis sported a first lieutenant's silver bar now, not the gold one he'd worn before. He still carried a Garand like an enlisted man, though: no faggy officer's M-1 carbine or Russian piece for him. "Ain't this fun?" he said.

"Now that you mention it, no," Cade answered. "If you want to ask me whether it's better than getting killed and having buzzards and stray dogs squabbling over your carcass, I may tell you something different."

"I wish we had some tanks," Sturgis said.

"Wish for the moon while you're at it," Cade advised. "And keep on wishing Stalin doesn't decide to send the Chinks some more. Wish hard on that one."

"Bet your ass, sir." Sturgis fired a couple of shots of his own. The clip on his rifle went dry and popped out with a distinctive ping. He slammed a new one into place.

Another soldier on Cade's right squeezed off a few rounds of his own. "There you go, Jimmy!" Curtis said. "Give 'em hell."

"Bet your ass, sir," Jimmy said, echoing Howard Sturgis. The soldier formerly known as Chun Wong-un was as foulmouthed as any American GI. More and more, Cade thought of him as if he were an American GI. The longer he stayed with the regiment, the more he acted like one.

Jimmy soaked up English like a sponge. He'd been a soldier of sorts even under a son of a bitch like Captain Pak Ho-san. Now, except for his flat face and narrow eyes, he made a near-perfect copy of a dogface.

Oh, there was one other difference. Most dogfaces wanted as little to do with officers as they could finagle. Jimmy thought the sun rose and set on Captain Cade Curtis. Cade had thought of rescuing him as adopting a puppy. Now he had a full-grown companion, but one who still didn't want to leave his side.

Sturgis didn't think of it the same way. "You know what he is?" the veteran said. "He's our *Hiwi*."

"Our what?" Cade didn't know the term.

"Our *Hiwi,*" Sturgis repeated. "Some of the krauts we faced in France, especially the outfits that came from the Eastern Front, they had these Russians attached to them, doing the cooking and the horseshoeing and the driving and anything else you can think of. *Hiwis,* they called 'em—it was their slang for volunteers. Sure, some of the Russians joined up to keep from starving to death in POW camps. But the rest were just like Jimmy. They weren't supposed to fight, but some of 'em sure as hell did that, too."

"But they were on the other side before, right?" Cade said. "Jimmy was on our team."

"Yeah. Or I guess so," Sturgis said. "You ask him how he liked it, though, he's gonna tell you it wasn't so hot."

Cade intended to do no such thing. Jimmy was working as hard as he could to forget the days when he was Chun Won-ung. If he could have turned his eyes blue to seem more American, he would have done it in a flash. In a way, that flattered the United States. In another way, it left the adoptive GI with a problem, one he might not have worried about yet.

"One of these days," Cade said, "this war'll be over and done with."

"You hope!" Sturgis said.

"Fuckin'-A, I hope," Cade agreed. "It'll be over, and we'll go home. Jimmy's not coming with us, not unless we stencil MEDICAL SUPPLIES on his forehead or something."

Sturgis chuckled. He also fired out at the Red Chinese before answering, "Maybe we *can* smuggle him into the States. Who the hell knows? Or maybe we can pass him on to some new Americans. There'll be some, bet your ass. We're gonna occupy this place like we did with Germany."

"Uh-huh. And look how great that turned out," Cade said.

"Captain," Sturgis said earnestly, "as soon as the troopship taking me away from here gets over the horizon, they can blow this whole motherfucking peninsula off the map, north and south together, an' I won't shed me one single goddamn tear." He jumped up onto the firing step, squeezed off two more rounds, and hopped down again.

Cade suspected most surviving Americans held a similar view. He didn't love Korea or Koreans himself; he was faintly embarrassed that at least one Korean loved him. But his view of the place would be forever tempered by remembering that this was where he'd gone from boy to man in any number of ways.

He took a few shots at the Red Chinese himself. They were already falling back toward their own holes and trenches. They'd shelled, they'd probed, they'd seen they weren't going to break through. They'd try something else somewhere else, or they'd wait a while and try something else here. They were getting to be pros.

Kaeryong was gone. Cade didn't know what had happened to Pak Ho-san, or care very much. He just wanted to hang on until America remembered a war was still cooking here and put in enough men and machines to win it. He had no idea how long that would take. Sure as hell, Jimmy might die of old age before he had to fret about getting separated from the regiment.

Another Jurassic tank park. Another tank-park sergeant smiling a smarmy, apologetic smile. Another dinosaur of a T-34/85. *"Yob tvoyu mat',"* Konstantin Morozov said, and the way he said it warned he was ready to take the tank-park sergeant apart. "I ought to tear your head off and piss in the hole."

"You shouldn't talk that way," said the tank-park sergeant, who'd obviously heard obscene suggestions from other tank commanders before Konstantin. "It's a fine machine, and—"

"I don't see *you* in the fucking antique," Morozov broke in. "Some other chancreface gave us one before, and it got killed out from under us in nothing flat. Just lucky the bazooka hit the engine compartment, or we'd be pushing up daisies right now—and you'd give this cunt to some other dumb prick."

"I don't know what you want me to do—"

"I want you to give us a real tank, not a kiddy car. The Hitlerites built better tanks than this, and that was years ago."

"Do you want to tell that to an officer, Comrade Sergeant?"

The question had cowed Morozov once. Not twice. "Bet your pussy I do, you assfucking whore." Konstantin didn't care what he said. Nothing a lieutenant or a captain could do to him was likely to be worse than sticking him in a T-34/85 again.

Biting his lip, the tank-park sergeant stomped away. When he came back, he came back not with a company-grade officer but with a gray-haired lieutenant colonel. Morozov's crewmen looked ready to let the dirt swallow them. He didn't worry about it. The man wasn't going to shoot him on the spot.

"So what are you giving Ninel a hard time about?" the senior officer demanded.

Ninel! The tank-park sergeant had had good Red parents. In the aftermath of the glorious proletarian revolution, quite a few Soviet babies got tagged with Lenin's name spelled backward. As far as Konstantin was concerned, though, it sounded precious if not swishy. And it had nothing to do with the price of sausage.

He spoke to what did: "What for, Comrade Colonel? Because my men and I don't deserve to die in this hunk of junk, that's what. Like I told your Ninel, we already had one of them smashed with us in it. I fought through the last war, sir. You want to see my scars? I had T-34/85s killed by the Hitlerites with tanks not half as good as what the enemy uses now. We go back into this clunker, it's murder, nothing else but. . . . Sir."

The lieutenant colonel glowered. "I can have you court-martialed and shot inside of fifteen minutes, Sergeant."

"Go ahead, sir. Whatever the pricks with the rifles do, it won't be as bad as when a Pershing slams a round through my glacis plate. And the round *will* get through, too, because that armor might as well be tinfoil. It can't keep anything out."

"What makes *you* deserve a T-54 and not somebody else?"

"I'm a damn good tank commander, Comrade Colonel, that's what. I've got a damn good crew. Give us a damn good tank so we have the chance to serve the Soviet Union the best way we can."

"You're living on borrowed time, Sergeant," the officer rumbled.

"Tell me something I didn't know, sir," Konstantin replied with a laugh. "The Nazis have blown me up. So have the Americans. If I'd been any closer to an A-bomb, I wouldn't be arguing with you now. But if you stuff me into this tin can"—he spat at the T-34/85—"all I've borrowed gets paid back right now."

He wondered if he'd overplayed his hand. By the way Vazgen Sarkisyan's eyes—and Demyan Belitsky's, too—bugged out of their heads, they were sure he had. The lieutenant colonel studied him. The burn scar on the side of the man's neck said he'd seen action himself, and probably been lucky to get out of a blazing tank.

He nodded to himself with the air of a man who'd made up his mind. "Ninel!"

"Yes, Comrade Colonel?" By the eager way the tank-park sergeant said it, he expected the next order to be *Place these men under arrest!* Konstantin more than half expected the same thing.

But the gray-haired lieutenant colonel said, "Put these men in a T-54. They won't need the bow gunner. We'll find a crew short a man for him."

Ninel stared as if he couldn't believe his ears. "Comrade Colonel?"

"You heard me. Do it." The officer waited.

"I serve the Soviet Union!" the tank-park sergeant choked out.

Konstantin clapped Ilya Goledod on the back. "Good luck, pal," he said.

"Thanks," Goledod said. "You, too."

They squeezed each other. Goledod said his good-byes to the other men in the crew. Konstantin rounded on the tank-park sergeant. "Come on, Ninel. Give us something that may keep us alive for twenty minutes."

"Take them to the one with *Za Stalina!* painted on the turret," the lieutenant colonel said. Ninel's face fell. If he'd planned to stick them with a lemon, he wouldn't get the chance now.

The T-54 was . . . a T-54. It wasn't new. Konstantin's nose told him another crew had been in there before his—had, in fact, been killed in there. Kerosene smelled better than spoiling flesh and blood.

Juris Eigims peered through the magnifying gunsight. "Well,

this is more like it," he said. "I've got a chance of hitting what I aim at."

"You never did get a shot off in the old sow, did you?" Konstantin said.

"Nyet." The gunner shook his head. But then he held up a hand. "Wait! I was going to say, the rocket hit us before I could. But I did blast that guy who shot us on the way to the regiment. I didn't fire at any enemy tanks, though."

"Oh, yeah, the other asshole with the bazooka. I forgot about him. How did I do that?" But Morozov knew too well how he'd done it. He'd been in so many tight spots, he couldn't keep track of them all any more. That had to be a bad sign. If it didn't mean death was gaining on him, he couldn't imagine what it would signify. Shaking his head, he used the intercom: "Fire this bastard up, Demyan."

"I'll do it, Comrade Sergeant," Belitsky answered. That told Konstantin the system worked, which was more than it had in the T-34/85. The big diesel behind the fighting compartment started right away. It sounded smoother than the relic's motor had. That was good, anyhow.

Morozov stuck his head out of the cupola. Ninel still stood beside the tank, looking as if he'd just swallowed a big swig of vinegar. "Where do we find regimental HQ?" Konstantin asked him. He had to shout; the engine's blatting seemed louder when thick steel didn't shield him from it.

"Eight or ten kilometers up the road, in Dassel," the tank-park sergeant shouted back, pointing to show the way.

"Spasibo," Konstantin said. He relayed the instructions to Belitsky. The T-54 got moving. It occurred to Morozov that dear Ninel might be lying. But if a tank couldn't take care of itself, what in this world could?

Dassel wouldn't have been anything much before the Red Army overran it. It was even less now. The defenders had fought fiercely to keep Soviet troops out, the Russians just as ferociously to break in. It looked to have been bombed and strafed a few times, too. Only a handful of scrawny Fritzes skulked along the rubble-strewn streets.

But the headquarters did lie at the western edge of the shattered town. The CO seemed glad to see Konstantin, and even gladder to see his T-54. He was a major named Genrikh Zhuk. He'd likely been a junior lieutenant last time around. "Do you come from the tank park off to the east?" he asked.

"Yes, sir," Morozov said. "Why?"

"How did you pry a real machine out of them instead of a retread?"

"I made a perfect son of a bitch out of myself, Comrade Major," Konstantin answered. "I've been in one of those old crocks this war. Two would've been too many."

"Sergeant, you're my kind of man," Zhuk said. "The more sons of bitches we've got, the better we'll do." They nodded to each other, both of them smiling.

AARON FINCH LIFTED PAPER BAGS from the shopping cart and put them into the Chevy's trunk. Ruth tried to help, but he wouldn't let her. "Keep an eye on Leon," he said.

Keeping an eye on Leon was always a good idea. For the moment, he was still in the little makeshift seat by the cart's handle. Look away from him for a second, though, and he was liable to go out headfirst before you looked back again.

"There," Aaron said a minute later. He slammed down the trunk lid. "We've got groceries, and Vons has our money."

Leon pointed to the big red letters that identified the supermarket. "Vons!" he said. "Vons!"

"He just read the sign." Aaron could hear the disbelief in his own voice. But he'd seen it. He'd heard it.

"He sure did." Ruth lifted Leon out of the shopping cart. Once she put him down on the asphalt, she held on to his hand to make sure he didn't do anything she'd regret. "He's a smart thing."

"Smart!" Leon agreed enthusiastically. He didn't know quite what that meant, but he'd heard it applied to himself a lot, and he thought it was something good.

"I feel like the hen that hatched the waddayacallit in that kid's book we got him," Aaron said.

"The Churkendoose!" Leon knew what you called it.

"He's so smart, he'll be rich. He can support us when we're old," Ruth said.

"If somebody doesn't pinch his little head off before we get old, yeah," Aaron said. His wife made a face at him. He used the key to open the Chevy—he was getting into the habit of locking it all the time. "Come on. Let's go home."

A couple of blocks from the Vons stood a big billboard that

at the moment sported a smiling portrait of Senator Joseph McCarthy. Aaron thought McCarthy looked even scarier with a phony grin on his mug than with his usual scowl. The slogan beside his face said REPUBLICANS! VOTE MCCARTHY JUNE 3 FOR FREEDOM AND VICTORY!

"I want to climb up there in the middle of the night and paint a Hitler mustache on him," Ruth said. "I can't stand that man."

"I never would have guessed," Aaron said. His wife poked him in the ribs. He didn't flinch; he wasn't ticklish. As he stopped at a light—Ruth's foot hit the imaginary brake, as usual—he went on, "That's not what I was thinking."

"*Nu,* what were you thinking?" she asked.

"I was thinking it's a good thing Leon can't read *that* yet because he doesn't spot lies the way grown-ups do," Aaron said.

"Don't be silly," Ruth told him. "If grown-ups could spot lies, McCarthy would be selling hot dogs from a pushcart, not running for President."

That was so cynical, Aaron might well have come out with it himself. "Well, it's not like you're wrong," he said. "But he can't take California in the primary, or I don't think he can. Looks like Earl Warren's got it sewed up. The pro-Taft delegation that Congressman's heading isn't going anywhere, either."

"I'm not worried about Taft. I don't like him much, but he doesn't scare me," Ruth said. "McCarthy, now, McCarthy scares me. The worse the war gets, the more he scares me, too. Whenever something blows up, he gets more votes."

She sounded like her cousin Roxane. Aaron started to say so, then thought better of it. For one thing, Ruth might well have been right here. For another, he was discovering, part of what went into staying happily married was *not* always saying the first thing that popped into your head. If it made your wife mad or hurt her feelings, you were better off keeping your big trap shut.

That wasn't easy for a Finch to figure out. It was even harder for a Finch to do. Marvin liked using Sarah for a punching bag. His and Aaron's father and mother had fought all the time till they finally separated. After staying single till he was middle-aged, though, Aaron had discovered he enjoyed domestic tranquility.

He turned left, right, and then left again. The last turn put him on the little street where the house was. He parked in front of it, set the hand brake, put the car in neutral, and killed the engine.

Ruth got out on the passenger side, then reached into the back seat to extract Leon. Leon plucked a dandelion on the front yard. "Flower!" he said. Just yesterday, it seemed, Leon had gone *Flarn!* because he couldn't say it right. Now he could. Kids made you feel old, old, old.

His wife took Leon into the house. She left the front door open behind them. Leon knew he wasn't supposed to run outside while his father brought in groceries. Ruth kept an eye on him just in case, but he really was good about that.

Aaron opened the trunk, picked up a bag of groceries with each hand, and carried the stuff into the house. Then he went back and did it again. When he came out for one more trip, he saw a Mexican-looking kid, maybe fourteen, quickly walking down the street with one of the sacks from the trunk.

"Hey!" Aaron yelled, and took off after him. Empty-handed, the kid would have got away with the greatest of ease. Burdened by the groceries he was swiping, he didn't have the speed or the moves he needed. Aaron caught up with him just before the corner.

As he did, he wondered what would happen if the kid dropped the bag of groceries and pulled out, say, a switchblade. Aaron had a pocket knife in his pocket, but it was a tool, not a weapon. Against six inches of steel with a real point, a paper clip would have done about as much.

But the kid had no switchblade, just a scared, scrawny, miserable face. "I'm sorry, Mister," he said, looking on the point of tears. "I been so hungry since the fuckin' bomb came down an' made us clear out. . . ."

He'd probably lived in Chavez Ravine, just north of downtown. That had been a solidly Mexican, and terribly poor, part of town till the A-bomb fell. The people from there who'd lived through the blast had come farther north yet, into Glendale. Maybe this guy's older brother was the so-and-so who'd made the family Nash disappear.

But how could you stay mad at a skinny fourteen-year-old who so badly needed the stuff he'd walked off with? Aaron tried. He couldn't do it. "Give me back the groceries, son," he said.

As the kid handed over the Vons bag, he really did start to

snuffle. *"Mierda,"* he said, more to himself than to Aaron. "I can't even steal right."

"Oh, for God's sake!" Holding the bag in the crook of his elbow, Aaron dug his billfold out of his back pocket. He pulled out a five and handed it to the kid. "Buy yourself some chow with this. Nobody should have to steal for food. Go on, beat it."

The kid looked at the bill as if he couldn't believe his eyes. "You don't gotta do that, Mister!" he blurted.

"Never mind what I've gotta do. Get lost. Amscray," Aaron said. The kid stuck the fin in the pocket of his faded, ragged jeans and took off like Jackie Robinson swiping second. No, Aaron never would have caught him if he hadn't had a burden.

Shaking his head, he started back to the house. Ruth was standing on the walkway. She must have come out when he didn't bring in the next load.

"What was that all about?" she asked as he drew near.

"A hungry kid," he said, and hefted the sack. "I don't care how hungry he is, he's not gonna eat what we bought."

"No, huh? How much did you give him there?"

She'd seen more than Aaron had figured. "Five bucks," he answered sheepishly. He would have kept quiet about it, but he didn't like to lie point-blank.

"That's more than what's in the sack is worth," Ruth said, which was true. She started to laugh. "You're such a softy! I didn't think so when we got married, but I know better by now."

As he had with the kid, Aaron tried to get mad. As he had then, he failed. How could he do it when she was so obviously right?

Marian Staley took a copy of the *Weed Press-Herald* from the stack on the counter at the Rexall. She slid the druggist a nickel. "There you go, Mr. Stansfield," she said.

"Thanks," he answered. "Want to read about poor Leroy, do you? That was a terrible thing."

"Everybody in town is talking about it," Marian said. Leroy van Zandt had driven a truck for National Wood and Timber, another logging outfit based in Weed. He'd swerved on a twisting road to try to miss a deer, and gone down a steep slope. His rig caught fire when it hit the bottom. He dragged himself out of the upside-down cab, but not soon enough. He died in the back of Doc Toohey's car on the way to the hospital in Redding.

Heber Stansfield pursed his lips. "He might've been lucky to peg out at the end, you know what I'm saying? If Doc had got him to the hospital, chances are he just would've suffered longer and then died."

"I won't try to tell you you're wrong," Marian replied. "But it's still a crying shame there was no ambulance to pick him up and no hospital here to bring him to. That might have done him some good."

The druggist nodded. "You don't hardly got to read the *Press-Herald* now," he said. "You and Dale Dropo, the two of you're on the same page."

"We need those things. I'm new in town, and I can see it. I'm not surprised the guy who runs the paper can, too," Marian said. "The lumber-company bosses get rich off the loggers. They ought to take care of them better when they get hurt."

"That's a fact, and I won't try and make like it isn't," Stansfield said. "But I will tell you, you better be careful who you say it to. It gets back to the people you work for, you won't work for 'em no more."

"I understand that. Oh, boy, do I ever!" Marian said. "They've got Weed sewn up tighter than Boeing did in Seattle before the bomb hit. But if nobody ever tells them what they need to hear, another Leroy van Zandt is just waiting to happen."

"Yes, ma'am." Heber Stansfield's bespectacled stare reminded Marian of that of an old, old tortoise that had seen too much of this wicked old world. He went on, "But you got yourself a young 'un—pretty little thing, she is. You ever tell her the fairy tale about the mice what voted to bell the cat? They're still waiting for a volunteer, an' so're we."

On that cheerful note, Marian took the paper and the bottle of aspirin she'd gone in there to buy and walked back to the Studebaker, which was parked three stores down the street. Linda was waiting inside. She . . .

Marian stiffened. Linda had rolled down her window. In spite of all Marian's warnings about never talking to strangers, she was in animated conversation with a man. Marian broke into a run.

And then, three steps later, she slowed again. Panic faded. Only one man in town wore an old-fashioned tweed cap, what they called a newsboy cap. And Fayvl Tabakman, while he might be a great many things, wasn't a stranger to Linda. Except for Marian, she'd known him longer than anybody here.

The cobbler turned. He touched the brim of the cap in his familiar greeting gesture. "Hallo," he said. "I saw your little girl, and I thought I would keep an eye on her till you got back."

"Thanks." Marian believed him. She still didn't know whether she felt anything for him, and what it was if she did, but she was sure she didn't worry about him near Linda. Weed was a pretty safe place. She wouldn't have left her daughter alone for even a few minutes if it hadn't been. But an adult eye didn't hurt.

Tabakman pointed at the newspaper in her hand. In the sunlight, Marian saw that his forefinger had more scars than she could count—marks of how he'd learned his trade and of slips after he did. He said, "It's a terrible thing about that poor van Zandt man."

"It is." Marian nodded. "Mr. Stansfield and I were talking about that in the drugstore just now."

"Terrible," Tabakman repeated: and if anyone here knew about terrible, he was the man. "And it doesn't got to be this way. A hospital? A hospital, I don't know about. Is expensive, a hospital."

"I know," Marian said sorrowfully.

"But an ambulance, an ambulance we could do," Fayvl Tabakman said—or maybe it was *Weed could do.* "An ambulance is what? A few t'ousand *taler*? Can't be more. We got lots lumber companies here. They split the cost, not so real much for anyone. A few *hindert taler,* a t'ousand tops. They could. Only they don't want."

"You're right." Marian hadn't looked at it from that angle. "It wouldn't take more than a fleabite out of their bottom line."

"Mommy," Linda said, "can we go home now? I have to tinkle."

"Okay." Marian realized that listening to grown-ups talk about things that didn't matter to her couldn't be very exciting for a little girl. She said her good-byes to Fayvl Tabakman and got into the Studebaker.

Even after she made dinner—lamb chops, which she could do quickly on top of the stove—Tabakman's idea stayed in her mind. The more she thought about it, the better it seemed.

Except for one thing. *Who'll bell the cat?* Heber Stansfield's question stayed in her mind, too. Whoever did try to bell the cat wouldn't just be belling one cat, either. That person would have to go to all the lumber bosses in town. The more who said no, the more each of the rest would have to pay. How soon would that be enough to scupper the project?

And if her own boss said no, she might very well be tossing her own job down the drain. She didn't want to take the chance. Anyone who was a kid during the Depression learned that, when you had work, you hung on to it the way an abalone hung on to a rock.

So, instead of talking to Mr. Cummings or the other big shots, she spent two or three days contemplating ways and means. Then she paid a call on Dale Dropo. "A friend of mine said that, if all the lumber companies chipped in on an ambulance, it wouldn't cost any one of them too much," she told the editor of the *Weed Press-Herald*.

He scratched his cheek. "You've got a smart friend," he said after a moment. "Who is he, she, whatever, if you don't mind my asking?"

"Fayvl Tabakman, the cobbler," she said. "But talk to him before you put his name in the paper, okay?"

"I will, honest injun," Dropo said. "It's a better scheme than trying to get any one outfit to cough up the dough, that's for sure. Who does the dirty work, though?"

"Here's what I was thinking," Marian said—the result of her contemplation. "If you put petitions in the paper and almost everybody in town signed them, wouldn't the lumber companies have to notice that?"

"Lumber companies don't *have* to do a darn thing," Dropo replied. "But the people who run them, if they don't want their neighbors smearing dog poop on their windshields or slashing their tires in the middle of the night, they've got to think about it, anyway."

"That's how it looked to me, too," Marian said. "I'm glad you see it the same way."

"Worth a try. If they ignore the whole thing, we're no worse off than when we started—and maybe they will get their tires slashed. What the heck? I can probably find a knife or an ice pick myself." Dale Dropo eyed her. "I know you and that Tabakman guy both came out of the camps by Seattle. This town may be lucky you decided to stop here."

"Thank you. It's a nice place," Marian answered. "If we can make it a little better, well, good."

"No guarantees," Dropo warned.

"Oh, I know. When are there ever?" *No guarantees your house doesn't get blown up,* Marian thought. *No guarantee your husband comes home. No guarantees at all.*

American 105s and 155s howled down on the Soviet positions. Ihor Shevchenko huddled in his foxhole, praying inexpertly but with great sincerity. The last time around, the Nazis hadn't enjoyed this kind of artillery support. The Red Army was the one that lined up guns hub to hub and blasted its foes to jam and sausage meat.

Red Army gunners had done the same thing this time . . . till the A-bombs in far western Germany and along Soviet supply lines gave the edge back to the imperialists. The Hitlerites hadn't had the atom bomb, either. A good thing, too, or Byelorussia, the Ukraine, and Russia at least to the Urals would have turned into a radioactive wasteland.

Well, here it was, only a few years after the Fascist beasts were ground into the dirt. Here it was, only a few years after fraternal socialist regimes in Eastern and Central Europe gave the USSR a giant glacis against any future invasion from out of the west. And . . . ?

And Byelorussia, the Ukraine, and Russia at least to the Urals had turned into a radioactive wasteland. Hitler might have been more thoroughly, more savagely, destructive than Truman. But Truman was doing fine on his own.

Ihor dug the foxhole deeper. He flipped the dirt up onto the western side. When the shelling let up, he'd use bushes and branches to camouflage the foxhole's lip. For now, that could wait. Sticking any part of himself above ground was asking to get that part mutilated.

Anya'd been lucky. Without her horrible cold, she would have gone into Kiev the day the Yankees visited fire upon it. Ihor had been lucky himself. If he hadn't sat on that stupid broken bottle, he would have been at the front, not behind it, when more atomic fire fell from the sky.

His entrenching tool clanked against something. He dug more carefully than he needed for ordinary excavation. His amateur archaeology unearthed a sharp, curved chunk of rusty shell casing from the last war. Was it German or American? Or had the English dueled with the Nazis in this part of Germany? He didn't know. Even if he had, it wouldn't matter now.

After all, what did one more shell fragment prove? Only that this war wasn't the first time people had tried to kill one another here. A musket ball would have shown him the same thing, in case he didn't already know it. So would an arrowhead. So would a spear point, or an axe blade, or a club made from a stone fastened to a length of wood by sinews. People had been trying to kill one another here for as long as people had lived here.

Had he done some digging in the black soil of his collective farm outside Kiev, he would have come up with the same kind of lethal hardware going back to the dawn of time. People there had tried to kill one another for as long as people dwelt in those parts, too.

People everywhere had done their damnedest to kill one another for as long as they'd been around. The story of Cain and Abel distilled a lot of truth down into a teacup.

These days, though, the would-be murderers had better tools than they'd enjoyed in Biblical days. Even as Ihor dug to strengthen and deepen his hole, nearby shell bursts threatened to collapse it on him. Earth tortured by high explosives sprang into the air in anguish. Clods and pebbles came clattering down onto his helmet. He rubbed at his nose and wasn't surprised to find it bloody. Had one of those 155s hit a little closer, blast might have killed him without leaving a visible mark on his carcass.

And, of course, everything didn't turn to sunshine and roses the instant the shelling stopped. In case any of the men in the company were too stunned to remember that or too stupid to know it, Lieutenant Kosior called, "Be ready to fight! They'll be coming now!"

Ihor heard him as if from five kilometers away. He wondered how far his ears would recover. He made sure he had a round chambered in his Kalashnikov. That wouldn't help his hearing, either. It would help him stay alive, though, which also counted.

Or it might. The Americans knew how to play this game. They sent tanks forward with their foot soldiers. German panzers, all slabs of steel and sharp angles, looked more frightful than these beasts. But thick armor and a high-velocity 90mm gun were nothing to sneeze at. If that gun sneezed at you, there'd be nothing left.

Against the panzers, though, Russian foot soldiers hadn't had any weapons but magnetic mines and Molotov cocktails.

To use either, you had to sneak suicidally close to your target. If the bastards inside the panzer didn't get you first, the infantry shepherding them would.

The game was different now. A Red Army man launched an RPG at an oncoming Pershing. The rocket fell short, and the tank fired two rounds of HE at his foxhole. Ihor hoped he stayed alive. Whether he did or not, though, that trail of fire would make all the Yankee tank crews who saw it thoughtful.

They came on, anyway. Like their Soviet counterparts, they had their orders. They'd catch it if they didn't follow them. And they paid the price for courage or obedience or whatever it was. Another Red Army man waited till the American tanks reached the forwardmost Soviet foxholes. Then he launched his RPG. It burned through a Pershing's side armor and set off the shells inside the steel box.

Flame and smoke shot out of the turret. The tank stopped. It would never go again. The crew probably died fast. All the questions that had vexed philosophers and prophets since men wore skins? Whatever the answers were, those Americans had just discovered them.

Ihor squeezed off a quick burst in the direction of the advancing infantry. When he came up to shoot again, he wasn't quite in the same place. A good thing, too, because a bullet cracked past his head. He ducked down again in a hurry.

A crashing clang told of an RPG deflecting off a tank it didn't hit squarely. HE rounds from the tank's cannon said that the man who'd loosed the rocket-propelled grenade was paying the price for failure.

Maybe he'd be able to talk it over with the crew from the incinerated Pershing. Or maybe there was just nothing. One way or the other, he knew now. Ihor didn't. Nor was he anxious to find out, not in any final way.

Another American tank brewed up, and then another, both of them spectacularly. Soviet artillery woke up to the idea that the sons of bitches on the other side were attacking. Shells started falling among them—and short rounds started falling among the forward Red Army troops.

"You stupid cocksuckers!" Ihor screamed when a shell from his own side left him stunned and deafened. Your friends could kill you every bit as dead as the enemy could. He laughed as he tried to shake himself back to usefulness. Anatoly Prishvin might be telling the Yankee tank crew and the RPG man all about that right now.

Someone peered over the edge of the foxhole. Evidently all the artillery fire had chewed up the ground enough so the spoil Ihor had thrown out didn't seem anything special. The shape of that helmet was wrong—too much dome, not enough brim. Ihor fired a burst at point-blank range. The American groaned and sagged. Barring Resurrection Day, he wouldn't rise again. When things calmed down a bit, Ihor would rifle his pockets.

One more Pershing went up in fire and smoke. The Yanks seemed to decide that, if they were going to move forward, they weren't going to do it right here. Sullenly, competently, firing as they went, they pulled back.

"*Urra!* for the *rodina*! *Urra!* for the great Stalin!" Lieutenant Kosior shouted. "They shall not pass!"

"Urra!" Ihor said. He had schnapps in his canteen. He drank greedily.

Like vodka, schnapps was good for what ailed you. It might not fix anything, but making you not care worked just as well. Ihor wondered how the great Stalin would have done in one of these foxholes. Not so well, was his guess, even if he couldn't tell anyone about it.

He'd solved the problem of peace! Put the leaders in the trenches and the war wouldn't last five minutes! The only problem with that was, who could do it? But if you wanted to worry about every little detail . . .

Luisa Hozzel's stomach growled. She was so worn by another day out among the pines, she was ready to fall over during the evening count. She wanted to eat. She wanted to go back to the barracks. She wanted to sleep. Since the Russians threw her into the gulag, her horizon had shrunk to that. Supper. Her bunk. They would both be bad, but bad was better than none.

The guards prowled up and down. They looked angry and jumpy. The count kept coming out wrong. Luisa hated days like this. Piling the stupid guards' incompetence on top of all the other *Schweinerei* here just seemed like too much.

Beside her, Trudl Bachman murmured, "They should take off their boots so they can count with their toes."

"No." Luisa almost imperceptibly shook her head. "One of them will have got a toe shot off in the war, and that will mess things up worse than ever."

Even though a nervous guard prowled past not three meters

away from them, he didn't turn his head or snarl at them to shut up. By now, practice and need had turned them both into fine ventriloquists. *Give me a dummy—one of these guards, say—and I'll go on stage,* Luisa thought.

"I hate it when they have kittens over nothing," Trudl said.

"I know. Doesn't anybody here know how to count?" Luisa answered. They weren't the only *zeks* grousing, either. As time wore on and the women still weren't allowed in to eat, grumbles in both German and Russian grew more and more audible. Even the bitches were getting angry.

The two top guard sergeants put their heads together. At last, one of them slowly and unhappily clumped off to the administrative office, so it wasn't over nothing after all.

The man came back with a lieutenant: a man who had a hook where his left hand should have been and whose eye patch didn't come within kilometers of covering all the scars on the left side of his head. He looked fearsome enough when he wasn't irked. When he was, as he was now, he would terrify children. He scared Luisa. She hadn't seen many men in Germany more horribly mutilated. He was lucky to be alive, though she wasn't so sure he would call it luck.

"We have had an escape," he said. Something was wrong with his voice, too. It sounded more like the scraping of sandpaper on hard-wood than anything that should have come from a human throat. He went on, "The count is five short. You will be interrogated to discover who helped the criminals abscond with themselves. For now, go to your barracks at once."

"What about supper?" Nadezhda Chukovskaya spoke for all the hungry, weary women. Since she was neither a political nor a German, she thought she could get away with the question.

"We have had an *escape,* you stupid, worthless cunt," the mangled officer said in tones of cold fury. "I don't give a fuck if all of you starve to death. Then we can count you, anyway. Dismissed to your barracks! Now, damn you!"

"I hope they get away," Luisa said as they dejectedly did what the lieutenant ordered them to do.

Like her husband, Trudl Bachman was a very practical person. "I hope they weren't from our work gang," she said.

"Five? They couldn't have been—could they?" Luisa said.

"I don't *think* so. But would I swear?" Trudl shook her head. "I didn't pay any attention on the way in tonight. I was so worn out, all I could do was keep putting one foot in front of the other."

"Same here," Luisa agreed. "You'd think the guards would have noticed, though. That's what they're there for."

"Maybe they were too stupid," Trudl said. "Or maybe the women who escaped paid them off."

With what? Luisa started to ask. She didn't come out with the question. Not much in the way of cash or valuables circulated in the gulag. Most of what there was was in the hands of the bitches and the inside workers, the people with the least incentive to flee. But a woman who was desperate enough to do anything to get away always had a coin she could offer a man. All it would cost her was her self-respect. If losing that meant getting out of this horrible place, it might be a small price to pay.

She guessed she'd be too hungry to sleep. She wasn't, as she hadn't been too tired to eat a few times after tough days in the taiga. As soon as she lay down on her bunk, her eyes sagged shut. The next thing she knew, a guard was banging on the shell casing to summon the women for the morning count.

Then she realized how hungry she was. She did notice that two of the escapees came from her barracks: a German and a Russian political. They didn't belong to her work gang.

Once the guards were satisfied no one else had flown the coop during the night, all the gangs except the one from which the five women had fled were allowed to go to breakfast. Luisa ate every scrap of the nasty fare set before her, and felt as hungry afterwards as she had before. The luckless members of that work gang who'd got kept out there had to be hungrier yet. The guards would be grilling them—and, no doubt, their comrades who'd taken more women out into the woods and brought fewer back.

No one went into the woods after the quick and noisome latrine call. The guards separated the women into their gangs, but they stayed on the flat ground where they lined up.

Some of the women from the first gang came out of the administrative building. Some didn't, at least not where Luisa could see. She guessed they went straight to the punishment cells.

Her gang got summoned next. She drew the mutilated lieutenant as her interrogator. He started in Russian, but soon saw she didn't have enough of the language to follow his questions. She also acted dumber than she was, which turned out not to help. He switched to rasping German: "Bauer and Nekrasova were from your barracks, *nicht wahr*?"

"If those were their names, sir," Luisa answered. "I didn't know either of them, really. They were just—faces." That wasn't altogether true, but the less she admitted, the better off she was.

Or so she thought. "Then you don't need to worry about betraying them," the lieutenant said. "Did you hear them conspiring to steal themselves from Soviet custody?"

Luisa thought that a peculiar way to put it, one more thing she didn't say. She did say, truthfully, "No, sir. I paid no attention to either one of them."

"Then you should have. Ignorance is no excuse," he said, glowering at her with his surviving eye. "Five days in a punishment cell to remind you to respect the Soviet state and its regulations." He raised his ruined voice: "Guard!"

The guard hustled her to the punishment block. The cells there were too low to stand up in and too small to lie down in. She had to fold herself up in a corner. There wasn't even a bucket. When she needed to ease herself, she'd have to use a different corner. The stench in the cell said she wouldn't be anywhere close to the first who had.

She got water and black bread—precious little of either. The guards yelled abuse at her and the other luckless women in the cells both day and night. She'd never been through anything like that before. It made ordinary camp life seem like a *Kraft durch Freude* cruise by comparison. In her maddest nightmares, she'd never imagined anything could do that.

When they opened the cell's door to let her out, she had trouble crawling out. She had even more trouble standing up. The outside world was too big, too wide, too open.

Three doors down from her, Trudl Bachman also came forth. The two women from Fulda nodded to each other. Before her confinement, Luisa had hoped the escapees got away, but she hadn't *hoped* they had. Now she did, with all her might. Let them be gone for good! She was sure Trudl felt the same way.

24

VASILI YASEVICH AMBLED along the road, the track, whatever you wanted to call it, that connected Smidovich and Birobidzhan. He'd never been to the capital of the Jewish Autonomous Region. Few people from Smidovich had. Birobidzhan held thirty-five or forty thousand souls. To the locals, that made it the big city.

It wasn't the big city to Vasili. He was supposed to come from Khabarovsk, which had been quite a bit larger till the American A-bomb cut it down to size. And he really knew Harbin, which had been larger still. Of course, by China's anthill standards, even Harbin was only a third- or at best a second-rate town.

Having grown up among Harbin's teeming hundreds of thousands, Vasili was amazed at how much he enjoyed getting off by himself. When he went a few kilometers down the road, he might have been the only man in the world. All he could hear were birdcalls, the wind soughing through the pine branches, and his own footsteps. No, he could hear one thing more. He could hear himself think in a way he couldn't in a crowd.

A squirrel gnawing on a pine cone paused to chatter at him. It sat on a branch fifteen meters up a tree. He couldn't have hurt it if he tried. It told him off just the same. Then, with a flirt of its plumy tail, it was gone.

He wagged a finger at it. "Better be careful, *Tovarishch.* They'll collectivize you and your pine cones if you don't watch out." He could make jokes like that so long as only a squirrel heard him. If anyone in Smidovich did, he'd find out all about what *they* did to people.

On he went. In a jacket pocket, wrapped in newspaper, he had a sandwich of rye bread and smoked salmon and onions.

The people on this side of the Amur smeared creamy cheese on their bread when they made that kind of sandwich. He didn't. He had the Chinese view of cheese: that it was nothing but rotten milk. If the locals noticed how he fixed his food, they might think he was odd. They wouldn't make any more of it than that.

There was the fallen tree he remembered, with the orange and yellow lichens growing on the trunk. It was the perfect place to sit and eat and smoke and let his thoughts go where they would for as long as they felt like going there. Then he'd get up, take a leak against a sapling, and saunter back to Smidovich.

He'd taken two bites out of the sandwich when a noise from deeper in the woods made him turn his head away from the dirt road. Something good-sized was moving in there. People in Smidovich talked about wolves. Vasili had never seen one, or even seen tracks in the soft ground. He suspected all the talk was only that and no more.

But he might have been wrong. He set the sandwich on the colorful tree trunk and reached for the Tokarev automatic he'd taken from Grigory Papanin. It wasn't accurate out much farther than he could piss, but the report ought to scare away a wolf.

Or a tiger. People in Smidovich talked about them, too. Vasili had more trouble taking that seriously. Still, his father had charged the Chinese in Harbin through the nose for medicines made from ground-up and dried tiger parts. He must have got them from somewhere.

What came out of the forest, though, wasn't a wolf or a tiger. It was a human being, though a scrawny one with cropped hair and such cheap, shabby clothes that Vasili wondered for a moment. Then he saw that the jacket and trousers had a number written on them: Б711. He realized what kind of human being it must be—a *zek,* straight out of the gulag.

At the same time as he saw Б711, the *zek* saw the sandwich he'd just started and pointed at it. "*Bitte*? Uh, *pozhalista*?" the *zek* said. Only when Vasili heard the voice did he realize it was a woman. The ragged, quilted jacket and baggy pants hid whatever curves she owned.

"Go ahead," he said. She had to be starving. He wouldn't waste away for want of a smoked-salmon sandwich. He waved in invitation, in case she had trouble with his Russian—it plainly wasn't her first language.

"Danke schön! Bolshoye spasibo!" she said, and engulfed the sandwich like a snake engulfing a rabbit. When it was gone, her bony, filthy face lit up. *"Ach, wunderbar!"* She pointed at her own chest. *"Ich heisse Maria Bauer."*

"I'm Vasili," he said. She had to be speaking German. He'd picked up a few Yiddish phrases in Smidovich, but only a few. He asked, "How much Russian do you speak?"

She held her thumb and forefinger not far apart. "Little bit," she said.

Vasili nodded. "Did you run away from the gulag?" he asked. Maria Bauer looked alarmed. He held up his hand. "Don't worry. I won't turn you in. Fuck the Chekists!"

That, she understood. "Fuck Chekists, *da*!" she said fiercely.

"How did you get away?" he asked.

She laughed. "I fuck Chekist. Five of us, we do. We go, we split up, they not maybe all catch. I here." She paused. "Where here?"

"Near Smidovich," Vasili said. Plainly, it meant nothing to Maria.

"What do you of me—to me—with me?" she asked. "You not give me Chekists, I you fuck, too." With her rudimentary Russian, she couldn't be anything but blunt.

Right this minute, he had no trouble shaking his head. She might clean up nicely, though. Feed her, let her hair grow out, and she wouldn't be terrible. He couldn't take her home with him any which way, not when he lived in a dormitory. All of a sudden, he started to laugh.

"Chto?" she asked, her voice full of animal wariness.

"I have a friend in town." He spoke slowly and clearly, to make sure she could follow. "I will go see him. I think—I hope—he can take you in. I will come back tonight. I will bring food. I will take you to him if he says yes. If he says no, I will give you what I can to help you get away."

"How I know you it?—it you?" she asked after he'd repeated himself and gestured several times.

He whistled a tune that had been popular in Harbin before the Russians drove the Japanese out of the city. "I'll do that when I come," he said.

Maria Bauer nodded. *"Khorosho."*

Vasili went on whistling as he walked back to Smidovich. A couple of trucks passed him. He assumed Maria had had sense enough to hide from them. If she hadn't, she was too dumb to deserve help.

He knocked on David Berman's door, hoping the old Jew hadn't gone anywhere. Sure enough, Berman was home. "Vasili Andreyevich!" he said, smiling in surprise. "What are you doing here?"

Looking inside the cabin, Vasili saw it was even grubbier than it had been the last time he visited. "How would you like a maid to help you straighten up this joint?" he asked.

Berman frowned. "What are you talking about?"

"Well, I met somebody in the woods. . . ." Vasili told the whole story. If David Berman went to the MGB, he was history. But Berman didn't seem that kind of man. Vasili was willing to take the chance.

And the old Jew said, "Well, I got no use for Chekists or camps. Who does? But you want I should take a young girl into mine house? Into this?" His wave took in all the neglect. "And a *German* girl? *Vey iz mir!*"

"She's not *that* young, David Samuelovich. She's my age, give or take a little," Vasili said. "Believe me, next to the camps, what you've got here is great. And see? You'll be able to talk to her better than I can. You can call her your niece or your cousin or something, visiting from the real Russia."

"She's your age? That's young. Believe me, that's young," Berman said. "But I'll do it. If she gets caught, we all go to the gulag. For you, for her, it's a worry. For me? I don't care what happens to me no more."

"I'll bring tonight," Vasili said. "You can keep her a secret till she grows some hair and gets some clothes that don't have a number on them."

He feared Maria Bauer would have fallen asleep by the time he came back up the road whistling his song. But she came out at once and walked to Smidovich with him. "A Jew?" she said when he told her David Berman's name. "I go to a Jew?" She laughed.

"He thinks it's funny, too," Vasili told her, which didn't stretch things . . . too far.

He knocked on Berman's door. The old man opened it. Maria stumbled inside. Vasili went away. Either he'd just done something marvelous or he'd wrecked three lives. Well, you could only try.

* * *

Simon Perkins was already at work compounding medicines when Daisy Baxter came downstairs. Grinding away with a big brass mortar and pestle, he might have fallen through time from the Middle Ages. Even the faintly camphory, faintly sulfurous odor of the chemist's shop suggested bygone days. Only his waistcoat, necktie, and gold-framed bifocals argued for 1952.

"Good morning, Mr. Perkins," she said, as cheerfully as she could. She didn't feel she knew him well enough to use his Christian name. She wondered if anyone in the world did.

"Good morning, Mrs. Baxter," he answered, not stopping what he was doing.

Did he bear down a bit on the title that showed she was, or at least had been, a married woman? She didn't want him to be difficult. Yes, he was generous, to give shelter to someone who'd lived through the disaster that crushed Fakenham. But couldn't he leave it there?

Evidently he couldn't, because he went on, "You got in late last night—or I should say, this morning."

"I'm ever so sorry if I bothered you coming up the stairs," Daisy said, pretending not to hear any larger meanings in his remark. "I tried to be as quiet as I could."

"I wasn't awake very long," he said grudgingly. "But what can you and your Yank be doing that keeps you out till half past two?"

He sounded as if he honestly had no idea. Daisy didn't know whether that made her want to laugh or to cry or to do both at once. *What are we doing? We're screwing like bunnies* was the first thing that leaped into her mind. However tempting it was, though, it would only make things worse.

"We have a good time," she said. "We enjoy each other's company." And the North Sea was damp, and the flash when an atom bomb went off was bright. Words were useless for some things. If you hadn't experienced them, they couldn't mean anything to you. She did try to sound as innocent as she could. For that, words were worth something.

"I daresay," Simon Perkins replied. Perhaps she sounded less innocent than she hoped.

"It's really between Bruce and me, don't you think?" she said. Before he could tell her whether he did think that—she would have bet against it—she added, "I'm going out for some breakfast. I'll see you later."

Out she went. She could feel his eyes boring into the small

of her back like awls. She was glad to close the door behind her. She wondered whether she ought to look for another room. She didn't want to. Even with as little in the way of worldly goods as she had, moving was a bloody nuisance. But if Mr. Perkins was going to get his nose out of joint whenever she and Bruce spent time together, she might not have a choice.

She bought scrambled eggs and chips and her morning cuppa at a place around the corner from the chemist's shop. She had a hot plate in her room; she could brew tea there. She could even cook if she had no other choice, but a little experimenting had shown that anything beyond tea or heating tinned soup was more trouble than it was worth.

The town hall had gone up in the 1880s. It was brick and granite, built with smug Victorian confidence that it would still be an important place two hundred years from when it went up. Back then, the British Empire had been the unchallenged, the unchallengeable, mistress of the world. Here it was, only a lifetime later, and the Empire was a tattered ruin of its grander self. The home country, still in the grip of crippling austerity after the last war, had been hit again, harder, by this new one.

People nowadays laughed at how smug and certain their grandparents had been. No one now was certain about anything—and how could you be, when the town where you lived might get seared out of existence in the next moment? But that sureness that their achievements would last forever made Daisy envy her ancestors . . . and also made her want to weep at the foundering of all their hopes.

Inside the hall, signs with arrows directed people to where they needed to go. By now, she knew which window to visit without resorting to them. The window had a newly printed sign held in place above it by sticky tape: FAKENHAM SURVIVOR BENEFITS. This was where the government gave what it could spare to the townsfolk the Russians hadn't managed to murder with their atom bomb.

The clerk looked up from a form he'd been filling in. "Ah, Mrs. Baxter," he said. "How are you this morning?" His smile and something in his voice told her he liked the way she looked.

She smiled back, not quite with the same warmth. He was polite, which made his regard more a compliment than an annoyance. She wanted to keep it that way. "I'm fine, Mr. Jarvis, thanks," she said. "And you?"

"I'm very well, very well indeed," he replied. "You've come for the weekly allotment?"

"That's right." She wondered why else she or anyone else would come to this tan-painted, poorly lit corridor. Unless you had to be here, you'd stay as far away as you could.

"Here you are." He handed her an envelope. She looked inside to make sure the money the state said she was entitled to was in there. When she saw it was, she signed the line on the allotment roster that also held her typewritten name. She turned to go, but Mr. Jarvis said, "Wait a moment, please."

"Yes?" Now she didn't sound one bit warm. Was he going to prove a bother after all?

But all he did was hand her another envelope. "This came in for you yesterday. As you'll know, the post to Fakenham has been, ah, rather badly disrupted since the, ah, unfortunate incident."

"The A-bomb, you mean," she said. Government officials thought they could hide the mushroom cloud behind a thicker cloud of meaningless words.

"Well, yes." Mr. Jarvis didn't care to admit it but couldn't very well deny it.

"Thank you very much," she said, giving him credit for admitting it and more because he wasn't in fact trying to urge himself on her.

Sure enough, the envelope had gone to the Owl and Unicorn's address in ruined Fakenham. It was from her insurance company. *Bloody took them long enough,* she thought as she opened it.

It has come to our attention that the property at the abovementioned address may have been adversely affected by the unfortunate events of 11 September 1951, she read. A soft snort escaped her. The insurers talked as if they wanted to be bureaucrats. She waded through a couple of paragraphs of turgid drivel before she got to the meat. *As acts of war and acts of God are specifically disallowed under the provisions of Clause 6.2.3.a.3 of your policy, we regret to inform you that we have no financial obligation in the matter of damages suffered on or about the above-mentioned date in regard to the unfortunate events thereof.*

A scribbled signature followed. She read it again. *No financial obligation.* Yes, it still said the same thing. No, she hadn't read it wrong. They weren't going to pay. She only wished she were less surprised. Insurance companies were there for themselves first and you only later, if at all. They were very good at taking in premiums. Sending money the other way? That, they weren't so happy about.

She knew what Bruce would say if she showed him the letter. He'd note the London address and offer to make a special bombing run for her. He couldn't do it, but the offer would be nice. Unless the government did more for her and her townsfolk than it had so far, the offer would be all she got.

What the company said might be legal, but it hardly seemed fair. She'd just had her pub in the wrong place at the wrong time. Was that enough to ruin her for life? The insurance outfit thought so.

With sudden startling clarity, she realized letters like hers were how the Bolsheviks got started. When the ones above you didn't give a damn about what happened to you, what did you do? You got rid of them. *Good God! I've just turned Red myself,* Daisy thought—proudly.

Harry Truman had eaten rubber chicken at more political dinners than he could remember, let alone count. Sometimes it was good rubber chicken. The fried drumsticks he'd had in Kentucky on his 1948 reelection campaign he did still remember, and fondly. The stuff he'd downed in Reno on that same campaign he also recalled, but not so happily. He'd had the trots for most of a week after that banquet.

What was on his plate here in Buffalo tonight wouldn't go down in either of those columns. He could eat it. It wasn't interesting. If it had been a baseball player, it would have been a backup infielder with a decent glove who hit .250 but had no power. Serviceable. Not memorable.

A local politico named Steven Pankow stood up to introduce him. Pankow aspired to be mayor of Buffalo after the next election. He might well make it. He had the self-confidence, the glibness, and the money he'd acquired from a successful career selling cars.

"Ladies and gentlemen, it's my great privilege to present to you the President of the United States, Mr. Harry S Truman," he said from the lectern. He also had a slight Polish accent, which in this part of the country was in itself a political asset of sorts.

"Thank you very much, Mr. Pankow," Truman said as he walked to the lectern. Then he said it again into the mike. He got a warm hand from the crowd of dignitaries and other prosperous upstate Democrats. Applause never went stale. He went on, "Thank you all for coming to the museum today to take a look at the dinosaur."

That won him a laugh, maybe a bigger one than the joke deserved. But many a truth was spoken in jest. He'd volunteered for his own political extinction, but he would have been pushed if he hadn't jumped.

"The cast always changes, but the show goes on," he said. "It has to. We need to elect as many Democrats as we can in November, from the top of the ticket all the way down, to make sure the so-and-sos on the other side do as little damage as possible. The way things look, the Republicans seem to be running on the slogan 'Throw the rascals *in*!'"

He got another laugh for what looked like another jesting truth. The real problem, or what looked like the real problem to Truman and the rest of the pols in the room, was that the Republicans were all too likely to throw their rascals in and the ones who were Democrats out.

"We've held the White House and Congress for the past twenty years," Truman went on. "Oh, the Republicans took Congress a few years ago, but they made such a do-nothing mess of it, the people made them give it back two years later."

They blistered their palms clapping for that. Had the President been in the audience instead of giving the speech, he would have clapped, too. He'd won the tag *Give 'Em Hell Harry* not least by tearing into the Republican-led Congress when he was running for his own term in 1948. That had gone a long way toward giving him the election.

"They say we can't win this upcoming Presidential race. They sure do say a lot of stupid things, don't they?" Truman grinned out at the crowd. "I say they're full of hooey. I'd say they were full of something else, something from the barnyard, but we have ladies present. I do want to remind you of a picture somebody took of me four years ago. I was holding up a copy of the *Chicago Tribune* with a big old headline—DEWEY DEFEATS TRUMAN. So tell me, folks, did Dewey defeat Truman?"

"No!" everybody shouted.

"That's right. Dewey didn't defeat Truman. If he had, you wouldn't be here today putting up with my hot air," Truman said. "And whoever gets our nomination this time around can win the same way I did. All he has to do is work hard, never give up, and remember he's running for the little man, not for the fat cats. Fat cats always vote Republican. They've got other things wrong with 'em, too."

They whooped and hollered. They liked him fine when he was laying into the GOP. When he had to talk about the war and the punishment America had taken and how things in Europe and Korea were going . . . No, he wasn't so popular then. If he had been, he would have run again. So he steered clear of anything that had to do with foreign affairs as far as he could—which wasn't far.

"We've got us a fine field of candidates," he said. "The way it looks to me is, we've got a better field than they'll run in the Kentucky Derby next week. This is the state Averell Harriman comes from, of course. He's a fine man. Since he spent time in Moscow as a diplomat during the last war, he knows the Russians as well as any American is likely to. If I haven't found peace by the time I leave office, I know he'll make a good one."

No, he couldn't ignore the wider world, however much he wanted to. He won more applause, tentative at first but then growing. Everyone wanted a good peace. Finding terms both sides could accept was the hard part.

"Now, I wouldn't mind if Mr. Harriman were to be the nominee, but I also wouldn't mind if any of the other leading candidates got the nod." Truman liked Harriman at least as well as any of the others, and better than most. But he wasn't about to endorse him publicly. As near as he could tell, his endorsement would be the kiss of death for whoever was unlucky enough to get it.

"The most important thing is, whichever candidate wins the nomination, we all have to get behind him and work for him as hard as we can. No Dixiecrats this time around, please. No so-called Progressives. We're all Democrats together, consarn it, and we've got to stick together as Donkeys against whichever jackass the Elephants run against us. Thanks very much, folks!"

He got a laugh and applause this time. It looked more and more as if the junior Senator from Wisconsin would bear the Republicans' standard. Without the war, Truman would have bet on Eisenhower. But a general's luster tarnished when men were fighting and dying all over again. Senator Taft kept trying to pretend Senator McCarthy didn't exist. It wasn't working.

Well, this bash cost twenty-five bucks a plate. Some good, solid cash would flow into the Democratic coffers from it. You needed ward-heelers to campaign for your candidates, not just the national ticket but the local men like Steven Pankow as well. You needed flyers and pamphlets and billboards. You needed more money for radio spots. And, in this modern world, you needed more money still for TV ads. Politics had never been cheap. These days, getting somebody elected was ridiculously expensive.

As the gathering started to break up, Truman pressed the flesh and chatted with his supporters. That was also part of the game. If they could imagine they knew you, they'd work harder on the campaign.

"Nice introduction," the President said when he clasped Pankow's hand. "You kept it short, and that's the most important thing."

"My pleasure, sir," Pankow replied. "Keep walloping the snot out of those damn Russians—that's all I've got to tell you. And never trust 'em further than you can throw 'em. They'll cheat if they get half a chance. A quarter of a chance, even."

"I have noticed that, yes," Truman said. A man who spoke with a faint Polish accent might well be one of the few people on earth who trusted Russians even less than Truman did. His reasons would be personal and historical, not political, but that only made them more sincere.

A limousine with a police escort took Truman to the airport. Red lights flashed, clearing traffic from the road. It was after midnight; there wasn't much traffic to clear. Spotlights guided the limo to the waiting *Independence.* As soon as the President climbed the wheeled stairway and boarded the DC-6, its engines thundered to life and the big props began to spin.

The plane rolled down the runway. It smoothly climbed into the air. Truman leaned back in his seat with a weary sigh. Washington soon, Washington and the war.

Boris Gribkov peered out through the Tu-4's Plexiglas windscreen. All he saw was ocean. Waves in the North Atlantic rolled on endlessly from the northwest toward the southeast.

He circled between Norway and Iceland, low enough and far enough away from land that radar sets on Jan Mayen and the Faeroes wouldn't spot him. Patrol planes . . . Patrol planes were a chance he simply had to take.

Although the sun had set, it was a long way from dark. He was up near the Arctic Circle, farther north than Leningrad and its famed white nights. That was another chance he had to take. He wouldn't have had to worry about it during the winter. It was May, though. Things happened when they happened, not when it was most convenient for them to happen.

He spoke to the radar operator over the intercom: "Anything?" It wasn't the first time he'd asked the question, or even the tenth.

"No, Comrade Pilot. I'm sorry," Arkady Oppokov replied. The first few times, he hadn't apologized.

Muttering to himself, Gribkov spoke to the navigator instead: "We *are* where we're supposed to be?" It wasn't the first time he'd asked that question, either.

"Yes, Comrade Pilot," Svyatoslav Filevich replied.

"You're sure?" Boris knew he wouldn't have asked that question of Leonid Tsederbaum. He'd had confidence in the Jew. He might not have asked it of Yefim Arzhanov, either. But they weren't here. Filevich was.

"Yes, Comrade Pilot," he repeated. It also wasn't the first time Gribkov had asked him that.

Boris fumed. That was all he could do. No, he could also eye his fuel gauge and worry. If his crew didn't find a milch cow pretty soon, he'd have to abort and fly back to Murmansk. That would effectively end his career. They wouldn't blame his crewmen. They wouldn't blame the milch cow's pilot. They'd blame *him,* for not flying the mission he was ordered to fly. He had the responsibility, and blame was the other side of that coin.

He was about to query Oppokov yet again when the radar operator suddenly exclaimed, "I have a target, Comrade Pilot! Bearing 270, speed 300 kilometers an hour, range fifteen kilometers, altitude . . . a long piss above the sea. That's got to be why I've had so much trouble picking it up."

"Here's hoping." Gribkov swung the Tu-4 west. He wasn't much more than a long piss above the sea himself. His last couple of practice runs at in-flight refueling had been low-level missions. He knew how to do it. He'd done it. It still made him nervous every time.

He also hoped the plane Oppokov's set had found wasn't another thirsty calf. That would be a colossal balls-up. He didn't know what he'd do then. Head back to Murmansk, he supposed, and try to take his medicine like a man.

But the pilot of the Tu-4 ahead waggled his wings when he spotted Gribkov. The tail gunner flashed a green lamp. Anton Presnyakov answered with a red one. Here, milch cow and calf had to connect without radio contact. The Soviet Union didn't control this stretch of ocean, which was putting things mildly. The enemy was bound to monitor every frequency.

Up Boris came, taking station astern of the milch cow. Its pilot deployed the filler cable. Lev Vaksman used his own to catch that one and guide it to the wingtip recess where it needed to go.

"We *are* taking on fuel, Comrade Pilot!" the engineer said. He didn't sound amazed the way he had the first time, but he still seemed excited.

"My gauge also shows it," Gribkov replied. "Wait till we're good and full before you turn loose of it."

"Yes, *sir*!" There was an order Vaksman agreed with.

Uncoupling went as smoothly as the rest of the process. Boris waved to the milch cow's pilot as he pulled away. He didn't know whether the other man could see him, but he made the effort.

That milch cow kept circling. Boris didn't know how many calves it could feed. What he didn't know, no interrogator could tear out of him. On the kinds of missions he flew, capture was only too possible.

"What's our course now, Svyatoslav?" he asked the navigator.

"Comrade Pilot, I suggest 225. That will send us out into the wider ocean about equidistant between the Faeroes and Iceland," Filevich replied. "We want to stay as far from land as we can."

"Think so, do you?" Boris said dryly. "Good enough. Course 225 it will be." He swung the Tu-4 to the southwest.

Every kilometer brought deeper darkness as the sun sank farther below the horizon. That was all to the good. The Americans and English could read a map. They knew where the ocean gaps were. Aerial patrols and radar-carrying picket ships watched them. But if the Tu-4 stayed low, an enemy plane's radar looking down from above had trouble telling its echo from that of the Atlantic. Picket ships couldn't spot it from very far away. Its IFF insisted it was an American plane itself.

On and on. On and on. No attacks. No challenges. They'd made it through one danger zone. The next one, the bad one, was still hours away. After a while, Presnyakov said, "It's a big ocean, isn't it?"

"Not next to the Pacific," Boris answered. He'd made that flight. He'd come back from it, too. Maybe he could do it again. *That* would be something to brag about! (Though poor Tsederbaum would tell him otherwise.)

On and on. He swallowed a benzedrine pill, then another one. They would have their way with him later, if there was a later. For now, they kept him awake and made him alert. On and on. He saw no freighters heading for England. With luck, no freighters saw him, either.

"We are approaching the East Coast of the United States," Filevich reported some time later. He sounded awed. "We should make landfall over Atlantic City, New Jersey."

Before long, Gribkov saw lights ahead. The Yankees didn't bother with a blackout in this part of the country. Radar made navigation easier, but lights helped. The Tu-4's IFF went right on claiming it was just another B-29 on its lawful occasions. Why a B-29 would be roaring along without lights at an altitude that made skyscrapers dangerous and heading straight for the capital of the USA was a question the IFF couldn't answer.

They crossed the Delaware Bay, then zoomed low over Dover, Delaware. Another stretch of water—the Chesapeake Bay. Annapolis, Maryland, was a small town.

Faizulla Ikramov, the radioman, knew some English. "They seem to be wondering about us, Comrade Pilot," he reported. "They don't know what we are, though. We're so low and so hard to pick up, they aren't sure we're anything."

"Good," Boris said. Washington was only a few minutes away. "We put it between the White House and the Capitol, if we can," he reminded navigator and bombardier. "They've tried to kill the great Stalin. Now we go after Truman."

The little river called the Anacostia guided them. At Filevich's word, Gribkov turned west before it joined the Potomac. As soon as the bomb fell free, he swung north and jammed the throttles past the red line. There'd be enough delay to let the Tu-4 get clear . . . if everything went well.

Unlike his crewmen, he'd been through atomic explosions

before. He rode out the hideous flash and the shock waves, then went east, back toward the Atlantic, again. "They're going crazy, Comrade Pilot!" Ikramov told him. "Crazy!"

"Good," Boris said once more. "If they don't come to their senses till we're out over the water, we may even get away with this." A submarine from the Red Fleet was supposed to be waiting at a precise point of latitude and longitude. If it was, if he could ditch this Tu-4 as he had the other after bombing Seattle, he and his crewmates might see the *rodina* again.

Seven and a half minutes after they bombed Washington, another great flash of light came from behind them. *"Bozhemoi!"* Anton Presnyakov exclaimed. "What was that?"

"Another dose of the same medicine," Gribkov answered. "Can't be anything else. The imperialists gave Moscow three. Washington deserves at least two."

"Oh, yes, sir," the copilot agreed. "I didn't know another plane was on the way, though." He laughed a shaky laugh. "Security!"

"That's right. Security." Boris hadn't known, either. The other blast might have knocked down his Tu-4—or he might have taken out the other one. But neither mischance happened. Both planes carried out their missions. Now they had to live through them.

SOMETIMES HARRY TRUMAN could sleep on the *Independence* despite noise and turbulence. When you were flying nonstop from one coast to the other or crossing the Atlantic, you had to be able to do that. For a trip from Buffalo home to Washington, the President didn't feel like making the effort. He'd sleep after he got to the White House.

Or so he thought. The Presidential airliner was about fifteen minutes—say, fifty miles—from landing when an aide came back from the direction of the cockpit. "Excuse me, Mr. President, but Major Pesky says there's some kind of flap about the airspace over Washington," the man said. "We've been asked to divert to Richmond."

"I don't think Richmond is even slightly diverting," Harry Truman said. The aide winced, which was what puns were for. Truman continued, "Some kind of flap, you say? Does the pilot know what's going on?"

"Sir, I told you as much as he told me," the man said.

"Well, go back up and find out why they've got their knickers in a twist," Truman said. "I don't want to head for Richmond unless we've got to."

The aide had just started up the aisle again when sudden harsh glare burned away the night and blazed in through every window on the DC-6, swamping the airliner's lighting system. Truman sat frozen in his seat. He knew—knew too well—what that flash had to mean. Somehow or other, the Russians had got through.

That was his first thought. His second one made him bury his face in his hands. Bess and Margaret hadn't come to Buffalo with him. His wife and daughter were waiting back at the White House.

Or they had been. He couldn't let himself contemplate his

own troubles, though. The country had just taken an uppercut to the chin. Truman stood. He pushed past his aide and stuck his head into the cockpit. "Major Pesky, don't take me to Richmond. If you can't land in Washington, go to Baltimore. That's close enough so I can get to Washington in a hurry—by helicopter, if I have to."

Without looking back at him, the pilot answered, "Sir, I'd rather not. They may hit Baltimore, too, while they're less likely to go after a smaller city like Richmond. Since I don't know how bad the casualties are in Washington, I'm obliged to keep you as safe as possible. I may do best just to circle as long as I can."

He made more sense than Truman wished he did. Was Alben Barkley still alive? How much of the Cabinet was left? What about Congress? Only this political junket had kept Truman from being in Washington. He might have lived through the blast. He probably would have, in the bomb shelter in the White House basement, had he got any warning. Had Bess got any? Had Margaret? Had anyone?

"What are you hearing on the radio?" Truman asked.

"They're scrambling fighters, sir," answered Captain McMullin, the copilot. "The Pentagon is directing—" He broke off. "Mr. President, I'm getting reports of a blinding flash in New York City. It—" He stopped again, and swore loudly and fluently. "Boston, too, damn them."

"Christ!" Harry Truman said. Marshall had assured him the Russians couldn't reach the East Coast. Even the august and brilliant Secretary of Defense didn't know everything there was to know. Truman hoped Marshall had survived the attack. He'd help pick up the pieces better than anyone else was likely to.

If there are any pieces left to pick up. Truman had had that thought before. What brought it on this time was another flash ahead. They were closer to Washington for this one. It seemed fiercer and brighter than the first. Something buffeted the *Independence,* as if a big dog were shaking a mouse.

Pesky and McMullin both cursed. They fought the DC-6 back under control. "Pentagon just fell off the air, Mr. President," McMullin said. "Everything's going to hell, sounds like."

The Tempest tolled in Truman's mind like a funeral bell:

The cloud-capp'd towers, the gorgeous palaces,
The solemn temples, the great globe itself,

Yea, all which it inherit, shall dissolve;
And like this insubstantial pageant faded,
Leave not a rack behind.

What had Will known? How had he known it? Washington's proud towers were capped by clouds, all right—mushroom clouds.

Pesky's thoughts ran on more pragmatic lines: "Sir, I am going to stay airborne as long as I can. I have fuel for another couple of hours. That should give us some kind of chance to sort out what's going on."

"Do that, then," Truman said heavily. "If you get . . . any word of how things are at the White House, please pass it on to me."

"Of course, sir," pilot and copilot said together. McMullin sent a sympathetic glance over his shoulder.

"We'll make the Russians pay for this," Pesky said.

"Oh, yes." Truman nodded. But Stalin had been making America pay for what B-29s did to the Soviet Union. Where did it end? Did it, could it, end anywhere except with both sides too battered and devastated to throw any more haymakers, as if two weary pugs in the ring knocked each other out at the same time?

Slowly, reports filtered in as the DC-6 droned through the sky. A Superfortress that had to be a Bull in a lying paint job was said to have gone down outside of Philadelphia. No one had shot it down. It was flying so low, it clipped something tall and crashed in flames. If it was carrying an A-bomb, which seemed a good bet, the infernal device hadn't gone off. Philadelphia lived.

Truman stayed by the cockpit, hoping to hear something about his wife and daughter. He didn't. News came in from the outskirts of both Washington blast areas, stories of fires and burns and wreckage. Plainly, the White House wasn't on the outskirts of either. Truman ground his teeth. His dentist would have clucked. He cared nothing for what his dentist thought.

"If you land in Richmond when we run low on gas, Major, can I get a helicopter or a light plane to take me over Washington after sunup so I can see what's happened to it?" he asked the pilot.

"Sir, I don't think you'd be helping the country right now

by going up in anything with only one engine," Pesky said. "That goes double for those newfangled flying eggbeaters, but it holds for Piper Cubs and the like, too. If you want, though, we can refuel there and I'll take you over myself."

"Thank you. That should work," Truman said. "In the meantime, I'll get off the plane at the airport and get on the telephone and see what I can do to let the country and the world know I'm still in business."

Major Pesky nodded. "Sounds like a good idea."

The President wasn't so sure. If Washington and New York were down for the count, he wouldn't have an easy time getting word out. The *Washington Post,* the *New York Times,* the *Wall Street Journal,* the hubs of all the radio and television networks . . . Gone now, probably.

He gulped coffee for an hour and a half. Then Pesky smoothly landed the *Independence.* Reporters snapped photos of Truman as he got off. A boss' phone in the terminal did very little for him or the country. He couldn't make the connections he needed, and the local operators didn't know enough to be helpful. Frustrated, he retreated to the airliner and drank more coffee.

As soon as the sky grew light, the DC-6 flew north. It wasn't far from Richmond to Washington. Ninety years before, Abe Lincoln and Jeff Davis had both fretted about that. Now . . . Now Truman watched smoke from fires still not quenched rise high into the air. Was what he breathed getting more and more radioactive as he neared the capital? He could wonder, but he didn't know—or care.

He'd seen photos of what A-bombs did to cities. He'd visited the West Coast in the wake of the Russian attacks there. Now he saw it again, with that smoke still swirling up and up and making him cough as the *Independence*'s ventilators sucked it into the fuselage. The Washington Monument was a melted, toppled stub. Not much was left of the Pentagon—part of one side of the five. The Capitol's shattered dome lay on the Mall, in front of what remained of the ravaged, burnt-out building. Of the White House he could make out nothing at all.

And he flew three miles above the disaster. Burned and charred and blinded and radiated people in terrible anguish, tens of thousands of them, were too small to make out at such a distance. So were the dead: more tens of thousands.

But they were there. Truman knew they were. Some of them were his. All of them were somebody's.

"Stalin will pay, all right," he whispered. "Oh, how he'll pay!"

Commander Alexei Vavilov raised a glass in salute. "Congratulations!" he told Boris Gribkov. "To the glory and vengeance you and your crew have given the Soviet Union! To victory over the imperialists!" He tossed back his shot of vodka.

Gribkov's copilot stood up and hoisted his glass. "To Commander Vavilov and the splendid *S-71*!" Anton Presnyakov said.

He drank. So did all the flyers. So did Vavilov and the other officers serving on the Red Fleet submarine. On and under the sea as in the air, the USSR learned from its foes. Just as the Tu-4 was a virtually identical copy of the American B-29, so the submarines that came out of Red Fleet Project 613 borrowed heavily from German Type XXI U-boats.

The Yankees, at least, had also got good use from their heavy bombers. The Hitlerites developed the Type XXI too late for their fancy new subs to take more than one or two combat cruises. But the design made all previous boats obsolete. It had tremendous batteries, a snorkel to power the diesels and charge those batteries while most of the submarine stayed hidden beneath the water, and such perfect streamlining that it was faster submerged than on the surface.

As German U-boats had before them, attack submarines like the *S-71* harried the lifeline between America and Europe. Unlike the *Kriegsmarine,* the Red Fleet didn't delude itself into thinking it could starve England into surrender. But it could sink enemy ships full of food and weapons and men, and it could make life difficult for the ones that did manage to cross.

And its submarines could rescue bomber crews if not bombers, and take them back to the *rodina* to fly more missions in new planes. That was what the *S-71* was doing, along with Gribkov didn't know how many other boats. Some of them would head back to Murmansk and Arkhangelsk with no airmen aboard. Not all the bombers that struck at America would have reached their oceanic meeting points. Not all of them would have reached their targets, either.

War was like that, however much people wished it weren't. Things went wrong. The bastards on the other side proved more clever than you thought they would. You lost friends . . . or they lost you.

Briefly, Boris thought of Leonid Tsederbaum again. Now he had Washington on his conscience along with Paris and the rest of the places he'd smashed. The old navigator hadn't been able to stand it. The fighting went on without him.

As if to prove as much, Commander Vavilov's executive officer rose to make another toast. Lieutenant Yuri Krasnov lifted his glass and said, "To Comrade Filevich, whose navigation put you down right where it should have!"

The men gathered under the conning tower—the only place in the boat with room for them all—drank together. Svyatoslav Filevich offered his own toast: "To the brave submariners who take all this crowding not just to save us but to carry the fight to the foe!"

Everyone in the Tu-4's crew drank. So did the submarine's officers, but they seemed amused. "If you think this boat is crowded," Vavilov said, "you should have seen the ones we used during the Great Patriotic War. We were as bad as the Germans. The junior ratings slept on top of the fish in the forward torpedo room till we used a few and gave them more room to swing their hammocks."

"Maybe it was worse then, Commander," Gribkov said. "I mean no disrespect when I tell you it's still pretty bad."

The boat was divided into three pressure compartments. Going from one to the next meant slithering through a round hatchway not much wider than a man's torso. That might have been the smallest breach practicable in a bulkhead, but it was far from convenient. Corridors were so narrow, two men going in opposite directions had trouble squeezing past each other. Every so often, metal things with corners and edges stuck out into them. The top of the pressure tube made a low ceiling. The pipes running along it had valves and fittings that could knock an unwary man in a hurry for a loop.

Boris and the rest of the flyers kept quiet about one more aspect of how crowded the *S-71* was. The boat stank. It smelled of dirty sailors and dirtier socks, of food going off and of heads that had backed up, all mixed in with the heavy reek of diesel fuel. The men wore shabby clothes and let their beards grow while they were at sea. Shaving soap was a luxury judged needless. By the fug, so was any other kind of soap.

As a man familiar with commanding and maintaining one kind of complicated mechanism, Gribkov used his time as a passenger aboard the *S-71* as a chance to watch another skilled professional in charge of a different, perhaps even more complex, piece of machinery.

On the Tu-4, what the pilot and navigator could see was still an important part of completing a mission. Except when making an attack run with periscope raised, Alexei Vavilov depended almost completely on his sensors. Men with earphones constantly monitored the passive sonar, listening for any warning that U.S. Navy or Royal Navy vessels were near enough to be dangerous.

"I don't expect to surface till we're up in the Arctic Ocean," Vavilov told him. "We'd be asking for it if we did. The snorkel will keep the diesels going and the batteries happy. If we show ourselves on the surface, even at night, the enemy's radar will spot us and he'll send out planes after us."

"More and more gadgets," Gribkov said. "It's the same in the air. Pretty soon the gadgets will do all the fighting, and the crews will just come along for the ride."

"Or there won't be any crews," Vavilov replied. "Think of a *big* rocket, one like a V-2's big brother. It'll fly thousands of kilometers, not hundreds. It'll be powerful enough to do that with an A-bomb on the head of its dick. And it'll land within a hundred meters of where somebody aims it. As soon as they build it, you'll be out of work."

Boris hadn't thought of the future of war in those terms till now. As soon as he did, he realized the submarine skipper was bound to be right. "Your job won't last much longer than mine," he said.

"You never can tell," Vavilov said. "Mount those rockets on a submarine, and it'd pop up and launch them before the enemy realized it was in the neighborhood."

"You could do that, couldn't you?" Now the bomber pilot saw what might be the future of war spread out for him, almost as if in a religious vision. He shuddered. That future held even more deaths than he'd already dealt out.

The current state of the art faced them the next day. Alexei Vavilov had explained that the *S-71,* like its Type XXI ancestors, ran much quieter than earlier models. Enemy ships detected the boat anyhow, and attacked. Vavilov dove deep and sneaked away. Depth charges burst in the sea above the boat, close enough to be alarming but not to put it in serious peril.

"How's this stack up against antiaircraft guns?" the skipper asked Boris in a low voice—silence was literally a matter of life and death.

"As far as I'm concerned, you can keep them both," he whispered back.

Vavilov nodded. "About what I figured. This, this isn't too bad. They don't really know where we are, and the charges foul up their sonar something fierce. Slow and steady, and we'll get away. Once we slide through the gap between Britain and Iceland, we're just about home free."

"I used that gap flying south to strike Washington," Boris said.

"I'm not surprised. It's there to be used," Vavilov said. "We'll get you back, and they can pin some more medals on you."

"Who cares about medals? I just want to live through the war."

"Well, so do I. Who doesn't?" Vavilov said. "But when you serve the Soviet Union, you get what the *rodina* needs, not what you want." It was Boris Gribkov's turn to nod. He'd already worked that out for himself.

Whenever Aaron Finch wasn't at work or asleep—and he slept as little as he could get away with, or rather less than that—he sat staring at the television set in his living room. TV in and around Los Angeles had gone cattywumpus when the A-bomb leveled downtown: it took out most of the local studios.

TV here was back in business now, and relayed from the East Coast to the West more horrific images of what atomic war did to great cities. The Empire State Building and the Chrysler Building both wrecked and toppled, *Old Ironsides* burnt to the waterline in Boston harbor, the glassy wasteland that had been the White House . . .

Seeing the damage to what had been national monuments was bad. Seeing and hearing about the damage to what had been people was worse. It had a horrid fascination to it, though. Aaron found he couldn't look away.

The television reporters understood that only too well. A man with a jacket and tie would go up to a scorched or bandaged woman who'd somehow been pulled alive from a ravaged Manhattan apartment house and stick a microphone in her face. "Excuse me, Mrs. Torres," he'd go, or it might be *Mrs. Lombardi* or *Mrs. Callahan* or *Mrs. Rabinowicz,* "but could you tell me what happened to you and what you're feeling now?"

And Mrs. Torres or Mrs. Lombardi or Mrs. Callahan or Mrs. Rabinowicz would break down and sob and say something about her parents or husband or children or all of the above who hadn't escaped or who had but who were hurt worse than she was.

Every so often, whichever network Aaron was watching at the moment would cut away to a makeshift headquarters in Philadelphia. A tired-looking reporter—sometimes a tired-looking reporter with a cigarette in his mouth—would give the latest estimates on numbers of the dead and amount of damage. Those amounted to hundreds of thousands of people and billions of dollars. Once Aaron knew that much, he knew everything he needed to know. Precision hardly mattered, though the reporters kept trying to provide it.

They also kept posting lists of Senators and Representatives known to be dead. Most Congressmen and -women had Washington digs not far from the gutted Capitol. Most of the time, that meant they could easily get to work. Now it meant that large numbers of them would never run for reelection, or for anything else, again.

Robert Taft and Joe McCarthy were both on the lists. So were Hubert Humphrey and Estes Kefauver. Averell Harriman was known to be dead, too; he'd been at a hotel in Manhattan that the falling Empire State Building drove into the ground like a sledgehammer hitting a railroad spike. George Marshall had been working late at the Pentagon. His diligence meant only that nothing of him was left to bury.

Of the Federal government's leading organs, the Supreme Court came through best. Seven of the nine Justices were at a lawyers' conclave in St. Louis when doom fell on the capital. Naturally, that was the branch of government with the least to do with setting policy or carrying it through.

Harry Truman still lived, too, but the more Aaron saw him the more he thought the President wished he didn't. Truman looked suddenly, cruelly, old. Some of that might have been that he wasn't bothering with makeup any more before he came in front of the cameras. More, though, had to come from the loss of his wife and daughter.

"I brought the United States into this war. God has given me my own full measure of the nation's grief. The Psalms tell us that the judgments of the Lord are true and righteous altogether. I bow before those judgments. I see nothing else that I can do. The Bible also says that vengeance is the Lord's. There I must respectfully disagree with the Good Book."

Listening to the way Truman came out with that, Aaron felt a chill run up his back. "I wouldn't want to be in Joe Stalin's shoes right this minute," he said to Ruth.

"I wouldn't want to be in Stalin's shoes any time at all," she answered. "They'd probably steal my toes."

"I wouldn't be surprised," Aaron said. "Or else paint 'em red. But you do that yourself, at least with the nails."

"You're crazier than I am," Ruth said, not without admiration.

"I try," Aaron said. But with the stricken President on the screen in front of him, he couldn't stay lighthearted. "That poor man. He's lost his family, and Pearl Harbor looks like a pinprick next to this. And somehow he's got to go on."

"We face a crisis in our system of government," Truman said. "Neither house of Congress has enough members for a quorum. Governors may appoint Representatives, but Senators must be elected. All of that will take time, time we don't have in the middle of a war. I've spoken by telephone with Chief Justice Vinson, who was in St. Louis when Washington was attacked. He assures me that I may continue carrying out policies I find necessary, both at home and abroad, even without Congressional approval, because of the national emergency. 'We have to move forward,' was the way he put it. He's right—we do. And we will, with God's help and with the help of the American people."

His face disappeared from the TV. Ruth said, "He sounds like he wants to cry but won't let himself, not where anybody can hear him do it."

Aaron nodded. "You're right. That's just what he sounds like. I heard something in his voice was odd, but I couldn't put my finger on what." He sent her an admiring glance. "You're as smart as you are pretty."

"Break out the shovels, boys!" Ruth said. "It's getting pretty deep tonight." Aaron laughed, very fond of her in that moment.

Again, though, laughter couldn't last. The picture cut away

to a field—the reporter at the edge of the field said it was five miles west of New Egypt, New Jersey. Aaron had never heard of New Egypt, New Jersey, till that moment.

"This is the final resting place of the Bull bomber that crashed before it could deliver its cargo of death to Philadelphia, less than thirty miles away," the reporter said. "None of the eleven Russians who made up the crew survived. Because they perished, all of Philadelphia's more than two million people still live. America's third-largest city escaped the tragedy that struck Boston, New York, and Washington."

The bomber's tail had broken off from the rest of the fuselage. It stood upright amidst the grass and bushes, almost like a cross marking a grave. The star on the vertical surface looked the same as the ones on U.S. Air Force planes.

"Russian Bulls are modeled after American Superfortresses, and look nearly the same," the reporter said. "The Russians often paint them in our colors to help fool our air defenses."

Did B-29s on their way to Moscow or Kiev bear Soviet markings? The reporter said nothing about that. He was a propagandist. If the Reds did it, it was a dirty trick. If the USA did it, it was a ruse of war.

Men wearing gas masks and what looked like rubberized suits were moving about near the wreckage. The reporter did talk about that: "This Bull *was* carrying an A-bomb. Obviously, it didn't explode, or I wouldn't be standing here talking to you now. But it did release a certain amount of radioactivity because of the crash. The authorities have assured me that I am at a safe distance from the crash scene. The experts in the protective clothing are making sure that the bomb is secure and that the radiation is properly contained."

How much were the authorities' assurances worth? Aaron wouldn't have wanted to trust somebody who might not know what the dickens he was talking about—or who might be lying through his teeth. The guy with the mike and his camera crew couldn't have been more than a couple of hundred yards from the Bull's wreckage.

They had a job to do. They were doing it. Reporters didn't face danger as often as soldiers did, but they did face it. Aaron just wanted to do his job, too. So did most of the people in the world. But how could they, if it was going up in radioactive fire around them?

* * *

Rolf Mehlen scratched himself under his left armpit. It was only an itch. Not six weeks after the last war ended, he'd given a doctor two cartons of Old Golds to cut away the blood-group tattoo every *Waffen*-SS officer carried there. It hurt like a son of a bitch after the novocaine wore off, but the scar was almost invisible now.

In *Leibstandarte Adolf Hitler,* he'd been a *Hauptsturmführer,* the SS rank equivalent to captain. In this new, half-assed West German army, he was just a guy named Rolf. A rifleman. A spear carrier. It was better this way. Nobody asked a whole lot of questions about a private. That suited Rolf fine.

He wrapped some oil-soaked cloth around the end of his cleaning rod and pushed it through the barrel of his Springfield. Except for firing a cartridge of different caliber, the American rifle was as near the same as his old Mauser as made no difference.

Sitting across the little fire from him, Max Bachman took care of his own Springfield. Bachman had served in the *Wehrmacht,* not the *Waffen*-SS. His politics weren't just soft. They were squishy. When the *Führer* was running things, the *Gestapo* would have had a little talk with him, or maybe not such a little one. Back then, though, he would have been smart enough to keep his big yap shut.

To give him his due, he knew what he was up to when he fought. Anybody who'd lived through a stretch on the Eastern Front had the soldier's trade burned into him, whether he made social-democratic noises or not. If you didn't know how, you died. It was that simple.

You might well die even if you did know how. Especially toward the end, there'd just been too goddamn many Russians. Skill gave some defense against numbers, but only some. The way the Ivans used their guns and rockets, you needed luck on your side, too.

Rolf oiled the bolt and checked the Springfield's action once he had it reassembled. When he was happy, he lit an American Lucky to celebrate.

"Let me have one of those, will you?" Max said.

"Knock yourself out." Rolf tossed him the pack.

"Thanks." Max eyed the red circle on the pack with *Lucky Strike* in black on it. He took a cigarette and got it going. Then he said, "I know some English. 'Lucky' is *glücklich.* From what they're saying, the Amis' luck has run out."

"Just like Gustav's," Rolf said.

"Uh-huh. Just like Gustav's." Max's cheeks hollowed as he sucked in smoke. "He was a good guy, Gustav was. Had a nice wife, too. Pretty gal. I hope Luisa's all right, and my Trudl. Fulda's been Russian too long now."

"Everything west of Russia's been Russian too goddamn long now," Rolf said. "And so the Americans had some cities hit? Big deal. They're—what? Ten times as big as we are? Twenty times? Maybe more, I don't know. They had some places nailed last year, and some more now. They bombed us harder than that themselves a little while ago, and we're supposed to be on their side."

Bachman blew a stream of smoke up into the darkness. "You love everybody, don't you, Rolf?" he said.

"Just like I love you," Rolf answered sweetly.

Max chuckled. "Christ have mercy on the rest of the poor buggers, then!"

"Let Him worry about that. I sure don't." But Rolf got more serious after a moment. "I love Germany. I love the *Reich.* The rest of the world? I don't give a shit about the rest of the world. It can goddamn well take care of itself."

"It can take care of us, too. It can, and it has. This is three times in less than forty years it's jumped all over us with hobnailed boots," Max said. "We would've been better off if the Kaiser and the *Führer* never started their wars."

"How about this last one?" Rolf said. "You gonna blame this one on us, too?"

"Nah. We were just in the way this time," Bachman replied. "The first two World Wars, we were a great power. This time, we're chopped in half and the real powers bump into each other where we are. Ever wonder if that ought to tell you something?"

"It tells me we should have won before," Rolf said.

"If it tells you how we should have, I'm all ears," Max said. "After Stalingrad, after Kursk, after the Anglo-Americans made it into France, anybody with his eyes open could see we were fucked. But we kept fighting anyway, you and me and all the other fools."

"What were we going to do? Surrender unconditionally? I don't think so!" Rolf said irately.

"Well, we wound up doing it whether we wanted to or not. How many more soldiers got killed on account of that? How many more towns got leveled? How many more women got gang-banged?"

Rolf only shrugged. He ground out the cigarette on half a brick. "We didn't know that would happen. We thought we'd step on the Ivans. They're like cockroaches. That's all they deserve."

As if to say the Red Army had a different opinion, Soviet guns thundered to life. Rolf cocked his head to one side, gauging the reports and the howl of the shells through the air. He had a foxhole only a jump from the fire, in case he needed it. Max had dug one, too. No wonder he'd made it through the last scrap and into this new one. One of the things that helped you get to be an old soldier was digging a hole wherever you were first chance you saw.

He was listening, too. "Those are 155s. They've got more of them and fewer 105s than they did before, I think."

"I think maybe you're right. More of them self-propelled, too." Rolf let out a sour laugh. "Guys who'd gone through the Kaiser's war would have talked the same way, except with them it would have been 105s taking over for 77s or 75s, depending on which side they were on."

"Here's one for you," Max said. "I wonder if we've got anybody who's been in all three World Wars. A kid in the trenches in 1918, a captain in 1939 who somehow managed to live through it, maybe a colonel or a *Generalmajor* now."

"It could be," Rolf said. "Getting through the second one if you really fought, that's the hard part. Somebody who was on garrison duty in Norway or Holland would have a better chance." He hawked and spat. Anyone who didn't see the *Ostfront* hardly counted as a soldier to him.

"The Tommies didn't have as tough a war as we did," Max said. "They're bound to have people like that—maybe even a top noncom or two."

Rolf only grunted. He'd come up through the ranks himself. But the men who stuck at senior sergeant were the ones who didn't have any imagination. All armies needed people like that. They steadied the show and kept junior officers from doing anything too spectacularly stupid. But routine had a way of ruling what passed for their souls.

American guns fired back at the Russian artillery. Rolf had had to learn their reports during this war, whereas the Red Army's artillery pieces were almost old friends. He'd known

German guns even better, of course, but those hadn't come to this party.

"It's a bitch," he said, "when we turn into a football pitch for two other sides to play on."

"I told you—that's what we get for losing twice before." Max took out a fresh Lucky. "See? I'm stealing another smoke from you. Can I ask you something while I do it?"

"You can always ask. If I want to, I'll tell you to go fuck yourself."

"And that's supposed to surprise me? What I want to know is, what are you doing here? This isn't the Germany you fought for last time. It never will be, either. You know that, right?"

"*Ja,* I know it." *And I hate it,* Rolf thought. But that was for him to know and for Max to guess at. He held out his hand for the cigarettes. Max flipped them back. After he'd started one, he continued, "No, it's not the *Führer*'s Germany. All that matters these days is getting by and making money. We want to be America, but we can't. You know what, though? I don't care. It's still Germany, and I still love it."

"Deutschland bleibt Deutschland," Max said, and Rolf nodded—Germany *did* stay Germany. Max sketched a salute. "Well, we aren't so far apart after all, are we?"

"Not on that," Rolf said. Now Max nodded. Yes, there were a few—million—other things.

ALONG WITH DOLORES and the rest of the women who typed and filed and answered the phones in the Shasta Lumber Company's front office, Marian Staley walked down the long hallway to Mahogany Row. Each of them carried a copy of the ambulance petition from the *Weed Press-Herald*. Taking all the petitions together, they had several hundred signatures.

Dolores looked at the others. "Well, here goes nothing," she said, and knocked on Carl Cummings' door.

"What is it?" the executive said, his voice muffled by the barrier. Thus encouraged, Dolores opened the door. Seeing the crowd in the hall, Cummings raised an eyebrow. "Looks like Grand Central Station out there," he remarked. "What's going on?"

"Mr. Cummings, sir, you'll have seen the petitions for an ambulance in the paper," Marian said, hoping she sounded less scared than she felt. "We need—uh, Weed needs—ambulances for when bad things happen, so they won't be as horrible as they were with poor Leroy van Zandt. We've all gathered signatures for these petitions, and we wanted to give them to you so you can see how the whole town feels about it."

"That's right," Dolores said. The other four women nodded.

"If Shasta Lumber joins up with the other outfits in town, it won't cost any of you too much money, and it'll save lives for years," Marian finished. "Who knows, Mr. Cummings, sir? One of them might even be yours."

"So that's what we're here for," Dolores put in. "We want to give you these here petitions, like Marian said. Just so you know, sir, I've got Doc Toohey's John Hancock on mine. He thinks it's a great idea, Doc Toohey does."

She walked into the paneled office. The rest of the clerical workers followed her. One by one, they set the petitions on Cummings' desk. That was also of mahogany, unlike the cheap painted-steel desks at the other end of the hall.

"I did know about the petition drive, yes. I couldn't very well not know about it, could I?" Cummings paused to glance at some of the sheets of newsprint. Marian's petition had, among other people's, Dale Dropo's signature, and Fayvl Tabakman's, and Babs' from the diner, and that of Miss Hamilton, who was Linda's teacher.

"Have you, um, talked with people from the other lumber companies, sir?" Marian asked, that seeming more polite than barking *So what are you going to do about it, you filthy capitalist, you?*

"As a matter of fact, I have," Carl Cummings said. Marian braced herself for what she feared was coming next. *And you're all fired, for having the gall to try to tell us what to do* was what that boiled down to. The executive paused to light a Pall Mall, which only made her want to fidget more. After his first drag, he went on, "And we all think it's the best idea anybody's had for years. We know we've got a problem here. This lets us take a shot at fixing it without costing anybody too much. We've already started talking with an outfit down in Sacramento that sells ambulances. One ought to be here inside of a month."

"You do?" Marian hardly believed her ears.

"You have?" Dolores sounded just as astonished.

"It will?" So did Claire Hermanson, who ran the switchboard.

"Absolutely," Cummings said, and all at once he didn't seem anywhere near so filthy to Marian. Still a capitalist, yes—who but a capitalist in Weed would have worn such an elegant gray pinstripe suit (or any kind of suit, for that matter: jeans and Pendletons were the usual menswear)? But maybe not one to spark a proletarian uprising. He nodded to Marian. "You know this Tabakman fellow who came up with the notion, don't you?"

"Uh-huh." She nodded, still dizzy at how easy it had turned out to be. "We knew each other up in Washington before the bomb hit, and in the camp there afterwards."

"Good for you. Good for him. He's got a head on his shoulders—not like Dale Dropo." Carl Cummings rolled his eyes. "That maniac thinks he can say whatever he wants because he runs the *Press-Herald*. He doesn't understand that it's a newspaper, doggone it, not a blackjack."

Marian prudently kept her mouth zipped tight. Without the petitions in the *Press-Herald,* the lumber bosses might well have gone on thinking they could ignore what Weed needed. The blank forms in the paper must have been enough to get them going. They hadn't waited for the ones full of signatures like those on Cummings' desk.

"You've given us good news, Mr. Cummings, sir. Thank you." Dolores still seemed flabbergasted, too. "I guess we'll go back to work now."

"Okay." The executive nodded briskly. "Why don't you close the door again on your way out?" He was already reaching for the telephone as the clerical staff beat a retreat.

Out in the hall, with the solid door closed behind them, the women clasped hands and hugged. "We did it!" Marian exclaimed. "We really did it! We went and belled the cat!"

"Yeah!" Claire Hermanson started back to her station. "I'm gonna call Doc Toohey. He'll shit a brick when he hears, swear he will!" Marian wouldn't have put it that way, not even after her spell at Camp Nowhere, but that didn't mean she thought Claire was wrong.

At lunch, she headed for the diner to tell Babs the news. Babs had already heard, which wasn't a shock, either. "That skinny Hebe made the big shots act like they weren't jerks," the waitress said. "Who woulda thunk anybody could?" She eyed Marian. "Tabakman, he's sweet on you. You know that?"

"Who, me?" Marian said. Babs cackled. Marian went on, "Yes, I know. He knows I know. I'm still putting myself back together, though. He understands that. He doesn't rush me or anything."

"Don't wait too long," Babs said. "Men ain't patient critters." That was bound to be good advice, even if Marian wasn't ready to take it yet.

She stopped at the Rexall on the way back to work. As she had in the Shasta Lumber hallway, she said, "We *did* bell the cat."

Heber Stansfield was the one who'd first used that figure of speech. He nodded now. "That's good. That's mighty good. They got to do it without looking like they was bending too much. But with the whole world coming to pieces around our ears, who knows how much it'll matter in the end?"

A radio behind the counter was giving the news. "What's the latest?" Marian asked. "Do I want to know?"

"Murmansk. That Archangel place—somethin' like that, anyways. Odessa." Stansfield spoke of death and devastation with sour approval. He could afford to. He'd never known for himself what an atom bomb was like. "And they're shootin' looters in Boston and Washington."

"Not in New York City?" Marian asked.

"From what the radio reporters say, in New York City, the looters, they shoot back." The druggist spoke as if no iniquity coming out of New York City was too big for him to credit.

Marian bought a package of Life Savers to keep him sweet, then walked down the block to Fayvl's cobbler's shop. He looked up from an upside-down logger's boot. "Hallo, Marian," he said. "It's an ambulance."

"It sure is!" she agreed. "Everybody in town is going on about how smart you are, to come up with a way to make it an ambulance."

"Foosh!" Tabakman waved that aside. "Anybody what thinks I'm smart, himself he ain't so."

"Don't sandbag." Marian wasn't sure he'd get that. But he did. She realized that if he'd played a lot of cards to get his stake to come here, he would have to. She added, "I think you're way too smart to be doing this for a job."

"Why for you think that? It's honest work. It ain't such a bad living. And I enjoy it. So why I shouldn't do it? What should I do instead?"

"I don't know, not when you put it that way," Marian said.

"Anything I used to did, I would think it was from God a blessing. Then the Nazis came, and God forgot about us if He was ever there at all," Fayvl said. "So now I do what I feel like doing because I feel like doing it. It's the same as before, only without God and without the blessing. I get by."

Without God and without the blessing. Marian found herself nodding. "Me, too, Fayvl. Me, too."

Vasili Yasevich wanted to pay a call on David Berman to see how the old Jew's "niece" or "cousin" or whatever they decided to call her was coming along. He knew better than to do it, though. Unless Berman found work for him to do, someone would wonder why he was visiting him. He didn't want anybody asking himself a question like that.

He might not have lived in the Soviet Union for long. He knew how police states operated, though. The Japanese in Harbin had been at least as ruthless as the MGB was here. So had Mao's men, once Manchukuo went back to being Manchuria. The best way to get along with secret police was never to draw their notice.

So he did his odd jobs. He kept an eye out for Grigory Papanin, but Papanin seemed to have decided leaving him alone was the better part of valor. He also kept an eye out for Gleb Sukhanov. Whether he'd wanted to or not, he'd already drawn that Chekist's notice.

Vasili stood in the town square, listening to Radio Moscow's news broadcast coming out of the speaker mounted on the pine pole. Roman Amfiteatrov alternated between bragging about the ruin Soviet bombers dealt to cities on the East Coast of the USA and moaning about the ruin American bombers had visited on Russian cities in response.

If you listened to Amfiteatrov, the Soviet bomber crews were heroes. They represented the vanguard of the proletariat and struck a mighty blow on behalf of the oppressed masses and the advance toward a classless society. The Yankee bomber crews, by contrast, were the lapdogs of plutocracy and warmongering imperialists who delighted in massacring workers and peasants and their children.

If you listened to Amfiteatrov . . . Vasili could see that, regardless of ideology, when you dropped an atom bomb on a city you knocked it flat and killed tens if not hundreds of thousands of people. How many others here could see the same thing? Either there weren't very many of them or most of them, like Vasili himself, knew better than to show they could think for themselves.

"*Zdrast'ye,* Vasili Andreyevich." There was Sukhanov, right beside him. While he'd been listening, he hadn't been watching. The MGB man went on, "He sure does talk funny, doesn't he?"

"Oh, hello, Gleb Ivanovich." Vasili did his best to sound as if Sukhanov were an ordinary friend, one who had nothing to do with the Ministry of State Security. "He doesn't have an accent like mine, that's for certain. Your jaw still doing all right?"

The Chekist touched the side of his face for a moment. "Hasn't given me any more trouble since Yakov Benyaminovich yanked that stupid tooth, thank heaven. But I want to thank you one more time for the poppy juice you gave me. That kept me going till he was able to work on me. I owe you a big one there."

"Nah." Vasili shook his head, even as he was thinking *Bet your dick you do. Will you remember when it counts?* If you had to ask yourself a question like that, chances were you wouldn't like the answer. Still casually, Vasili asked, "How're things otherwise?"

"For me? Well enough. And you?"

"Not too bad, thank you very much," Vasili said.

"I'm glad to hear it," Sukhanov said. "I need to tell you something you may not be so glad to hear, though."

"Oh? What's that?"

"You were listening to Radio Moscow just now. The war keeps going. It's heating up, in fact. The way the Americans kill cities, they may as well be tigers killing elk," the Chekist replied. Did he remember that the USSR had also struck at the USA? If he did, he didn't show it. He went on, "Conscription calls are heating up, too. The ever-victorious Red Army has to get more men if it's going to keep winning those victories."

"If the *rodina* needs me to serve it again, of course I will serve it again." Though Vasili bore down on the lying *again,* he wasn't at all sure he meant that. Mean it or not, he had to say it. Saying anything else meant he'd serve the Soviet Union in a gulag like the one from which Maria Bauer had escaped—maybe in that very same one.

"Khorosho," Gleb Sukhanov said. "So far, your name hasn't shown up on any lists. If it does, maybe I can lose it. But I can't promise I'll be able to do that. All I can do is try."

"Whatever you manage, I'll be grateful for." Vasili wondered whether he'd be better off letting the Red Army draft him or disappearing into the woods if it did. Either way, he was much too likely to have unfriendly strangers shooting at him.

"The other possibility I need to warn you about is, I may not be able to do anything at all for you. I may not be here to do anything for you," the MGB man said. "My name may be on those conscription lists, too."

But you're a Chekist! Vasili thought. Then again, that might not matter. How many Soviet cities had the Americans incinerated? The ever-victorious Red Army did have to get its men somewhere. If it couldn't lay its hands on enough ordinary people, chances were it would start grabbing secret policemen.

Aloud, Vasili said, "It's a rough old world, Gleb Ivanovich." He wanted to sound sympathetic without sounding as if he were criticizing Stalin. If you did that, you were unlikely to make any other stupid mistakes afterwards.

"It sure is." Sukhanov set a hand on Vasili's shoulder. *Maybe he* does *like me,* Vasili thought in surprise. The MGB man added, "Take care of yourself," and ambled off.

Roman Amfiteatrov was still blathering away. He'd worked through the world news while Vasili talked with Sukhanov. Now he was praising the record aluminum output from shock labor gangs in Omsk. That did tell Vasili Omsk probably hadn't made the acquaintance of an atom bomb yet. Whether the shock workers had really made all that aluminum was a different question. So was whether they even existed.

Down a side street off the square was one of the little unofficial markets the authorities grudgingly allowed. Babushkas sold strawberries and eggs and onions and golden cheeses they'd made themselves: that kind of stuff. You had to spend money there, but you could find much nicer things than you could in the state-run stores.

There stood David Berman, hefting a big white onion as if it were a grenade. "*Dobry den,* David Samuelovich," Vasili said. "How's the world treating you?"

"Oh, hello," the old Jew said. He looked less . . . less disheveled than he had when Vasili brought Maria to his door. His clothes sat on him the way they were supposed to, and Vasili thought he'd run a comb through the scraggly tangle of his beard. "The world is . . . not too bad for me, anyhow. How is it for you?"

" 'Not too bad' sounds right." Vasili drew Berman away from the onion stand so the babushka wouldn't overhear. "And how's your niece from way off in the west?"

"She seems to be settling in pretty well, thanks," Berman answered. "You know how it is with young people. Or maybe you don't, since you are one yourself. Sometimes it's like we don't quite speak the same language. But she's a nice girl, mighty nice. She's friendly." He nodded, as if pleased with his own choice of words. "Yes, very friendly."

"Good. I'm glad for you," Vasili said. If that meant what he thought it meant, Maria was fucking David till he couldn't see straight. And if it didn't mean that, too bad for him.

"Don't just walk off with that onion there," the babushka said. "You want it, you got to pay for it." Pay for it David Berman did. Vasili thumped him on the back. He lit a Belomor, happy with the way that was working out.

Daisy Baxter stood outside the chemist's shop, waiting for Bruce McNulty to pick her up. She could see a few of the brighter stars—Mars shone bright and bloody, low in the southeast—but it wasn't true dark yet. It wouldn't be for a while, either; as spring advanced toward summer, twilight lingered late and then came again early the next morning.

Not many motorcars moved along East Dereham's narrow, twisting streets. Civilians had a devil of a time getting petrol. Bruce, of course, was no civilian. He could fuel whatever machine he got at the unfailing tap of a U.S. Air Force motor pool. If he wouldn't be using it for military purposes . . . he didn't care.

Air-raid sirens began their warbling screech. Daisy said something that would have made Simon Perkins look as if he'd just bitten into a green persimmon. The Russian Beagle bombers got bolder by the day. They zoomed across the skies of eastern England like malevolent bats, dropping bombs here and there and then disappearing.

"Run for the shelter!" a man who was taking his own advice shouted to Daisy.

Antiaircraft guns went off in the distance. The tracers arcing across the sky put her in mind of Guy Fawkes' Day. She knew she was taking a chance staying out in the open. But it wasn't a big chance. A Beagle *might* target East Dereham. There wasn't anything about the place that would really tempt one of the marauders, though.

Here came a jeep. "Hey, good-lookin'!" an American voice called. "Wanna come for a ride with me?"

"I'd love to!" She hopped in. She was getting used to the right side's not holding the driving seat. She leaned over to kiss Bruce—who would see her while she did it?

He put the jeep in gear. More antiaircraft guns bellowed. More tracers scribed lines of fire overhead. Bruce chuckled. "Maybe we should've worn—what do you call 'em over here?—tin hats, that's it. Don't want fragments coming down on our heads."

"I wasn't fretting about it," Daisy said. "All I was thinking about was you, and us, and us later on."

She could still see his grin. "I like the way you think, babe." He swung the jeep onto the road that led southwest. "And now, on to wonderful, historical Watton."

"Oh, rubbish!" Daisy said. "There's no history to any of the little towns and villages around here. That means Fakenham, too, or it did before the bomb hit. People live in places like these because they want nothing to do with history. Only sometimes it comes calling whether you want it or not."

"I guess so," Bruce said. How much history had he carried in his B-29's bomb bay? On whom had it fallen, whether they wanted it or not? He wasn't thinking about that now. He went on, "The combo playing at the dance is Freddy Cullenbine and His Smokin' Five. How come that sounds familiar?"

"Weren't they the band at Yaxham, the first time we—?" Daisy felt herself blushing. She didn't go on.

"You could be right." Bruce set a hand on her knee. "I wasn't paying much attention to what their name was. I had other things on my mind." The hand moved higher.

With a laugh, Daisy knocked it away. "While you're driving, kindly drive."

Watton was bigger than Yaxham, smaller than East Dereham. It thought it had history—it boasted, and boasted of, a clock tower from the seventeenth century. A sign in front of the tower—barely readable now, as the light was failing—said the clock had got a new face in the 1930s. The dance was at the town social hall, a few doors down from the gray stone tower.

Freddy Cullenbine did prove to be the pot-bellied trumpeter who wished he were Satchmo. If he lacked genius, he and his bandmates had plenty of enthusiasm. Bruce steered Daisy out onto the dance floor.

"You're perkier than you were before," he said after a while. "You don't fold up after a couple of numbers the way you used to."

"I've got my strength back, or most of it," she said.

He squeezed her. "I'm darn glad you do."

"I wouldn't mind sitting the next one out, though," Daisy said. "I could use a pint of bitter—maybe even two."

"Now you're talking, honey!" Bruce said.

This was better bitter than they'd served in Yaxham, though not, to Daisy's thinking, a match for what she'd sold at the

Owl and Unicorn. To Bruce, who'd grown up with bilgewater like Pabst and Schlitz, all English bitter was a revelation. He downed two pints in quick succession.

"It's stronger than you think," Daisy said. "Will you be all right to drive?"

"I'd worry about it if there was gonna be any traffic," he answered. "The way things are, the biggest thing I've gotta watch out for is running over a sheep in the dark."

She laughed. "Fair enough."

Sweat gleaming on his broad expanse of forehead, Freddy Cullenbine worked as hard as any of the dancers. He eventually took a break and got himself a pint. "Louis Armstrong would never do that," Bruce said, clucking in mock disapproval. "He'd have a bourbon instead." That made Daisy laugh some more. She liked laughing with someone. She squeezed Bruce's arm.

Then jet engines roaring low over the social hall made everyone inside think twice about the contrast between the good time they were having and the deadly game of hunter and hunted in the sky above. "I hope they get him," Daisy said.

"Yeah, me, too," Bruce replied. But how far did he mean that? The Russians in their Beagles were part of his guild, as it were. The RAF and USAF fighter pilots belonged with the men in MiGs who harried invaders of their airspace. Daisy started to ask him, then decided she didn't want to know after all.

Getting out of the crowded, smoky, sweaty social hall was a relief. It was a relief in several senses, in fact; Daisy paused to spend a penny in the ladies' loo. Bruce smoked a cigarette waiting for her to come out. "You should have eased yourself, too," she said.

"I'm okay," he answered. "I can always stop and go behind a tree if I have to." He drooped out his tongue like a panting dog and mimed lifting a leg. She giggled.

It was cool and clear outside. The moon had set not long before. With lights all across the country blacked out, though, stars sparkled bright and clear. The Milky Way gleamed, ghost-pale. Daisy squeezed Bruce again. They'd just driven the jeep out of town when more jet engines howled and antiaircraft guns thundered rage at them.

"Maybe it's not such a hot night to stop anywhere," Bruce said. "If you want, I'll take you straight back to your place."

"Don't be silly!" Daisy shook her head. "You'll do no such thing!"

"Okey-doke." This time, he slid his hand under the hem of her dress and slid it up her stockinged thigh toward his target. He knew all about bull's-eyes, too. "Then we'll do something else."

Which, when they found a secluded lane near a pear orchard, they did. More fireworks kept going off in the sky, but they had fireworks of their own. Daisy hardly noticed the show overhead, or even the roars of bombs going off. If Bruce did, he gave no sign she could sense, and all her senses were straining.

Afterwards, though, he did say "Lousy Beagles are busy tonight" as he peeled off his rubber. Then he laughed. "Now, if you'll excuse me, I *am* gonna walk over to one of those nice trees. Beer does take its revenge."

Daisy's manners were too good to let her tell him *I told you so.* She was distracted a moment later, anyhow. Another jet roared low over the quiet English countryside. Two more were right behind, shooting off machine guns and underwing rockets.

One of those rockets scored a hit. The fleeing plane—the Beagle?—blew apart in midair. Flaming wreckage pinwheeled toward the ground. One big blazing chunk flew straight at the jeep. Daisy watched it, open-mouthed . . . for a split second too long. Then she started to jump out.

Lieutenant Stanislav Kosior ran around keeping an eye on the men in his company like a mother hen herding along a new brood of chicks. "Come on!" he called. "Come on, come on! Into the trucks! Hurry up! Pile on in! You can do it!"

"Do you know what's going on, Comrade Lieutenant?" Ihor Shevchenko asked him.

"They're pulling this whole division out of the line," Kosior said. "They have some other duty in mind for us. What that is, they haven't told me yet. Whatever it is, I serve the Soviet Union, Comrade Corporal, and so do you."

"Yes, sir." Ihor thought of the move a little differently. Whatever it was, he was stuck with it. He helped some of the guys from his squad climb aboard a truck, then scrambled in himself. It was getting dark outside the canvas-covered bed of the truck. That pleased him. Motor convoys on the road in broad daylight made tasty, tempting targets for fighters with guns and rockets.

Away they went. In the darkness, of course, the driver couldn't see the potholes and dodge them. Ihor suspected he could barely see the road—or maybe the trouble was that he barely knew how to drive. They headed east when they set out, which made sense: everything west of where they had been belonged to the imperialists. But they kept going, much farther and much longer than Ihor had expected.

"I think we're back in the German Democratic Republic," one of the soldiers said after a while.

Ihor needed a few seconds to remember that that was the official name for the part of Germany the USSR had kept after the Nazis got finished off. German Communists ran it these days, but Communists from the Soviet Union ran them. None of the Soviet satellites could do much without permission from Stalin and his henchmen. The German Democratic Republic could do next to nothing.

The soldiers piled out at a town called Jüterbog. A man who'd fought in Marshal Koniev's army had gone through it in 1945. He said it lay south of Berlin. Ihor couldn't see much of it. What he could see told him the Fritzes hadn't rebuilt it since Koniev's troops overran it.

They got black bread and salted herrings there, with tea to wash them down. Once they'd eaten, the lieutenant gathered the company together. "Well, boys, now I know what we'll be doing next," Kosior said.

"What's that, sir?" several men asked, Ihor among them.

Kosior paused to light a match to get a *papiros* going. The flame briefly lit his earnest features from below and made him look harder and tougher than usual. "There's a reactionary uprising in the Polish People's Republic," he answered. "The crypto-Fascists have been lying in wait, hoping for their chance. Now they think they've found it. They want to detach Poland from the roster of progressive states and bring back the squalid military dictatorship from the years of Pilsudski and Smigly-Ridz. But we won't let them get away with it, will we?"

"No, Comrade Lieutenant!" the Red Army men chorused. Ihor made sure Kosior heard his voice. The less eager you really felt, the more eager you had to show yourself to be.

"*Khorosho. Ochen khorosho.* I wouldn't expect anything less from good Soviet men like you," Kosior said. "Now I need to tell you, along with counterrevolutionary soldiers you may also find reactionary civilians they've seduced with their lying propaganda. Some of them may speak Russian. Pay no attention to anything they tell you. They're in the pay of American and English spymasters. We liberated Poland from the German Fascists in the last war. Now we have to clear out the Polish Fascists who hid their venom till they thought they could hurt us the most."

"We serve the Soviet Union!" the soldiers said as one.

They got to unroll their blankets and stretch out on the ground in Jüterbog. That beat the devil out of trying to sleep sitting up in a truck bouncing along rough roads. After more bread and herrings and tea in the morning, they got rolling again. They were far enough inside the zone of Soviet control to make attack from the air only a small fear.

As soon as they got into Poland, the paving petered out and the road turned into a dirt track. They hadn't gone far before Ihor, looking back through the opening in the canvas at the rear of the truck, saw a burnt-out T-34/85 in a field. It *might* have been sitting there since 1945. But that was about thirty tonnes of steel. They would have salvaged it between then and now . . . wouldn't they? And the carcass looked fresh, not all rusty and dusty.

Bare-chested Red Army artillerymen served 105s and 155s in gun pits plainly just dug. The guns boomed. Cartridge cases jumped from the breeches. Loaders slammed in fresh rounds with fists clenched so they wouldn't snag their fingers in the mechanism. Ihor remembered noticing that trick during the last war.

Then a machine gun opened up on the front of the column. It was an MG-34, the MG-42's older and almost equally fearsome cousin. Maybe that meant the Poles using it were indeed Nazis. Or maybe it just meant they could get their hands on leftover German hardware.

Whatever it meant, Ihor's truck jerked to a stop. "Out!" he said. "Out and down! We'll hunt the fucker to death!"

Not fifteen seconds after the soldiers bailed out of the truck, a burst from the machine gun punched holes in the canvas cover—and, by the clanks, in the driver's compartment and engine as well. Ihor cautiously raised his head a few centimeters as he dug in with his entrenching tool. Flashes came from behind some bushes in the meadow.

"There it is!" he yelled. "Riflemen, make the gunners keep their heads down. Submachine gunners, forward with me!" With his Kalashnikov, he could have hung back and fired from this longer distance. But the red stripe on each shoulder board told him he had to set an example.

Bullets cracked past him. He flopped down after his rush and squeezed off a short burst at the MG-34. The guys with PPDs and PPShs were firing, too, but they were too far away to have much chance of hitting anything. He wasn't.

"Go home, you Russian pigs!" a Pole yelled. Ihor had no trouble following him. He wasn't so sure the Great Russians could. The Pole sounded more Ukrainian than Russian. Maybe he'd come from eastern Poland when it turned into the western Ukraine after the revived Polish nation saw its borders shift several hundred kilometers westward.

"Keep going! Fire and move!" Lieutenant Kosior called. The veterans in the company already knew how. They'd done it before often enough. The machine gun didn't have enough friends and couldn't fire every which way at once. Before long, three dead Poles lay behind it.

"Murderers! Russian fucking bandits!" other Poles shouted. "Freedom for Poland! Freedom, damn you!"

"Death to the Fascists!" Lieutenant Kosior shouted back. Some people truly believed whatever their superiors told them.

He did succeed in infuriating the Poles who were trading fire with the Red Army men. "Fuck Stalin!" some of them yelled, while others shouted, "Death to Stalin!" One man added, "He's a worse Fascist than Hitler ever was!"

"What are you bastards doing shooting Poles inside of Poland?" still other rebels called. "This is our country. It's not yours. Go home!"

Ihor wouldn't have minded. Only the certainty that an MGB man would put a bullet into the back of his neck without even smiling if he tried to abandon his post kept him banging away with his Kalashnikov—that and the equally grim certainty that the Poles *would* shoot him if he didn't shoot them first.

"No one insults the great Stalin!" Stanislav Kosior dashed forward with his PPSh, as furious as if the Poles had cursed his mother, not his political boss. Then he spun and crumpled. He tried to drag himself back to cover. Two more bullets slammed into him and made his body jerk. He lay very still after that.

Another old German machine gun in Polish hands snarled to life. Ihor dug like a mole. *These are our socialist allies, too,* he thought as the dirt flew. *Christ have mercy if our enemies ever get this mad at us!*

Read on for an excerpt from
the stunning conclusion to the Hot War Trilogy.

Armistice

THE HOT WAR

By Harry Turtledove

Published by Del Rey

SOMETHING LIKE GLASS CRUNCHED under the soles of Harry Truman's shoes as he walked through the ruins of Washington. Two men with Geiger counters walked ahead of him. They both wore gauze surgical masks that covered their faces south of the eyes.

They'd offered him one, too, but he'd turned them down. He'd had all he could do not to laugh at them. He was breathing in radioactive dust? He might die sooner than he would if he didn't filter it out? To say he didn't give a good goddamn showed how little language could really do.

Close to half of him already wished he were dead. Then he could have Bess and Margaret for company again. He'd been flying back from a political rally in upstate New York when the Russians hit the center of Washington with one A-bomb and the Pentagon with another. If there'd been any air-raid alarms at all, they hadn't come soon enough to let his wife and daughter make it to the shelter under the White House.

George Marshall had been positive the Soviet Union didn't have the air-to-air refueling capability to let its Tu-4s (monkey-copied B-29s with Russian nameplates and hood ornaments) reach the East Coast of the United States. The Secretary of Defense had had the courage of his convictions. He'd been working late at the Pentagon when the second bomb hit. Like most of the enormous building (not like all of it—the Pentagon had been too vast for one atom bomb to destroy it completely, a scary thought if ever there was one), he'd gone up in the fire and smoke and ash and dust.

Turning his head for a moment, Truman looked back toward the Capitol. The blast that leveled the White House had also smashed Congress' longtime home. It knocked off the Capitol's dome and left it lying, shattered and broken, on the Mall below. Seeing it there reminded the President of what happened when a tank turret took a direct hit from a large-caliber shell.

"What a mess," Truman muttered. "What a fucking mess!"

One of the men with the Geiger counters turned his way. The morning sun glinted off the fellow's steel-rimmed specs, making him look even less human than he would have otherwise. "What did you say, sir?" he asked.

"I said, 'What a mess,'" Truman answered. "And it is." He'd been an artillery captain during the First World War. He knew how to cuss, all right. But he didn't swear all the time, and he mostly didn't do it for show. He wasn't sorry the Defense Department technician hadn't heard him this time.

"Oh." The man gave back a grave nod. Truman still couldn't see what color his eyes were. He went on, "It sure is. 'Course, we're still hitting those Red bastards harder than they're hitting us."

"Uh-huh." Truman nodded in return. From everything he knew—and he knew more than anyone except perhaps Joe Stalin—that was true. However true it was, it offered scant consolation to him, or to the hundred thousand or so who'd died here along with his wife and daughter, or to the additional hundreds of thousands who'd perished in New York City and Boston, or to their friends and relations.

Philly would have got it, too, only the Tu-4—the NATO reporting name was Bull—with its bomb had gone down short of the target. For the first time since the turn of the nineteenth century, Philadelphia was the de facto capital of the USA because it hadn't got hit.

Not that the United States had one hell of a lot of government to put there. Truman was still alive, but he didn't take up much room. Seven of the nine Supreme Court justices survived; they'd been at a legal convention in St. Louis when the bombs dropped. But Congress was gutted like one of Hemingway's marlins after he finally dragged it into the boat.

Neither House nor Senate had a living, breathing quorum. Governors could appoint new Senators to complete unfinished terms. If you listened to the Constitution, Representatives had to be chosen in special elections. That took time, and time was in desperately short supply in the United States right now.

More glass clinked under Truman's feet. Till the A-bomb

fused it, it had been dirt or sand or concrete. It was glass now, almost the color of a Coke bottle but less transparent and full of imperfections. He stooped, picked up a piece, and held it in his palm. "How hot is this thing?" he asked the men from the Department of Defense. He wasn't talking about the temperature.

They eyed each other. "Well, let's see," said the one with the glasses. He aimed the business end of his Geiger counter at the chunk.

Truman heard a click, then another and another. They came faster than they had when the technicians were just sniffing the air, so to speak. "What does that mean?" the President asked.

"About what you'd expect, sir," the man said. "It's more radioactive than the air—this has to be somewhere close to ground zero—but it isn't hot enough to hurt you in a hurry. You can keep it if you want to."

"No, thanks!" Truman had a hard time imagining anything he wanted less. He threw away the atomic glass as hard as he could. It shattered into half a dozen pieces. Sadly, he shook his head. *A tiny bit of destruction on top of the big blast,* he thought. *Looks like destruction is all people are good for.*

But it was an ill wind indeed that blew nobody any good. Among the elected officials the Soviet A-bomb had incinerated was the junior Senator from Wisconsin. Joe McCarthy had been the favorite to grab the Republican Presidential nomination at the upcoming convention. Truman knew too well that, given the Democrats' popularity on account of the war, whoever the GOP chose was odds-on to breeze to the White House (or wherever he'd stay till there was a White House again) come November.

Well, it wouldn't be Tail-Gunner Joe. Truman suspected Stalin has saved America from swallowing a good stiff dose of Fascism. Now . . . Robert Taft had also died. That should have left the field wide open for General Eisenhower. Truman didn't like Ike, but also didn't think him a bad man.

But McCarthyism seemed to be a vampire that hadn't yet had a stake pounded through its heart. A young Senator from California had taken up the cudgels for the late, unlamented (at least by Truman) Joseph McCarthy. Dick Nixon's nose reminded people of Bob Hope's. Nixon might be a lot of things, but funny he wasn't.

That, however, was the Republicans' problem. The Democrats' problem was that their leading candidate still among the living was Adlai Stevenson. Truman admired his principles and his brains. The combination had taken Stevenson a long way (his being the son of a prominent politico hadn't hurt, either). But he was not the kind of man to whom the average little guy readily warmed. And, like every other Democrat in the race, he ran with a uranium-weighted anvil on his back.

Quietly—almost whispering, in fact—Truman said, "It seemed like a good idea at the time."

"Sir?" asked the technician with the specs. Truman still hadn't seen what color his eyes were.

"Nothing," the President said hastily. "Never mind." If those weren't the saddest nine words in the English language, what would be?

He hadn't thought Stalin would retaliate if he used A-bombs in Manchuria to gum up the Red Chinese supply lines and keep Mao Tse-tung from gobbling up all of Korea after his men destroyed the UN force near the Yalu. But Stalin must have decided that letting the United States beat up his biggest ally without hitting back would cost him too much face. And here Truman was, a year and a half later, shuffling through the wreckage of Washington, D.C.

"Ask you something, Mr. President?" that Defense Department man said.

"You can always ask. I don't promise to answer," Truman said.

"Sure." The fellow nodded. His eyes were gray, gray as skies that threatened rain. He went on, "Is it true that the Russians' satellites are getting frisky? You gotta understand, sir: my last name is Plummer, but my old man changed it from Plazynski."

Had Truman had a nickel for every time he'd heard a story like that, he would have been too rich to worry about politics. "They're frisky, all right," he answered. "We aren't quite sure how frisky, but enough to make the Russians wish they weren't."